# Claremont Tales II

## Richard A. Lupoff

Golden Gryphon Press • 2002

LIBRARY OF CONGRESS CATALOGING-IN-PUBLICATION DATA
Lupoff, Richard A., 1935–
   Claremont tales II / Richard Lupoff — 1st ed.
   p.     cm.
   ISBN 1-930846-07-X (alk. paper)
   1. Fantasy fiction, American.   2. Detective and mystery stories, American.  I. Title.

PS3562.U6C57  2002
813'.54 – dc21                           2001055523

Contents

This book is dedicated to the honorable editors who brought each story to its first publication:

Chester Anderson
Scott Aniolowski
Mike Ashley
O'Neil DeNoux
Edward Ferman
Maxim Jakubowski
Keith Kahla
Marvin Kaye
Gary Lovisi
David Pringle
Mike Resnick
Roy Torgeson
Gary Turner
Sean Wallace
Ted White

. . . and to those responsible for the stories' new life in *Claremont Tales II*: my editor and publisher, Gary Turner, the wonderful illustrator Nicholas Jainschigg, and those generous souls, T. Goto and Priya Monrad, who checked and corrected my poor phrase-book Japanese . . .

. . . to the founder of Golden Gryphon Press and initiator of this project, the late James Turner . . .

. . . and to my very own "first reader" and indispensable encourager and companion, Patricia Lupoff.

# Foreword: No Long White Beard

**F**UNNY HOW MEMORIES STICK WITH YOU. ESPECIALLY the memories of first encounters or of experiences lived only once. I can summon up with vivid exactitude the flavor of the first pear I ever bit into, the sensation of climbing onto a piano bench when I was so small that I did—literally—have to climb onto it, the precise shade of yellow in a paint set I owned as a child, the smell of machine oil on my first typewriter, the terror I felt when I heard that the Japanese had attacked Pearl Harbor, and my shock and grief when I learned of my mother's death.

I can remember the Sunday afternoon I sat in a wooden booth in a little café near my school, quaffing a juicy, ketchup-laden cheeseburger, the metallic clicks and chimes of a pinball machine in the background, while I read Jack Williamson's *The Legion of Space* in a kind of ecstatic trance.

Oddly, I can't remember the first time I kissed a girl or the identity of my partner in that experiment, but whoever she was and wherever she is today, I send her my gratitude and I wish her well.

The school I attended as a small child and the experiences I had there, the synagogue my parents took me to, the posh pseudo-oriental décor of the movie palace where my brother brought me to see Basil Rathbone and Nigel Bruce in *The Hound of the Baskervilles*. They're all part of my world, after half a century and more. They're part of my life.

The wonders and terrors and joys of a lifetime.

One thing I remember is a group of us, perhaps five years of age, discussing our families. One of my friends described his grandfather. "He's more than fifty years old, and he's still alive!"

It was startling.

I was a precocious child, for years the youngest member of my class, the younger of two sons in my family, for decades the junior-most this or that. And for what seemed a very long time, the youngster who hero-worshipped the novelists and short story writers whose works he doted on.

Then one morning you wake up and discover that you're a senior member of the fraternity. Reviewers start referring to you as a seasoned veteran instead of a promising youngster. Fans send you letters saying, "I've been reading your books since I was a little kid." Worse yet, when you meet them you discover that they're middle-aged.

Word gets back to you of conversations in which someone asked, incredulously, "Is *he* still alive?"

Well, hang in there, Bunky. As our Muslim brethren say at certain of life's crucial moments, Only God is immortal.

I wrote my first story, if you could call it writing, sometime around 1940. I knew from a very early age that I was going to be a storyteller. One of my earliest memories is of learning to read. I couldn't wait for school, I campaigned relentlessly until my Grandma sat down with me and patiently explained the letters of the alphabet and the sounds they made, and from there on I was on my own.

From reading to writing was the next step, and from writing to publishing was the next, even if it meant "publishing" in an edition of one copy, hand made, crayon on construction paper. Then it was on to school and summer camp newspapers, professional journalism, magazines, and finally volumes of my own.

Copies of my first book are now hawked for hundreds if not thousands of dollars—more than I earned for writing the thing!

When you reach a certain point in your life and your career, you inevitably pause to look around and take stock. Sixty years a writer. Fifty years a professional. A "mere" thirty-five years of turning out books. I've lost count of the number of books I've written, probably somewhere between forty and fifty; plus a hundred or so short stories, assorted screenplays, comic strips, broadcast scripts, reportage, speeches, essays, and even a couple of scraps of doggerel.

Is this any way for a nice Jewish boy to spend his life?

I think it is. I ponder the other careers I might have pursued, the paths not taken, and none of them, I think, would have brought me the satisfaction that my career as a writer has brought me.

But I haven't written these millions of words for my own amusement. There's something of the performer in the writer. Without an audience the performer is nothing and without a reader the writer is nothing.

*Claremont Tales II* is the third major collection of my short fiction. The first was *Before . . . 12:01 . . . and After* (1996), then came *Claremont Tales* (2001) and now, the final volume in what I consider a pretty comprehensive overview of my works. In fiction. In less-than-novel length. There have been several other volumes of my short stories, notably *The Ova Hamlet Papers* (1979) and *One Murder at a Time: The Casebook of Lindsey and Plum* (2001). What remains uncollected is for the most part either pretty minor or of inferior quality. Or else it's something that slipped my mind while I was rooting around, exclaiming with variously delighted or horrified expressions when I unearthed yellowing periodicals and anthologies from the 1950's, 60's, 70's, 80's, and 90's.

Throughout the decades that I've spent as a writer I've worn other hats, including those of critic and teacher. I think these have been valuable activities—valuable for my readers and my students, or at least I hope so, but valuable for me as well. Moving through these different roles, one gets to observe both the process of writing and the product of that process from varied perspectives.

As a teacher—at the University of California and elsewhere—I must confess that I've offered my students a somewhat mechanistic concept of the writing process. It goes something like this:

- Start with a basic idea.
- Populate that idea with a group of characters whom it will effect.
- Place those characters in an appropriate setting.
- Work out a plot line that flows logically from the nature of those characters, the situation in which they find themselves, their relationships to one another, and the impact of that basic idea.

In practice, I'm afraid that my own method is a lot more chaotic than that. Characters scurry through my mind; events wake me up, startled, in the middle of the night; images flash before me; bits of dialog or description occur to me at odd moments and I jot frantically to prevent their being lost. My wife knows the signs now: there's Dick with his little notebook and that cheap pen that he stole from a motel, scribbling away in a noisy saloon, a darkened movie theater, a bustling restaurant, or wherever we happen to be.

Somehow it all comes together, sometimes well and sometimes not so well. Usually I do a lot of revising, but the revisions are of the nature of word choice or punctuation, polishing here and fine-tuning there. I seldom make major changes to a story. Once written, it's either right or it's not.

Upon reexamining the product of a lifetime in order to select the contents of these three volumes, I've been pretty pleased with what I found. It's true that some stories just didn't hold up, either because they weren't very good to start with (but then why did the editors buy them?) or because they represented a phase, a tentative direction in my work, that proved unsatisfactory and that I abandoned after a while.

But the good ones . . .

It's a pleasant experience to reread something that you wrote thirty or forty or fifty years ago and decide that, Hey, this is pretty good work! It's a pleasanter experience to reread something that you wrote last year—or last week!—and decide that, Hey, this is better than my old stuff.

I feel very sorry for those artists, whether writers, musicians, or athletes, who "peak" with their first efforts and never again match their initial accomplishments. Looking back at my own earliest efforts—at least, the earliest ones that still survive—I've come to the conclusion that they're not so bad, but that I have learned a lot over the years, and I am satisfied that my recent works are superior to my earlier ones.

But that's just my opinion. The author (or any other artist) may not be the individual best qualified to judge his own work. In fact, he may be the worst qualified. He's so close to the process, he has been so concerned with the problems of the project and the ways that he resolved them, that he lacks the perspective of the reader. The reader, after all, was not there with the author, did not sit at his elbow as he researched and planned the work, did not sweat with him as he struggled to *get it right*, as he tore his hair over second, third, fourth, or ninth drafts, did not agonize with him as he waited for the response of his editor, the critics, and the authentic human beings whose opinions really, really matter.

The reader just has a book in his lap, and loves it or doesn't love it.

That's what it comes down to. A man or a woman or a child sitting with a book and reading, and coming to the end of the book and saying, "That was really great."

Or not.

As the case may be.

I hope I've still got your attention, although if I haven't, if I'm sitting here talking to myself, that's okay, too. It means you were eager to get on to the stories, and the stories, after all, are what this book is *really* all about.

But if I've still got your attention, I'd like to say a few things about categories of fiction. Millions of words have been spoken and written on this subject. Some authors proudly claim the label of *mystery writer, western writer, romance writer, horror writer,* or whatever. Others turn purple and begin to froth at such titles. "I'm a writer, period," they exclaim. "Labels are limits. I don't want to be labeled."

Well, fair enough, but labels are useful, too. If you doubt that, imagine browsing through the canned goods at your local grocery store if there were no labels.

Right, works of art are not canned goods, I know, okay, point taken. I still say labels are useful.

And there are those who hold that the distinction between category or genre fiction, and general or mainstream fiction, is highly arbitrary and more a marketing device (or a pejorative, depending on who's calling whom a what) than a literary difference. Of those who do make a distinction between the two, I think my favorite is Joyce Carol Oates, who maintains that the difference is one of expectation and realization.

The genre reader, she believes, expects a formulaic exercise leading to a clear-cut conclusion. And the genre reader is entitled to what he or she pays his money for. A mainstream reader, on the other hand, does not have such an expectation, and would more likely than not be disappointed if he or she did. Things are too messy in mainstream fiction, and unsettling elements are often left unresolved.

Hmmm.

Maybe.

But there's something to be said for the "marketing device"

theory. Some years ago I came across two excellent books more or less simultaneously. One was labeled as fantasy, the other was unlabeled but was packaged and marketed as a mainstream novel.

When I read the so-called "fantasy novel" I was unable to find any fantasy content. It was an adventure story set in a generic, woodsy, bucolic, pre-industrial Western Europe. Could have taken place at any time between the fall of the Roman Empire and the Renaissance. People riding around dark forests on noble steeds, camping out at night and worrying about their enemies in the castle. Everybody wearing soft green or brown leggings and jerkins and caps. That sort of thing.

But the author had a "track record" as a fantasy writer and her publisher was known for its fantasy line, so the book was published as a fantasy.

The second novel was *full* of fantasy elements. A mysterious magic mirror, its origins lost in an ancient Oriental land, finds its way to twentieth-century America. It is delivered to a bride on her wedding day. She passes through its surface and travels backward into time. I think in the end she winds up becoming her own grandmother. Something like that. Forgive me, I read it a long time ago.

Actually a darned good book. And pure-quill fantasy. But its author already had a reputation as a mainstream novelist, so the book was published as a mainstream novel.

Go figure.

For what it's worth, I've gone through the stories in these three collections — *Before . . . 12:01 . . . and After, Claremont Tales,* and *Claremont Tales II* — and tried to sort the stories by genre. It hasn't been easy. Some of them are mysteries with science fiction elements in them . . . or science fiction with mystery elements in them . . . or mainstream stories containing a touch of fantasy, or crime, or horror. Not to mention parodies and pastiches.

Hard to tell.

But just for my own satisfaction I took the three books — forty-seven stories in all — and made little tick marks on the tables of contents, and wound up with the following totals:

- nineteen science fiction stories
- eight crime/mystery/detective stories
- thirteen fantasy and/or horror stories
- seven mainstream stories

And what do those numbers tell you? That I'm a science fiction, crime/mystery/detective, fantasy-horror, mainstream author? Does that mean *anything*?

To be candid, I have mixed feelings about the issue.

Several years ago, when I was working as a book reviewer, an author sent me a copy of his pride 'n' joy in hopes of scoring some ink. I wrote to him and explained that, Sorry, I just wasn't interested in military science fiction, thus didn't feel that I could do justice to his grand opus, and therefore did not intend to review it.

He sent back a poignant note reeking of injured resentment (and maybe a smidgen of anger), asserting that his book was not military science fiction at all, it was a *novel*, period, and would I please give it another look. And a fair chance.

Not an unreasonable request, so I did.

And the book was all about people in spiffy uniforms and zooming rocket ships and life and combat in the armed forces of the distant future as our heroes and heroines battle their way to death and glory in outer space or on alien worlds.

At least that's what I recall of the thing. I don't have the book any more, it left my house in one of my periodic de-cluttering campaigns, somewhere along the way from then to now. I'm probably being very unfair to the author, which is why I don't mention his name or the title of his book. And also because I don't remember them.

To say, "This is a war novel," doesn't have anything to do with the quality of the work at hand. "War novel" covers everything from *The Naked and the Dead* to *Patriotic Blaster Brigade Smashes the Commie Pinko Terrorist Liberal Rats of Doom*. One is serious literature and one is pandering garbage. You can read Norman Mailer's masterpiece or you can read Tom Clancy's propaganda spew, but they're both still war novels.

"It's broccoli, dear," the review-seeking author asserted. But, "I say it's spinach," your servant replied, and I trust you know the rest of that quotation.

And I say that the stories in the book you're holding right now, and its two predecessors, are "just stories." Yes. Stories with ideas in them, and people and settings and plots. But they are also science fiction stories and mystery stories and fantasy stories— and mainstream stories.

And what do you want to tell me in return?

Well, as the queen of punk divas, Patti Smith, once growled to a room full of unruly druggies and drunks (I was there, yes), "If you have something to say to me, I have just one thing to say to you first, and that is—*Don't be polite!*"

Richard A. Lupoff
Berkeley, CA
May, 2000

# Claremont Tales II

Ino Hajime, the diffident little Japanese/Martian with the polished pate and the mutton-chop whiskers, made his debut several years ago in a story called "Black Mist." In that story he was called Hajimi Ino. Okay, the version of his name used in "Green Ice" is the correct one. We live and learn.

The first Mr. Ino story was a calculatedly traditional, by-the-rules tale of detection. "Green Ice" is not merely a different case but a different kind of case. Among other changes, it's much more "Japanese" than its predecessor, but you need not have read the earlier story, nor be familiar with the Japanese language, to understand "Green Ice."

It's my conviction that authors don't really create their stories. At best they find them. Perhaps, in the last analysis, it is the story that writes the author rather than the other way 'round. The fact is that I was thoroughly surprised by "Green Ice."

I've long been suspicious of authors who include stories in their collections, proudly proclaiming, "Never Before Published!" More often than not, this means that the author saw a chance to clean out his desk, get an unpublished puppy into print and make a few shekels into the bargain. But you have my word of honor that "Green Ice" is not such a story. I wrote it especially for this book with my editor/publisher, Gary Turner, standing over my shoulder and applying the knout whenever I faltered.

Honest.

# Green Ice

I N THE DAZZLING GLARE HIS EYES WERE HALF BLIND-
ed, his vision tinted a rich green. He held his heavily gloved
hands before his face, squinting at his fingers. Was he solid or
liquid, flesh or water? Were his surroundings green crystal as hard
and as brilliant as emerald or were they soft and flowing like the
green waters of the Sea of Japan?

Where did the light come from?

He tried to tilt his head so he could see its source but the
spacesuit was too heavy and too rigid to permit. Instead he twisted
his body, shoving with his arms to turn himself. He had struggled
forward in a prone position but now he was able to turn on his
back and stare upward. The orbiting station that wove its way
through the moons of Jupiter was somewhere overhead but he
could not see it. Perhaps it was millions of kilometers away, weav-
ing its complicated path from moon to moon, taking observations
now of Ganymede, now of Callisto, now of Io. Or perhaps it was
overhead, closer to his position on Europa than to any of the other
satellites, but lost, invisible to his milky eyes, a speck too small to
be seen against the rosy majesty of the great planet.

He felt dizzy, disoriented. Perhaps he could achieve immortality, unity with the green ice, the *midori no koori* that surrounded him.

If he closed his eyes, removed his helmet, let himself swim away into the green glory of the Pwyll caves, all troubles would cease, all pain would disappear. There would be green glory forever. He would breath in the ice, become one with Europa, one with the universal truth that he had resisted.

*Okasan, yurushite kudasai.*

*Otosan, yurushite kudasai.*

Mother, forgive me.

Father, forgive me.

He raised both hands, placed them on the latches that held his helmet in place, that sealed his spacesuit against the frigid green ice of Europa. His fingers were still fingers.

"Am I dead?"

"Not yet."

"Ah." The voice was weak, the movement of the lips barely visible. "But soon."

"It is not for me to say."

"You are not a doctor?" The eyes were narrow and clouded. The figure lying supine upon the bed shifted, craning its neck as if to get a clearer view of the newcomer. If such was the purpose of the movement, the eyes were not totally useless.

"I am not a doctor. My duties are other."

Again, "Ah." The figure moved again, as if a tension were leaving its body. A pale lavender sheet covered the body from the neck downward. The head rested on a soft pillow of the same tint. The arms lay on the sheet but they were covered by a thin garment suggestive of the color of a kumquat but far more pale. The hands were covered in bandages. Only the patient's face was exposed, swollen and distorted to the point where it was impossible to tell whether the patient was male or female.

"Mr. Nishiyobi," the newcomer began once again.

"Who are you?" The words were little more than a whisper.

"Ino." The newcomer bowed politely. Although he was of higher standing than the patient, he felt that he could grant this extra courtesy. The dead and the dying were due respect. "Ino Hajime."

Nishiyobi exhaled and once more nodded almost imperceptibly. "Who are you?" he whispered once again.

One would have thought that a weight lay on Nishiyobi's chest, that he strained to draw each breath and to speak each syllable. Mr. Ino considered his own weight. At home on his tiny island north of Hokkaido, he had weighed some fifty-five kilograms. On Mars his weight had been drastically reduced and on the moon Phobos, where last he had worked, it was reduced further. Now on *Tsuki*, the home planet's own moon, his weight was little more than nine kilos. He wore heavy protective garb, but even so its weight was negligible. The difficulty of wearing it arose from its bulk and the clumsiness that it imposed on its occupant.

Had Nishiyobi spoken again? Had he whispered an interrogative "Eh?" or had Mr. Ino merely imagined the sound? The protective garment was of necessity fully sealed. The face mask was transparent, but for hearing it was necessary to utilize small microphones on the exterior of the helmet and corresponding speakers within.

"I have come in the hopes that you will explain things to me," Mr. Ino said.

Did Nishiyobi smile at that? Did the muscles of his face still respond to his emotions and to his desires, or had Mr. Ino imagined the tiny, fleeting rictus as he had, perhaps, imagined the soft syllable that preceded it.

He shifted his weight. Even in *Tsuki*'s light gravity his muscles cramped uncomfortably when he stood too long in one position. "You were on Europa," he said. He knew that a bead-microphone within his helmet picked up his words and that a speaker on the exterior of his suit spoke the same words to Nishiyobi. Still, he wondered what he must sound like, how he must appear to this dying man. A strange figure in a white costume, a dark face peering out through the transparent mask, a mechanical voice uttering words. If Nishiyobi were floating in the dreamlike semiconsciousness that Mr. Ino had come to believe the dying experienced, what must he think of the figure standing beside his bed?

"You were on Europa," Mr. Ino repeated. "You and your companions. All of them have died, Mr. Nishiyobi. Some were dead when the rescuers arrived, others lived but briefly. Only you have survived this long. We need to know your purpose in entering Pwyll. How you infiltrated the institution, how you took control of our orbiting station, what you were after on Europa."

"*Poa,*" Nishiyobi whispered. "*Poa.*"

Mr. Ino shook his head, then realized that Nishiyobi could not see the movement within his protective helmet. He said, "I am puzzled. Please, explain."

"*Poa,*" Nishiyobi repeated. "To save all. To save the universe. *Poa.*"

Mr. Ino raised a hand to scratch his bald pate, then realized that he would have to wait to do so. He saw Nishiyobi reach for him, saw the other man's raised hand move toward his arm. He could have drawn away but instead watched in horrified fascination as Nishiyobi grasped his wrist. Even through the bandages on the man's hand he could see the nodulated texture. Even through his protective garment he could feel the hard substance of the man's flesh.

For a moment Nishiyobi clung to Mr. Ino's arm. Then his grip relaxed. His hand fell back, not onto the lavender bed covering but straight down beside the mat on which he lay. There was a last exhalation and the faint glow of life and awareness disappeared from his cloudy eyes. The air escaping his lungs seemed tinted, a pale color so subtle that Mr. Ino could not be certain that he saw it at all. It faded away quickly.

Mr. Ino lifted the bandaged hand and laid it across Nishiyobi's body. The hand and arm seemed abnormally heavy. He circled the bed and repeated the gesture with Nishiyobi's other hand. He leaned across the body, peering into the face, trying to read in it a message, an explanation that would tell him why Nishiyobi and his companions had given their lives.

In this he failed. Instead he raised his own heavily gloved hand and lowered the swollen eyelids over Nishiyobi's now lifeless eyes. He exhaled, a slow and silent sigh, straightened, and made his way to the same sealed hatch through which he had entered the room. He paused and raised his eyes to the monitoring equipment clustered near the bed, striving to read and to understand the lines and numbers, the glowing characters and colored lights.

He knew that they meant one thing. Mr. Nishiyobi was dead.

Miss Sabi looked up from her work as Mr. Ino entered her office. Mr. Ino could see that she had been watching a *bokushingu* match on a deskside monitor. She switched it off. He bowed to Miss Sabi and she returned the gesture. It was no longer as unusual as once it had been for a woman to become a manager in the corporation.

"Please." She nodded toward a chair beside her desk.

Mr. Ino seated himself. He wore now only the comfortable *zubon* and *wai-shatsu*, soft trousers and thin shirt, common within the corporation's lunar station. Once spacesuits had been required for daily use, but the structure's strength and the reliability of its seals were such that workers no longer worried about a leak of air and sudden suffocation or freezing. A direct meteor-strike would of course smash the structure, but in that case a spacesuit would do little to protect its wearer.

Miss Sabi offered Mr. Ino a cup of hot tea and he indicated

his acceptance. To his surprise Miss Sabi turned before pouring his tea and filled another's cup. There was a third person in the room, so unobtrusively seated that Mr. Ino has not noticed her presence.

"This is Miss Kawamichi," Miss Sabi said. "She will assist you." Miss Kawamichi rose to her feet and bowed.

Mr. Ino responded, his bow nearly as deep as that of Miss Kawamichi. He was not comfortable with the new ways by which men and women related. It was not that he considered women his inferiors, as it had been argued in past years that men were likely to do. Rather, he had been raised in the northernmost quadrant of the home archipelago where old ways persisted. There the roles of men and of women were clearly defined, and one would no more infringe upon the duties of the other, Mr. Ino had often thought, than a seal would attempt to become a pelican.

A transparent panel filled part of the wall behind Miss Sabi's desk, a sign of her status within the installation. Through it Mr. Ino could see the home world, mostly in darkness at this angle, the illuminated portion brilliant nonetheless with the reflected light of the sun. He imagined that he could make out the tiny island of his birth, a conceit which he realized at once was purely the creation of his own wishful imagination. Even so, it would be winter in his home village. The mountains that towered over the village would of course be white with snow, the roofs and streets of the village would be frosted, and flakes would likely be falling upon the black waters of the sea. Families would be huddled over small fires, bundled into their warmest clothing, sipping o-cha or sake. Parents would hold their children in their laps, tempting them with tidbits of nourishment while the children held small wooden toys carved for them by their elders.

With a soft sigh Mr. Ino returned to the moment. He hoped someday to return to the home planet, the home islands, and the home of his childhood, but the present was not the time for such an event.

"Miss Kawamichi," he whispered. "Kawamichi-san."

"Mr. Ino. Ino-san." She was dressed as he was. On the home planet he had been 1.6 meters in height. During his years of life in the low-gravity environments of the moon, of Mars, and of Phobos, he had grown nearly three centimeters. Miss Kawamichi was taller than he, but whereas his build was stocky hers was slim and angular.

"Mr. Ino," Miss Sabi spoke. "Please tell Miss Kawamichi what you observed in the isolation chamber."

"Mr. Nishiyobi," Mr. Ino complied. "He was very ill when I arrived, and very weak. We spoke briefly and he held my wrist. Then he died."

Miss Kawamichi nodded. "You saw his hands and feet? His eyes?"

"His hands and feet were bandaged. They appeared swollen and deformed, yet when he grasped my wrist his hand was as hard as broken rock, and as heavy. At the moment of his death a pale green exhalation escaped his nostrils. It reminded me of a soul leaving a body."

"And his eyes," Miss Kawamichi prompted.

"They were milky. At first I thought that he was blind, but he followed me with his eyes and I do not believe that he was blind. At least not entirely."

"Yes," Miss Kawamichi said, "he could see, I am sure of that." She sipped at her tea, then lowered the cup to a tray that stood on Miss Sabi's desk. Miss Kawamichi's manner was not that of a subordinate, but rather that of a guest or associate. Mr. Ino wondered if his bow to Miss Kawamichi should have been deeper.

Miss Sabi said, "Miss Kawamichi has come from the home planet. She is employed by the government. There is great concern over events on Europa. Since the orbiting installation there is under control of the corporation, the government has asked for our cooperation, and we are of course pleased to offer all possible assistance."

"Mr. Ino," Miss Kawamichi said, "what do you know of Aum Shinrikyo?"

Mr. Ino wrinkled his brow in thought. "Little or nothing. I remember the name."

"You have heard of one who calls himself *Atarashii Sendachi?*"

"The new guide. It could be a name or a title. What does the phrase mean?"

"What of Matsumoto Chizuo? Are you familiar with that name?"

"Alas, I am ignorant."

"Asahara Shoko, then."

"Yes. I know the name. A religious leader, was he not? Of a century ago or longer."

"Indeed." Miss Kawamichi sipped tea. "Matsumoto Chizuo, Asahara Shoko. The same person. He was born nearly two centuries ago. His eyes were clouded. From birth he was able to see but little. As a young man he was a petty criminal, a peddler of worthless medical nostrums, on occasion a jailbird. All of this until the day he was visited by Shiva."

"Shiva? The Hindu deity?"

Miss Kawamichi smiled wryly. Her eyes, when she did so, shone with a deep beauty and warmth. "Matsumoto or Asahara was a mystic. He created a religion called Aum Shinrikyo, the teaching of universal truth. He borrowed ideas from Hinduism, Buddhism, Christianity. His followers obeyed him without question. Many donated their all to Aum Shinrikyo and lived communally. Matsumoto was a brilliant student of the cult phenomenon, or perhaps he had an instinctive grasp of the principles of control. He kept his recruits awake for long periods of time, using fatigue and brainwashing to win their unquestioning loyalty. He gave them drugs that opened their minds and he poured himself in."

Mr. Ino had heard of such cults and their leaders. In the past he had encountered criminals and had uncovered plots by no less than the Yakuza, but cults like Matsumoto's seemed even more dangerous. Even so, even so. "But he must be dead. You said he was born two hundred years ago."

"Nearly so. He died long ago, but Aum Shinrikyo lives, and *Atarashii Sendachi* claims to be the reincarnated spirit of Asahara Shoko. Of Matsumoto Chizuo."

"And you believe that Mr. Nishiyobi was a follower? That he was in thrall to an *umarekawa-ri*, a revenant?"

Behind her desk Miss Sabi had risen to her feet and stood with her hands clasped in the small of her back. The angle of her neck indicated that she was gazing through the transparent panel. Perhaps, Mr. Ino thought, seeking her home as he had sought his own. Perhaps thinking of her mother or her father, or of friends from her school days.

"Aum Shinrikyo lives." Miss Sabi had now turned to face the others. Her face was drawn. "*Atarashii Sendachi* has become its leader. We do not know where he is. Aum Shinrikyo has continued to find followers since the days of the first Asahara Shoko. There are cells in many cities of the home planet, and we know there are followers here on *Tsuki* and elsewhere. Perhaps on Mars, on Phobos. On *Ryo no Hae* and on Europa itself."

"Mr. Nishiyobi was brought here from Europa."

"He was. There is trouble on Europa. We fear a coup."

Mr. Ino shook his head. "Is that not the concern of the government?"

Miss Sabi's expression was guarded. "The government, Ino-san, the corporation. Would one survive without the other?"

"Mr. Nishiyobi will tell us nothing now," Miss Sabi pointed out. "The dead do not speak to the living."

Miss Kawamichi made a sound of discomfort.

"Yes?" Miss Sabi nodded encouragingly toward the taller woman.

"I would not wish to disagree but—" She halted.

Miss Sabi now appeared uncomfortable. "Please."

"The dead indeed speak to us," Miss Kawamichi supplied. "It is often difficult to understand what they are telling us, but if we are skilled enough, patient enough, determined enough, often we can comprehend."

She bowed her head.

Miss Sabi nodded. "Continue."

"The condition of Mr. Nishiyobi's extremities tells us much."

"And that is what?"

"Surely you are aware of the crystalline matter found on Europa, in the region known as Pwyll."

To Mr. Ino it seemed that Miss Kawamichi took special care in pronouncing the European names for the distant moon of Jupiter and its region marked with ridges and caves of ice.

Miss Sabi drew a startled breath. "How do you know about Pwyll?" Her pronunciation sounded less comfortable than that of Miss Kawamichi, but her meaning was clear. "Information from Europa has been restricted to those authorized and needing to learn of events there."

Miss Kawamichi shook her head. "It has always been the case. Those in authority try to keep information to themselves. Especially in the sciences they hoard what they learn, they exert their efforts to prevent others from finding out. But when we ask, Sekai, the nature of being, answers. When we observe, Sekai reveals. We need only ask the right questions, in the right ways, and Sekai replies."

Miss Sabi curled her lips in annoyance. "Philosophy, Kawamichi-san. I will not say, maundering, but—"

"But that is your meaning." With a visible effort, Miss Kawamichi withheld further comment.

Mr. Ino cringed in embarrassment.

Miss Sabi brought the subject back to its former focus. "Tell us, then, what the unfortunate Mr. Nishiyobi can tell us, now that he is no longer alive. He had little enough to reveal before his death."

Miss Kawamichi said, "I trust that Mr. Nishiyobi's body has been frozen?"

"That is the normal procedure."

"If he was frozen soon enough after death, his extremities will retain their hard, crystalline form. If not, they will first soften, then sublimate."

"They will not putrefy in the normal manner?"

"They will not." Miss Kawamichi shook her head. "Mr. Nishiyobi was a victim of conditions on Europa. He entered the ice caverns of Pwyll, did he not? The lure of the *midori no koori*, the green ice, was too great for him to resist. It cost him his life. Or perhaps he was not lured by the ice, perhaps he was dispatched by his superiors in Aum Shinrikyo."

She turned, smiling, toward Mr. Ino.

"What do you think, Ino-san? Have you an opinion, a hypothesis to venture?"

Mr. Ino pressed the heels of his hands against his eyes. Sparks danced in the darkness. "I want to know what will happen to Mr. Nishiyobi's remains, now that he is no longer living. What will happen, especially, to his extremities."

Miss Kawamichi said, "As long as the remains are refrigerated, they will be preserved."

"In what form?"

"Did you not see them, Ino-san?"

"They were bandaged. I saw the shape of his hands. They were formed like flat crystals. I felt them. They were as hard as broken rocks. I did not see them."

"They were like emeralds, Ino-san. Brilliant and beautiful. If they are allowed to warm they will sublimate into a green gas and disappear, but anyone who inhales the gas runs the risk of infection. His eyes will grow clouded and his extremities will become like Mr. Nishiyobi's. This is a dangerous contagion. An alien disease that would spread on the home planet until our very species was threatened, if it once got loose on the planet."

Mr. Ino bowed his head. He clenched his teeth and let his breath out between them with a soft hissing sound. "You know about the gas that escaped Mr. Nishiyobi at the moment of death."

"His *tamashii*," Miss Kawamichi said.

"Are you serious?"

"No, no, not really. We're all good, rational materialists nowadays, aren't we?"

"Perhaps." Mr. Ino turned toward Miss Sabi. She had sat

quietly, her teacup held to her lips, during the dialog between Mr. Ino and Miss Kawamichi. "And your wish, Sabi-san?"

"You are to investigate, Ino-san. Miss Kawamichi is your technical associate. She will accompany you and provide information and assistance as needed."

Miss Kawamichi said, "Aum Shinrikyo was discredited more than a century ago. Their theology called for the annihilation of the human species, all except a chosen few who would survive and build a utopia on the ruins of the world. They were able to find followers in all countries. They were known to be buying nuclear weapons from clandestine peddlers, to be building hidden factories for the manufacture of poison gases and deadly disease toxins. They went so far as to release gas in the subways of the home islands. All under the leadership of their half-blind prophet."

Mr. Ino let his eyes drift from the face of Miss Kawamichi, back to the transparent panel behind Miss Sabi. Through the panel the home world was visible. A great storm system swirled over the northwestern Pacific Ocean, hiding all but the southernmost of the home islands. He thought of his father and mother, huddled over a charcoal fire. Snow would be falling outside, there was no chance today to seek fish in the waters off their little island.

They should have enough to eat. That, at least, was a comfort to Mr. Ino. His salary was more than sufficient for his modest needs, and the rest was remitted by the company to his parents. They were old but they both insisted on working, his father as a fisherman, his mother cooking, caring for their small home, sewing clothes for herself and her husband, sitting with the other women of the village when it was time to mend the nets that their husbands used in their daily work.

*Otosan, Okasan.*

Miss Kawamichi was still speaking.

"The Aum Shinrikyo still exist in cities across the home planet. Governments have tried to wipe them out, but they survive. They attract the usual variety of misfits, neurotics, sociopaths. But they also attract intelligent and well-educated individuals. Mr. Nishiyobi was a brilliant technician, a space traveler and explorer, but if he could have, he would have spread the infection of the green ice from Europa to the home planet."

"Europa should be quarantined," Mr. Ino suggested. "For several reasons. Is there native life there?"

Miss Sabi frowned.

Mr. Ino awaited her answer.

"Observations of the surface of Europa show only ridges of ice."

Mr. Ino nodded, then bowed his head. "Forgive me, Sabi-sama. Forgive me, but I believe your answer is an evasion. I put my question to you once more. Is there native life on Europa?"

Miss Sabi lowered her cup angrily, striking it against the top of her desk. "Perhaps," she said. "That information is classified. As for quarantine, that is beyond our authority. You must work to uncover the plans of Aum Shinrikyo so they can be frustrated."

Mr. Ino bowed his head.

To Miss Kawamichi he said, "We had best be on our way, Kawamichi-san." The tall woman lowered her teacup quietly to the corner of Miss Sabi's desk. She bowed to Miss Sabi who returned the gesture. Mr. Ino also offered his respects to Miss Sabi. The gesture with which she responded was curt.

Together, Mr. Ino and Miss Kawamichi left the office.

The shuttle that carried Miss Kawamichi and Mr. Ino to the surface of the home planet was small and operated efficiently. They traveled with minimal belongings. The reaction mass needed to lift it from the surface of *Tsuki* was slight and for its landing on the home planet it acted as a glider rather than a ballistic object.

The landing field was operated by the company. It stood on the Iberian plain some forty kilometers to the west of Barcelona. Mr. Ino and Miss Kawamichi were met by a representative of the company, Mr. Kemuri. Miss Sabi had radioed word that Mr. Ino and Miss Kawamichi were to be afforded all assistance during their visit. Their status was not specified; Mr. Ino suspected that Mr. Kemuri would think they were investigating financial peculations. Mr. Ino was willing to permit Mr. Kemuri to think that.

It was difficult for Mr. Ino to so much as stand upright in the gravity of the home planet. He watched Miss Kawamichi struggle to function. He managed to smile encouragement to her.

As they left the terminal Mr. Ino halted in his tracks. A great blazing ball in the sky blasted down at him. He threw his hands over his eyes. Mr. Kemuri handed him a pair of darkened spectacles, apologizing for his thoughtlessness. Tears were streaming down Mr. Ino's face. Even to lift his hand to wipe them away required an exhausting expenditure of energy. Beside him, Miss Kawamichi was clearly experiencing similar difficulties.

Mr. Kemuri apologized again and ushered them toward a ground vehicle but Mr. Ino paused first, overcome by emotion.

This was his first visit to the home planet in—how many years?—he could not remember. True, Cataluña was far from the home islands and Barcelona, he knew, would be a metropolis bearing no resemblance to his small fishing village. Yet here he stood on the surface of the home planet. The area outside the aerospace terminal was paved but green shoots had poked up through cracks in the tarmac.

Mr. Ino stood, enchanted. Then he bent to touch the living plant with his fingertip. When he tried to rise he required the assistance of Mr. Kemuri. Dizzy, he raised his eyes to the sky again, turning away from the brilliance that he now realized was *Taiyo*—the sun. Through the dark lenses he gazed at the sky, an astonishing shade of blue dotted with incredible bits of floating white cloud. Again tears rolled down his face, this time not caused by the brightness of the sun.

They rode to the city and to the corporate office on Carrer Pontanella. In Mr. Kemuri's office they were seated in comfortable chairs and offered a choice of tea, *sake*, or a regional red wine. Mr. Ino explained to Mr. Kemuri that he represented the highest levels of corporate management. Miss Kawamichi was his confidential aide. They would draw upon the resources of Mr. Kemuri's office as needed, but would spend little time there.

Mr. Kemuri obviously had difficulty in restraining his curiosity, but Mr. Ino had made it clear that further information would not be forthcoming, and that further inquisitiveness would not be welcomed. Mr. Kemuri had arranged a suite for Mr. Ino and Miss Kawamichi at the city's finest hotel, the Imperial Nippon. Mr. Ino drew a sizable financial advance from the office's funds and left with Miss Kawamichi.

Departing the office they declined Mr. Kemuri's offer of a limousine and driver and settled for an electrically powered *kuruma*. This course of action had been planned with Miss Sabi before leaving *Tsuki*. Following Miss Sabi's advice, Mr. Ino gave the address of the Hoteru Melía Mahakaruna. They checked in as husband and wife, workers returning to the home planet on vacation from the research station on Phobos.

These identities would explain their weakened muscles and unfamiliarity with local customs. Neither of them spoke the language of Cataluña, but the language of the home islands had by now become the *lingua franca* of the planet and its sparsely scattered expatriates; there would be no difficulty on that score.

In their suite Mr. Ino and Miss Kawamichi arranged their few belongings and lay down to rest. Mr. Ino slept soundly, dreaming of his home and his parents. He awoke to find Miss Kawamichi wearing fresh *wai-shatsu, zubon* and *kutsu.* She was seated in an armchair watching him. "I purchased clothing and toiletries for us. I will retire while you refresh yourself."

Mr. Ino bathed and donned the light clothing that Miss Kawamichi had purchased. He moved his heavy body to the door of their suite, then accompanied Miss Kawamichi to the lobby and the street outside their hotel. They hired a ground conveyance and Miss Kawamichi surprised Mr. Ino by speaking to the driver in Catalan.

Shortly they entered an establishment over whose entrance a dingy sign read, *Sakana's Go Parlor.* The establishment was furnished with rough-hewn wooden tables and frame chairs with woven straw backs and seats. They were led to a table where they played the ancient game of lines and stones while awaiting their dinner. Despite the unfamiliar weight of his body, Mr. Ino was very hungry. The local cuisine of langouste with chantelles and rice served with *rioja* was welcome and startlingly vivid to his palate. How long had it been since he had tasted real food, prepared over an open flame, served in an iron bowl and eaten with new, wooden *hashi*?

An unseen musician added to the ambiance, offering a solo rendering of a composition by Albenez upon a koto.

As Mr. Ino lifted a bit of dripping, tasty food to his mouth Miss Kawamichi gestured, tipping her head inconspicuously. Mr. Ino glanced in the indicated direction. At an adjacent table sat a rough-looking individual, unshaven and wearing a ragged linen *uwagi,* sipping *sake.* He wore peculiar, old-fashioned metallic buttons; one of them was coming loose; it hung by a long, fraying bit of twine. A *go* board stood before him but he had no companion. Even so, from time to time he would move a stone. Mr. Ino wondered if the man had memorized classic games and was practicing his skills.

At length Mr. Ino turned back to his own companion, lifted his wine glass, then turned back once again toward the stranger. There was something odd about him. His whiskers were scraggly, his hair was wild, but neither of these was the feature which captured Mr. Ino's attention. It was the man's eyes. They were milky white, like the eyes of the unfortunate Mr. Nishiyobi.

Miss Kawamichi had said that the founder of Aum Shinrikyo had been partially blind from birth, his eyes clouded white. Mr.

Nishiyobi, the disfigured disciple of Aum who had been returned from Europa to *Tsuki* only to die in a sealed isolation chamber, had been the victim of a similar handicap.

And now the ragged stranger in the *go* parlor . . .

Mr. Ino turned away from the stranger, but not before they had locked glances for a fleeting instant. The sensation of communion with the ragged man sent a chill through Mr. Ino. He swallowed a warming slug of *rioja* followed by a hearty dollop of langouste.

The stranger shoved his chair back from his table with a loud noise and rose to his feet. He turned and approached Mr. Ino and Miss Kawamichi. Mr. Ino half expected the man to make an uncouth remark or to misbehave in some other manner, but to his surprise the stranger bowed courteously and muttered a polite greeting. Mr. Ino returned the gesture.

"May I join you?" the stranger asked. He waited a moment before, receiving no objection, pulling his chair to Mr. Ino and Miss Kawamichi's table. He turned it backwards and seated himself, arms folded, leaning against its back. "I apologize for imposing my presence on you. I noticed your style of *go* play. Your skill and courtesy impress."

The stranger's manners were an odd mixture of the deferential and the aggressive. Mr. Ino wondered if customs on the home planet had changed during the years of his absence in such a manner that this man's conduct was considered acceptable. He felt like an alien on the world of his birth, physically uncomfortable and socially out of place.

Miss Kawamichi lowered her eyes, conducting herself at least in this small degree in traditional fashion.

Mr. Ino rose and made a small bow. It remained to be seen if the stranger should take offense at the gesture. Apparently he did not, returning the bow with one equally—perhaps slightly less—shallow. The stranger reached inside his ragged *uwagi* and withdrew a business card. He presented it to Mr. Ino, making another *ojigi* as he did so. Mr. Ino read the card. It was printed in both traditional and western characters: *Asobi Yoi*, followed by an address on Carrer Girona in the city of Barcelona.

Returning the *ojigi* Mr. Ino presented the stranger with a business card of his own. Miss Kawamichi watched the silent exchange. Out of the corner of his eye Mr. Ino saw Miss Kawamichi's own gaze flick toward the card. He knew, of course, that it read *Koga Isoruko, Kobe*. Miss Kawamichi did not react at all to sight of the card. Mr. Ino introduced her as his wife.

The stranger said, "Perhaps you would be interested in visiting a more exclusive *go* parlor than this. Mr. Sakana is a businessman, of course, and must cater to that trade which he can. But the class of customers in this district leaves much to be desired."

Indeed, thought Mr. Ino. He gazed at the stranger. "Mr. Asobi," he said, "*Tsuma* and I are fatigued. We have just completed a journey."

Asobi nodded. "Kobe is distant from Barcelona."

"It is."

Mr. Ino rose from his seat; Miss Kawamichi followed his example. "Perhaps another evening. Please accept our apologies but we must rest now."

Asobi pushed himself up from his chair. "I will meet you here at the same hour tomorrow, Koga-san."

"If you wish."

In their hotel suite Miss Kawamichi poured herself a glass of cold water. Mr. Ino opened the window. Their room faced to the east, toward the harbor and the Mediterranean Sea.

"Mr. Asobi was right. We are far from Kobe. Farther still from my village. And you, Miss Kawamichi?"

She smiled. "Did you recognize my accent? You surprised me, Ino-san. When did you have that business card made?"

Mr. Ino turned back to face the room. It was furnished in gray with trim of a creamy shade. The effect was restful to the eye. A few prints of classical paintings were hung from the walls.

"Miss Sabi arranged the card. As soon as I heard you speak, I realized that her choice was by no means random." He turned once more to the window, inhaled deeply, then strode across the room and seated himself. "I have read that the sense of smell is the most ancient and deeply-seated of the human senses. Do you agree, Miss Kawamichi?"

"I've never thought about it."

"The newborn infant is blind, of course. He has tasted nothing. The first sensation is that of odor. The most deeply embedded human memory is that of the scent of the mother."

He peered out into the night. It was winter in Cataluña. It had been years since Mr. Ino had lived in an environment where the seasons were meaningful. On Mars the periodic dust storms inhibited surface travel, but normal life took place beneath sealed domes. On Phobos or on *Tsuki*, of course, there were not even the faint seasonal differences that were known on Mars. But on the home world—

Ah, on the home world there were seasons, there was weather, snowfall and rainfall, wind and air that carried odors of brine or of forest or of grain. Returning to the home world was an experience that provoked emotions Mr. Ino had not known himself capable of.

"The scent of the sea, Kawamichi-san, is to me like the scent of its mother to an infant."

Miss Kawamichi said, "Do you plan to return to the *go* parlor tomorrow night?"

"Oh yes. Without a doubt."

"And during the day, what do you propose?"

"We are a touring couple, visiting Cataluña from the home islands," he smiled.

"Truly?"

"To the world. I propose that we behave as tourists tomorrow. Take a light breakfast in our hotel, stroll the streets, visit a museum."

"But we are not tourists. We are here to learn what the Aum Shinrikyo is up to." Miss Kawamichi had retrieved a small *denwa* from her sparse luggage. A message light pulsed red. Miss Kawamichi's eyes widened; she touched a fingernail to the *denwa* to open a secure link to *Tsuki*. She looked up. "Ino-san, do you wish to speak with Miss Sabi?"

Mr. Ino nodded. He began a verbal report but Miss Sabi cut him off.

"You are doing as you ought to. We are increasingly concerned. Europa reports unauthorized landings and departures. We know that Aum activity centers in Cataluña. You must act quickly."

"*Mochiron desu!*"

"Have you made contact with Aum?"

"*Hai.*"

"Very good. A warning. Do not trust Mr. Kemuri. Do not trust any of our company's people in Barcelona. You are on your own."

Mr. Ino raised his eyebrows, glanced across a polished wooden desk at Miss Kawamichi.

As if she had read his mind, Miss Sabi said, "Miss Kawamichi is reliable. I was not referring to her."

"*Naruho do.*"

"Learn what you can. Communicate with me when you have anything for me."

The light blinked off and the *denwa* became dormant.

Miss Kawamichi said, "I am very tired. I will shower now and then retire."

Mr. Ino waited for her to finish, then stood under a stream of hot water, soaping himself luxuriously. Like so many other things taken for granted on the home planet, a hot shower was a precious luxury on *Tsuki* or Mars, nothing more than a fond memory or a dream on Phobos.

In the morning they breakfasted on tortillas made with fresh eggs and morels and *shoku-pan* with marmalade and drank steaming coffee and freshly squeezed orange juice. They dressed in warmer clothing, for the winter morning in Cataluña was brisk.

Like married tourists they strolled from the hotel, gazing at buildings that had stood since the fourteenth century and those constructed in the twenty-second.

The morning was clear and brisk. The city was filled with residents going about their business. A fresh breeze came off the Mediterranean. Somehow they found themselves in the Plaça Santa Maria. They entered the Basílica Santa Maria del Mar. Mr. Ino watched the morning light through ancient stained glass. He edged into a pew, seated himself, then leaned forward to rest his head on the polished wood of the next pew. The walk had tired him.

He repeated to himself, *Ore wa mushukyo da.* I am not religious. Certainly he was no Christian, but the church was pleasant. It had stood for almost a thousand years. He felt the weight of the centuries and yet in the tall, open space of the basilica he began to feel lighter.

Miss Kawamichi edged into the pew beside him. He felt the warmth and pressure of her presence at his side.

After a time they left the basilica and walked again. In his fantasy they were what they pretended to be, a married couple on holiday enjoying the exotic sights of Cataluña. Phobos was a distant memory. *Tsuki* was a lovely object that appeared in the night sky. Aum Shinrikyo was an aberration of history. Mr. Nishiyobi was dead.

Later they found an outdoor *chamise* and rested. Time had passed and appetites returned. Miss Kawamichi ordered *tsukemono* with *hiya-yakko.* Mr. Ino chose *hayashi-raisu.* They shared a steaming pot of *ryoku-cha.*

They rode the subway to Carrer Veguer in the Barri Gòtic and the Museo d'Història de la Ciutat. Mr. Ino preceded Miss Kawamichi through the great carved doors. The museum was filled with artifacts from Barcelona's past, Cataluña's glory some eight hundred years ago, its repression under Philip V and its restoration in the new millennium.

To Mr. Ino's startlement Miss Kawamichi took his hand and led him down a passageway. They emerged into a glowing Palatine chapel, passed through it and down, seemingly, into the earth itself. They emerged in a carefully preserved Roman chamber. Other tourists shared the space, and groups of students. Without their presence, Mr. Ino felt as if he could tumble backward through the centuries to Barcelona's golden age and then still farther back to its days as an outpost of the Roman Empire.

But there was an explosive thump and the room's glowing light was stained a sickly green. Men shouted, women screamed, children cried out in terror. There was a rush to return to the chapel. A mother swept a child into her arms and shoved her way through the crowd. A man in a ragged *uwagi* bowled Mr. Ino over. As he tumbled he grasped the man's garment and came away with an oddly made button attached to a fraying thread. He found himself on the floor, surrounded by scuffling *kutsu* and dusty *zori*.

The green gas burned his eyes. His skin itched as if he had fallen into a briar patch. He struggled to his feet. He spotted Miss Kawamichi. She was peering around herself, a frantic expression on her face. There was no way that he could make himself heard by her above the hubbub, but he managed to reach her side and they were swept from the room by the crowd of sightseers.

Green gas was billowing behind them, filling first the chapel and then the main hall of the *museo*. Guards were hustling people out of the building.

Outside a first aid station was quickly established. A dousing with fresh water relieved the burning of Mr. Ino's eyes and reduced the itching of his skin. An emergency worker furnished a few breaths of pure oxygen from a tall tank and Mr. Ino's lungs returned to normal. With a skirl of sirens, ambulances and cars of the *guardia civil* converged on the *museo*, but few casualties needed to be evacuated.

A uniformed *guardia* pointed out his commander to Mr. Ino. The commander was a square-faced, moustachio'd man. He appeared to be an occidental, probably a Cataluñan, but he spoke the universal language. Mr. Ino had reached him by flashing his credentials at the uniformed *guardia*. He had no authority in Barcelona but he had long learned that impressive credentials and an authoritative manner could carry him into or out of most circumstances.

The commander appointed a uniformed *guardia* to escort Mr. Ino back into the *museo*. The *guardia* had arrived equipped with breathing gear and eye covering; a set was provided for Mr. Ino. It became obvious that the *guardia* spoke only Catalan and Spanish, but he accompanied Mr. Ino to the Roman chamber.

A technician there armed with tongs was just placing a metal canister in a containment device. The air was still discolored but was visibly clearing even as Mr. Ino watched. The technician did speak Mr. Ino's language. Already he had tested the gas; it was nothing but pepper spray tinted with an inert vegetable dye. The canister would be studied for DNA traces or other evidence, but the technician doubted that anything useful would be learned from it.

Mr. Ino left the *museo*. He found Miss Kawamichi helping a mother to calm a pair of panicked twin children. They made their way along Carrer Veguer to the Placa Sant Felip Neri. They sat beneath the ancient saint's monument.

"Thus we see the work of Aum Shinrikyo," Miss Kawamichi pronounced.

"So it would seem. But are you certain?"

"I know their history."

There was a silence. Then, "Please."

"Their greatest atrocity was the release of poison gas into the subway in Tokyo in the home islands. It was an act of mass murder. They had plans for far greater catastrophes. They were trying to purchase nuclear weapons, biological weapons. Their leader was arrested."

"Matsumoto Chizuo."

"The one."

"But why? Who is their enemy? What is their purpose?"

"*Poa.*"

"Mr. Nishiyobi said that. He repeated it shortly before he died."

"It is at the core of their beliefs. They are truly out to save the world by destroying humanity except for the chosen few, themselves."

"Then why set off this gas? The *guardia* technician told me that it was harmless." He managed a wry grin. "Relatively speaking, of course."

"You were distressed."

"You dealt with it better than I."

She did not reply.

"But why, then? Why set off a gas bomb that would create panic in a museum but do little or no harm?"

She shook her head. "That puzzles me, Ino-san. I have studied the Aum Shinrikyou for twenty years. I wrote my doctoral dissertation on them." She laughed softly. "But I don't understand them fully. Truly I don't."

A wave of fatigue swept over Mr. Ino. He suggested that they return to their hotel. When they arrived he composed a report on the day's events and transmitted it to Miss Sabi on *Tsuki*. He shut off the device and showered, then collapsed onto his bed. He turned on the monitor and was treated to the story of a gory murder and then was urged to purchase a reliable fuel-cell powered *torakku* to haul materials for his business. He closed his eyes on mixed images of corpses and happy vehicle owners and slept soundly and dreamlessly.

When he awoke the room was dark. Beyond its windows the sky was dark. Night came early in winter. The stars glittered hypnotically. The moon blazed like a cold, miniature sun. Was Miss Sabi truly there? Were the remains of Mr. Nishiyobi preserved, or had they by now been destroyed?

Mr. Ino rose and donned fresh *zubon* and *shatsu* and a warm *seta*. He had no idea where Miss Kawamichi had gone until she returned to their suite with a fresh spray of flowers pinned to a *seta* of her own.

"Are you ready?" she asked.

"For what?"

"We promised Asobi-san that we would meet him at Sakana's Go Parlor. And I am hungry."

Mr. Ino was not at all hungry. The pepper spray he had breathed had reached his stomach as well, and such appetite as he might have had was gone. But this was work as well.

They reached Sakana's and looked around. Mr. Asobi was nowhere to be seen. They found a table and set up a board for *go*. Mr. Ino drew the black stones; Miss Kawamichi, the white.

Play had barely begun when a ragged form approached from the shadows to loom over the board. Mr. Ino craned his head to see Mr. Asobi, an intense expression on his face.

"Asobi-san."

"Koga-san." Mr. Asobi made a polite *ojigi*. "It pleases me to see you and your wife once more. You are both well?"

"Thank you. Yes."

"I was concerned. There was an incident today. A disturbance. I know you are both strangers in Barcelona, I was concerned for your well-being."

"Thank you. We are both well."

"I heard there was an attack at the Museo d'Historia. I worried that you were among those injured."

Mr. Ino shook his head. His neck was becoming sore from tilting to face Mr. Asobi. He dropped his glance to Mr. Asobi's disreputable *uwagi*, expecting to see that one of the buttons was now missing entirely. It was not; instead, one of the odd metallic buttons of the *uwagi* had been replaced by an ordinary one of plastic.

"Are you hungry, Koga-san? You or *okusan?*" He cast a glance, not disrespectfully, toward Miss Kawamichi.

"No."

"Ah." Mr. Asobi reached behind him and dragged a chair to the table, turning it as he had the previous night so that its back was to the table. Once more he straddled it, leaning on folded arms atop its ladder back.

"Even so, Koga-san, there are better places than Sakana's Go Parlor, more rewarding places for strangers in town to spend their evenings. Do you get to Barcelona often? Are you here on business or as tourists?"

"Not often." Mr. Ino waited for Asobi to speak further.

"Are you religious persons?" Asobi asked.

*Ore wa mushukyo da,* Mr. Ino thought, but instead he made a noncommittal response. "Who knows? Under the right circumstances, who is not?"

Mr. Asobi smiled. *"Tashi kani!* I have lived in Cataluña for some years now. I miss the home islands, but my affairs are here. If you would both honor me with your company, I would be grateful. And we can find better surroundings than Sakana's."

Mr. Ino pushed his chair back from the table. He gestured to Miss Kawamichi, who did the same. Their *go* contest would have to await another occasion.

Mr. Asobi preceded them to the doorway and into the street. To Mr. Ino's surprise a car was awaiting them. A uniformed driver held the door for them and Mr. Ino and Miss Kawamichi climbed into the backseat. Mr. Asobi climbed into the car and seated himself in front of them. The driver closed the doors and they proceeded.

The night streets of Barcelona were nearly as bustling as those of daytime. Lights flashed on restaurants and theaters. Mr. Ino suspected that music poured from clubs but the car was closed and no sound penetrated the tonneau from outside.

Barcelona was not without its industrial areas, sections of warehouses and small factories darkened for the night. The car pulled into an opening and plunged down a ramp. The driver pulled to a halt and opened the doors for Mr. Ino and Miss Kawamichi.

Mr. Asobi exited the car and disappeared. The driver bowed and indicated that Mr. Ino and Miss Kawamichi were to follow him.

The interior of the building was plain, the walls of stucco and the floor of rough wood. The ceiling was high and lost in darkness. They were led through a doorway and down a long hall. The lighting was dim and uneven. A faint tang came to the nostrils. There was distant music, so faint as to cause one to wonder if it was imaginary.

They entered a room hung with embroideries. A raised platform was covered with dark cloth; upon it was a throne, and upon the throne, richly robed in green cloth stitched with gold, Asobi Yoi.

"*Heiwa.*" Asobi bowed his head to Mr. Ino and Miss Kawamichi. "Surely you guessed before now who I am."

"I suspected. *Atarashii Sendachi.*"

"Yes. But Asobi is good."

"This is Aum Shinrikyo. This is your *kyoto.*"

The other spread his hands. "Our *Bukkkyoto,* our *Kirisutokyoto,* our *Hindukyoto.* All religions are one. That is why we are the people of the universal truth."

"You kill."

"We save."

"You set off the bomb at the Museo d'Historia."

Asobi smiled. "Not I personally. I was there, but it was another who set off the bomb. No one was injured seriously." He pushed himself upright and took a few steps toward them, descending from his throne and from the platform on which it stood.

"Ino-san, Kawamichi-san, why have you come to me? Do you wish to join Aum Shinrikyo? You would be welcome."

He had called them by their true names. So much for Koga Isoruko and his wife, of Kobe. He knew who they were. How much else did *Atarashii Sendachi,* the new guide of Aum Shinrikyo, know about them?

Mr. Asobi made an *ojigi* before them, then straightened. Mr. Ino found himself returning the polite bow, saw Miss Kawamichi at his side do the same. In the dim light he could see that Mr. Asobi's eyes were milky, like those of Mr. Nishiyobi.

"Come." Asobi gestured. "Let's be comfortable." He walked straight at a cloth-shrouded wall, parting the draperies before him to show the way into another room. Mr. Ino and Miss Kawamichi stepped through. The draperies fell into place behind them. They were in an ordinary room made in the style of a simple residence in the home islands. There was comfortable furniture, and all were seated on cushions surrounding a low table. The floor was covered with *tatami*.

"Of course Miss Kawamichi is not your wife."

Mr. Ino did not respond.

"You would be fortunate if she were." Asobi smiled.

In the light of this so-ordinary room his eyes appeared to be clear, bright, sharp. His unkempt hair and scraggly beard were transformed into handsome array. His ragged *uwagi* was nowhere to be seen, replaced by the robes of *Sendachi*, the guide.

An iron pot and three small porcelain cups decorated with gilt herons stood on the table. Mr. Asobi looked away, then back at his guests. A slim woman in traditional garb of the home islands appeared and poured tea for all. In an instant she was gone, as if she had never been present.

Mr. Asobi lifted his cup. "*Heiwa. Heiwa wo ki shite, Kampai!*"

Hooray for peace indeed.

"Ino-san." Mr. Asobi sipped, then lowered his cup. He smiled again at Mr. Ino and Miss Kawamichi. "You aren't drinking your tea." He frowned. "Oh, you fear—what? Poison? Drugs? Aum has placed a hypnotic chemical in your tea and if you so much as accept a sip you will be helplessly enslaved forever?"

He shook his head. "No. Here." He placed his cup on the table, lifted another, sipped from it. Then from the third. "You see? Nothing harmful. I am not dead. Of course I could have arranged for your own deaths earlier. I wish you no harm. But I am curious as to why you came seeking Aum Shinrikyo. Why you came seeking *Atarashii Sendachi*. Here I am, you see, neither god nor saint, a mere man. What do you want?"

"What is Aum Shinrikyo doing on Europa?"

"Ah! Very good. At last you speak sensibly."

"I await your answer."

"But who are you to question me? I am an ordinary man. Aum Shinrikyo is a religious movement. I serve its members. What have we to do with some icy globe billions of kilometers from Earth?"

"There have been deaths. There have been perilous doings. Most recently, the death of Mr. Nishiyobi. There are dangerous materials on Europa. Caves of *midori no koori*, of green ice."

"So I have heard."

"Green ice of incredible beauty, said to have amazing qualities. But only stable at extremely low temperatures. Warmed, the ice sublimates into a deadly toxin that bears a resemblance to a virus. It kills, and it spreads after the victim's death. His *tamashii* escapes from his mouth or from his nostrils, his extremities become hard and brittle and themselves turn to *midori no koori* that must be refrigerated or it will sublimate and spread the plague."

Mr. Asobi laughed. "What a fairy tale."

For the first time, Miss Kawamichi spoke up. "It's true, *Sendachi*. Ino-san has seen it with his own eyes. I have seen it with mine."

"False, false, false." Mr. Asobi shook his head vigorously from side to side. "But even if true, what affair is it of your company?"

"Our company operates the *uchuukichi*, the great station that orbits Jupiter. The expeditions to the moons, including Europa, are ours. We are responsible. We might be responsible for the welfare of the species. Or its demise, Asobi-sama."

The erstwhile ragged Asobi covered his mouth with one hand and rocked in place. "You do not understand *Poa*, do you?"

*Poa* again. *Poa*. Mr. Ino admitted that he did not.

"You are from the home islands, Ino-san. Did you practice any religion at home?"

"There was a Shinto shrine." Mr. Ino felt himself blushing. He had spoken truthfully but had committed an evasion of the type for which he had challenged Miss Sabi.

"Did you believe?" Mr. Asobi persisted.

"I was a fisherman." Mr. Ino clenched his teeth.

Asobi laughed. "Very good. You are a man of subtlety, Ino-san."

"I try to be a man of simplicity, Asobi-san."

"Do you believe that Asahara Shoko was a god? A saint? A madman? A criminal?"

"I try to do my work, to please my employer, to bring some justice to the world."

"Ah." Mr. Asobi sucked air between his teeth. "An idealist."

Mr. Ino was silent.

"Do you believe in *karma*, then? In sin? In salvation?"

Mr. Ino shook his head. "I leave such questions to others."

Mr. Asobi raised his hand and signaled to someone outside of Mr. Ino's vision. There was the sound of stockinged feet, the swish of draperies. Mr. Asobi addressed Miss Kawamichi, asking about her own upbringing.

Shortly a young woman in traditional garb brought trays. She knelt beside the low table and served food and drink. There was *gomoku-soba, yasai, kaibashira, kare-raisu, sake, mizu.*

Throughout the meal Mr. Asobi guided the conversation between talk of the day's events, references to traditional culture, the teachings of Aum Shinrikyo. The cult seemed strange to Mr. Ino, but no stranger than other religions. Its members sought to save others from committing *tsumi*. Each sin not only harmed its victim but the sinner as well. In fact, in the long run, it harmed the sinner far more than the victim, for it stained his soul, his *seishin*, his *tamashii*. The victim would recover, in another life if not in the present one; the sinner would suffer.

Moreover, the *karma* of the world was damaged by each *tsumi*. If only there were no sinners, all would be well. If the world were populated only by beasts, there would be no sin, for only those capable of understanding the difference between right and wrong could possibly be guilty.

Did Ino-san not agree?

Did Kawamichi-san?

Miss Kawamichi seemed convinced.

Mr. Ino kept his own counsel.

Mr. Asobi rose and led them to another room, a modern chamber equipped with monitors and communication devices. "You see, we religious are not primitives."

"I never thought that of you." A smiling face and a friendly voice urged consumers to purchase Bombay *momoiro ganyaku* for cure of toothache.

A pleasant haze had come over Mr. Ino. He cast his gaze at Miss Kawamichi. She had, somehow, switched from her western-style shirt and trousers to traditional garb. Mr. Ino looked around for a mirror. He found none. Instead he raised his arm so he could see his garment, bent to see his shoes clearly. His ears pounded so he raised his head once more only to find it floating in the air above his body.

He shook his head and opened his mouth to speak but was unable to do so.

Miss Kawamichi placed her hand on his arm. She appeared concerned. "Ino-san?"

Mr. Asobi was speaking, not to Mr. Ino but to Miss Kawamichi. Mr. Ino tried to understand what he said, but could hear only a buzz of syllables. Miss Kawamichi took him by the elbow. Mr. Asobi, *Atarashii Sendachi*, levitated from the floor. The young woman who had brought their dinner or another woman identical to her took Mr. Ino by the other elbow. He turned his head to look at her. She had black, glossy hair, graceful features, smooth skin. She could have been a young woman from his home island. She could have been his wife, but Miss Kawamichi was his wife, he knew this, they were so recorded at the registry of their hotel.

He was Ino Hajime.

He was Koga Isoruko.

The two women, each of whom could have been his wife, were guiding him . . . somewhere. Neither was his wife. He had no wife. But the tall Miss Kawamichi, the petite—what was her name?

He opened his mouth to ask her name but there was no wind in his chest. Of course not. His head was not connected to his body. He did not know the name of his own wife, the lovely petite woman who wore her traditional garb with such charm. He did not even know her name. He began to weep with shame for not knowing his own wife's name.

The two women were guiding him through a doorway, leaving the building. He had to lower his head to the level of his torso to fit through the doorway. They were in the street now, outside the lovely *kyoukai* of Aum Shinrikyo. He did not want to leave the temple, did not want to part from the presence of the saint, of Asobi-sama, of *Atarashii Sendachi*, but he had no power.

He turned his eyes downward and saw that his feet were moving, first one and then the other.

If there were no *tsumi*, no sin, then the world's *karma* would rise, the world would be saved. If there were no sinners there would be no sin. But—a brilliant thought came to Mr. Ino—if a group could remove all others from the world, there would be fewer sinners. If a smaller group could remove them from the world there would be still fewer. And so on.

In due course there would be only one person left, one holy person to remove all the others. By so doing he would free the world from sin. He would take the heavy *karma* of the others upon himself, and by so doing would commit an act of selfless sacrifice that would save the world. Surely then he himself would be taken up into heaven. He would be the savior of the world.

It was all a familiar story, strange and oddly shaped, but familiar nonetheless.

*Kami o shinjiru.*

*Kami o shinjiteiru to omou.*

*Atarashii Sendachi wa kami da.*

I believe in god.

I think I believe in god.

Asobi-sama is god.

He began to weep uncontrollably, ashamed, the weeping adding to his shame.

He was whirling, surrounded by colors that were sounds, sounds that were patterns, patterns that spelled out strange words that he could read but not understand, that he could understand but not read. He tumbled into the words and found himself in a black space, cold, helpless, omnipotent, wise, mad, ecstatic, bursting with laughter, wracked with sobs, rolling in a sea of white writhing worms that turned into lovely women with pointed teeth and long black talons that raked his flesh. They pulled his soul from within him and fought for it among themselves, devouring him bit by bit, smiling and licking their red lips with each morsel of his being.

A thousand-kilo hammer smashed into the back of his skull and shattered him into a million pieces.

He was dead.

He was in a metal coffin.

The coffin was not a coffin, it was a storage locker.

A worker clad in dark green coveralls had opened the lid of the coffin that was not a coffin and was peering at him through milky eyes. The worker nodded his head. "Koga Isoruko."

Who was that? Ino Hajime blinked. The worker was bathed in a liquid haze of whiteness.

"Koga!" The voice was neither friendly nor solicitous. Ino Hajime was suddenly aware of his helplessness. He was weak and naked. He tried to rise but had difficulty. He was afraid that the worker in the green coveralls would be angry with him and punish him. But he was not Koga. Who was Koga?

The worker took him by the shoulders and pulled him upright. He was sitting in the locker now. But he was confused. Where was the ceiling, where the floor? He was light-headed and dizzy, nauseous. He felt his stomach heave and a burning substance pump up from his gut.

At this the coverall-clad worker leaped backwards.

The lid on the coffin slammed shut. He was in total darkness, the metal of the coffin cold and clammy around him, the remnants of his vomitus burning his mouth and the stench of it searing his nostrils.

Time passed.

He was awakened by water running cold and rapidly over him. He feared that he was drowning but then realized that the water was flowing over him, washing away the accumulated filth. When the water stopped the lid of his coffin was opened once again and he saw another face, another individual wearing dark green coveralls. The face was surrounded by a pale nimbus, the eyes milky.

This time he was able to sit up unassisted. The burning taste in his mouth was gone. He was dripping wet.

"Koga Isoruko, arise. Koga Isoruko, born again into Aum Shinrikyo." The face was smiling.

Now he remembered who Koga Isoruko was. It was he. Yes. Ino Hajime had been his old identity. Ino Hajime had been an employee of the company and a foe of Aum Shinrikyo. Koga Isoruko was part of Aum Shinrikyo, was part of the salvation of the universe.

In due course he was wearing green coveralls of his own, white *kutsu* covered his feet. Everything was strangely pale and unclear. He knew that if he could find a mirror he would see that something had happened to his eyes, that they were milky like those of the *kami-seijin,* the god-saint, Asahara Shoko.

He was alone in a metal room that reminded him of the metal coffin or storage locker from which he had been summoned — how long ago? A few minutes, a thousand years? His time-sense was confused. All his senses were confused. Colors shifted one into another, shapes altered, large objects were suddenly small and endearing, tiny ones monstrously huge and terrifying.

He wandered from the room and found himself in a corridor. Men and women, all of them clad in green coveralls, bustled past him, ignored him. Clearly they were intent on urgent yet mysterious missions of their own.

His surroundings, at first strange, became gradually more familiar. He had been in a place like this before, had been in places like this more than once. It was — he almost had it but the idea slipped away like a dream lost upon awakening.

Sounds came to him and he followed them until he found himself standing in the entrance to a hall filled with long tables and benches. Men and women were seated at the tables, chattering to one another. There were bowls and cups and pairs of wooden *hashi* that men and women manipulated with skill, transferring food from their bowls to their mouths, sipping beverages, laughing.

Laughing.

If they were laughing they were happy and this must be not so bad a place. Perhaps it was *tengoku.* Heaven.

A woman sitting with her back to him must have sensed his presence. Perhaps he had made a sound that caught her attention, although it seemed peculiar that such would be the case above the jumble of voices in the hall.

The woman smiled and gestured to him. She lifted one hand

and drew him into the hall as if by a puppeteer's strings. He walked carefully toward her. She slid aside, making room for him at her table. A man sat beside her. He moved in the other direction.

Koga Isoruko made a polite *ojigi*. The others smiled and returned the gesture as best they could without rising from their places. He introduced himself, reflexively reaching for a business card that was no longer part of his accouterment.

Someone handed him a bowl, someone else ladled hot *miso shiru* into the bowl. Koga lifted the bowl gratefully. The steaming soup had a delicious odor. Tiny yellowish cubes and bits of green floated in it. He essayed an experimental sip and found the soup offered a splendidly rewarding flavor. He finished the soup and set the bowl back on the table.

The table was metallic in nature, bolted to the floor as were the benches.

His bowl was filled again, this time with *yaki-onigiri* and *hamachi*, or at any rate with things that resembled these items. He added *shoyu* and *wasabi* and fed himself with fresh wooden *hashi*.

He had not realized how hungry he was. Prior to this meal he had not eaten in—how long? he wondered. He had no idea. He remembered awakening in his metal coffin. Had it been the only one in the great coffin-like room, or had there been others? He had not noticed.

He had awakened once and been sick and lost consciousness. He had been awakened the second time by water rushing over his body, and had found his way to this refectory hall.

He had been so busy with his meal, so obsessed with his hunger and thirst that he had neither participated in the conversation of his companions nor listened to their words. His consciousness had been limited to food and drink.

Now his companions were finishing their meals, laying their implements on the table. He emulated them, still vaguely hungry but ashamed to request more food when the others were clearly preparing to move on to other activities. He would wait for another opportunity to satisfy his appetite.

He raised his eyes, embarrassed, from the table with its dining implements and the remnants of the meal, to the faces of the men and women around him. They seemed unconcerned with his arrival and his conduct, perhaps mildly welcoming and surely not hostile.

Above the table the ceiling was curved and transparent. The sight was hauntingly familiar. Had he beheld such a spectacle before? His vision was milky, but rather than annoying him this added a pleasing quality to what he saw.

Through the transparent ceiling he could see blackness and distant points of light. The image rolled slowly past as if a diorama were unfolding beyond the transparent material, then he realized that the image was not moving so much as he was, the whole room was, the whole—whatever the room was part of—was rolling.

A blue-and-white disk came into view, and beyond it a much smaller white one. The disks looked familiar. He knew what they were, or at least he knew that he knew what they were, if only he could summon up the understanding, but he could not. He knew he had been there. He had been on that blue disk and on the white one, if only he could remember when that had been and why he had been there, and what the disks represented.

The vistas continued to change until the blue-and-white disk and smaller white disk disappeared. A brilliant flaming disk slid into his view. The transparent ceiling altered, darkened. The flaming disk was dimmed.

Now he dropped his gaze to return to the men and women who had surrounded him. While he had sat transfixed by the sights beyond the transparent roof they had departed.

Where had they all gone? Why had he been left alone? Was he supposed to return to his coffin now? Was he dead? Had he been summoned back from beyond the world of the living to enjoy a final meal, only to return now to the coffin where he would lie for all eternity?

He wandered corridors until he found someone. He did not know this person, did not know even if he had met a man or a woman. He stood facing the other, somehow calm, passive, feeling neither discomfort nor pleasure. With milky eyes the other looked into his face, then nodded, took him by the shoulder and led him to an area where coverall-clad figures worked over machinery.

He was shown a simple job and set to performing it over and over. How many times he repeated his task he had no idea. He may have felt hunger or thirst, fatigue or the pressure of bladder or bowel, but he continued the simple repetition. Finally a signal must have been given, although he was unaware of it. Workers around him laid down their tasks and shuffled away.

It was mealtime again, then time for rest. They moved in a body, women and men, chatting among themselves. They reached a dormitory, bathed in groups, then lay down. The water with which they bathed was tepid and smelled unpleasantly, as if it had been recycled many times and imperfectly purified.

Koga Isoruko spoke to no one. Occasionally someone would speak to him, simply and slowly, telling him what to do. Disrobe now. Stand beneath the shower now. Soap and scrub, rinse yourself, stand in drying chamber. Now don undergarments. Now climb into bed and sleep.

Thus the cycle. Rest, work, eat, work, bathe, rest.

When he saw the sky turning slowly past he was filled with strange feelings, vague yearnings, distant memories that retreated when he tried to capture them, returned when he gave up the attempt.

Each time he slept he had no idea how long he remained unconscious. There was neither day nor night. Hours could be years; centuries could be moments. Each time he woke he searched for the blue disk, the white disk, the burning disk. Each time he found them they had become smaller.

The hundredth time he peered through the transparent ceiling something new appeared. Slowly Koga Isoruko had begun to regain his awareness of himself and his surroundings. The first time he spoke was at refectory. He turned to the woman beside whom he had taken every meal since his first awakening in the metal coffin and asked her for *wasabi*.

She exclaimed in astonishment and spoke rapidly to others at their table. Koga Isoruko asked again. "*Wasabi, onegai shimas.*"

Suddenly they were talking to him, asking him his name, his home, how he had come to be aboard this *uchuu-sen*.

He had been on spaceships before. He remembered. He had traveled from—that was a puzzle. Someone even mentioned the name of this *uchuu-sen*. It was *Kaigun-Taishoo Shigamitsu*. He knew the meaning of the name. The *uchuu-sen* was named for an Admiral Shigamitsu, but he had no idea who that might be.

Their meal was of *hiyashi-chuka* and *gyoza*, dumplings with cold noodles. He wanted some *wasabi* to add flavor to the bland dishes. His name was Koga Isoruko.

His neighbors introduced themselves. He found himself reaching automatically for something—something to give them—something to tell them who he was. He had told them, Koga Isoruko, but propriety required that he give them—give them—what? A book, a letter, no, a card. A business card.

With his name engraved on it in traditional characters, *Koga Isoruko*, and the name of the company. But something was wrong. His name was not Koga Isoruko, and the name of the company was—he could not remember. And none of this mattered as he had no cards to give them, nor they to give him.

He reached for the *wasabi*, added it to his noodles and dumplings, ate them, drank tea.

It was time to work.

But he knew that he was aboard an *uchuu-sen*, a spaceship, and the transparent ceiling was a panel in the hull, provided to help space travelers remember that there was a universe outside their ship. What lay beyond was *uchuu*, was space, was the sky. He had seen something new in the sky. The blue disk and the white disk no longer appeared. The burning disk was tiny now, no larger than a grain of rice. Only the shining points of light were unchanged in the transparent ceiling.

After two more sleeps he saw the new thing in the sky again. It was larger now. It was another disk, neither blue nor white nor burning, but red and glowing, like a coal removed from a furnace and placed on an iron grille.

Somewhere inside his head were memories. He pounded his skull with his fists. He was at his work now, a simple task that required little attention and less thought. He spent the time of his work trying to think, trying to remember.

Was he Koga Isoruko or was he someone else? He was certain that he was someone else but he did not know who.

Every so often, after a work time and a meal, they did not bathe and sleep but marched to a hall where a leader lectured them. The man who was not really Koga Isoruko tried to understand the lectures. Behind the speaker was a huge portrait of a man with milky eyes. He was clad in the fashion of a past century.

Not-Koga had trouble understanding the lectures. All those around him seemed to understand. He did not question. He sat and listened and tried to comprehend something called *Poa* but he could not follow the lecturer's logic.

The pace of life aboard the *uchuu-sen* increased. Something important was happening. Not-Koga tried to ask but his speech was still halting, flawed, his vocabulary broken by ideas for which he could not recall the words. When he tried to ask a question and found that he could not express himself he felt a pressure mounting in his head, a ringing in his ears. His chest tightened with the difficulty of breathing until he abandoned the effort and permitted the moment to pass with some trivial comment, some small talk, or with simple silence.

His refectory companions were pleasant but he was unable to join fully in their conversations. He did not speak at work or at bathing or rest times. When the lectures occurred he sat and listened, trying to understand.

What was *Poa?*

In time he realized that it was at the heart of universal truth. Aum Shinrikyo. If he could understand *Poa* he would understand Aum Shinrikyo. He thought he had understood it once but in a different time and place, a time and place now lost to him.

Men and women were running in the corridors. The *uchuusen* was preparing to dock. The great glowing disk in the sky had resolved itself into a seething red ball. He knew that he knew what it was but he could not remember. His task was not vital to the docking operation and he sat beneath a transparent panel watching the approach of something—of something—

And he knew what it was. It was the *ookii kokai,* the great station that the company had placed in a complex orbit around the great red planet Jupiter, an orbit that wove among the countless moons and the small rings that circled that planet like a minor solar system.

There was the *uchuukichi,* dead ahead of *Kaigun-Taishoo Shigamitsu.* The big spaceship was drifting slowly toward the orbiting station, slowly approaching the station's docking port. The closer it approached the more gigantic did not-Koga realize the station must be. Now it filled the sky, like a world in its own right, and now with a whirl of gyroscopes and the soft pressure of compressed gases *Shigamitsu* touched the docking grapples of *uchuukichi* and halted with a great, relieved groan of weary metal.

In that moment not-Koga caught a glimpse of himself, not in the polished glass of a mirror or metal of a bulkhead, but in the depths of his mind. The milky stuff that softened the focus of his vision and of his mind cleared and he remembered his name and his mission, but as quickly and as dazzlingly as he had regained his knowledge of self, that knowledge was lost again.

The milky whiteness returned.

They were leaving the great *uchuu-sen* now, marching in orderly ranks into the chambers and corridors of the orbiting *ookii kokai.* The space station, like the spaceship, was fitted with large transparent panels, making it possible to see the universe outside the machine.

That universe was dominated by the great red ball that was Jupiter with its swirling bands of brighter and darker color, its roiling storms big enough to swallow a planet the size of Earth as a koi-pond would swallow a pebble tossed by a child, and with as little effect.

He found himself in a briefing room with a score of others. A woman entered and stationed herself on the platform. She was there to explain their new duties to them, but first she would call roll. When she came to Koga Isoruko he uttered a loud grunt, *Hai*, receiving an acknowledging nod from the woman.

He was Koga Isoruko. He had come from Kobe in the home islands. He had a profession, an employer, a home and wife. He had—but he could not recall them clearly. A face rose before him, the strong face of a tall woman, a woman with long glossy hair and good bones. Her name was—he almost had it, but it slipped away.

His profession was—

The company by which he was employed was—

He shook his head despairingly.

It was no use.

The woman at the front of the room had spoken for some time. Now assistants rolled a machine onto the platform. Each of them carried an odd-looking tool. With the tools they demonstrated the purpose of the machine. The woman continued to speak.

After a while they left the room, followed leaders to other places in the orbiting *ookii kokai*, were given food and permitted to wash and change their clothing once again. They were fitted with sealed suits and breathing apparatus. Then they were led to a small *uchuu-sen*. It was little more than a sled with open seats and grips for passengers.

The sled dropped away from the orbiting station.

Jupiter loomed overhead like a giant red sea. Its face was covered by storms, but rather than marring its appearance the waves and swirls of color added to its terrible beauty. As the sled accelerated the thin rings of Jupiter enveloped them, then passed behind as they approached first one, then another of the magnificent planet's moons.

Koga Isoruko saw the moon Europa ahead. The little sled was headed toward the moon. Koga Isoruko became disoriented; the meanings of up and down kept shifting. He tried closing his eyes to combat the vertigo and nausea that assaulted him, but they only grew worse when he plunged himself into darkness. He dared not vomit inside his sealed suit; somehow he knew that to do so would clog his air lines and he would die.

How did he know that, he wondered. Mr. Koga of Kobe—how did he know that? Truth approached him like a shark swimming through warm water, then flicked its tail and sped away just at the moment when he was about to get a clear glimpse of it.

The sled now passed between the great planet and the small moon. Koga Isoruko tried to decide: Was Europa beneath the sled and Jupiter hovering massively in the sky like a giant red fist ready to smash down on the tiny sled, or was Jupiter beneath the sled while little Europa hovered overhead?

The pilot of the sled decided that once for all by swinging the tiny spacecraft into a gentle approach path to the moon. The icy ridges and plains of Europa became visible beneath the sled. Not a word had been spoken since leaving the orbiting space station, or perhaps it was the case that the sealed suits of the passengers had no means of transmitting or receiving speech.

The sled dropped closer to the surface of Europa. Mr. Koga recognized the topography, recognized the region of Europa called Pwyll. This was an area of icy ridges, fissures and caves. Beneath the icy covering of Europa a sea lay in wait, lay in wait for visitors, for life—unless it already contained life of its own.

No one knew.

Or—did someone know? Not-Koga almost remembered a conversation he had held long ago on the subject. The question had been asked but he could not recall the answer.

A small collection of buildings loomed ahead. The sled touched down on ski-like runners. Mr. Koga had skied in the home islands, sliding down the snow-covered slopes of beautiful mountains on holiday. Or had he? Was this a false memory? Was he a denizen of Kobe, an urban man raised in a towering apartment block, traveling to school as a child and to work as a young man by speedy public conveyance?

He thought that was the case, but another set of memories struggled to reach the surface of his mind, a set of memories in which he lived in an humble dwelling on a far northern island, raised by *Otosan* and *Okasan*, taught to ply the icy waters of the northern sea, to catch fish for food and for exchange with the bigger boats that came to the island to trade.

Koga Isoruko had a wife. Where was she?

Not-Koga was unmarried. Where was he?

They were trudging from the sled now. Beneath the feet of Koga the surface of Europa was like the face of a mountain in the home islands. Europa revolved on its axis and Jupiter was now below the moon's horizon. The hot face of the planet had appeared frightening while it was overhead, but now that it was not to be seen the moon was more terrifyingly desolate than ever.

They were taken into a barracks-like shed and handed tools. These were the tools that they had learned to use during the brief demonstration before boarding the sled that had brought them to Europa.

A voice crackled inside Koga's helmet. One question was answered, then. It was possible to receive speech while wearing the sealed suit. Whether it was possible to make oneself heard by others was another matter. Koga was inclined to test this but felt somehow constrained; instead, he held his silence.

From the shed they marched to a pit. The milkiness in Koga-not-Koga's eyes came and went. Now the face of Europa was lighted only by the sun, brilliant but distant and tiny. Koga-not-Koga was one of a group of workers. They might have been his erstwhile companions, the same men and women with whom he had traveled aboard the great ship *Kaigun-Taishoo Shigamitsu*. They all wore protective suits like his, suits sealed against the vacuum of Europa, warmed against its cold, fitted with breathing tubes that furnished oily-smelling air.

They stood at the edge of the pit. A faint light rose from it, spreading only a short distance. Not-Koga stood peering into the pit, then raised his eyes in faint curiosity to the plain surrounding it. He turned his head. In the distance he could see the shed from which he and his companions had come. The surface of the moon was visibly ridged, its lined face looking like a crude fabric woven by the hands of a giant.

He raised one hand to his head, an unconscious gesture, the revenant of a life past and forgotten. To his surprise, through gloved fingers he felt a switch on the side of his helmet. He snapped it and a lamp burst into being, casting light on the ground before him. All around him his companions were making the same discovery, turning so that their lamps cast ovals of light on one another and on the surface beneath their feet.

Bending so as to illuminate an area directly ahead of him he saw a white surface. Was this truly the icy face of Europa or was it something else? He bent and touched it with a gloved hand. It was rough and unyielding; like a vampire it sucked warmth from him, even through the insulated glove. He stood upright.

They were proceeding into the pit now. As they moved along they were issued simple tools, pointed pickaxes and baskets. The light from within the pit had a greenish tinge.

Soon they were at work, like subject peoples laboring in the darkness and danger of deep mines on the home planet, working to extract riches for the betterment of their oppressors and at the risk of their own lives.

The pit had led to a tunnel. The walls glittered in the light of their helmet lamps, reflecting light that could turn darkness into glare when the angle was right. The material they were mining was hard and came away in sheets and crystals when struck with their pickaxes. Whenever a basket was filled with green crystals it was passed back to the entrance of the pit to be carried away by other workers.

When a large crystal came away from the tunnel wall Koga-not-Koga laid his pickaxe aside and hefted it in both hands. In the light gravity of Europa its weight was slight but he could feel its heft and mass as he handled it. As he bent to examine the crystal his lamp flashed deep into the crystal and it reflected his image in a deep green tint.

Not-Koga's helmet, like those of his fellow workers, was furnished with a transparent faceplate. His helmet was reflected by a flat plane of green crystal, and for a moment, through the milkiness that obscured his vision, he caught a clear glimpse of his face.

It was the first time he had seen himself since leaving the *Kaigun-Taishoo Shigamitsu.* His cheeks were sunken, what little of his hair that he could see was mostly gray, as was the ragged beard that had sprouted on his chin. He raised a hand to feel his features but his gloved fingers encountered only helmet and faceplate.

He dropped his head toward the crystal, resting the forehead of his helmet on its surface. A sudden pain brought him to himself. Another worker—this must be a boss—had struck him across the back with a slim rod. The boss pointed, his meaning clear.

Not-Koga resumed his work.

Night and day alternated on Europa as periods of glaring red from giant Jupiter filling the sky and periods of blackness punctuated by brilliant points of light. There was no conversation. Meals were tasteless, fed through tiny locks in workers' protective suits. Sanitation was minimal.

Not-Koga lay on a hard pallet, resting between shifts of work. He lived with his own stink inside his protective suit. He wondered if he could remove his helmet. If so death would be quick. Every time they were awakened to return to the pit there were fewer workers. He saw one worker raise a hand, find a toggle and carefully lift helmet away from suit collar.

The worker was a woman. Her long hair was swept from the suit by the rush of air. He could see the moisture as it was expelled from her lungs. The sight was striking. The breath emerged as a visible mist of a distinctive green hue. In the frigid vacuum droplets of moisture crystallized instantly and fell like emerald sleet. Her death took but a moment. Not-Koga smiled. There was escape, then.

He stood over his dead companion's body, studying her face, pursuing a fugitive memory. He reached for her hand and removed the glove. Her hand had been transformed into a thing of green crystal.

He returned to work.

He had not seen the sled return from Europa to the orbiting *ookii kokai*; it must have done so while he was at work in the pit, or perhaps while he was sleeping. But he saw it return, a new crew of workers in their protective suits riding down from orbit to land on Europa. He wondered how long a worker was expected to last in the pit, how many had died before now, what was done with the remains of those who died of exhaustion or starvation or who simply opened their helmets to escape their labors.

On his next shift he made it his business to work farther into the tunnel than any of his fellows. There was no competition for the role of "leader" of a work party. Their efforts were equally demanding, the bosses equally harsh. The only requirement was that they keep at their tasks, chipping crystals, filling baskets, passing them to the rear.

Not-Koga lacked even the curiosity to wonder what became of the crystals after they were passed from the tunnel, or what they were used for. When he handled one he could see by the light of his helmet-lamp, could sense that there was a living force within the crystal, a green, pulsing power. It had something to do with Aum Shinrikyo, he thought, something to do with *Poa*. He knew this but he did not understand it.

Sometimes he wondered who he was.

Sometimes he worked unthinkingly, a robot that he knew would soon wear out and be scrapped in favor of a newer unit. It did not matter to Not-Koga.

But not this day. This day he was aware, his mind less numb than it had been for a long time. He pushed on ahead of his work party. He expected to feel the blow of the boss's rod on his back at any moment, but it did not come. He tilted his head to get a clear look at the tunnel ahead of him. Some days his vision was less clouded by the milky whiteness in his eyes than others. Today his vision was fairly clear.

The tunnel was no taller than a man, little wider. Was it a product of the moon's history or had it been carved out by workers like himself? It might have been the burrow of life native to Europa. There might have been life on the moon, might still be in the sea that rolled beneath the ridged, icy crust of the moon. There might be some way to tell, but if so it was a mystery to him.

He could feel the shock of workers' pickaxes as they chipped away green ice for their masters, the vibrations of the impact transmitted by the crystalline structure of the tunnel. He reached for his helmet and clicked the lamp into darkness. At first he seemed to be in perfect darkness. A sense of peace descended upon him. His body was light, his suit gave him protection, all was silent and black and calm. He lay face down on the floor of the tunnel, thinking that he might drift there from the peace of the moment into the peace of eternity, but the chill of the tunnel floor leached warmth through his suit and he pushed himself once more to his feet.

His eyes had accustomed themselves to the darkness of the tunnel and he realized now that the darkness was not perfect, that the crystals which formed the walls and floor and roof of the tunnel glowed with a soft green light. The longer he remained there without the light of his helmet-lamp, the brighter the crystals glowed, or so it seemed.

He strode onward through the tunnel. To this point it had followed a single course but now it branched. He chose a path and followed it until it, too, divided. He smiled. The tunnel might lead to a maze in which a wanderer would be lost. Unable to return to the pit and thence to the workers' shed, he would wander until his air gave out, then lie down and fall asleep and never awaken.

Again he smiled.

He turned slowly. He made his mind a blank. He lost track of the direction from which he had come. He started along a tunnel. More branches offered themselves, some leading not merely to left or right but rising from the tunnel or descending from it. He gave himself to the moon, to the green ice, wandering as impulse dictated.

He was not Koga Isoruko. This he knew. But who was he? He might stop, sit on the tunnel floor and ponder that question. But he suspected that if he did so he would lose himself in the labyrinth of his mind as he had already, deliberately, lost himself in the labyrinth of green ice.

He was not ready for that fate. He was—he shook his head, blinking his eyes, striking at the crystal wall of the tunnel with his pickaxe held in both gloved hands.

He was Ino Hajime.

He was Ino Hajime, son of humble fishers from the far north of the home islands.

He was Ino Hajime, investigating the activities of the Aum Shinrikyo and he was lost in the green-ice caves of Europa, a moon of Jupiter.

He leaned against the wall. His pickaxe was embedded in the crystal and he used it to steady himself as he gazed upward. Through the green ice, through the ridged surface of Europa he could see a reddish glow. Jupiter was in the sky; this was the day of Europa, such as it was.

He held a gloved hand against the wall, hoping to pick up some vibration that would be an indication of his fellow workers, or some life or activity within the labyrinth. He had changed his mind, he did not wish to find eternal oblivion here in this tomb of green ice.

Nothing.

He tilted his head, staring through milky whiteness at his pickaxe. Its point was embedded in the tunnel wall, its haft stood upright. He leaned toward it and laid his helmeted head against the haft. He detected sounds.

But where were they coming from? He had lost all sense of the path he had followed through the labyrinth. He worked his pickaxe loose, walked forward for a while, then struck it into the wall again. Was the sound louder or fainter? If louder, he was headed toward it.

He had no idea how long he made his way through tunnels, he was beyond hunger or thirst, far beyond fatigue. He knew that as long as his air supply lasted, he would continue. When his air was exhausted, he would lie down and die, or perhaps he would undo the seal on his helmet and expire in a rush of stale air, his breath turning to a sleet of green ice as the breath of his fellow worker had done.

He held his hands in front of his face, studying them to see if they had turned to masses of green crystal or of broken rock. Inside their heavy gloves they looked normal. They felt normal.

He worked his pickaxe loose from the wall. Ahead of him the tunnel branched. He walked a short distance down one branch, tested for sound, returned and tested the other branch, made his decision and walked on.

The sound was louder now. He could tell what it was. Voices. It was the sound of voices.

He continued until he could see a darkness looming ahead in

the tunnel. He thought, *If the voices had stopped before now, I would be hopelessly lost.* But the voices had not stopped, and something dark was looming ahead of him in the tunnel.

It was a door.

He walked more slowly now, striving to be silent. He could not hear the voices from beyond the door. When last he had heard them there was a rhythm to them. No words were discernible, but the voices were rhythmic. They might have been engaged in spiritual chanting.

He reached the door. He switched his helmet-lamp on and studied the door. There was a handle and a mechanism. Around the edges of the door he could see a heavy, soft seal. He tried the mechanism and was able to open the door. He was brushed by the outward rush of air.

He stepped into a small room and closed the door gently behind him. The only illumination here was that provided by his helmet-lamp. A gauge recorded the pressure in the room, rising rapidly from zero even as he watched.

On the opposite side of the room he found another door, another soft seal, another mechanism. He opened it and stepped through, closing the door gently behind him.

He was in a temple. Robes hung from a wall, *zouri* lay beneath them. He removed his protective suit, donned robe and stepped into *zouri*. He could smell the staleness of his own body but the freedom from the protective suit was exhilarating. Should he return to the tunnel now or to the surface of Europa he would die, he knew, as the female worker had died in the shed. It seemed not to matter.

He could hear the chanting.

He moved forward, parted curtains and found himself standing in a magnificent sanctuary. Rich tapestries hung from the walls. Men and women knelt in orderly rows. Incense rose from burners. The chanting continued, soothing his pained soul.

He was Ino Hajime.

At the opposite end of the room on a raised platform was a throne. A resplendently garbed man sat upon it. As Ino Hajime advanced into the sanctuary the enthroned man raised his face and peered at him through milky eyes.

Ino Hajime halted in astonishment.

"Asobi-san."

The man smiled gently. "I welcome you."

"You know me. You remember me."

"Of course."

"Koga Isoruko," Mr. Ino said, introducing himself, reaching reflexively for a business card that was not there.

"*Boku na koto.*" Asobi Yoi rose to his feet and made a deep *ojigi.*

Mr. Ino returned the bow.

"Nonsense," Asobi repeated. "Not Koga Isoruko. Ino Hajime. You are Ino Hajime. You are the *Atarashii Sendachi.* You are the new messenger, the new leader, the new Asahara Shoko. You are the new giver of Aum Shinrikyo."

He bowed once again, more deeply than before. He stepped from the platform. He walked through the kneeling, chanting worshipers. He halted before Ino Hajime and bowed still again, took him gently by the hand and led him to the platform, to the throne at the front of the sanctuary.

"You are the new messenger," Asobi repeated, "the *Atarashii Sendachi.*" Gently he turned Ino Hajime and pushed him backward so the edge of the seat pressed against the backs of his knees. He moved his hands to Ino Hajime's shoulders and pressed downward, nodding his head as well to indicate that Ino Hajime was to be seated.

Gently Asobi took the pickaxe from Ino Hajime's hands. "Ino-sama, do you understand *Poa* now?"

"*Iye.* I do not."

"Asahara Shoko teaches us to raise the karma of the universe by preventing the commission of bad acts. That is the message of Aum Shinrikyo. Look at these *gakusei* of Aum. Each has taken upon himself the bad karma of many. We have saved millions of souls over the centuries. We have taken it upon ourselves to prevent others from committing bad acts by sending them to their next lives. We have taken many guises, worked our beneficence in many places."

Ino Hajime shook his head. "By killing?"

"By sending to the next level."

"But killing is a bad act, Asobi-san."

"*Yoi!*" the other leaped joyously. "You see, then. This is *Poa.* By sending them onward we prevent all further bad acts. We take their karma upon ourselves, and what nobler, what holier act than to sacrifice one's own karma for the salvation of another's *tamashii.*" He shook his head. His long hair flew around it in the light gravity of Europa. "Who were the greatest figures of history, Ino-sama? I will tell you. Temujin. Tojo. Hitler. The lovely Stalin. The glorious Truman. The holy bin Ladin. The greater the killer the higher the karma. This is the meaning of *Poa.* To understand

*Poa* is to understand killing. To understand killing is to understand *Poa*."

He stepped from the platform, lifted a large covered chalice from a table nearby and removed the lid. He carried it to the kneeling worshipper nearest him. He held the chalice as the worshipper sipped a green fluid from it. The worshipper, Ino Hajime saw, was a lovely woman, little more than girl. She raised her face to Asobi Yoi. Her face was brightened by a beatific smile. She exhaled, a delicately green-tinted mist, and fell forward.

Asobi Yoi moved to the next worshipper and the next, continuing until all had sipped from the chalice and toppled to the floor.

Now Asobi Yoi stood before Ino Hajime. "You see? Each of them had taken the bad karma of others. I have taken it from all of them." He smiled. "My soul is heavy, but you may save me, you may take the karma from my shoulders onto your own. Only you, Ino-sama, *Atarashii Sendachi*, can do this. Only you have the spiritual strength. Only you have the holy force."

He turned to peer into the chalice, then tossed it aside. Ino Hajime saw it bounce off the wall, then clatter across the floor, empty.

Gently Asobi Yoi hefted Ino Hajime's pickaxe, held it toward Ino Hajime, haft first. "I beg you, Ino-sama, *Atarashii Sendachi*."

Dazed by what he had beheld, Ino Hajime took the pickaxe. Asobi Yoi knelt before him, a keening sound coming from his throat. Ino Hajime lifted the pickaxe, then brought it down with all his strength, in a single stroke.

He rose to his feet, doffed the ceremonial robe and *zouri*, found his protective suit and boots, helmet and gloves, and donned them. He made his way through the sealed inner door, then the outer. He was in the ice tunnel again.

Bright rays sparkled off crystal surfaces. He looked up and realized, to his surprise, that he must be near the surface of the Pwyll plain for he could make out, murkily, the giant red disk of Jupiter. It was brighter than he had ever seen it, its intensity seemingly focused by the green crystal walls and floor and roof of the ice cave.

In the dazzling glare his eyes were half blinded, his vision tinted a rich green. He held his heavily gloved hands before his face, squinting at his fingers. Was he solid or liquid, flesh or water? Were his surroundings green crystal as hard and as brilliant as emerald or were they soft and flowing like the green waters of the Sea of Japan?

Where did the light come from?

# News from New Providence

H IS ROYAL ROBES WERE HEAVY, HEAVY. AND SO HOT! Why was it so hot in the Cathedral? It was only June. Why could the Archbishop not complete the crowning and the anointing, the blessing of the monarch, the placement of scepter and orb? Then he would present his Queen Consort to the nation and the empire and be damned to the PM and the rotten dog-collared clergy, that bloodless superannuated fool Cosmo Lang, and—

—and suddenly he was looking up at the high ceiling above his bed, where the broad blades of a slowly-turning fan could do little more than stir the hot, moist air of this damned backwater island. The dream was gone, the dream that had come and gone so many times, and he was King no longer. He was Governor-General of a string of rocky protuberances that poked out of this Caribbean backwater and gave home to a couple of thousand colonial expatriates, white chicken farmers and black fisherman.

And his aide was standing just inside the doorway of the bed-room fidgeting like a schoolboy and clearing his throat desperately to get the Duke's attention.

He pushed himself upright in bed. His silk pajamas, the light-est pair he owned, were stained with perspiration. The tropical sun beat through window curtains and turned the room into a blaze of daylight.

The Duke reached for a cigarette, struck flame from a lighter embossed with his coat of arms, and drew in a deep draught of smoke. "Yes, Deering?"

"Something terrible, sir." Deering shifted his weight from foot to foot. He still carried the rank of colonel in the guards but he maintained a wardrobe of mufti at the Duke's suggestion. "Something terrible has happened."

"Well?"

"It's Sir Walter, sir. Sir Walter Maples. At The Tradewinds, sir."

"Thank you, Deering, I know quite well the name of Sir Walter's home. The Duchess and I stayed there at one time, you will remember."

"Yes, sir."

The Duke drew on his cigarette, waiting for Deering to go on. The dream came every night now, or so it seemed. It left him high-strung and unrested each morning and a cigarette helped to calm his nerves.

"Sir Walter, sir—"

"Spit it out, Deering."

"He's dead, sir."

The Duke hesitated for a split second. Then, "Who knows?"

"His houseman found him, sir."

"Oh, that fellow, yes. What's his name?"

"Plum, sir. Stolid black chap. Not too bright an individual. Skin the color of his name. Marcus Plum, I believe it is."

"Who else?"

"Sir Walter was alone, sir. Lady Margarethe is off the island. In Canada with her daughter. The only other white man in the house was Mr. Harrel. Plum fetched him and—"

"Her Royal Highness has not been disturbed, I hope."

"No, sir. As soon as Mr. Easton—"

"You didn't tell me that Easton knew."

"Beg pardon, sir. It seems that Mr. Harrel telephoned the commissioner as soon as Plum sounded the alarm. Mr. Easton felt that the Governor-General should be informed at once."

"Well, very rightly so, Deering, very rightly so."

"Yes, sir."

The Duke climbed out of bed. He drew one final puff on his cigarette and crushed out the butt in a massive cut-glass ashtray.

He smoothed his rumpled pajamas, running his hands down the silken legs.

"Close the door, will you, Deering? No need to waken the household."

"Yes, sir." Deering complied.

The Duke stepped into his lavatory and doffed his pajama shirt. "All right, Deering, I can hear you from in here. You were saying—?"

While his aide spoke, the Duke filled a glass with fresh tap water, wetted his toothbrush and sprinkled tooth-cleansing powder on its bristles. He gave his teeth a thorough brushing. Having rinsed his mouth, he instructed Deering to provide a step-by-step review of the sad events at The Tradewinds.

"It's unfortunate that we have to rely on the Negro's version, sir."

"Nevertheless, Deering, nevertheless."

"Yes, sir. Yes. Well, apparently Sir Walter indicated that he wanted to spend the day fishing."

The Duke shook his head. "Indicated how, Deering? To whom? You must be specific."

"I apologize, sir. I assume that Sir Walter would have spoken with Plum the previous evening. Last evening, sir."

"Are you unaware, Deering, that Sir Walter hosted a small dinner last night in honor of Her Highness and myself, at The Tradewinds?"

"No, sir."

"No?" The Duke raised an eyebrow. "No, you were unaware? Or no, you were not unaware?"

"Sorry, sir. I meant to say that, no, sir, I am not unaware of that fact. That is, I am quite aware that the Governor and Her Royal Highness dined at The Tradewinds. As I recall, sir, the guest list was quite small, just Sir Walter Maples, Mr. Harrel, Count Grenner, and Sir Walter's son-in-law, M. Delacroix. Her Royal Highness was the only lady present."

Of course. The Duchess was at her best surrounded by male admirers who sought her favor and attention. She did not care for female companionship; it smacked inevitably of competition.

"Yes, M. Delacroix," the Duke said. "Why the Vichy authorities didn't slap him in irons, I shall never understand. Or turn him over to the Germans. The Gestapo would know how to deal with M. Antoine Delacroix, you can rest assured of that, Deering."

Deering ran his finger around his collar uncomfortably. He

wished he could switch to clothing more suited to the climate of these islands, but the Duke was adamantly opposed to the relaxation of Britannic propriety. More likely, Deering thought, it was the Duchess's iron will rather than the Duke's adherence to tradition that was at play.

He suppressed a sigh.

The Duke asked, "Who else, Deering? You said that Commissioner Easton, Harrel and this Negro, Plum, know about Maples. Who else?"

"That's all, sir."

"Well, why the devil didn't Easton telephone me? Why didn't he come straight to Government House and inform me? Who does he think he is, some ha'penny gumshoe? Who does he think I am?"

Deering bit back an impulse to answer the question and instead waited for the Duke to continue. But the Duke emerged from the lavatory wrapped in a heavy chenille robe.

"Damned place, damned job, can't even get a reliable dresser to tend to my needs. Deering, fetch me an outfit from the wardrobe and be quick." The Duke gestured, then waited for Deering to select a medium tan silken shirt, regimental tie, pleated trousers and light linen jacket. He dressed carefully but swiftly, knotting the tie in the pattern he had himself invented and that bore his name worldwide—his personal contribution to sartorial posterity.

"One thought that His Royal Highness might see fit to take a personal hand in the case," Deering ventured.

"Yes, certainly, capital idea. I shall want to speak with Commissioner Easton first."

"Yes, sir. And I thought His Highness might wish to question Mr. Harrel and the houseman, Plum, as well."

"Why in the world would I want to—oh, you did say that he found Sir Walter's, ah, remains, did you not? Well, I suppose it might be a good idea. Deering, you'll have to learn to order your thoughts, don't you know? You're much too confused to deal with a crisis such as this. Well, get Easton on the telephone. Have him come here at once. Bring Harrel, of course, and that black fellow. Where is he? Where is Easton? I suppose I must break the news to the Duchess. I don't know how she's going to take this."

Deering stepped out of the Duke's path, bowing slightly as the Duke brushed past him.

The Duke tapped gently on the door to the Duchess's boudoir. He pressed his ear to the tropical wood. Was that a slight stirring? He tapped again. "Are you awake, my darling? May I enter?"

After a lengthy silence he heard her muttering. He scampered back to his own quarters. Deering was using the telephone. The Duke signaled to his aide. Deering uttered a few more syllables and lowered the instrument. "Yes, sir."

"See to it that the Duchess has her tea and toast. I don't understand this household, can't keep up the most elementary level of service."

Deering flushed. "At once, sir."

The Duke waited outside the Duchess's chambers until a servant approached bearing Her Highness's breakfast tray. "I'll take that." The Duke carried the tray into the boudoir and placed it carefully on the bed, its folding legs holding it at a level comfortable for Her Highness.

She sipped at the tea, swallowed and lowered the cup. The china was of course imported from England and bore the Ducal crest. "Now, David, what is the fuss?"

He looked around for a chair, asked permission to be seated, drew it close to her bedside. "I have dreadful news, my dear. Sir Walter Maples is dead."

The Duchess raised her chin. "Walter? What happened?"

"His houseman found him in his room this morning. Called Chris Harrel, he was staying over at The Tradewinds. Harrel phoned Ray Easton, then phoned here. Deering gave me the news. I hope you won't be too upset, my darling. If there were a way to spare you this I should have done so."

"But that's terrible, David." The Duchess nibbled a corner of her toast. "Absolutely terrible." She washed the toast down with another sip of tea. "You've got to tell me everything."

Before the Duke could answer, Deering rapped his knuckles on the Duchess's door. "Beg pardon, sir. Madame. Commissioner Easton is here, sir. And Plum."

"Have them wait in my office downstairs. I shall be there as soon as possible." He turned back toward the Duchess.

"Has anyone told Margarethe yet?" the Duchess asked. "She has to know. Poor thing. All their years together. And she put up with so much from him. You know, David, he was not an easy man. Not easy at all."

The Duke looked away. "I shall send your maid up to dress you, my dear."

"Yes, please."

As he descended the broad flight of stairs he wondered what his brother was doing at this moment. Adjusting for the difference in time, it would be late in the day in England. The Nazis had refrained from bombing Buckingham Palace for more than a year after the commencement of hostilities, and they might never have attacked, might never have needed to attack, had the Duke remained upon the throne. Had he not allowed himself to be shipped off to this lonely exile. New Providence, Grand Bahama, the rest of the islands of his Lilliputian realm — they might as well be Elba and St. Helena.

Ribbentrop had been quite reasonable, after all. And his boss, Herr Hitler — well, a decidedly peculiar chap. Not a pleasant person, very poor manners. But then what could one expect of an individual with his lowly origins? But their ideas had not been so far apart after all. They recognized the twin perils to Mankind, Bolshevism and Jewry. Why should the great Nordic peoples, the Anglo-Saxons and the Germans, be at each other's throats while the lesser races stood by waiting to pick at their carcasses?

It didn't make sense, and he'd tried to make the politicians see that it didn't make sense, but Baldwin and Chamberlain and Churchill were all such a gang of stiff-necked fools, they either could not or would not recognize the reality that confronted them — and England.

Deering held the door for him as he entered his study. Ray Easton, Christopher Harrel, and the Negro, Plum, had preceded him, per his instructions. When the Duke entered the room Easton sprang to his feet; Harrel rose lazily to his. Plum was already standing. Easton was a big-boned man. He affected a tropical linen suit and plain black tie. Harrel was attired in a colorful shirt, rough trousers and sandals. Hardly proper attire. The Negro wore not a houseman's outfit of black trousers and white jacket but a fisherman's faded trousers and open-necked shirt. He held a battered fisherman's cap in one hand.

The Duke shook his head in despair.

He circled the others and seated himself behind his desk. He waved to Deering and the latter closed the office door, remaining inside.

"Now, what is this about Sir Walter Maples, Commissioner?"

"If I may, sir—"

The Duke gestured Easton to a seat, Harrel to another.

"Plum here found him," Harrel volunteered. "Soon as he fetched me I could see poor Walt was as dead as a doornail. Look on his face as if he'd seen a ghost. More like he is one, now, eh? Blood spattered all over the walls, coverlet soaked, what a mess, what a mess."

"Thank you, Harrel," the Duke nodded. He kept to himself his opinion of the man, that Harrel was an unspeakable wretch, little better than cockney trash. But he was one of the colony's wealthiest and most influential citizens, a force in the legislative council. One put up with what one must.

The Duke asked the houseman, "What have you to say for yourself, Plum?"

The Negro closed his eyes as if gathering his thoughts. He held his fisherman's cap in both hands. He shifted his weight from foot to foot. How like Deering, the Duke thought.

"Well?"

"Sah, Sah Walter ask me last night. Your Highness and Her Highness takes your partings and leaves Tradewinds for Government House and he ask me, can I take him out this morning. Early, 'fo sunrise."

"Yes. And did he say what the destination was to be?"

"Chub Cay, sah."

"Chub Cay?" The Duke appeared startled.

"Yes, sah. I reckon, we could pick up a nice easterly this time of year, make it to Chub by midmorning, easy."

The Duke lifted a briar pipe from the rack on his desk. He held it in one hand and tapped its bowl in the palm of the other. "Did Sir Walter say what he wanted to do at Chub?"

Plum shook his head from side to side. "No, sah, he did not. He is my employer, sah, and he is entitled. He was my employer, I should say."

"Quite. Well, go on, Plum."

"I woke up and went to Sir Walter's room. I knocked on his do'—"

"What time was this?"

"I don' know the hour, sah. I just know, when I went to bed, I tol' my mind to wake me up good an' early cos' Sir Walter want to get an early start. But he didn't answer my knock, so I went in, Sir Walter's door wasn't locked, and that was when I found him. Sah."

The Duke returned the pipe to its place in the rack. He slipped a cigarette case from an inside pocket of his jacket, extracted a cigarette and lit it from a heavy lighter before Deering could spring across the room and hold a flame for him.

He blew a plume of smoke into the air. "Mr. Harrel, what can you add to this?"

"Not much, Your Highness. I was sleepin' like a log."

"Where is the room in which you were staying?"

"Crost the hall. Down the way from poor old Walt's."

"Do you stay often at The Tradewinds?"

"After last night I didn't want to drive home. Hard to get petrol these days, eh?"

"Indeed. Well, continue."

"So Walt, he said he was a bit low on petrol himself so he couldn't drive me home, eh, so put me up in his guest room."

"This was solely for the purpose of saving petrol?"

"Well, I'll level with you, Governor."

"Please."

"I was kind of, well, two or three sheets to the wind. Had a couple of drinks before the meal and a few glasses of wine and a snifter afterwards, Your Highness. So I thought it wasn't such a grand idea to drive, you see."

"I do indeed. Commendable of you not to risk it. Commendable of Sir Walter to put you up. Were you part of this plan to visit Chub Cay?"

"Not as I can remember."

"Did you and Sir Walter stay up talking last night?"

"Not as I can remember."

The Duke turned sharply toward Plum once again. "You're sure that Sir Walter made no mention of his purpose in visiting Chub Cay? Think hard, Plum."

The Negro scratched his head. "I think he might 'o said something, sah."

"Well, and what was that something?" The Duke made an effort to contain his impatience.

"Something about countin' on it, sah."

"Counting on it?"

"Somethin' like that, sah."

"It couldn't have been something about the Count, could it? Count Grenner?"

Plum looked as if he was going to explode from the strain of concentrating. He held his breath until his eyes bulged, then exhaled explosively. "Sir Walter, he might could have said, 'Count When.' I thought he said, 'Count When.' Like when you pourin' a drink fo' yo' frien' and you say, 'Say when,' he might could have said, 'Count When.'"

"Thank you, Plum." The Duke closed his eyes and pondered. He realized now that it might have been better had he questioned Plum in private. Count Max Grenner was to be his partner and front man in the development of Chub Cay. The Duke, Walter Maples, and Count Grenner.

It all had to do with the economy of the colony. The Bahamas had been a sleepy backwater for many years, until the Americans had put in their law prohibiting the manufacture and sale of alcoholic beverages. Then, ah, then the Bahamas had boomed! Whiskey was imported from Britain, schnapps from Germany, wine from Italy. Freighters docked in the Bahamas, their cargo off-loaded onto small, fast craft and smuggled into the States via Florida.

It was saddening to realize that a single slip of the tongue, an exercise of candor when discretion should have dictated a wiser course, could bring one down. There was that American who had parlayed capital raised running rum into a fortune in film production and risen to the Ambassadorship at the Court of St. James, only to be laid low by a single foolish remark regarding the inefficacy of democracy.

The fact that he was right did nothing to alter the circumstances.

The Duke addressed the houseman once more. "I want you to take me where you were to take Sir Walter."

Plum said, "You want to go to Chub Cay, sah?"

"That is correct."

Plum tilted his head, obviously deep in thought. "I s'pose I c'd take you, sah. My boat, she's all outfitted. I was plannin' to take Sir Walter this mo'nin', I c'n take you instead, sah."

"Very well, then." The Duke stood up. Commissioner Easton leaped to emulate him, Christopher Harrel lazily following suit. "Easton, Harrel, you will hold yourselves in readiness should I need to question you further. Deering, you may return to your duties. Plum, you shall await me on the verandah of Government House."

"Yes, sah!"

The others stood, heads slightly inclined, as the Duke strode from the room.

He climbed the broad staircase leading to the family quarters and tapped once more on the Duchess's door. Her familiar voice called out, "Come!"

He found her within, reclining on a chaise lounge, garbed in a Mainbocher dressing gown of pale blue silken faille. She wore matching blue mules, each topped by a fluffy cotton pouf. A star sapphire pendant rested against her throat and a cuff of matching stones circled one wrist.

"My darling," he said.

"Yes, David, what is it?" He observed that her breakfast tray had been removed and the bed straightened.

"I don't suppose, my dear, that you would care for a brief sail today?"

"A sail? You just told me that Walter Maples was dead. And you're going sailing?"

"I am investigating his death, my dear. It appears that he came to a dreadful, bloody end, but he had planned an expedition this morning to Chub Cay and I thought to follow his planned route, don't you see."

"I see plenty, David. I see you trying to play Sherlock Holmes. Don't we have our own little Inspector Lestrade on this dreadful island? Can't you leave the investigation to the official police?"

The Duke frowned. "You forget, my darling, that as Governor-General I am the colony's chief law-enforcement officer."

"Yes, and you're the commander of its military force, but I don't see you drilling recruits on the parade ground."

The Duke blinked. Her Royal Highness was in one of her moods. Well, who could blame her? Being awakened to the news of the murder of one's closest friend—well, one of one's closest friends, anyway—would surely put any sensitive person into a state. He drew a breath, waited until he was certain that she was not going to speak further, and resumed.

"Walter was my friend as well as yours, my dear. Not to mention a prospective business associate. This war is not going to last forever, you know. We have to think of the future."

"You know what our future should have been," she grumbled bitterly. "We should be at Belvedere if not Buckingham this very moment instead of that stammering weakling and his simpering little wifey. If you weren't such a fool—"

"Stop it!" He felt the pressure within his head and knew that his face had turned a bright red. Rarely did he stand up to the Duchess, but there was a single topic on which he would not brook her criticism. "He is my dear brother!"

"And see how he treated you once you had made him Caesar," came the hissed reply.

"My family is sacred. That is the end of it."

He spun on his heel and left the room.

He found Plum awaiting him downstairs, standing respectfully near the tall cut-glass doors. The Duchess of course was right. It was such a tragically far cry from Buckingham and Belvedere and the life of pomp and privilege they had known before the abdication, to this hot and isolated post. If only he could go back and change things—but he could not.

"Pardon, Governor sah, but yo' shoes—"

The Duke managed a rueful grin, the first of the day. Of course. This would be no Mediterranean cruise such as he and the Duchess had shared on the palatial *Nahlin*, nor a Caribbean jaunt like those hosted by Max Grenner aboard *Stella Australis*. What could poor Plum own but a little sailing dinghy?

"Have you suitable footwear for sailing, Plum?"

"Sah, I sails barefoot."

"Then I shall do the same," the Duke rejoined, grinning broadly.

They strode side-by-side between the white pillars of Government House, past the Duchess's precious Buick sedan and down sleepy Blue Hill Road toward Prince George's Wharf.

Plum's craft was as the Duke had expected. The Duke removed his shoes, socks and garters and left them on the quay. He waited while Plum climbed into the dinghy. Plum helped him into the boat, cast off the painter, then used a pair of heavy oars to propel the dinghy away from the quay.

Plum raised a much-patched sail, swung the dinghy to port, caught a late-morning breeze and guided the craft through the narrow channel separating Nassau from Hog Island.

A few scrawny goats wandered the hilly island, cropping sparse vegetation. As the dinghy rounded Hog Island and swung to the north, toward Chub Cay, the Duke permitted himself a fantasy. A U-boat would rise from the sparkling turquoise sea. Its captain would emerge from the conning tower, take the Duke onboard and return with him to a subdued Britain where he would resume his temporarily abandoned throne.

He would offer his brother and his consort better treatment than the stammerer had offered him and his wife. That much generosity he could afford. Wrongs would be righted, mistakes would be corrected, injustices would be undone. The rightful king would reign once again!

"They be Chub!"

The Duke abandoned his reverie with reluctance, but there indeed was the Cay where he and his partners had planned to build their resort once the war had ended. When the Americans repealed their prohibition of alcohol they had crushed the booming economy of the Bahamas, but there was another prohibition in the United States, against gambling. It was carried on legally in one of the arid western states, he recalled, and was winked at in the city of Miami.

But a full-scale luxurious casino in the style of Monte Carlo, located in the salubrious surroundings of the Bahamas, would be his bonanza. His and the Duchess's, of course, assuming that she did not abandon him for a fresher and more energetic companion, as she had previously abandoned one husband for a second and that husband for himself. She'd already picked out her fourth mate, the Duke suspected, but that liaison had been scotched, there was no longer any danger from those quarters!

"This where Sah Walter was wantin' to go this mo'nin', sah." Plum was standing at the tiller, a line in one hand running to the little dinghy's boom. "You want me to put in, sah?"

The Duke shook his head. "No, Plum, there will be no need for that. Could you circle the Cay, I'd like to survey it today, then return to port."

As the man moved to obey, the Duke questioned him. "You say Sir Walter had bled copiously when you found him, Plum."

"Sah?"

The Duke blinked. "You say there was blood spattered all over the room."

"Yes, sah."

"I didn't think a bullet to the brain would cause such bleeding."

"Bullet, sah?"

"Yes. Was Sir Walter not killed by a gunshot?"

The black man shrugged. "That man's throat be slashed and his belly sliced open. Whoevah done in Sir Walter was one mean person. I didn't see no bullet hole, sah."

After a moment the Duke asked, "Do you sleep at The Tradewinds, Plum?"

"No, sah." Plum shook his head. "I go home every night to sleep, I come back to The Tradewinds every mo'nin'."

"So you would not have heard a gunshot. And Chris Harrel was drunk."

Beating back through Nassau Harbor, the Duke half expected to see Max Grenner's *Stella Australis* moving majestically toward the open sea, but she was nowhere to be seen, nor was she tied up at Grenner's usual dockage. Come to think of it, the grand yacht had not been at her place when the Duke left Prince George's Wharf hours earlier with the Negro Plum.

Once again shod, the Duke returned to Government House and telephoned the Harbor Master. He learned that *Stella Australis* had sailed at daybreak. Only the Count and Countess Grenner were on board, aside from the crew, of course. No, sir, the Harbor Master did not know their destination, although he thought it might be either the Count's villa at Tampico or his mansion at Veracruz.

The Duke slammed the telephone down. Damn Grenner! He and Maples had been the main financiers of the planned casino at Chub Cay. The Duke's allowance from the Crown was a precarious pittance, hardly enough to cover the Duchess's clothing budget. And his brother, he knew, was plagued with constant health problems. Should he die the scepter would pass to his elder daughter, and who knew how she would treat himself and the Duchess? They had been close when he was Prince of Wales but cracks had appeared in the family structure during his brief reign and since the abdication he had not seen either of his nieces, nor received as much as a greeting card from them on his birthday.

He had to make a go of the casino! Now that Maples was dead, Max Grenner's role was more important than ever. It was vital.

The dead Walter Maples had come from humble enough roots: a rough diamond prospector, he had found a mother lode in South Africa and made his fortune. That would pass now to the detestable Lady Margarethe, maybe even fall into the hands of the son-in-law, the vile Delacroix. There was no counting on that money any longer.

Grenner's fortune was even more unsavory. He maintained his residency in neutral Sweden, built guns and sold munitions to both sides, cash and carry, no questions asked. The Crown was after him, the PM had personally sought his extradition, but the Duke exercised his official prerogatives and gave Grenner free run of the Bahamas.

But what if Grenner had heard of Maples's death early this morning? What if word had spread even before notification reached Government House? Grenner held the exchequer for the planned casino, including the portion put up by the Duke. The amount was modest enough by the standards of the likes of Walter Maples or Max Grenner. The Duke's chief contribution to the scheme was the prestige of his name, the glamour that he and the Duchess would provide to the eventual establishment, that would draw wealthy gamblers from the entire Western Hemisphere if not from Europe.

But he had insisted on putting up a share of the capital that represented a huge investment by his standards. Had Grenner decamped for Mexico with all the money?

The Duke raced up the broad staircase to his wife's boudoir. She was not there.

He found her shortly in the garden, sunning with her terriers. She had changed her costume to a day-frock of cornflower blue linen. A broad-brimmed hat protected her delicate skin from the rays of the sun, and she wore a pair of oversized spectacles of smoked-glass in harlequin frames of jewel-decorated tortoise shell. She was seated beneath an oversized parasol, a cold glass beaded with condensation at her elbow, a novel opened in her lap. She looked up as the Duke literally ran to her.

"What is it, David? You're as pale as a ghost!"

"Where were you last night?" the Duke demanded.

Behind her dark glasses, did he detect a blink? In her always-confident voice, did he hear a hesitation? "Why, I was with you at dinner, of course. Colonel Deering drove us there in the Buick."

"Afterwards, afterwards."

"Why, we returned here, David. What's the matter with you?"

"You did not go out again? You did not return to The Tradewinds and—and see Walter Maples?"

"David, don't make an ass of yourself. What are you implying?"

"I am implying that you took the Buick. Late at night. Quite late at night. You took a knife from the pantry here at Government House and drove yourself back to The Tradewinds and entered the house. Only Chris Harrel was present, other than Walter Maples, and Harrel was immobilized with liquor. You made your way to the master bedroom. You found Maples dead to the world and with the knife you slashed his throat and belly."

"David," the Duchess laughed nervously, "why would I do such a horrible thing?"

"Because Maples was your lover and he was losing interest in you. You follow the same pattern, my dear, but this time you couldn't simply divorce me and move on. You couldn't continue to satisfy Maples. I know you, I know you now, at last. Perhaps you hoped for a reconciliation but when you couldn't even waken him you flew into a rage and used your knife on him."

She removed her sun glasses, folded them and placed them in the gutter of the open book in her lap. She glared at him coldly. "He would not even stir," she said.

"That was because there was a bullet in his brain already." The Duke started to walk away, then halted and turned back to face his wife. He stood beside her, aware that to her eyes he was a menacing black silhouette against the blazing Caribbean sun.

"Max Grenner and the Countess are gone. Sailed away with Walter's money," he paused dramatically, "and ours."

She gasped and started to rise.

He placed his hand on her shoulder, pressing her back into her seat. "It seems that we are fated to remain together for the rest of our lives, my dear. We deserve each other."

When I sent this story to David Pringle, editor of the superb magazine Interzone, he liked it at once and stated that he wanted to get it into print before the end of 1999. There was one problem. The story was originally called "12.31.99"—a title that would have been perfectly sensible for Americans, but which would have been gibberish to British readers. Pringle himself is Scottish, Interzone is published in England, and to most of Interzone's audience, the original title would mean the twelfth day of the thirty-first month of 1999. Could we, Pringle asked, put the title in the British format rather than the American?

I thought that was a splendid idea, the story was published as "31.12.99" and since I rather liked that title, I've retained it for the story. Please note, however, that it takes place on the thirty-first of December, not the twelfth of—Whatever.

But, come to think of it, "The Twelfth of Whatever" does have a ring to it, don't you agree?

I may just take a crack at a story with that name.

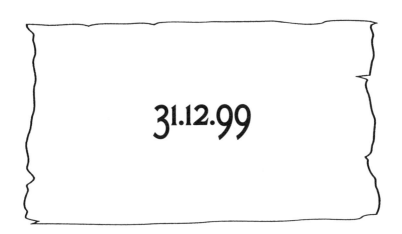

**31.12.99**

**W**ALTER PUSHED HIMSELF UPRIGHT AND WALKED slowly to the window, drawn by the sound of shots and sirens. He wasn't really old, it was just that everything seemed an effort since Meg's death. It was if he had to debate with himself before he took the smallest action.

Should I take a drink of water?

Well, I think I will.

Why should I?

I'm thirsty.

Oh, all right, then I'll take a drink of water.

Should I scratch my nose?

Why should I scratch my nose?

It itches.

Oh. But maybe it will stop by itself.

No, I think I'll scratch. It will stop itching sooner that way. Besides, I don't see why I shouldn't scratch it.

All right then, scratch.

It went like that. Every action, every decision. It was as if he'd lost the driver inside that had propelled him through his life.

"Darling, don't."

He paused and looked down. His sister was seated on the sofa beside her husband. She reached toward Walter.

"Stay away from the window, darling. It could be dangerous. You could be—" She stopped, realizing that she was stirring up painful recollections. Recollections that were all too fresh to start with, images that she knew tormented her brother.

"It's all right, sister. It's all right, Allie. What if I get shot, eh? Do I care?"

The night outside was clear and a bright moon hung over the Mississippi. A freak cold spell had brought a rare sprinkling of snow to New Orleans, and revelers in the French Quarter regarded it as an omen. Something special for this very special night.

"Look at that." Walter smiled wanly, his hand pressed against the window sash.

Allie and her husband, James, remained seated.

Walter turned back toward them. He shook his head slowly. "There's nothing to be afraid of. No more than there is any time, anywhere, any more." He gestured. "Come and take a look."

A group of revelers had decided to get themselves up as cartoon characters, and were parading through the streets in outlandish costumes, drinks in hand. They were led by Wonder Woman in full regalia, in her abbreviated costume of patriotic colors, her boots, her long blue-black hair surmounted by her golden tiara.

She had her magic lasso in her hand. She was leading a muscular young man wearing black tights with white skull and crossbones on his chest.

Walter sensed Allie and James behind him, one just to his left, the other just to his right. He felt Allie take his free hand. James put his own hand on Walter's shoulder.

"You see that fellow?" Walter asked. "He's dressed as the Black Terror. Pretty obscure reference. They must be pretty serious collectors to have a Black Terror in their gang."

The moonlight might have glinted off the window of Walter's apartment, here on the second story above the book shop that he would have to operate alone now, now that Meg was dead. The killer had fled and Walter had called 9-1-1 and the police had got there fast.

There was nothing they could do for Meg, for all that they'd gone through the motions of applying pressure to her wound and attempting resuscitation. Walter knew she was dead and the paramedics confirmed it when they arrived. Still, they'd taken her to the hospital and an MD on duty in the ER had made it official.

It could have happened to anybody.

James was talking about the university, his classes and faculty maneuverings and campus politics back in Chicago. It was his way of trying to give comfort, Walter knew. He let them lead him back to his easy chair and guide him into it, and James was telling some dull story about the history department and Walter nodded from time to time as if he actually cared about what his brother-in-law was saying, even though he didn't.

Allie said, "What about something to eat? Or drink? It's chilly in here, you don't have any heat, Walter. I always told Meg, you should have heat in this place. What if I make a pot of tea, would you like some tea?"

Walter waved his hand. "If you'd like some. Not for me. Or have some brandy. You want some brandy? Allie, James?" Walter's sister Alicia was Allie but his brother-in-law James was only James not Jimmy or Jim or Jay. "Maybe a glass of scotch. We should have champagne to welcome the new millennium but I don't have any, I didn't get to the store."

He meant Jenkins's grocery across the street. He'd got to his own store, the bookstore. Meg had died there. Meg's full name was Margaret. Meg had died in the store and the killer had panicked and fled with nothing to show for his efforts except a murder on his conscience.

And of course the police looking for him, but Walter couldn't give much of a description and there were no other witnesses. The book shop hadn't been busy on December 30. People don't come to New Orleans to scout used books anyway. Walter and Allie had operated the shop for years, barely earning back their expenses. They both drew pensions and the store didn't have to do much more each month than earn its own modest rent. It gave them something to do, brought a small trickle of interesting people to their door, kept them alive in a way.

Until it brought Meg her death. James said, "I will have a glass of brandy, if you don't mind."

Walter went into the kitchen and reemerged bearing a small tray. Three glasses and a bottle of brandy stood on it. He set it on a low table and went to the wall and turned on some music. "Mozart," he said. "Meg's favorite." He tilted his head, then nodded when he'd identified the piece. "The Jupiter. It's a real war-horse, isn't it, but there's no finer music in the world."

He poured a small glass of liquor for each of them. Allie and James lifted theirs and looked expectantly at Walter.

Raising his own glass he said, "It was very good of you to fly down here on such short notice."

They answered simultaneously but he was able to sort their words from the jumble.

"Darling, poor, poor Meg. Such a terrible thing to happen. Such a terrible thing."

"Of course we came, there was never any question. The airline was very helpful. They said they understood."

"I told her time and again, if they want money let them have it. We were held up once before, did you know that? Almost. Some thugs came in, a couple of children really. Meg was in the back and I was behind the counter and two thugs came in, they looked like skinny children, they couldn't have been more than eleven, twelve. They said, 'Give it over, give it over all your money.'

"I thought they were playing a joke. I started to laugh, then the bigger one pulled a gun out of his pants and pointed it at me. Just then a cop walked in. He must have been driving past and saw them through the window and he came in with his own gun and took them away. The kid had a toy gun. I had to testify at their trial. Not a trial, a hearing. They were children. They were released to their parents. They said they were going to come back and kill us but I never saw them again."

James asked, "Could they be—could one of them be the one who—who killed Meg?"

Walter shook his head. "They were black. This one was white. I could tell that much. He wore a ski mask but I could see around his eyes and mouth and his hands. He was white."

He turned away from Allie and James and went back to the window. He could see the clock in Jenkins's window, a neon advertising clock. It was a quarter to midnight. The revelry in the streets was growing wilder. He saw more costumes. A woman in an abbreviated outfit, of shimmering black satin complete with gloves and boots and mask, was trolling slowly up the street on a huge motorcycle. Her skin looked as white as death.

Walter murmured, "The Black Cat."

"Eh?" Walter turned and saw James's questioning expression.

"Just another old character. I loved the adventure characters when I was a boy. It's nice to see them now. Meg always thought I was childish. She preferred real literature. What she called real literature. You know the last sale we made? The last sale we made before the killer came into the store?"

Allie and James sat holding their glasses before them. The

Mozart played on. Across the street, the neon advertising clock in Jenkins's window edged closer to midnight.

"A set of cheap paperback novels. Someone collected them. Nine little books from a company in Chicago, not one book you ever heard of, not one author. There's no book in the world but somebody loves it."

Suddenly he was overwhelmed by his rage and his outrage at what had happened. "There are monsters all around us," he shouted.

His sister looked alarmed. His brother-in-law started to rise. Walter inhaled sharply, searching for control of himself. "When the children were here and the police came they told us to give any gangster anything he wanted, it was better than getting killed. Meg knew that. She wasn't trying to defy him. She was reaching for the money box. We don't even have a cash register. The business we do, who needs it? We keep the receipts in a box. She reached for the box and he yelled at her. He called her something terrible. He must have thought she was reaching for a gun and he panicked and killed her and then he ran away."

Allie was holding him and he was shaking. He didn't know what to do with his brandy glass so he just dropped it. Maybe it would stain the rug. It didn't really matter.

"You know, such a little thing. She could have said . . . She could have said . . ." He stopped, gasping. He freed himself from Allie's embrace. "She could have said, 'Look, mister, the cash is right here, right here in a box under the counter. You can come around and get it yourself, you don't trust me.' And he could come around the counter and take the cash, what did we have, thirty, forty dollars? What does it matter? But she went to hand it to him. Maybe we could change it. I could go back somehow, it was only yesterday. Meg."

He fell to his knees, weeping.

"My Meg."

His sister knelt and held him.

He said his wife's name and cried.

His brother-in-law put strong hands on his shoulders and helped him back to his chair.

"Every hundred years," James said. "The end of every century, crime rises, religious madness, anarchy, violence. And the end of the millennium. The year 1000, you know, people thought it was the end of the world, the Second Coming, there were mass suicides, madness. Now it's happening again."

The historian, doing his best, trying to give comfort he didn't know how to give.

Walter said, "Allie, Allie the physicist."

She smiled and held both his hands in one of hers, pressed the other to his cheek.

"Help me go back and fix it."

She shook her head sadly.

After a while he said, "You can't."

"No."

"There's no way."

She said, "There might be other universes, other realities. Quantum theory is so strange. Nothing is true or false, Walter, everything is either probably true or probably false. Or probably probably true or not so probably true or not so probably false. Every particle in the universe, every time it wiggles, it creates another whole universe. There are an infinity of infinities of universes. Maybe there's one where she said that. Where she lived."

He sighed. "I would give my life. I would have died for her. If I could just stand up and walk in the next room and there would be a golden shimmering, a shimmering or glimmering, and I could step into it and she was there, she was alive."

Margaret stood looking out the frost-rimmed window, watching a few white flakes drift from the sky. They settled onto the lawn and yesterday's still unshoveled snow, onto the tree still decorated with its colorful lights, onto the Santa with his sleigh and reindeer. If only Walter were here to watch. If only he were here at her side.

She turned and nodded to her sister-in-law and brother-in-law seated side by side on the expensive yet comfortable sofa. Behind them a fire crackled on the flagstone-flanked hearth. She brushed something or nothing from the front of her black dress.

Her sister-in-law, Allie, said, "Meg, come and sit with us. Come, darling, sit with us."

Robotlike she obeyed. What did it matter? Sit or stand, walk or lie down, live or die.

Actually it did matter. It would be much better to die than to live. She had only to find the strength to die.

She stared into the fire. After a little while she became vaguely aware of music and voices. She knew it was James's choice of music. He was the historian and he liked everything that was not of the present. He had what he called his creeping deadline. Anything that was fifty years old was worthy of consideration, and as he got older himself, the fifty-year line crept along behind him.

Nineteen forty-seven. Nineteen forty-eight. Nineteen forty-nine.

Now it was just minutes before the clocks struck midnight and it would be the new year, the new century, the new millennium. The millennium was making its way around the world, time zone by time zone. In a little while it would reach Chicago and we would be living in the year 2000.

But Meg would be living in the year 2000 without her husband.

"Meg, dear?"

It was her sister-in-law, Allie. Alicia.

"Are you all right, Meg?"

"Of course not," she ground bitterly.

"I know. I'm sorry. I was just —"

"No." Meg shook her head. "I'm the one who should — I mean, you and Walter — you took me in. I'm nothing to you. I —"

"You're our family."

"I should have done what he wanted."

Allie and James were silent. The fire hissed and popped. Softly, a woman's voice came from concealed speakers. In a moment of peculiar clarity Meg identified the woman as Jo Stafford, the song as "I'll Be With You In Apple Blossom Time." The recording was old enough to meet James's fifty-year rule. Old enough and then some.

She would not be with her husband again, not in apple blossom time or any other time.

"I should have done what he wanted," she repeated. "He wanted to move, did you know that? We used to take vacations. New York, Los Angeles, Montreal. New Orleans was his favorite city. Funny, the first time we went there he didn't want to go. It was my idea. I talked him into it and he fell in love with the city. When we both retired and got our pensions he wanted to go there and open a little book shop, but I wouldn't do it so we stayed in Chicago and now he's dead."

"It wasn't your fault, Margaret." Walter had called her Meg, Allie called her Meg, James always called her Margaret.

She looked into his face, challenging him to say more.

"It was a heart attack, Margaret. He was a heavy man, he went outside in below-zero weather and shoveled snow. It happens every winter, you hear it on the news all the time. It was nobody's fault. Certainly not yours."

James stood up and walked to the sideboard. An engraved platter stood there, with good wine and crystal glasses and cheese and three small Limoges dishes and three tiny silver forks. Three of each, not four. "You should take a glass of wine, Margaret."

She shook her head.

"Alicia?" He tried his wife.

"You go ahead, James."

The wine had been breathing since afternoon. He poured himself a glass and raised it. "Better days," he said.

The women stood watching as he downed half the wine, studied the glass, then lowered it to a monogrammed coaster. If he had sought something in the glass he gave no indication of finding it, or of failing to find it.

With a muffled boom, fireworks exploded over Lake Michigan. You couldn't see the lake itself from James and Alicia's large Tudor revival house, but from the front windows the fireworks were visible, rising like backwards meteors into the black sky and then exploding into multiple ribbons of color.

"Is it midnight already?" James asked. Then, after studying his pocket watch—he must be the last man in Chicago to wear a vest and keep a pocket watch in its pocket—he answered his own question. "No. Some eager beaver must have jumped the gun. Well, it will be 2000 soon enough."

He stood up and assumed the voice that he used when he lectured a class at the university. "Of course, the millennium won't really start for another year. There was no year zero, the first millennium started with the year one and second millennium started with the year one thousand and one and the third millennium will start in two thousand one, but they want to celebrate now."

The two women ignored him.

Allie saw the movement of Meg's shoulders and hurried to her, put her arm around her. She said, "Meg, Meg."

The widow raised her eyes to meet Allie's. "I can see him there." She pointed at the window, at the snowy scene outside. Lights twinkled up and down the street. Beyond her fingertip a line would have reached her own house, the only darkened house on the street. She had lived with her husband less than fifty yards from Walter's sister and her husband. They had been best friends since they were in their twenties. James and Allie's children had played at their house. Childless, they had reveled in the role of aunt and uncle to the other couple's children.

Those children were grown now, grown up and independent and gone away. In recent years the two elder couples had passed from maturity to middle age, to the early slope of old age, four friends, four of them living in proximity and contentment, and now there were three.

"I can still see the place in the snow," Meg said to Allie. "See there, beside the little lamp near the curb. See, Allie? He pulled on his boots and his Mackinaw and he tramped down the path to the sidewalk. He always did that. Every winter. He always liked to start at the sidewalk and shovel back toward the house. He always said it was just coming home, he never minded."

"Come away, dear." Allie tugged at Meg's hand, trying to draw her away from the window. "Come and sit by the fire, it's too chilly here."

Instead, Meg took another step toward the window. "If I squeeze my eyes closed and then open them just a slit, I can see him through the tears. I can see him fall down just like he did. He didn't move. Not a muscle. He just fell down dead. But if I try hard enough I can see him, I can make him get up again. It wasn't a heart attack. It was an icy spot and he slipped. He twisted his ankle. He stepped on a rock. Some child left a toy there and the snow covered it up. I can make him do it. I know him so well, his glasses fall halfway off and he uses the snow shovel to brace himself and he gets up and fixes his glasses. He brushes himself off, the snow off his Mackinaw, and he waves to me, I'm standing in the window and he waves to me so I'll know he's all right. He looks embarrassed. He thinks he looked foolish falling down and he's embarrassed."

She turned away from the window and took Allie's upper arms in her hands. Allie could feel Meg's fingers, as hard and as cold and as sharply pointed as icicles, digging into her arms. This time Meg let Allie lead her back to the sofa. She let Allie seat her beside James, then Allie sat sideways beside Meg so she could hold her hands and speak with her.

"Do you think," Meg asked in a peculiar voice, "if everyone in the city of Chicago concentrated at the same time, they could generate enough mental energy to make Lake Michigan boil?"

Allie smiled, bemused.

James looked baffled.

"Maybe." Allie touched Meg gently on one cheek.

"Do you think if everyone in Chicago believed strongly, strongly enough that Walter was alive, he would be alive?"

James frowned.

Allie said, "I don't think so, Meg. Not really."

There was a silence among the three of them. Through it, the voice of Jo Stafford sang, "Autumn Leaves." But autumn was over and winter was here.

The log crackled and a bright ember fell through the andirons and landed on the flagstones and exploded with a hollow pop and a small shower of sparks.

"But I read a piece about something called consensus reality." Meg nodded for emphasis. "Didn't I read that piece? The authors said that the universe only exists as percept. It's just the way it is because we all agree that's the way it is. If everybody believed that the sky was green, then the sky would be green. That's what the authors said. Don't you agree with them, Allie? Did you see the article, James?"

James pulled his pocket watch from his vest pocket and studied it for a long time. Meg could never understand why it took James so long to read the time from his watch, but finally he slipped it back into his pocket and said, "Nearly midnight. Consensus reality isn't my field." He could change topics like that without missing a beat. Sometimes Meg found it amusing; other times, annoying.

"But I agree with Dr. Johnson when he refutes Bishop Berkeley," he continued. "If you don't think the physical world is real, just kick a rock. The harder the better."

He was able to chuckle at his own wit.

"You don't think that we can change reality?"

James rose and walked to the fireplace. He kicked the gray stone framing it. Grinning, he said, "Ouch." Then, more seriously, "I'm sorry, Margaret. Truly I'm sorry. But I just can't buy it. If this consensus reality idea were true, then where did the world come from? Did Adam and Eve dream it up out of their own minds? Or did God dream it up out of his? Does Counter-Earth exist? Does Vulcan? Are there worlds circling distant stars? Are there people in Antares and Orion? Are they there only because we believe in them, and if we didn't believe in them they would just disappear —*poof*?"

He paced back and forth, lecturing again.

"And if half of us believe in Counter-Earth and the people who live there, and the other half don't believe in Counter-Earth, does it half-exist and half-not-exist? No." He shook his head and made a sound, something like *Pah!* "And if they half-exist, and half of them believe in *us* and the other half don't—do we exist or don't we? Or do we half-exist for the Counter-Earthlings we believe in but only half of them believe in Earthlings?" He laughed out loud. "You see, Margaret, don't you? It just won't hold water."

Allie said, "You know James, you have a remarkable intuitive grasp of quantum theory."

James said, "Any time I need some grounding, my dear, I just kick a rock."

There was a loud boom and all of them turned to peer out the window, toward Lake Michigan. A great roiling sphere of light and glowing water was rising into the air. At least, that was what it looked like.

"Allie, James," Margaret asked, "was that Lake Michigan boiling just now?"

James said, "Just more fireworks." He pulled his watch from its resting place on his belly then, and studied it.

Meg said, "Excuse me." She crossed the room, turning her back on the windows and the Santas and the seasonal lights, on the display rising over Lake Michigan, and on her own house just across the street and down a little ways.

In the doorway, before leaving the room, she stopped and turned back. Even from where she stood, it was possible to see the window, and beyond the window in the distance the colorful display, and much closer the darkness of her own house.

She stepped from the stone-floored living room into a small foyer. The floor here was flagged as well. The walls were of half-beamed plaster. There was a closet door and there was an outer door. Each was of wood, fitted with antique iron hinges and apparatus, the metal all greened by age or perhaps by the artisan's hand.

She reached for a metallic door handle but an obstacle retarded the movement of her hand. She didn't feel it, at least she didn't feel it at once. She could see it, but she wasn't even sure she could see it. It was vaguely oval or egg-shaped, or probably vaguely oval or egg-shaped, or probably not not-oval or vaguely egg-shaped.

And it was golden, or it was probably golden, or probably not not-golden.

Its edges were fuzzy, and she could see into it, or probably see into it, or probably not not-see into it. People and buildings and furniture and clothing and the sky. It was daytime or probably it was daytime or nighttime or probably probably-not not-day or—

Behind her the booming of fireworks grew louder and she looked around for a clock. It was midnight, or at least it was probably not not-midnight, and it was the new millennium, or at least it was probably the new millennium if everybody in the city of Chicago agreed that it was probably the new millennium here on

Earth and maybe on Counter-Earth as well, or maybe not.

In New York or maybe San Francisco, James and Allie's grown-up children met them at the airport.

James and Allie's daughter had moved to New York to pursue her career as a designer. She'd got a job, found a loft in Tribeca, run through a series of lovers, become celibate for a year while she cleared her mind and body of distracting influences, resumed dating, made her choice and settled down.

Their son had moved to San Francisco, taken work with an investment firm in the financial district, spent his days at the stock exchange and his nights South of Market trying to decide who he was and what he wanted to do and to achieve in the world. He was at first amazed, then briefly pleased, then profoundly disquieted to learn how many of his fellows shared his own sense of uncertainty.

The huge jet touched down and James and Alicia waited while the flight attendant got their warm coats and hats from the little closet where first class passengers' outer clothing was stowed during lengthy flights. James had consumed four scotches during the flight, but he walked steadily. Allie had stopped after three. It was a function of body mass, she told him. Your body mass is one-third greater than mine so it will take you four drinks to achieve the same level of anesthesia that I can reach with three.

Their heavy winter footwear sounded hollowly as they made their way up the jetway, no one ahead of them, another perquisite of traveling first class.

Their son and daughter met them at the gate and they exchanged kisses and embraces. Neither of the younger pair had brought a lover, spouse, or significant other to the airport. They had driven together. Their car was nearby in short-term parking.

Their son went with them to help them ransom their hastily-packed bags while their daughter retrieved the car and brought it to the portico. Their son stowed their bags in the trunk and James and Allie climbed into the back seat of the car. It was a comfortable, full-size sedan.

James grunted, "Nice car. I didn't know they even made these any more."

Their son spoke in fragments. "The police. They said you'd have to. They were here on holiday. Walter and Margaret. Uncle Walter. Aunt Margaret. We had a tree-house. In their backyard. But they wouldn't let us. They said family. We told them. They said we weren't close enough. We didn't. Qualify. Dad, Mom. Uncle Walter's sister. They said. Mom. Can you do it?"

Allie shuddered. "What time is it? I forgot to reset my watch, I'm still on Chicago time."

Their son told her the time. "Morgue. The morgue. Still open."

"Let's go."

James turned to her. "You don't mean that, Alicia. Take us to a hotel, please. Alicia needs a good night's rest. We both do. Then we can go, we can do this in the morning."

"No!" Allie's voice was shrill. There was silence in the car, and for the first time she realized that her daughter had turned on the radio, perhaps to pick up traffic bulletins. Only there was music playing, a soprano saxophone playing Cole Porter's song, "Every Time We Say Good-bye I Die a Little."

Again, James said, "Please, a hotel."

"No," one of their children said, "you won't stay at any hotel. Not now. The least we can do is have you with us. You can use the master bedroom. There will be plenty of room. You have to do this."

"Alicia?"

"All right. Thank you, darling. You are our blessing, you know, the two of you are God's blessing. If only Meg and Walter had had children. . . ." She let out a long sigh that was partly a sob. "But take me to them first. To do my duty. Please, I wouldn't sleep a wink if I knew I had to do this tomorrow. New Year's Day? The new millennium? Let the dying age bury its own dead. Please, James, you don't have to do this, he was my brother, I'll do what has to be done."

With James's assent, they proceeded to the morgue, to perform the heartbreaking task of formally identifying the bodies. Walter and Alicia had carried identification with them, it was found on their persons, there was no question, but the law had its requisites.

An hour later, or perhaps two, they sat in a living room, drinks in hand. No one was getting drunk. No one would get drunk. The liquor offered a little warmth; it took the edge off the ice-bladed scalpel cutting Allie's heart, and probably the hearts of the others.

James asked, "What happened?"

The scene at the morgue had at least been mercifully brief. The bodies had been shown to Allie and she had said, "Yes, that is my sister-in-law. That is my brother. Her husband." And the bodies had been taken away, and Allie had signed a few papers and James and their children took her away as well.

Now James said, "Tell us what happened. We're entitled to know what happened."

James and Alicia's children looked at each other. Then their son spoke.

"It was a fluke. They were in town on vacation. Well, I guess you know that." He had recovered himself sufficiently to speak in full sentences again.

"They were staying in a hotel downtown. They had dinner reservations and then theater tickets. They kept their dinner reservations. The police verified that. Walter had a card from the restaurant in his pocket and a detective checked and they'd eaten their meal and then the doorman got them a cab to carry them to the theater. They could have walked, it wasn't far, but it was such a miserable night, cold and wet, they didn't want to do it so they took a cab."

He heaved a sigh.

His sister said, "Do you want me to take over?"

He said, "No, I'll tell them."

She disappeared into the kitchen and started to make coffee.

He said, "Some skell carjacked a fancy sedan a block away. Pointed a gun at the driver and threw him out of the car and took off in it with a woman in the passenger seat and a little dog in the back seat. Woman starts screaming her head off, the dog gets upset and jumps up and sinks its teeth in the back of the jacker's neck."

Allie put her face in her hands, her elbows on her knees.

James sat upright, following the narrative.

"The guy must have been crazy, probably full of crack or PCP, I don't know, the cops said they'd run a test and let us know. For what it's worth."

"I want to know," James said.

"I'll call you," his son replied. Then he resumed the story. "He had to be crazy or hopped up or both. That time of night, that part of town, this time of year. Especially this year. He had to be crazy. Where did he think he'd get?"

James waited, his expression intent. Alicia pressed the heels of her hands against her temples, then slid them forward again until her face was concealed.

"When the dog bit him in the back of the neck he floored the accelerator. The man who owned the car was running in front of it, waving his hands, trying to flag down the jacker. He ran him right over and accelerated into the intersection. Against the light, of course."

A low moan emerged from between Allie's hands, the hands

that covered her face. She could see what was coming. It wasn't hard to see what was coming.

"Uncle Walter and Aunt Meg's cab was just going through the intersection. The car smashed into their cab broadside. It was going so fast by then, the cab flipped over. There was a bus in the next lane. The car crushed the cab against the side of the bus."

He smacked his palms together, unthinkingly adding a sound effect to his story. He realized what he'd done and stood staring at his hands as he held them in front of his chest.

"The carjacker was killed. He went through the windshield and was cut to ribbons. He'd already killed the owner of the car. The woman in the passenger seat died in the crash. Walter and Meg died. The cab driver died. No one on the bus was seriously injured. The little dog was okay."

Allie's shoulders rose and fell, rose and fell. Racking sounds came from between her hands. Her husband, James, put his arms around her and drew her to him. She hid her face in his shirt.

James said, "We'll have to arrange the funeral. Alicia can decide what she wants to do, ship the remains back to Chicago or bury them here."

Their daughter had returned to the room halfway through her brother's narration, when she had volunteered to take over the task. Now she said, "There's coffee, tea, I made sandwiches." She refrained from making a hysterical joke about airplane food and airline service.

Allie shook her head negatively.

James said, "I think you should have something, Alicia. Some little something. You need nourishment."

"I just keep thinking," their daughter said, "it was such a crazy accident. If they'd stayed at the restaurant five minutes longer. Thirty seconds longer! If they'd decided to have another cup of coffee. If they'd stopped to use the rest room. Or if they'd left the restaurant five minutes sooner. Or if they'd decided to walk to the theater. If they hadn't been able to get tickets to the show. If their driver had taken a different route. If he'd got stuck at a traffic light in the last block."

Alicia freed herself from her husband's embrace and took a few deliberate steps, left foot, right foot. She stood looking out the window. The streets were full of revelers, celebrants eager to welcome in the new millennium. She saw Richard Nixon wearing a huge rubber head. She saw Medusa with a head full of writhing snakes. She saw a giant blue alien with a globular body covered with artificial cilia.

James and Alicia's daughter had turned on soft music in the

house. Somehow it might lessen the deathly stillness and the cold, crushing grief. A torch singer was caressing the lyrics of a little known ballad, "I Don't Want to Cry Anymore."

The blue alien began jumping up and down, bouncing higher with each repetition. Shortly, Richard Nixon and Medusa closed in on him from either side and guided him away.

Alicia returned to the others. "You're right," she told her daughter. "If anything at all had been a little bit different, they would be alive right now. They might have seen the carjacking and they would have a story to tell for years to come. They could have told James and me when they got home. Instead, we'll take them home with us and bury them. I think we should do that. They have no one else. We'll take care of it."

She sank onto the sofa. James held the tray toward her and when she ignored it he lifted a sandwich and put it in her hand. She sat with her eyes fixed on it. The tip of a soya sprout stuck out between the slices of bread. A tiny tremor in her hand made it quiver. It seemed to bounce between two places a tiny fraction of an inch apart.

The music had changed again, to another old song, "The Very Thought of You." She thought of her brother and her brother's wife, of their long love story. Where were they now?

Dead. Nowhere. No one really believed that anything happened after death, that was a fairy tale for an earlier age, the threat of punishment and promise of reward used by priests to keep their flocks in line. Do as you're told or God will get you.

Nobody knew where anything was. That was the message of modern physics. Of Allie's chosen work. Everything was quanta. A quantum might be here, might be there, but never in-between. A muon here, a boson there, the physical universe had turned into Old MacDonald's farm.

When a particle disappeared, where did it go? Did it cease to exist? Did it pop into another universe?

She stood up again and went back to the window. When she felt a hand on her shoulder she shook it off. She tried to focus on the farthest, dimmest object her eye could discern. In the city sky there was too much glow to see truly faint objects.

She saw something that looked like a glowing oval. There were forms in it, vague and uncertain. She wiped a tear from her eye and the glowing oval disappeared or perhaps it grew clearer and brighter. A quantum particle might be here or there but never between here and there.

Here or there.

Here or there.

The late Louis Armstrong once startled his fans and admirers by stating that he admired Guy Lombardo's music. Armstrong was the most famous jazz artist of his day, while Lombardo was regarded as the ultimate in square, stodgy corn. Was Louis joking? No. As different as his approach to music was from Lombardo's, he could understand what Lombardo was up to and he could admire Lombardo's dedicated craftsmanship and execution.

Similarly, while my own mystery novels and short stories have for the most part been pretty far from the hardboiled realm, I do read and enjoy hardboiled crime fiction. My favorite crime writer — one of my favorite writers, in fact, regardless of category — is Dashiell Hammett, who pretty much invented "hardboiled" and was practicing the craft before Ernest Hemingway introduced it to the world of so-called serious literature. (Don't get me started!)

"You Don't Know Me, Charlie," is an exception, one of my few excursions into hardboiled crime fiction. It was written for O'Neil DeNoux's New Orleans Stories, but appeared more or less simultaneously in Gary Lovisi's aptly named Hardboiled magazine and Maxim Jakubowski's anthology Constable New Crimes.

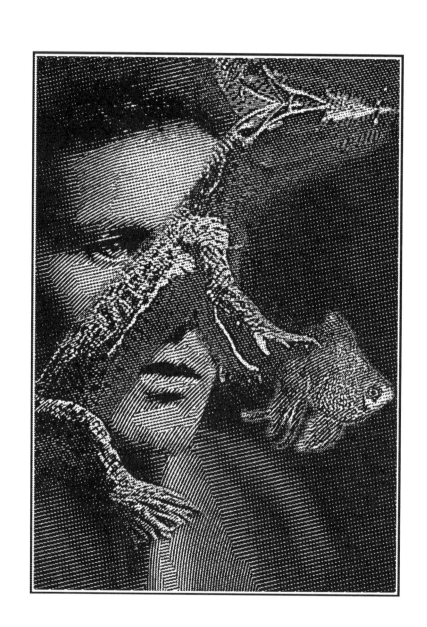

# You Don't Know Me, Charlie

B Y MORNING HE WAS AT MOISANT INTERNATIONAL Airport in New Orleans. The pilot announced that a cold front had beaten the jet down from Chicago and New Orleans had experienced a freak snowfall during the night, and everybody should watch out for slippery surfaces.

He rode into town in a van full of tourists, climbed out in front of a hotel in the French Quarter and just wandered away while the rest of them dealt with their baggage.

He walked in a straight line until he came to a broad thoroughfare. The street sign said Canal Street. He found a fleabag movie theater and bought a ticket and a hot dog and slathered relish and sauerkraut on the dog and sat in the dark, stale-smelling, mostly empty auditorium. He was too warm in the jacket he'd worn on the airplane, so he laid it across his lap for safekeeping. He ignored the movie, eating his lunch and trying to get his act together.

He'd walked out of the joint expecting to be met by a team of feds armed with a subpoena. It was going to be a matter of giving his testimony and then disappearing into the Witness Protection Program, and from everything he'd ever heard about the program he didn't want any part of it.

Instead he'd been met by a couple of guys in blue suits and

black glasses and whisked to Chicago by limousine, no less. A fancy dinner with the old guy in the soft houndstooth jacket and then it was another limo ride, this time to O'Hare with a couple of hundred fish in his pocket and a ticket on the redeye headed south.

The old guy kept making small talk and calling him Charlie and he kept telling him that his name wasn't Charlie but the old guy didn't pay any attention. The old guy did look familiar, but when he asked who he was all he could get was, "You don't know me, Charlie." He only asked once, and when he saw the look in the old guy's eyes he wished he hadn't asked at all.

In late afternoon he wandered through the French Quarter again. He let a barker lure him into a bar. Once he got inside the bar he scoped around. The place was full of people in T-shirts and short pants. He asked the bartender what kind of beer they had and he said to try an Abita and he said okay, and it was actually pretty good.

On his way out of the bar he bent over and picked up a square plastic badge. It said,

YO, DUDE!
YOU CAN CALL ME JOHN
OR YOU CAN CALL ME JOHN
BUT DON'T CALL ME LATE FOR COCKTAILS
WORLD CONSORTIUM OF Q-ZIX PROCESSOR ENGINEERS
NOVUM ORLEANSUS

It was a convention badge, and across the bottom where the date should have been was just a row of ones and zeroes.

He pinned the badge to his jacket pocket. It helped him blend in with the people wandering around getting drunk. He'd never heard of a place like this, but then when you've never been anywhere except Indiana, Ohio and Illinois in your life, and more than half of that in the joint, there must be a lot of strange places in the world.

He needed a place to stay and he needed a way to make some money. At first glance this town looked like dip heaven, all these overweight tourists wandering around, the men with their wallets in their back pockets and the broads with their purses on their arms. But he'd dipped a few times in his life and learned that it wasn't for him, he didn't have a light enough touch to be really good at it, and he didn't want to get picked up by the local minions of the law. Especially not on his first day in town.

Besides, there were too many blue uniforms in evidence, and

too many units visible on the streets here. It made sense. In a tourist town, keep the tourist neighborhood under control. Let 'em spend their green, the more the merrier. And look the other way if the girls in the bars want to cut their own deals with the visiting firemen, even if the powdered sugar that gets sold is maybe not just sugar.

But try to keep the dips and the muggers under control.

Somewhere along the line he'd attended enough school to know that New Orleans was on the Mississippi River but he was astonished to find himself looking at it. The water was yellowish-brown. He turned away and wandered down the street into a neighborhood dotted with warehouses and marine supply outfits and job printers. He stood across the street from a row of saloons and restaurants, studying them, trying to choose the one that would be just right.

He'd never seen so many liquor dispensaries in one town in his life, and they were all busy. He picked one that looked like it served food and booze both. The only thing he'd eaten all day was the hot dog in the movie house and it was squirming around in his belly now as if it didn't like him any better than he liked it.

He picked a place that looked right and crossed the street and stood on the sidewalk in front of the establishment. The air was warm and moist. His clothes stuck to his skin.

The front window was a big rectangle of plate glass with a tank in it half filled with water with a quarter-grown alligator in it lying on a rock. A few fat goldfish swam lazily around the alligator. He wondered if they even knew the alligator was there, and if the alligator knew the goldfish were there. The alligator looked like it was asleep until you looked at it closer, then you saw that its eye was open a slit and it was watching you. It had an expression on its face that said, *Come ahead, buddy, you look like you'd make a lovely morsel.*

The sign in the window said:

KING ARTHUR'S ALLIGATOR ROUNDTABLE

The place was cool inside and it wasn't as crowded as the restaurants and saloons that pulled in tourists in the French Quarter were. There was a single big room in the place, with a little office to one side and a couple of doors that must lead to the kitchen at the back. If King Arthur had a roundtable, it might have been any one of twenty or thirty tables that filled the big room. There was a bar running along the wall opposite the office, in the back half of the place. The ceiling was high, covered with patterned metal squares. Big wooden fans turned slowly above the customers' heads.

He slid onto a barstool and surveyed the room more closely in the back-bar mirror. He could see the office door in the mirror, and people eating an early dinner at four or five tables. It was too early for the real dinner crowd. These people must have a terrific appetite; maybe they were stoking up for a long night soaking up booze and jazz and the hot smell of strippers. They were eating some kind of stew, most of them, or some kind of mess of rice.

There were a few drinkers at the bar. A couple who looked like they were on their honeymoon, touching each other and drinking ridiculous drinks with pieces of fruit in them and whispering in each other's ears. A sad type who looked as if his wife had walked out on him leaving her mother in her place. He could have been the happy bridegroom, twenty or thirty years down the road, desperately trying to wash away a lifetime of mistakes with a glassful of bourbon.

There was a guy who looked a little smarter and a little tougher than the others. He had a double shot glass in front of him. It was mostly empty.

There was a woman at the end of the bar, with gray hair like steel wool and a blouse with some kind of collar that rolled away from her chest. She wore a bead necklace that disappeared into her cleavage. You couldn't help looking there. She must have been a looker twenty years ago. Now she looked like she was barely hanging on, one day at a time. Just like the AA people, only her one day at a time wasn't a day clean and sober, it was just a day.

She was drinking something that sent up steam. Maybe the air conditioning in the place was too much for her. Her drink looked like a hot rum toddy. It must be doing a swell job of keeping her warm because there was a sheen of moisture on her face.

He watched a drop of sweat roll down her neck and slide down her chest and disappear into her cleavage. It left a little trail behind it, a narrow stripe of skin washed clean of the day's accumulated grime.

She caught him watching her chest and gave him a peculiar look.

He said, "Excuse me."

She gave him some more of the look.

He said, "I'm sorry. I didn't mean to—"

She said, "Of all the gin joints in all the towns in all the world . . ."

The bartender looked at him. The bartender had a pale face, as if he never got out in the sun. It was almost a prison pallor. He had a fringe of black hair around his bald dome. His face was smooth. He was either old and well-preserved or young and prematurely bald, it was really hard to tell. "Something for you, Mack?"

He said, "Gimme an Abita." You had to like a town with its own beer, that was as good as this stuff.

The bartender put a bottle and a glass in front of him, took his money and slapped his change on the wood. He looked at it and thought about picking it up, then decided to leave it there.

In the mirror he watched a waiter come over and serve some food to a quartet of customers. They were all wearing little square plastic badges. They were all wearing I SURVIVED THE GREAT NEW ORLEANS BLIZZARD T-shirts. They were all overweight. The one who was most overweight was a woman. She caught his eye in the back-bar mirror. She wasn't wearing any brassiere. The two men at the table were smoking cigars and gabbing a mile a minute. They looked as if they were working on a business deal. The other broad was busy looking the waiters up and down but the waiters didn't look the least bit interested.

The fat woman without the brassiere smiled at him in the back-bar mirror. Christ, was she giving him the come on? Was she trying to get something on with him, right there while her husband yakked up a storm with the other broad's husband? That was all he needed. Christ.

The bartender said, "You want another one, John?"

He said, "Sure."

At the same time the guy with the double shot glass said, "Nope."

They looked at each other.

The bartender looked at the guy with the double shot glass and said, "Your name John, too?"

The guy with the double shot glass said, "Yeah."

The bartender said, "What a remarkable coincidence. I just read John's badge here." He took away the empty bottle, popped the cap off another Abita and clunked it onto the wood. He took the price of it out of the change that was left from the first Abita.

"Hey, John." The guy with the double shot glass looked at him. "What the fuck is a Q-Zix Processor? Sounds like some kind of ice box."

He poured a little Abita into his tall glass, watched it foam into a thin white head, said, "What ice box?"

The other guy laughed, if you could call one short, sharp bark a laugh. "And what the fuck is that one-zero-one-one shit?" He pointed to the badge.

Damn! Try and blend into the population and some wiseacre asks questions that you can't answer.

The woman with the steel wool hair saved him. She said, "Didn't you read about those Q-Zix people? Some kind of computer wizards. Hey, Johnny, you're the first one I've seen without a plastic pocket full of pencils."

He tried to keep quiet and ride this one out.

The woman with the steel wool hair said, "I thought you superbrains were all gone a couple of days ago. Doesn't that one-and-zero stuff mean the dates you were going to be here?"

He stole a glance at the badge himself, then tilted it up so he could read it upside down.

The bartender chimed in, "That's binary code. Lemme see." He scrounged around under the bar, came up with a plastic pen with a tiny woman trapped inside the plastic. When he held it one way she was wearing a green brassiere and panties. When he held it the other way the brassiere and panties slid down and you could see her tiny red nipples and dark triangle.

The bartender scribbled on a cocktail napkin. Then he said, "Yeah. Your convention ended last week."

Everybody seemed to be waiting for an answer.

The honeymooning bridegroom slipped his hand inside his wife's New Orleans Blizzard T-shirt and she squirmed and giggled. The older guy whose wife had left him gazed deeper into his shot glass.

"Yeah. The convention ended but I had a few extra days to kill. I'm taking a little rest. I been working too hard."

The giggling bride pulled her husband's hand out of her shirt and he dropped it into her lap. She squeezed her legs tight around his hand. She said, "We use computers all the time in my office. The boss says we're going to get a Q-Zix processor next year."

"I never talk about that when I'm on vacation." He fumbled with the plastic badge, undid the shiny metal pin that held it to his jacket and slipped it inside his pocket. He was still wearing his Chicago clothes. The jacket was too hot for this place and he pulled it off and laid it across his lap like he'd done in the movie theater.

The tough-looking guy said, "So you're John and I'm John. What a coincidence. But they call me Jack. And you're Johnny. That's good. That'll keep us separated okay."

He said, "Yeah. That's good. Jack and Johnny."

Jack said, "Pleased to make your acquaintance." He held his hand out.

Johnny hesitated a tick, then shook Jack's hand. Jack gave him a look. Johnny didn't like the look much. It was a funny look. It wasn't quite a faggot look. It was more a sizing-up look like new fish got when they hit the yard. There was nothing like the first day in a new joint. You look around for a familiar face and you sense the sizing-up that you're getting, from the jockers, from the killers, from the professional bullies, from the gang recruiters.

He didn't like the look.

Jack said, "You staying in the Quarter?"

Johnny said, "Maybe."

Jack held his head sideways. Johnny didn't like that look, either. Jack said, "You need a place to stay?"

Johnny said, "I'm set."

Jack lowered his voice. He said, "Just finish your beer and head up the street to the corner. There's a boarded-up gas station there. Take your time, Johnny." To the bartender he said, "I've had enough." To everyone at the bar he said, "Don't eat no yellow snow." Then he left the bar.

Johnny did a little mental math and ordered a bowl of the brownish stew. The bartender said it was gumbo. He ate it and drank another Abita.

A couple of times single guys dropped in to the bar, slid onto the stool next to the woman with the steel wool hair, and tried to pick her up. She brushed them off. She drank her hot drinks. Every time a drop of sweat rolled between her tits Johnny followed it with his eyes. The woman caught him looking every time.

He looked at a clock above the back-bar, slid off his barstool, pulled his jacket back on, found his way to the toilet and took a piss, then headed for the door. He stopped to look at the quarter-grown alligator. He counted the goldfish. A couple of them had disappeared but the others swam around looking as happy as ever. The alligator had switched ends of its tank. It gave him the same look it had given him before. Like it would still be glad to take off his hand for dinner. No couple of goldfish could satisfy this gator's appetite.

Outside in the street, Johnny stopped and looked at the sky. The sun was gone and a combination of low clouds and mist covered the stars. The moon made a pale, soft-edged blob over the Mississippi. His jacket felt like it weighed a ton but he had his hands free if he wore it and didn't carry it.

Jack was smoking a cigarette in the boarded-up gas station. He was wearing a blue Hawaiian shirt with hula girls on it. He was standing on a concrete island where gas pumps had been removed, leaving a couple of iron pipes sticking out of the island. He said, "Where you from, Johnny?"

Johnny said, "Chicago."

"What joint?"

"Fuck you."

Jack grabbed him by the front of his jacket. "Don't tell me fuck you, Johnny. I said, *What joint?*"

Johnny tried to get free but Jack wouldn't let go. Johnny said, "What makes you think I been in the joint?"

Jack shoved him away and Johnny stumbled over the concrete island. He caught himself without going down but now he was shaking a little. Jack said, "Don't shit me, it's all over you. I can see it. I can smell it. You got con stink on you, Johnny. What's this computer shit?"

Johnny said, "I found the badge."

Jack said, "You got a place to stay? You just got into town. You're dressed too warm. If you had a place you'd leave the coat in your room."

Johnny said, "I guess not. I'll find a place. You're not a cop."

Jack barked like he did back in the bar. "You'll stay with me. I got room. You can sleep on my couch."

Johnny looked around. He could see lights a couple of blocks away, back where the tourist crowds were dense. They were definitely out of the Quarter but it wasn't far away. It was darker here and there were no crowds. He could see the front door of King Arthur's Alligator Roundtable. The honeymoon couple were coming out. They headed the other way, toward the bright lights and the crowds. The guy had his hand on the broad's ass and he was squeezing as they walked.

Jack said, "Come on." He grabbed Johnny's arm. His fingers were strong. Even through the too-heavy jacket the fingers dug into Johnny's arm and hurt. Jack had a beat-up Plymouth Sapporo parked around the corner in front of a factory building. He unlocked it. Johnny stood next to the car. Jack said, "Fuck you, get in the damned car."

They drove under a couple of interstates and wound up on a street with old houses on both sides, scraggly lawns, a wide island in the middle of the street. Jack pulled the Plymouth into a driveway and led the way into the house. It was divided into apartments. Jack had a couple of rooms. The furniture was old and the place smelled of mildew and sweat. There was a kitchen sink and a counter with a hot plate and a small, battered-looking refrigerator in the room. There was a scratched-up TV in one corner with a coathanger for an antenna and a short metal shaft sticking out where the tuner knob should be.

Johnny took off his coat. He sat down hard on an overstuffed chair. There were stains on the upholstery and whatever color it might once have been had turned to a kind of neutral nothing. It was hot in the room and the chair felt damp and it smelled musty. He laid his coat over the arm of the chair. He said, "What do you want?"

Jack stood in the middle of the room. He looked at Johnny. He didn't say anything.

Johnny said, "You're not a fag. You're not a roll artist. You gotta be after something. You sure as hell didn't just take a liking to me."

Finally Jack said, "You got any money?"

Johnny said, "Maybe you are a roll artist. Why the fuck did you bring me here?"

Jack said, "I'm not a roll artist. You have some money or you wouldn't have spent like you did in Arthur's."

Johnny relaxed a little. "I got a few bucks."

"But not many or you wouldn't have been so eager for a free flop."

"Ain't you smart."

"Look, Bo, you're a con and you got a few bucks and you're new in town and you got no prospects. You want to make some green?"

Things were rolling his way, now. Jack wanted something. Johnny played it cagey. "What's your proposition?"

Jack said, "I need a helper."

"Sure you do. A helper with what?"

"Real easy job. A nice heist, real easy."

Johnny said, "Tell me."

Jack walked over and stood in front of Johnny's chair. He said, "Sure I'll tell you." He reached down and grabbed Johnny and pulled him out of the chair and spun him around and threw him against the wall. Johnny hit the wall face first with a crash. Jack said, "Position, fucker! You're too curious. You're wired."

Johnny put his hands on the wall and crossed one ankle over the other. Jack patted him down. He grabbed him by the back of the neck and threw him back into his chair. Johnny said, "No wire, okay?"

Jack said, "Okay. And no heat. Not even a shank. What the fuck—?"

"I'm clean. I just hit town. Whadda you expect?"

Jack lit a cigarette. Johnny held his hand out. Jack gave him one, threw a book of matches at him. "Christ, what happened to you? You get born this morning?"

"You're so fucking smart, I'm just out of the joint and I'm new in town. Okay, I need a score."

"You're no junky. I coulda spotted that."

"I need to score some bread. I got a little roll but it won't go far and there's no more coming."

Jack nodded. "Okay. What brought you into Arthur's?"

Johnny said, "Nothing."

Jack gave him a look.

"I wanted a drink and a meal."

"Arthur's is a little off the beaten track, Bo."

"That's why."

Jack looked at him. "Maybe you ain't so dumb." He drew on his cigarette, walked over to the sink and turned on the tap. He held the cigarette under it and when the water hit the burning tobacco the cigarette went out with a hiss. Jack threw it in a garbage pail under the sink.

Johnny crossed his legs and rubbed out his cigarette on the bottom of his shoe.

Jack said, "I been stopping in Arthur's pretty regular."

Johnny said, "So what?"

"How much money you think goes through that place every day?"

"I don't know."

"Want to guess?"

"I have no idea."

Jack said, "Call yourself a computer whiz."

Johnny said, "I told you, I found that badge. I don't know squat about computers."

Jack said, "Right." He said, "Stay put." He started looking for something, shoving piles of old *Times-Picayunes* around on top of a table and tugging drawers open and slamming them shut again. He grunted and came back to where Johnny was sitting. He sat on a chair like Johnny's. He had a yellow pad and a wooden pencil and a little calculator in his hand. He balanced them on the arm of his chair. He said, "Look at this."

Johnny grunted.

Jack said, "King Arthur's opens at ten o'clock every morning.

They serve breakfast, lunch, dinner. They serve dinners 'til ten-thirty at night. The bar opens when the restaurant opens and it stays open 'til eleven-thirty at night."

Johnny said, "I'd think they'd stay open later."

"If they was on Bourbon Street they would. Or Decatur Street. Anyplace in the Quarter. Maybe in the Garden District. But not in the Warehouse District. There's no foot traffic there late at night. Wouldn't pay 'em to stay open."

Johnny said, "Christ it's hot. Gimme a glass of water."

Jack said, "Take it." He gestured toward the sink.

Johnny opened a cupboard, found a jelly glass, filled it with tepid water and came back to his chair. He took a sip of water. "Wonderful," he said. "You planning to go in the restaurant business and you want me to manage the place for you."

Jack said, "Don't be so fucking smart. I asked you if you had any idea how much money goes through Arthur's every day."

"And I told you I have no idea what so fucking ever."

Jack was writing numbers on the yellow pad. He said, "Look, fuck-ass, here's how many customers Arthur's seats at the tables. Here's how many times they turn over those seats for breakfast on an average day. I been watching them, see? And I worked in a couple of saloons in my time, and a couple of dinner houses."

This time Johnny laughed. "I was right. You want to go in the restaurant business."

Jack hit him in the face with back of his hand, pretty hard. Not hard enough to knock him out of his chair, but hard enough to let him know he meant it. He said, "Pay attention."

Johnny rubbed his face. "Shit," he whispered. "Shit, shit, shit."

Jack said, "Here's how many lunches they sell. Same principle, you take the number of seats times how full they get times how many times they turn over."

Johnny said, "You really did work in one of those places."

"A lot of 'em. Shut up and pay attention. Don't interrupt me unless you don't understand something. Look, dinner's the big meal. They got a real long dinner hour in this town, the place gets the fullest then, and the meals cost the most. And the customers drink the most. You got to calculate bar business in there too. Sometimes that'll carry a dinner house all itself."

"Yeah. Yeah."

"Bar drinkers plus table service, figure they sell—hey, pay attention, shit head—you got straight drinks, you got mixed drinks, you got wine and beer. You—fuck, just sit still." He scribbled numbers, poked the calculator ON button and punched the keys, scribbled some more numbers, wrote the final total big at the bottom of the page.

There was a rattling sound.

Johnny jumped.

Jack said, "It's raining, that's all."

Johnny said, "I thought it snowed here."

Jack said, "That was a freak. It's raining."

"Okay." Still, a window was open and a cool, moist wind swept through it. The temperature dropped and Johnny was almost cold. It was still as moist as ever, close and sticky, but no longer hot.

Jack shoved the pad under Johnny's nose. "Look at the numbers, fuck-o. Look at the bottom number."

Johnny did. He nodded his head.

Jack said, "All right. I'm gonna watch TV. We'll talk some more tomorrow." He turned on the TV, jiggled the coathanger. The news came on. There was a story from Illinois about how the Feds were pissed at the local cops because they'd gone to pick up a con and the local guys had turned him loose an hour early and they couldn't find him.

Jack gave Johnny a sour look. He stood up and found a pair of pliers to turn the dial on the TV. "Nothing any good on. Fuck. If you ain't here in the morning I'll find your ass and I'll kill you, Bo." He snapped off the TV and disappeared into the other room.

The sun came through the window and hit him in the face and he sat up, startled. He blinked and Jack was standing there watching him, wearing a pair of stained khaki pants and an old-fashioned undershirt, smoking a cigarette.

Jack said, "All right. Here's how it works. All you need is a cosh, fuck-o."

"A cosh?"

"Christ! A sap. A blackjack. You're going to hit a guy on the back of the head. That's all you have to do and you get a quarter of that money we were talking about last night."

"A quarter?"

"Do you know how much that comes to? Are you smart enough to figure that out?"

Actually, Johnny hadn't figured it out. He looked around the room. Jack's yellow pad was still there. He looked at the bottom number, cut it in half in his head, cut it in half again. "If I'm your partner I get half."

"You're not my partner. You're my helper."

"Hey, if we take a fall I do the same time you do."

Jack hit him again, harder this time, right in the same place he'd hit him last night. "Shit head, I spotted this thing, I worked it all out, I made the plan and I'm running the job. All you got to do is do what I tell you. All you got to do is slug a guy. You got to do about ten minutes work. This'll be the best night's work you ever did."

Johnny said, "Who do I have to slug?"

Jack said, "You'll find that out later. You had breakfast yet?"

"How'm I gonna have breakfast?"

Jack sucked on his cigarette, took it out of his mouth and looked at the coal as if he expected to find a message there. He hung the cigarette from the corner of his mouth and squinted at Johnny through the thin column of smoke that twisted past his eye. He didn't say anything.

Johnny said, "You got any grub? And you got an extra set of threads I could borrow? I'm starting to feel a little ripe. I need some other stuff, too." He scratched the stubble on his face with the tips of his fingers. His face was sore where he'd taken those shots from Jack. He didn't say anything about that but he stored it away. He always stored things like that away.

Jack said, "I'll do better for you than that. You're gonna help me make a nice score, I'll front you the bread for a couple meals and a set of threads. Come on."

Johnny was sitting on the couch in his underwear. He pulled on his heavy pants and his shirt, his sweaty socks and shoes. While he rubbed toothpaste on his teeth with his finger, Jack boiled water on the hotplate. They drank some instant coffee. Johnny asked why it tasted funny and Jack said that was the chicory in it, you better get used to it.

They took Jack's struggling Plymouth down to Canal Street and Jack parked it and they went into a huge old department store that looked like they hadn't changed the stock in thirty years or the equipment in forty. Johnny still had most of his bankroll from Chicago but if Jack was willing to front him the cash for a couple of pairs of khakis and some Hawaiian shirts, that was fine with him. He picked up a toothbrush and a razor at Woolworth's.

Jack drove him back to his apartment and waited while Johnny shaved and washed the sweat off his body and put on new clothes. He felt a thousand times better.

They drove back downtown and ate lunch at Kolb's on St. Charles Avenue. Jack ordered red beans and rice. Johnny had a fried oyster po' boy. He drank a few beers with his meal and a cup of coffee after. They talked about great joints of America.

Johnny tried to be careful but Jack knew people he knew and the beers seemed to have more effect than they should. Maybe it was the hot, muggy weather. It was almost winter in Chicago and it should be getting colder in New Orleans, too, he thought, but you could take a bath in the steamy air.

Jack said, "I gotta piss." His chair scraped on the old tile floor and he strode away.

Johnny thought about just getting up and leaving. New Orleans was a big city. Jack wouldn't find him, probably wouldn't even try, and if he did, so what? But a score sounded good. His roll wouldn't last long, and Jack was the only person he knew in town. He signaled the waiter for another beer.

A couple of suits at the next table were looking at a copy of the *Chicago Tribune*. Wouldn't you know it. One of them was pointing to a story, saying, "You can bet he's dead. They'll fish him out of the Lake or maybe he's in New Jersey with Jimmy Hoffa. They'll never let that guy talk."

The other suit grunted. Then he said, "I don't know. More likely New Jersey. Yeah. They wouldn't want him anywhere close to home, not even dead. Draw too much heat."

"Yeah," the first suit said. "I'll tell you what I bet, they'll send him away someplace and set him up and just when he figures he's safe they'll take care of him. Serve the fucker right, anyhow." He laughed like he thought that was real funny.

The second suit said, "I guess you're right. Fuckin' criminals, deserve what they get."

Johnny felt like somebody had dropped an ice cube down his back. He looked away from the suits. There was no sign of Jack coming back from the pisser.

The first suit said, "Listen, we got one more appointment this afternoon and then we don't have to fly back 'til tomorrow. How do you feel about tying one on tonight? We can get a couple of bimbo's up in the room, a couple of bottles, maybe a little powder. Just keep the expense account clean. . . ."

Jack pulled out his chair and slid into it. "God, nothing like a good piss to make you know you're alive. You had enough? I haven't." He signaled the waiter and ordered a slice of cheesecake. He stuffed his mouth full of cheesecake and said, "How'd you work that thing in Illinois?"

Johnny shot a look at the suits. They were halfway to the front door, headed out of Kolb's. He said, "Work what thing?"

Jack put his fork down on his plate, loud. "Don't bullshit me. You saw the story on TV."

Johnny said, "I didn't work nothing. I served my time and I got my release. That's all."

Jack said, "Yeah." He chopped off another bite of cheesecake and shoved it in his mouth. He said, "Look, you can take the afternoon off. Do whatever you want. Go to the zoo, listen to some jazz, find a whorehouse. You want me to take you to one? Christ, I feel like your father." Some cheesecake crumbs fell on his shirt as he talked.

Johnny looked into his coffee cup. How long had it been? But he said, "Not yet. I want to keep my edge. Let's make this score, then I'll want a broad. I always like to get laid after a score."

Jack shoved the last of the cheesecake into his mouth. "Yeah. Don't I know it." He looked around for the waiter and signaled for their bill. He told Johnny he was lucky he'd cleaned up and put on his new clothes before they got there. He'd never have got into a place like this, looking like he did before.

Johnny said, "We need a schedule."

Jack nodded. He paused while a couple of working girls in tight skirts swirled past. "Look, you take the afternoon off. We're going back to King Arthur's tonight. Not for dinner. Ten o'clock. Make it ten-thirty. I wanna show you something. You know your way by now? I don't wanna get there together, that same name business last night was creepy. Sit at the bar and have a drink. You really like that Abita stuff, don't you? I wanna show you something."

He spent the afternoon in the movies again. He watched a pretty good flick about a corpse loose in a girls' school, lots of shots in the dorm and in the showers before the corpse killed his quota of teenagers and some faggoty-looking jock blew up the corpse.

After the movie Johnny worked his way down Bourbon Street. He picked up a street map. It was easy to get around in New Orleans, especially in the Quarter. He watched a few strippers, drank a couple of beers. Christ, but this would be heaven if he was still dipping for a living, but he kept his fingers to himself.

He cut over to Jackson Square on Saint Something street. He bought a hot dog from a vendor and sat on a bench watching a kid tap dance to a boom box until it was dark and the air was starting to cool off a little. He walked up Decatur, back to Canal Street, then crossed Canal to Magazine Street.

He stood opposite King Arthur's Alligator Roundtable and watched people go in and come out. Most of them looked like tourists, a few looked like locals. He tried to count the customers. Jack knew so fucking much about the restaurant business, why didn't he open a restaurant? In Chicago, he knew if the man in the soft houndstooth jacket wanted a restaurant, he'd send a couple of guys in blue suits and black glasses around and they'd arrange it.

He looked at his watch. It was a quarter after ten.

Jack's Plymouth wobbled past King Arthur's and disappeared around the corner onto Natchez. Ten minutes later Jack reappeared on foot smoking a cigarette. He crossed Magazine Street. Johnny ducked back into an alley. Jack walked past him, close enough for Johnny to reach out and touch him if he wanted to.

Jack reached the corner of Gravier, crossed Magazine again, and went into Arthur's.

Johnny gave him five minutes to get settled, then crossed Magazine in the middle of the block and looked through the window of Arthur's. The alligator was still in its tank. There was one goldfish left. The alligator gave Johnny the *you-look-good-enough-to-eat* look. Johnny said, "Fuck you, alligator." The alligator didn't say anything back.

Inside the place, Johnny could see Jack silhouetted against the far wall. He was sitting on a barstool with a double shot glass in front of him. At the near end of the bar the woman with the steel wool hair was on the same stool she'd been on last night. Johnny could see she was wearing a rusty-orange colored shirt and a pair of dark jeans. He couldn't see her drink but he thought he saw a little wisp of steam rising from it.

He pushed open the door and stepped inside. A party of two plain-looking women and a muscular guy with a dark mustache went by him, leaving the restaurant. A waiter spotted him and started to say something about the kitchen being closed but laid off when Johnny shoved past him and headed for the bar.

There were a couple of strangers soaking up booze but Johnny slipped into a seat next to Jack. He didn't look at Jack. He looked around, surveyed the other drinkers, zeroed in on the woman with steel wool hair. Tonight's shirt buttoned up the front and the top few buttons were open and she wasn't wearing a brassiere. Christ, she must have been something before she got so old.

She looked at him and made a little motion with her head.

Maybe she wasn't so old after all. What was the saying about how all cats were gray in the dark? All pussies. He smiled back at her. He felt a sharp pain in his side. He made eye contact with Jack in the back-bar mirror.

Out loud Jack said, "Hey, if it ain't Mr. Skeezix!" Under his breath he hissed, "Watch this, you fuck." He picked up his double size shot glass, laying one finger alongside it, pointing to the mirror.

Johnny watched.

The owner was coming from the far end of the dining room. One look, you knew this guy was the owner. King Arthur him fucking self. He gave the bartender the high sign and the bartender pulled his cash drawer out of the register and followed the owner into the little office. One of the waiters came over and took over the stick. None of the customers complained. Everybody drank his drink.

Johnny looked at his watch. It was eleven o'clock.

The office door opened and the bartender stepped out, carrying a cloth satchel. The owner came out behind him and stopped long enough to lock the door. Then he took the satchel from the bartender and headed for the door. The bartender followed him out onto the sidewalk.

Through the front window of Arthur's, beyond the alligator and its goldfish pal, Johnny saw the owner head up Magazine Street. The bartender waited a few beats, then followed him.

To Jack, Johnny said softly, "Is that all?"

Johnny said, "Shut up."

Jack drank his Abita and admired the tits on the broad with the steel wool hair. Christ, she was looking younger by the minute and better by the beer.

At twenty after eleven the owner and the bartender came back in, together. The owner disappeared into the office with the cloth satchel. The bartender took back the stick and the relief bartender disappeared into the kitchen.

They drove back to Jack's in silence, smoking cigarettes and listening to the radio. The disk jockey played nothing but punk rock. There was a news and weather break. The news was mainly about a political scandal in Baton Rouge, followed by a couple of sports headlines. The weather forecast was hot and muggy with a good chance of thundershowers blowing in from Lake Ponchartrain. Not a word about the missing witness in Illinois.

In the apartment Jack brought out a bottle of scotch and two jelly glasses and poured them drinks. They lit cigarettes. Jack said, "Did you get it?"

Johnny shook his head.

Jack picked up his hand like he was going to backhand Johnny again but he stopped. "Maybe I made a mistake. You're so fucking dumb."

Johnny put his glass down. He wasn't going to take a beating from this creep. "Can the tough talk and say it."

Jack looked at him with a little respect for once. "Didn't you understand what you saw tonight? Look, Arthur has a safe there in his office. Every couple of hours they transfer all the cash from the dining room register into the safe. Same for the bar register."

He dragged on his butt, swallowed a slug of scotch. "At eleven o'clock Arthur carries the last restaurant cash into the office, the bartender brings his cash drawer in. They total up the day's cash and put it in that satchel. Then they carry it to the night deposit at the bank."

Johnny nodded.

Jack said, "You're starting to follow, hey?"

Johnny said, "Yeah. Go on."

"Arthur carries the satchel. The bartender follows a little ways back. They don't look like they're together. If anybody tries to put the arm on Arthur, there's Arthur's little helper to the rescue. Any money comes in at the place, meanwhile, they put in the safe overnight. But that's peanuts."

Johnny rubbed his face. He'd shaved off the stubble and he was only a little bruised and swollen from Jack's backhand shots. You didn't know to look, you'd just think that he was kind of fleshy around the jawbone, a little fleshy and a little blotchy. He said, "You want to put the snatch on the receipts."

"You figured it out."

"Half."

"A quarter. All you got to do is slug the bartender. That comes first. Then I hit Arthur. Nice and quiet over there, not too light, nobody walking around. We come back here and split the green. Then, who knows, maybe we'll stay partners."

"Half."

"A third." They bargained a little more. It would be a good score. Maybe he could partner with Jack. This was a nice town, looked like there was plenty of loose cash around, he sure as hell didn't want to head back to Chicago. He didn't want to see the old guy in the houndstooth jacket again, or the guys in the blue suits and black glasses. So—why the hell not?

"Fuck you. A third."

They had a day to kill so they left the Plymouth in the alley by Jack's house and took the St. Charles streetcar out to Audubon

Park and walked around the zoo with the tourists and the school kids. They looked at tigers and bears and some alligators that could have swallowed the one in the window at King Arthur's in one bite.

They rode the streetcar back and sat in Jack's place and drank scotch and smoked cigarettes until it was time to go. Then Jack drove the Plymouth down to Magazine Street and parked around the corner from King Arthur's.

Jack provided the saps.

They sat at a table like a couple of guys in town for a convention or like two faggots celebrating the first week anniversary of their beautiful romance. Jack ordered a plate full of crawfish and Johnny ordered a blackened steak. Jack was still picking up the tabs, but he was keeping careful track of everything Johnny spent. Once they'd scored, he'd take it all back.

Somehow that made Johnny more confident. If Jack had been planning anything funny, he wouldn't be fronting cash. Would he?

Jack had his back to the street door so he could see the kitchen doors, the little office and the bar. Johnny could see the alligator tank behind Jack. He had a better angle at the bar. Steel wool hair was there as usual. She didn't seem to have noticed Johnny. She was wearing an off-white T-shirt with a picture of a spotted cat on the front. She must have picked it a couple of sizes too small. Her little tits were pointed and they looked really nice to Johnny. Maybe once he and Jack had made their score, there might be something there after all. The old ones were so damned grateful.

The waiter brought coffee with chicory and bread pudding. Jack looked at his watch. Johnny looked at the clock over the bar. They were running ahead of schedule. Shit, they didn't want to be conspicuous.

Jack signaled the waiter and said, "How about a liqueur?"

A liqueur, for Christ's sake!

The waiter brought over a bottle of Drambouie and a couple of tiny little glasses and poured them both drinks right there at the table and took the bottle away again. They nursed the Drambouie and that made the timing right. Jack paid their check and left a tip on the table and they walked outside, ignoring the bartender and the woman with the steel wool hair, past the sleepy looking alligator. There were no goldfish in the tank tonight.

Jack and Johnny walked up Magazine toward Gravier. Jack pulled Johnny into a narrow alley between two buildings. There was a flash of lightning and Johnny got a look up the alley before the thunder rolled in. The alley was filthy but otherwise it was empty. What a joke it would have been if they'd interrupted some conventioneer getting a blowjob from a whore when they were just there to knock off a restaurant's receipts!

The wind blew along Magazine Street, carrying some newspapers and fast food wrappers with it. It whipped around the corner, wrapping a piece of paper around Johnny's ankle. He bent over and pulled it off and threw it away.

Jack's sharp fingers dug into Johnny's arm. Johnny reached into his pocket and felt the sap there. He wrapped his fingers around it. He heard footsteps and in a couple of seconds King Arthur walked past the alley. There was another flash of lightning and Johnny could see the cloth satchel in Arthur's hand.

Arthur disappeared.

Jack shoved past Johnny and followed Arthur. If there was a flaw in Jack's plan, this was the moment it would appear. If the bartender saw Jack pop out of the alley and head after Arthur he might yell a warning or even pull a heater on Jack. As far as Johnny knew, Jack wasn't heeled except for a sap, just the same as he was.

If that happened, Johnny might still be able to sap the bartender, but it would be a messy thing, a risky thing. If that happened, he decided, he would just pop out of the alley and scamper off the other way. Forget it. Let Jack take the fall. Johnny still had most of his Chicago bankroll. He'd start over, maybe in New Orleans, maybe in some other town.

But Jack was gone and now the bartender moved past the alley. A gust of wind came up and brought the first rush of hot, fat raindrops spattering down as Johnny stepped out of the alley a few paces behind the bartender. He could see Jack farther ahead, and Arthur beyond him. Everything was working perfectly.

He raised the sap and brought it down very hard. The lead-weighted, spring-loaded, leather-covered sap smacked against the bartender's hairless skull. The guy didn't go straight down. It was funny. First he jumped like he'd been goosed instead of sapped. Then he seemed to go limp in mid-air. He crumpled to the sidewalk and he didn't make a sound and he didn't move.

Behind Johnny a woman's voice yelled and he turned around and saw a woolly-looking head silhouetted against a distant streetlight. The woman with the steel wool hair was running toward him. She had a rod in her hand. She was pointing it at Johnny.

She yelled again and he put his hands up and dropped the sap. He thought, fuck, fuck, fuck.

The woman was coming up fast and something spat past him and then he heard the shot and the woman hit the sidewalk with a dive and pointed her gun again. He couldn't figure out what was happening. Did somebody plug her? He started to turn around, to see where the shot had come from.

He saw Jack facing toward him, a heater in his hand. The guy was heeled after all. He saw twin flashes, one from behind Jack and one from Jack's gun. He saw Jack jump toward him as if somebody had punched him hard between the shoulder blades. He heard another crash, this one from behind him. He felt a whack as a round hit him. He'd already been turning and he didn't know whether Jack had shot him or the woman with the steel wool hair. He tumbled and rolled and felt a little shock as he fell off the edge of the sidewalk into the gutter. He lay on his back looking at the sky.

He lay in the street in the trash, waiting for the wail of sirens, feeling the hot, heavy raindrops on his face. He didn't think he was dying. He blinked and the woman with the steel wool hair was standing over him, the gun still in her hand. He wondered if she had shot him, or if Jack had. He wanted to ask her but he couldn't talk. He could hear footsteps pounding, and he knew they belonged to Arthur, not to Jack.

The rain was really coming down and the woman with steel wool hair's T-shirt was soaked and plastered tight against her skin and he could see that she still wasn't wearing a brassiere. He could feel himself bleeding and everything was starting to look a little fuzzy and now he wasn't so sure after all that he wasn't dying.

The woman bent over to look at him and there was a flash of lightning and he thought, *Christ, does she ever have beautiful nipples.*

*In the late 1960s and early 1970s the United States was torn by a crisis of conscience. The center of this crisis was the war in Vietnam, and while some Americans started out as "hawks" or "doves" and never budged from their positions, others faced a far more difficult problem in deciding whether to believe their government's pronouncements and the official optimism spouted on television night after night—or the far uglier, depressing, and ultimately enraging statements of the protesters.*

*I was one of those who experienced a terrible, wrenching change of conscience during the Vietnam War, and it should be no surprise that David Starke, the protagonist of "A Freeway for Draculas," serves as my stand-in.*

*The story appeared in 1973 in an anthology called* The Berserkers, *whose pages I had the honor of sharing with such distinguished colleagues as James Blish, Barry Malzberg, William F. Nolan, and James Sallis.*

# A Freeway for Draculas

HOW IT STARTED DAVID STARKE NEVER KNEW. HE rose and shaved, Bertha brought him coffee, balancing the delicate china cup and saucer in her plump hands, and he drank it. He pulled on his white broadcloth shirt, knotted his maroon J. Press tie, tugged once at the bottom of his gray suit jacket and left the house.

It was no different from any other morning, five mornings each week, forty-nine weeks each year.

He bent his stocky body and picked up the newspaper from his lawn. Without removing the rubber band that held it furled, he glanced at a few headlines: war, scandal, repression. He tossed the paper over his shoulder so it landed at the front door for Bertha to read later.

No different from other mornings.

At the end of the driveway he stopped, glanced at his watch to see how long before Rolly Poletsky's little electric Fiat would roll up for him. It was Rolly's turn to drive. Starke's watch said 8:24 — Rolly would arrive in two minutes, as he did every alternate morning, regular as clockwork.

As Starke dropped his hand the crystal of his watch caught the sun at an odd angle, reflecting the light into Starke's eyes. For a moment he staggered at the brightness, then stood blinking at the oddly colored afterimage that quivered momentarily on his retinas, expanding and contracting as it slowly faded.

He steadied himself against the mailbox, rubbed one hand against his eyes, then ran it through his thick, wavy hair and laughed. He glanced up the street, saw the light green of the Fiat and began to step forward.

Then he blinked. The Fiat was gone.

No explosion, no blinding flash—the pulsing afterimage of the glare in Starke's eyes did not recur. He stepped out into the little-used residential street to see if Poletsky had made a sudden and unexpected turn into one of the driveways feeding from the street, and as he did so the green Fiat drove into view, rounding the gentle curve a few hundred yards from Starke's house.

Starke shook his head and studied the little car as it purred smoothly to a stop a few feet from him. He leaned over as Poletsky reached across the cockpit and unlatched the passenger's door from the inside.

"Strangest thing," Starke said as he eased himself into the black leather bucket. He slammed the door shut.

"What's that?" Poletsky asked.

Starke laughed uneasily. "Strangest thing," he repeated. "I was standing next to the mailbox waiting for you the way I always do and I could have sworn I saw your car driving up."

Poletsky snorted. "I don't see what's strange about that. I *was* arriving. No?"

"Well, that's not quite it, Rolly. I'd looked at my watch and you weren't due for a couple of minutes. Then I saw your car, and then it was gone."

"Disappeared?"

"No. I mean, not in a puff of smoke or anything, it just wasn't there any more. And then—a couple of seconds later it was back again, coming around the curve." Starke felt himself pressed back into the bucket seat as Poletsky pressed down on the accelerator and the little car moved quickly forward.

"Upset about it?" Poletsky asked. He shot a concerned glance sideways at Starke, lines appearing in his slim, pale face.

Starke said, "I guess not." For a moment there was only the gentle hum of the little car, the crunch of its tires rolling along on the cold gravel of the bare winter street. "I just don't understand it," Starke said, "it was so odd. But I feel all right now." He stared through the windshield, took off his thick-framed glasses and studied them as if they might contain an explanation, put them back on and gazed, distracted, at the gray overcast sky.

They rolled through the little shopping center and Poletsky swung the Fiat onto the freeway service road, ready to head for 909 and the run toward the computer works.

"Come on, David," Poletsky said, "don't let it get you down. Here—" he reached past David's knee and punched the ON button of the sports car's Blaupunkt FM receiver. As the radio snapped to instant life he said, "See what you can get, will you? It's been as bad as AM lately. I think I'm going to throw it out altogether and get a tape rig for the car."

"Oh, sure, Rolly," Starke said, called back to the reality of the Fiat. The car's quad speakers were blaring the strains of Bach's seventh Brandenburg concerto as performed on an ARP synthesizer. Starke punched a news button and the synthesizer gave way to a low-interest-loan commercial. He punched again and a network news broadcast replaced the ad.

"Okay," Poletsky said.

They were stopped at the freeway entrance, waiting for a break in the morning rush-hour traffic. Starke used the momentary halt of the car to fine up the tuning of the FM set. The news was a standard Pentagon spokesman tape: so many missions by American aircraft against aggressive guerrilla forces designed to assure the survival of a peace-loving democratic regime, etc., etc.

"I'll be pleased when they get that automatic traffic channel on the air," David said. "Morning news is too much for me to take some days."

"You take it seriously," Poletsky said. "There's nothing you can do about it, is there? So why let it get you down?"

The announcer had finished the war bulletins and was turning to other topics, mostly more government handouts on improvements in environmental regulations. A high administration spokesman, the smooth voice was assuring its listeners, had told industrial leaders that the President would not let idealistic concerns for a few bugs and weeds interfere with the economic well-being of the nation.

"Take it seriously?" Starke reacted. "We both work for the same outfit, Rolly. Don't you think that all the talent that goes into our products could do something to help this situation? Don't we have a responsibility for what we create? Couldn't you grow those integrated circuit crystals for something better than weapons-control systems? Couldn't I design programs for something more constructive than government surveillance files? I mean—" He let his sentence fade out as the highway condition report finally began.

Freeways all the way from their present location to the computer works were crowded but flowing smoothly. Starke let the droning, surrounding voice fill the car while his eyes, bored with the sight of freeway traffic through the Fiat's windscreen, slowly rose to gaze, distracted, at the dully glowing sky.

Far ahead, over the downtown area, formations of long silvery shapes with huge tail fins swept silently across the sky. They came in herringbone rows, bright swept-back wings defining the relationship of one to another. High, high they were, barely distinguishable against the silver overcast.

The radio voice droned in the Fiat's cockpit; the hum of its mechanism and the gentle shushing of its tires against the freeway surface made a hypnotic wall of background noise. The aerial titans seemed almost to be standing stationary over the city, their arrangement in swept-back triangles led Starke's eyes through a dull iteration of their geometry: three aircraft placed at the apexes of an equilateral formation, and three groups of aircraft arranged to state the angles of a meta-formation. Three threes of three forming a meta-meta-formation.

The Fiat sped ahead, Poletsky intent on the freeway and the cars around his own, Starke staring distracted at the aircraft. Tiny specks of black seemed to fall from their bellies.

"Rolly," Starke heard himself saying, "they don't use those old B-52s any more, do they?"

"Huh?" Poletsky responded. "No, I think they junked the last few a couple of years ago. Why?"

Starke turned to face Poletsky. "Because there are some—" He looked back, trying to get a fix on the formation above the city.

"I thought—I could have sworn—" He leaned forward, bracing both his hands against the dashboard above the FM radio dial.

Poletsky's voice broke into his examination of the sky. "Are you sure you're all right, David?"

"Yes. I mean—" He stared at the sky, trying to see anything beside the gray wintry overcast. His neck felt very stiff and he leaned back in his seat; rubbed his neck with one hand.

"I could have sworn I saw a formation of B-52s over the city."

"Were they doing anything?"

Starke took off his glasses again, rubbed the bridge of his nose between thumb and forefinger. With his eyes still shut, the pressure of his fingers making vague red patterns swirl inside his eyelids, he answered. "It looked as if—as if they were dropping bombs on the city," he whispered.

Poletsky was silent. He reached across Starke and punched the music button on the FM receiver. The sounds of a Vaughan Williams symphony, its tones a tapestry of restraint, came from the speakers.

"Sounds like the *Antarctica*," Poletsky said. "Only two channels, they must have an ancient recording."

They drove along unspeaking, the notes of the orchestra filling the Fiat. "Yeah," Poletsky resumed, "that's the Seventh okay. Bet it's the old Adrian Boult recording."

"They wouldn't be bombing the city, would they?" Starke said. "I mean, there are no more B-52s anyway, and if there were they wouldn't be bombing *us*."

Poletsky said, "It's worth having only two channels to hear real instruments instead of synthesizers, don't you think?"

"Besides they'd have a bulletin on the radio."

"Some of those old performances have never been equaled. We're lucky they still exist, even in simple stereo."

Poletsky hit the turn signal and edged the Fiat into the freeway's exit lane.

Starke took a last look ahead of the car, toward the city, just before the Fiat rolled onto the exit ramp and down toward the service road. There was a moment of dazzling brilliance ahead, then a series of secondary flashes and a huge glowing cloud began to rise rapidly over the city.

The Fiat dived onto the service road, Poletsky pulling it skillfully into an opening between a huge Ford station wagon and a snappy Volvo 1800. Starke gripped the little courtesy handhold over the Blaupunkt. The afterimage of the flashes pulsed and faded in double exposure with the square tailgate of the Ford wagon. His ears rang, a muffled roar rising from somewhere inside his chest. Steadying himself on the handhold he twisted in his seat to look at Poletsky.

The Ford wagon pulled up at a stop sign where the freeway service road fed back into a commercial street; Poletsky braked the Fiat to a halt behind the Ford. Poletsky turned toward Starke. "What's the matter, David?"

Starke said, "Didn't you see it—see the sky?"

"I've been concentrating on the road. What was it?" He leaned forward, craned his neck to look straight up. "I don't see anything."

The Ford pulled away, turning into heavy street traffic. Poletsky followed, heading toward the computer works.

Starke punched the news button on the radio. A woman's voice was describing an international conference on abortion. He punched another button, got a commercial for a home air filtration system, tried the news again, then gave up and tuned back to the Williams symphony.

"Y-you didn't," he stammered, "you didn't see anything. And there's no bulletin on the radio."

"David, what is it?"

"I must be—there must really be something the matter with me. If I see things that nobody else can see, I mean."

"Oh, come on. This isn't a horror movie."

Starke removed his grip from the handhold in the Fiat, forced himself to lean back in his seat. Poletsky said nothing more. Starke closed his eyes and let the flowing texture of the Williams symphony fill his mind. A horror movie, he was acting foolish. Next thing he'd be seeing monsters.

He felt himself sway sideways as Poletsky pulled the Fiat out of the last traffic lane and up to the gate of the computer works. Starke watched him as he braked the little car at the guard station, reached into his jacket pocket and pulled out his identification badge. Starke did the same and leaned across the car to show the badge to the security guard.

The face of the guard, leaning down to peer at the badges through the car window, was a pale, cold white tinged slightly with a fungus-like green. Black shaggy hair was chopped off in a crude bang over his forehead, partially covering the terrible scar that ran from scalp to eyebrow. The guard's eyes glimmered with a terrible animal redness; a thin line of spittle hung from his narrow lips.

Pulling away from the car to stand upright again, the guard waved with one hand and said, "Pass right in, sir."

As the Fiat pulled away from the guard station Starke glanced back at the guard. Two small electrodes, their metallic finish shimmering in the brightly overcast morning, protruded from his neck.

In the reserved parking lot Poletsky pulled the little Fiat into a narrow space between two Detroit sedans and climbed out. Starke followed suit, slamming the door shut behind him. He stood still for a moment, the bright electrodes pulsing in afterimage. He steadied himself with a hand on the car's roof.

"David?" Poletsky said.

"Oh, uh, thanks for the ride, Rolly. I'll see you back here after closing, okay?"

"Are you sure you're okay?"

David shook his head. "Something odd but I'll be all right. Thanks."

He watched Poletsky stride across the parking lot and disappear into the engineering development wing of the building. Starke took a deep breath and walked toward the entrance of the programming center. Just outside the building he checked his wristwatch against the clock in the commercial tower across the street. There was no peculiar reflection this time and he pushed the twin glass doors open and walked in.

On the second floor of the programming center he stopped at the automatic vending machine, bought a cup of coffee, nodded a good morning to Angie Turner at her central secretarial station and walked into his own two-man office. He closed the door behind him, put his cardboard coffee cup carefully on his desk blotter and hung his coat on the corner rack.

He looked at the worker at the other desk, already immersed in stacks of computer printouts, felt-marker-scrawl-covered manuals, typewritten sheets and electrostatic copies. The other man looked slowly at Starke, pulled at his beard with his dirty fingernails and drawled, "Hi there, Starke. How goes it?"

At least Marston looked normal! But then so had Rolly and so had Angie, hugely overweight, stuffed into clothes that might have looked chic on a woman sixty pounds lighter and fifteen years younger. And Marston—slovenly, unkempt, the only employee Starke knew who didn't at least come near to the image of the bright professionals climbing through the hierarchy of the computer works—Marston looked no different than usual. Why had the security guard looked like a—Starke almost let go an incoherent exclamation—like a Hollywood horror film monster?

"Oh, it's, uh, okay I guess," David managed to blurt out.

"What's that?" Marston asked.

"Didn't you ask me how I was?" Starke replied. Marston looked at him puzzledly. "That was five minutes ago, pal. When it looked like you weren't going to answer me I went back to work."

Starke held onto his desk with both hands. "Sorry," he said. "I guess I was distracted. I feel a little odd today."

" 'S okay," said Marston. He turned back to his papers, reached into a lower desk drawer and pulled out a battered pipe.

Starke pulled a computer printout from his own *in* tray, flipped past the heading information and began to study the overnight machine printout on his new sort-and-retrieve model, series 10, Sarm-X. At least there had been a good machine run, he should be able to complete his development level study and begin a project report, with Marston doing the tech writing and documentation half of the job.

Funny, thought Starke, his forehead on one hand as he scanned the columns of machine print. Funny that a man like Mel Marston should reach his place in the world, a documentation specialist in the computer works where all the others followed the corporate model by keeping their personal grooming neat as a pin, their manner sober as a judge, their dress conservative as a Nixon.

Marston looked a mess, showed more interest in poetry than in technical writing, was known as an off-hours drinker and didn't even put much vehemence into his denial when someone suggested that he was a pot smoker. Yet, somehow, he had advanced to a responsible and well-paid position. Probably on the basis of sheer talent and competence, but it never ceased to leave Starke wondering.

He turned his attention back to the computer printout before him. The sort-and-retrieve program seemed to be working fairly well on the test information provided, an old company telephone directory sequenced by extension numbers. The calling sequence of the test specified abstracting all employees with six-, eight-, or eleven-digit last names ending in consonants from L to Z, then alphabetizing the names and printing them out.

Starke began to check the names: LANDOR L E / LAPTIPPE F T / LAZZARRA A J / LEACHPIT R P / LEACHPIT J F / LUTHER F X . . . wait a minute! LEACHPIT R P before LEACHPIT J F? The alphabetizing routine seemed to be shutting off after the surname, not continuing through the initials, else how could LEACHPIT R P come before LEACHPIT J F?

Starke reached for the telephone to check out the discrepancy with the linkage generator group in the next corridor, then decided to talk it over first with Mel Marston. He dropped the phone receiver back onto its cradle and said "Mel?"

The only reply was a muffled, "Mph."

Starke turned to look at Marston. Marston's collar-length hair had grown the better part of a foot, flowing wildly over his shoulders. It was held away from his face by a woven, bead-decorated headband, a huge turquoise peacock feather rising from the middle of Marston's forehead.

His small moustache and Vandyke had sprouted into a bushy, patriarchal beard.

His rumpled button-down shirt and tie had disappeared, replaced by a multicolored billowing shirt of some gossamer material over which hung a rawhide vest decorated with silver and blue jewels and leather fringes.

The blackened pipe that Marston habitually smoked at his desk had been transformed into a Persian hookah, its bottom a bubbling globe of water, its top an elaborate hammered-brass bowl filled with slowly charring shreds of something that Starke *knew* was not tobacco.

Marston turned to face Starke. He held a flexible tube toward him, one end connected to the hookah, the other ending in an ivory mouthpiece. As he leaned toward Starke he said, "Om."

Starke gasped, shut his eyes as tightly as he could, pressed the heels of both hands to his temples and ground his teeth together. He held the posture for seconds while the syllable faded from his ears.

Then it came again, only instead of "Om" it sounded more like "Hum," in Marston's voice, delivered with the usual drawl but with a questioning inflection on its end.

Starke opened his eyes, turned toward Marston prepared for the sight of the bizarrely arrayed apparition he had just seen. Marston was back at his desk, his hair back to its usual length, his costume back to its rumpled but relatively conventional composition, the pipe in his hand its old self, the odor of tobacco permeating the air of the small office.

"Mel?" Starke said.

"What is it, Davey?"

"Why, I was going to show you these test run results but for a moment you . . ."

Marston waited, then when Starke didn't resume, said, "For a moment I what?"

"You just looked a little odd, that's all."

"Come on, Starke, you're always after me about the old company tie and the old company white shirt. You know I'm not interested in that stuff."

"Not what I meant, Mel. I mean you." Again, Starke was unable to complete the sentence.

"Here, old chum, you'd better get it together a little more. Relax." Marston pulled out his bottom desk drawer, drew a brown bag from it, pulled out a thermos bottle.

He trundled his chair toward Starke's desk, unscrewed the stopper from the bottle and reached to refill Starke's coffee cup. "Don't see how you can drink that machine stuff anyhow," he drawled. "But then I never did understand you computer people no way." Marston laughed.

"Thanks," Starke said. He lifted his cup, sniffed the steam rising from it and shot an odd glance at Marston. "There isn't brandy in this stuff, is there?" he asked.

Marston shot back a look of mock surprise. "My innocence is deeply offended, sir. We are all thoroughly familiar with the company drinking policy."

Starke sipped at the coffee. "If this isn't spiked then I've never tasted alcohol."

"Even the walls have ears," Marston said, turning slowly to study the perimeter of the room.

Starke shut his eyes until the thought went away.

"But look, Davey, you really seem upset. Is it that dumb Sarm-X program? You really shouldn't let a little thing like a program bug get to you, you know."

"No, it's — something else. All morning I've been having, ah — odd things have been happening," Starke finished weakly.

"I don't know what you mean."

Starke pulled a fresh linen handkerchief from his pocket and wiped his brow. He removed his glasses and began painstakingly to clean them, first the left lens, then the right, then the left again and the right again.

"Om," said Marston; Starke looked quickly at him, saw the peacock-feather headband, the decorated vest. Or thought that he did, only fuzzily, with his spectacles in his hands. He slipped them back on, looked directly at Marston.

"Hm," said Marston, his tie slightly askew and his pastel, button-down-collar shirt rumpled as usual. "Hm, I don't think I quite understand what you mean, ah, by odd things happening. Sweet Angela didn't jump up and buss you on the way in this morning, did she?"

Starke felt his hands beginning to shake. A drop of cold sweat ran down the side of his neck. "I — I — "

"Say," Marston drawled, "do you want me to take you to the dispensary? Is it — are you sick?"

"I don't know. Maybe if I could — "

"How about Wally? You want to talk to the boss? Maybe you ought to check out for the day, go home and rest."

"No, it's — no, I have to work on Sarm-X, the deadline is almost here, we have to have the model running before the quarterly budget conference. I — Marston, tell me the truth."

"Of course."

"Latch the door first, will you?"

"Sure, David." Marston took the few steps to the door and clicked the security switch. "This is all mighty mysterious."

"You're a good deal younger than I am, Mel, and I think you're from a different school. More adventurous, less bound by tradition, willing to try anything."

"Not quite anything, but—?"

"What I mean is, ah—" He stopped, took off his glasses and wiped his forehead with the handkerchief again, then put his glasses back on. "I mean, with all the talk about drugs these past few years, I've never asked you if you've used them because it really isn't my business, but, ah—"

"Yes?"

"Mel, what do you know about things like, ah, LSD?"

"Oh, why lysergic acid diethylamide, discovered April 19, 1943, by a chemist named Albert Hoffman—"

"That's not what I mean."

"Oh. Sorry, Dave, that's the only LSD that I've ever heard of. Maybe there's another."

"No, that's the one I mean, the drug. I mean—ah, Mel, have you ever, ah, taken, ah—"

"The term is *dropped*, Dave, and I'm afraid when you ask me that, you're asking me if I've ever committed a felony, and I can hardly say yes to that, so suppose you ask me something else."

"What I mean is, ah, LSD is supposed to cause hallucinations."

"I've read the literature, it does say that, yes."

"Well don't be angry, Mel, but that coffee—you poured some for me yesterday and I thought it had a little funny taste."

"The literature says LSD has no flavor. Or so I've read."

"Don't play games, Mel. This is a serious matter!" Starke was sweating heavily now. His glasses had been steamed by the coffee Marston poured for him. He whipped them off and used them to point directly at the younger man. "I want to know if you put any of that stuff in the coffee you gave me. I don't care what you want to smoke or drink or stick in your veins, but I don't want anybody, ah, anybody—"

"I think the term you're looking for is dosing you, Dave. It has been known to happen, but most folks consider it unethical." He drew out the last word, giving each syllable separate emphasis. "I would never do such a thing. Assuming that I had any of that stuff to start with, of course, which I haven't said I do."

"Well I, ah—"

Marston said "I give you my word, David. I've never dosed

anyone in my life. Maybe I do put a tiny drop of brandy in the java some mornings, but that's the utter limit of it! Look!" And he put the thermos to his lips and drank.

"That doesn't prove anything," Starke said, "but I'll take your word. All right, then I wasn't drugged. Then what's going on?"

Marston re-stoppered the thermos, slipped it into its bag and put it in his desk. "You tell me, David. Is it all right if I unlock the door now?"

"I'm not sure. Oh, unlock it, certainly. I mean, I'm not sure what's going on. I was—this morning I thought I saw Rolly Poletsky's car before it arrived at my house."

"Trivial."

"And there were B-52s over the city."

"Oh?"

"And then the security man at the main gate—"

"What about him?"

"He was—he was—" Stark gulped once, "I could have sworn that he was Boris Karloff."

"Dead for years."

"In his Frankenstein makeup."

"Come off it, Davey."

"And then when I looked at you before I could have sworn you were dressed like some kind of hippie."

"I don't go for the white shirt dark suit thing but I'd hardly call these clothes hippie," Marston said, holding his fingertips to his shirtfront.

"No, I know you're not dressed any different from usual," Starke said. He looked at Marston. "You're dressed the way you always dress. But you *looked* different."

"Man, you are seeing things."

"That's what I'm trying to tell you. I can't figure out why. I thought maybe you had, ah, *dosed* me with LSD," he said. He felt uncomfortable using the unfamiliar term.

"Nope."

"Then I guess I'm just cracking up!" Starke put his head into his hands. "I'm just cracking up. I don't know why, I haven't been under any unusual strain, I *feel* normal. At least I felt normal until this morning. Now, all of a sudden, hallucinations. Why?"

"Not Sarm-X? Problems at home? Getting along okay with Wally Cheng?"

"None of those things. At least, I don't think it's any of them. I—I just don't know."

"Well, I'm afraid I can't do much for you right now, old friend."

Marston, standing, gave Starke's shoulder a friendly squeeze. "I've got one of those ridiculous meetings of all the documentation people. Wally asked me to give 'em a pep talk on the use of the subjunctive in discussing possible program errors, exciting stuff like that. Look, that's scheduled to break up by noon. You want to have lunch together? We can eat in the cafeteria or go out into the real world and grab something at Enzo's or at the Golden Garter."

Starke stared straight ahead, silently.

"How about it, David?"

He shook himself back from the moment of fugue. "Uh, yes, thanks a lot. I mean, uh, sure, I think it would be a good idea. To get away for a little while that is."

Marston picked up a clipboard from which flapped a mass of yellow-lined notepaper and left the room.

Starke worked over the Sarm-X test results the rest of the morning, receiving a few phone calls, making a couple. He looked at his wristwatch every few minutes. He felt jumpy and worried, but managed to keep his mind on the programming project and experienced no further hallucinations.

At twelve o'clock Marston walked back into the office, dropping his clipboard on top of his cluttered desk. The clatter jolted Starke alert. "Aargh!" said Marston. "Maybe those people know something about data processing, but how they ever got past junior high school without learning to write a simple sentence is beyond me."

He slumped into his chair, then sprang upright. "Come on, Dave, let's go scarf down some grub."

They made it outside and into the chill winter noontime. The sky was gray and a light sprinkling of snowflakes was falling. Starke wished he had worn his topcoat that morning. He and Marston broke into a trot as they crossed the company parking lot. When they passed the security guard's booth Starke steeled himself and cast a look at the guard: he was an ordinary man, middle-aged, black, with a neatly trimmed moustache and a neatly pressed olive uniform.

Across the street from the computer works the red and blue electric signs in Enzo's front window flashed on and off, throwing long, rippled reflections across the blacktop roadway wet with melting snow. Inside the restaurant Starke blew out the cold, wet air of the short walk from the programming center and drew in the warm, organic odors of wood and leather, hot food and human bodies.

They took the only empty booth in the room, nodding to other workers taking their lunch away from the computer works, ordered sandwiches for their meal. Starke called for coffee to go with his. Marston ordered beer.

"You just love to flaunt your independence, don't you, Mel?" Starke said to him.

Marston grinned a self-satisfied grin. "I figure, they pay me to edit a bunch of stuff and to write a little of my own. I figure, as long as I do a good job, they have no gripe with me, and any time I do a bad job, they can squawk."

Starke shook his head and sipped black, steaming coffee.

For ten minutes they munched silently on their sandwiches; Starke deliberately let his vision fall into a steady, almost hypnotic pulsation along with the neon flashes: red, blue, red, blue. The room was cozy and familiar. For the first time since leaving home that morning he began to feel comfortable and relaxed.

Again his mood was broken by Marston. "Figuring out your little puzzles, David?"

"Huh? Oh, no, I wasn't really thinking about anything."

"You really surprise me, you know? There are brigades of weirdoes in this business, God knows, but you've always struck me as totally stable — the last guy I'd expect to flip out."

Starke did not answer.

"Not that you're exactly running berserk, pal."

Starke laughed bitterly. "You're right about that. I always thought I'd come to work one morning and hear that you'd been carted away. Never thought I would!

"But I —" he made a helpless, appealing gesture with both his hands "— I *feel* perfectly normal. A little nervous about the whole thing, but I'm in control of myself, my thought processes seem normal, I'm not in a state of schizophrenic confusion or anything, I'm not frothing or screaming or attacking anybody with a knife."

He picked up the sharp, wooden-handled knife beside his plate, held it for a moment, then dropped it handle first to the wooden tabletop.

"I mean, can you be crazy," he paused, "in just one very particular way, like seeing hallucinations, and be perfectly normal in every other regard? Maybe I had a stroke. Maybe I ought to go to the doctor."

Marston replied, "If you think so. You don't seem crazy to me, though." He reached inside his jacket and pulled out a package of cigarettes. "You still off tobacco?" Starke nodded. Marston lit a cigarette. "Look, maybe if you try and think back to each, ah, anomaly, you'll be able to see a pattern in them. Do you think so?"

Starke considered. "Well, I was standing in the street waiting for Rolly and I saw him driving up. Or thought I saw him. Then his car disappeared and actually arrived a minute later."

"So you just anticipated what actually happened, right?"

Starke nodded.

"The second thing," he said, "was in the car. I looked up in the sky and thought I saw bombers over the city, then I thought I saw the city being destroyed."

Marston held his cigarette before himself and concentrated on its glowing tip. "Hmm. That sounds completely different. We know the city wasn't destroyed, we'd certainly have found that out by now. And there probably weren't even any bombers. Back at the office you said they were B-52s and there aren't any more B-52s."

"Okay, I'll buy that. Then what happened?"

Marston grinned. "I-da-know," he drawled, "maybe if you try and remember what you were doing or thinking just before you saw them."

Starke rubbed his face, reconstructing the moment in Poletsky's Fiat. "Rolly was driving." he said, "we had the radio on. There was a Vaughan Williams symphony, I think, then we got some news. They were talking about the war, about bombing the enemy, and then—" He looked at Marston, startled. "Is that it? Did I see the war? Or—what?"

Marston shrugged.

"All right. The third thing. We pulled into the company parking lot. I looked at the guard and he was Frankenstein."

Marston laughed again. "I'm sorry. No connection with anything?"

Starke considered. "It's really hard to remember." He picked up his coffee cup. It was empty except for a small, cold residue in the bottom. He drank even the dregs. "Just before we arrived at the gate I was talking to Rolly about seeing the bombing. He thought I was silly. He said that—" Starke brought his empty cup down on the saucer hard, sending a spoon clanking and clattering onto the floor. Two or three customers at Enzo's bar turned around to stare.

"Mel," Starke said, "Rolly thought I was just foolish. He accused me of seeing horror movies."

"Ahah! And then you did see one." He rubbed his hands together. "Now we're getting somewhere! And was there anything else?"

Starke put both hands to his face. "One more," he said. "In the office, I didn't tell you this. I had just arrived, I was looking at the Sarm-X test and I was going to show it to you. Before I did I thought about you for a second, wondered how a hippie like you could make it in the computer works, and when I looked at you, you *were* a hippie. You were dressed weirdly, you had long hair, and your pipe had turned into a hookah and you were smoking pot."

Marston slapped the table with both hands and roared with amusement. "Old hippie Mel! Not quite, friend. But that's all right, in fact that's just fine, that caps it. Don't you see the pattern?"

"No. I—what?"

"Why, you're up so close to it, you can't see the forest for the trees. Listen. First you were waiting for Rolly, thinking he was about due, then you saw him. Right?

"Then you heard about the war on the radio, you were thinking about bombing, and you *saw* bombing.

"Then Poletsky said you were seeing horror movies, and you thought about that, and then you saw Frankenstein.

"Finally, you thought I was a hippie, you looked at me, and you saw—what, beads and feathers, that stuff, right?"

Starke nodded, yes, yes, yes. "Well then, first you *think* about a thing. Then you *see* it. It's that simple."

Starke exhaled with a hiss, suddenly aware that he had been holding his breath while Marston spoke. "So I'm just—thinking about a thing, then I see it? But why? What's the trigger, and why is it happening to me?"

Marston shrugged. "Search me. Everybody must have a bunch of images in his head—stray thoughts, fragments of recollections, notions conjured by all sorts of external stimuli, full-fledged fantasies."

"Sure, of course. But these are externalized. Look, Mel, you can tell the difference between thinking about, oh, having the Chairman of the Board pull up a chair and join us for lunch . . . and *actually* having him walk in that door, come over to our booth here and sit down. No matter how vivid your thought was, you could still distinguish it from a real *occurrence*. You see? But if your theory is right, I *can't* tell the difference. That's what's happening to me."

"It isn't happening now, is it?"

Starke thought for a few seconds. "No. Everything is normal." He picked up his empty coffee cup, peered sadly at its dry bottom and put it back down. "What I mean is, everything *seems* normal. You know, once you start to have your doubts . . ."

"No. What?"

"Mel—how do I know I'm not still sitting upstairs waiting for you to get back from that editorial lecture? For that matter how do I know I'm not still at home and the whole day's been a dream?"

Marston stood up and began wrapping a striped scarf around his throat. "Sure, David, that's the classic dilemma. There's no logic to counter it any more than there is to knock down the old solipsist paradox. In fact it's really just solipsism turned around. All the reality you know is what you can see. Or feel, taste, whatever. You don't know that I'm really real, I don't know that you're really real. We all just have to take one another on faith and keep on truckin' if you know what I mean. Right?"

Starke assented dubiously.

"Come on, Dave. We'd better get back across the street."

Outside Enzo's the snow was still falling. The sky was darker now, the snowflakes heavier and thicker. A coating was beginning to accumulate on the sidewalks and the street. The automobiles in the computer works's parking lot were crusted over with white.

But the security man at the gate was still human, Starke noted gratefully, and inside the programming center everything seemed as usual.

He spent the afternoon conferring with the development programmers assigned to Sarm-X, going over the test data from the previous night's run. Marston sat in on the meeting, representing the documentation area.

The sort turn-off problem, it appeared, could be easily corrected in the next version of the program. Once the system was performing all functions according to specs they could bring their attention to improving performance time and trying to cut down on memory utilization.

It was a good meeting and actually ended before the scheduled quitting time for the day, a rare happening at the computer works.

On his way to the exit Starke passed the office of his boss, Wally Cheng, and stopped to mention the results of the Sarm-X meeting. Angie Turner wasn't at her desk outside Cheng's office. Thinking of Cheng's oriental coolness and authority and the amusing contrast of Angie's overweight attempts at glamour, Starke knocked once on Cheng's door, heard a calm "Come in," and opened the door.

For only an instant he saw Cheng garbed as a mandarin in silken cap and robe, Angie beside him wearing a high-slit *cheong-*

*sam,* Chinese writing brush poised over a sheet of parchment.

Starke leaned heavily against the doorjamb and shut his eyes. There was a rushing sound in his ears and he felt weak.

"Dave?" said Wally Cheng.

Starke opened his eyes. Cheng was seated at his desk in his usual herringbone suit and white shirt. Angie Turner, in the same outfit she'd worn that morning, was holding a brown wooden pencil and a stenographer's pad half covered with shorthand notes.

"Uh, just felt odd for a minute," Starke said. "I was going to bring you up to date on the Sarm-X thing."

Fifteen minutes later he was back in the passenger seat of Rolly Poletsky's green Fiat. On the way back home on 909 they made some small talk, then David turned on the Blaupunkt and found a station carrying the soothing melodies of Schubert's fourth, the pleasantly ill-named *Tragic.*

In front of Starke's house Poletsky stopped the Fiat. "I won't try the driveway tonight, Dave. The snow looks too slippery for me to get back up. You be able to get your car out tomorrow?"

Starke already had his hand on the door switch. "Nothing to worry about," he said, "local guy runs a private plowing service, solid as a rock. I'll pick you up in the morning."

He stood and watched the little green car round the corner, then made his way back to his house and Bertha.

That night, lying in the big double bed, he moaned and dreamed, reaching that half-awake state of knowing he was dreaming, being able to assess his own visions, yet not breaking from them into full wakefulness.

His strange malady did not disappear with the night's rest. Instead it spread, like a virulent plague, striking first his wife, his closest friends and coworkers at the programming center. Then it moved onward in successive waves as circles of acquaintances passed the infection to their own companions.

Everywhere the mental fantasies of the stricken appeared, externalized. Daily the number, the concentration, the variety of images grew greater.

Public places became filled with wild beasts of all eras; wolves and snakes, condors and tyrannosaurs; and imaginary creatures: griffins, unicorns, chimerae, basilisks, monstrous sandworms. Marilyn Monroe walked the streets, jostling a troop of Beatles, a brigade of John F. Kennedys, an army of Jesuses.

Not only did any figure appear when summoned by the fleeting thought of a mind: the same figure could be conjured up in endlessly replicated images by a single thinker or by any number independently. For not only did each person conjure his own fantasies. Now the fantasies of all coexisted, intermixing in a common conjoined reality.

Before long the thronging figures began to overcrowd all available space. A whole section of the municipal airport was filled with invoked images of the *Spirit of St. Louis,* of the infamous *Air Force One,* of the tragically remembered *Enola Gay.* Sports fans filled a giant stadium with Joe DiMaggios, Jim Thorpes, Jack Dempseys.

An entire jungle sprang up, populated by endlessly varied versions of Tarzan.

The sky was filled for an entire afternoon with muscular figures in variously colored costumes as a group of comic-book enthusiasts exchanged recollections of their respective favorites.

When an old Bela Lugosi film turned up at a revival showing, the theater was miraculously transformed into a huge, shadowy castle; a freeway leading to its creaking gate was filled with hundreds of caped and fanged images crowding to join the audience.

With a start David awoke.

He reached out and placed his hand on the figure of Bertha lying beside him in the bed. Somehow the familiar sensation of her skin beneath his hand seemed altered.

He switched on a bedside lamp and the room was flooded with a startling, pulsing, emerald hue.

He jumped from the bed, flung open the bathroom door and stared into the mirror.

He screamed and screamed until they came and took him away.

Even then the ride to the hospital was delayed for over an hour because of the crowd of Draculas jamming the freeway.

When *"The Devil's Hop Yard" first appeared in print, Theodore Sturgeon wrote a brief note about it, to the effect that I'd read H. P. Lovecraft's "The Dunwich Horror" at age nine, and never got over it. Since then I've done a little research and discovered that I read the Lovecraft story when I was eleven, not nine, but aside from that detail, Sturgeon was right.*

*The year was 1946, and for reasons too unpleasant to go into just now I was forced to attend services every Sunday at the Baptist church in our town. Not that there's anything wrong with the Baptist church, but I happen to be Jewish and I resented this "forced conversion" bitterly. (It didn't take, anyhow; I'm still Jewish.)*

*Each week I would sneak forbidden printed matter into church, hide it inside my hymnal, and read happily while the preacher promised that I'd spend eternity writhing in pools of flaming lava. I read "The Dunwich Horror" in a marvelous little book called* The Avon Ghost Reader. *"The Devil's Hop Yard" appeared in Roy Torgeson's anthology,* Chrysalis 2, *in 1978.*

# The Devil's
# Hop Yard

I T WAS IN THE AUTUMN OF 1928 THAT THOSE TERRIBLE
events which came to be known as the Dunwich Horror transpired. The residents of the upper Miskatonic Valley in Massa-
chusetts, at all times a taciturn breed of country folk never known
for their hospitality or communicativeness toward outsiders,
became thereafter positively hostile to such few travelers as happened to trespass upon their hilly and infertile region.

The people of the Dunwich region in particular, a sparse and
inbred race with few intellectual or material attainments to show
for their generations of toil, gradually became fewer than ever in
number. It was the custom of the region to marry late and to have
few children. Those infants delivered by the few physicians and
midwives who practiced thereabouts were often deformed in
some subtle and undefinable way; it would be impossible for an
observer to place his finger upon the exact nature of the defect,
yet it was plain that something was frighteningly wrong with
many of the boys and girls born in the Miskatonic Valley.

Yet, as the years turned slowly, the pale, faded folk of Dunwich continued to raise their thin crops, to tend their dull-eyed
and stringy cattle, and to wring their hard existence from the
poor, farmed-out earth of their homesteads.

Events of interest were few and petty; the columns of the Aylesbury *Transcript,* the Arkham *Advertiser,* and even the imposing Boston *Globe* were scanned for items of diversion. Dunwich itself supported no regular newspaper, not even the slim weekly sheet that subsists in many such semi-rural communities. It was therefore a source of much local gossip and a delight to the scandal-mongers when Earl Sawyer abandoned Mamie Bishop, his common-law wife of twenty years standing, and took up instead with Zenia Whateley. Sawyer was an uncouth dirt farmer, some fifty years of age. His cheeks covered perpetually with a stubble that gave him the appearance of not having shaved for a week, his nose and eyes marked with the red lines of broken minor blood vessels, and his stoop-shouldered, shuffling gait marked him as a typical denizen of Dunwich's hilly environs.

Zenia Whateley was a thin, pallid creature, the daughter of old Zebulon Whateley and a wife so retiring in her lifetime and so thoroughly forgotten since her death that none could recall the details of her countenance or even her given name. The latter had been painted carelessly on the oblong wooden marker that indicated the place of her burial, but the cold rains and watery sunlight of the round of Dunwich's seasons had obliterated even this trace of the dead woman's individuality.

Zenia must have taken after her mother, for her own appearance was unprepossessing, her manner cringing, and her speech so infrequent and so diffident that few could recall ever having heard her voice. The loafers and gossips at Osborn's General Store in Dunwich were hard put to understand Earl Sawyer's motives in abandoning Mamie Bishop for Zenia Whateley. Not that Mamie was noted for her great beauty or scintillating personality; on the contrary: she was known as a meddler and a snoop, and her sharp tongue had stung many a denizen hoping to see some misdemeanor pass unnoted. Still, Mamie had within her that spark of vitality so seldom found in the folk of the upper Miskatonic, that trait of personality known in the rural argot as gumption, so that it was puzzling to see her perched beside Earl on the front seat of his rattling Model T Ford, her few belongings tied in slovenly bundles behind her, as Sawyer drove her over the dust-blowing turnpike to Aylesbury where she took quarters in the town's sole, dilapidated rooming house.

The year was 1938 when Earl Sawyer and Mamie Bishop parted ways. It had been a decade since the death of the poor, malformed giant Wilbur Whateley and the dissolution — for this word, rather than *death,* best characterizes the end of that monster—of his even more gigantic and even more shockingly made twin brother. But now it was the end of May, and the spring thaw had come late and grudgingly to the hard-pressed farmlands of the Miskatonic Valley this year.

When Earl Sawyer returned, alone, to Dunwich, he stopped in the center of the town, such as it was, parking his Model T opposite Osborn's. He crossed the dirty thoroughfare and climbed onto the porch of old Zebulon Whateley's house, pounding once upon the gray, peeling door while the loafers at Osborn's stared and commented behind his back.

The door opened and Earl Sawyer disappeared inside for a minute. The loafers puzzled over what business Earl might have with Zebulon Whateley, and their curiosity was rewarded shortly when Sawyer reappeared leading Zenia Whateley by one flaccid hand. Zenia wore a thin cotton dress, and through its threadbare covering it was obvious even from the distance of Osborn's that she was with child.

Earl Sawyer drove home to his dusty farm, bringing Zenia with him, and proceeded to install her in place of Mamie Bishop. There was little noticeable change in the routine at Sawyer's farm with the change in its female occupant. Each morning Earl and Zenia would rise, Zenia would prepare and serve a meager repast for them, and they would breakfast in grim silence. Earl would thereafter leave the house, carefully locking the door behind him with Zenia left inside to tend to the chores of housekeeping, and Earl would spend the entire day working out-of-doors.

The Sawyer farm contained just enough arable land to raise a meager crop of foodstuffs and to support a thin herd of the poor cattle common to the Miskatonic region. The bleak hillside known as the Devil's Hop Yard was also located on Sawyer's holdings. Here had grown no tree, shrub or blade of grass for as far back as the oldest archives of Dunwich recorded, and despite Earl Sawyer's repeated attempts to raise a crop on its unpleasant slopes, the Hop Yard resisted and remained barren. Even so there persisted reports of vague, unpleasant rumblings and cracklings from beneath the Hop Yard, and occasionally shocking odors were carried from it to adjoining farms when the wind was right.

On the first Sunday of June, 1938, Earl Sawyer and Zenia Whateley were seen to leave the farmhouse and climb into Sawyer's Model T. They drove together into Dunwich village, and, leaving the Model T in front of old Zebulon Whateley's drab house, walked across the churchyard, pausing to read such grave markers as remained there standing and legible, then entered the

Dunwich Congregational Church that had been founded by the Reverend Abijah Hoadley in 1747. The pulpit of the Dunwich Congregational Church had been vacant since the unexplained disappearance of the Reverend Isaiah Ashton in the summer of 1912, but a circuit-riding Congregational minister from the city of Arkham conducted services in Dunwich from time to time.

This was the first occasion of Earl Sawyer's attendance at services within memory, and there was a nodding of heads and a hissing of whispers up and down the pews as Earl and Zenia entered the frame building. Earl and Zenia took a pew to themselves at the rear of the congregation and when the order of service had reached its conclusion they remained behind to speak with the minister. No witness was present, of course, to overhear the conversation that took place, but later the minister volunteered his recollection of Sawyer's request and his own responses.

Sawyer, the minister reported, had asked him to perform a marriage. The couple to be united were himself (Sawyer) and Zenia Whateley. The minister had at first agreed, especially in view of Zenia's obvious condition, and the desirability of providing for a legitimate birth for her expected child. But Sawyer had refused to permit the minister to perform the usual marriage ceremony of the Congregational Church, insisting instead upon a ceremony involving certain foreign terms to be provided from some ancient documents handed down through the family of the bride.

Nor would Sawyer permit the minister to read the original documents, providing in their place crudely rendered transcripts written by a clumsy hand on tattered, filthy scraps of paper. Unfortunately the minister no longer had even these scraps. They had been retained by Sawyer, and the minister could recall only vaguely a few words of the strange and almost unpronounceable incantations he had been requested to utter: *N'gai, n'gha'ghaa, bugg-shoggog,* he remembered. And a reference to a lost city "Between the Yr and the Nhhngr."

The minister had refused to perform the blasphemous ceremony requested by Sawyer, holding that it would be ecclesiastically improper and possibly even heretical of him to do so, but he renewed his offer to perform an orthodox Congregational marriage, and possibly to include certain additional materials provided by the couple *if he were shown a translation also,* so as to convince himself of the propriety of the ceremony.

Earl Sawyer refused vehemently, warning the minister that he stood in far greater peril should he ever learn the meaning of the words than if he remained in ignorance of them. At length Sawyer stalked angrily from the church, pulling the passive Zenia Whateley behind him, and returned with her to his farm.

A few nights later the couple were visited by Zenia's father, old Zebulon Whateley, and also by Squire Sawyer Whateley, of the semi-undecayed Whateleys, a man who held the unusual distinction of claiming cousinship to both Earl Sawyer and Zenia Whateley. At midnight the four figures, Earl, Zenia, old Zebulon, and Squire Whateley, climbed slowly to the top of the Devil's Hop Yard. What acts they performed at the crest of the hill are not known with certainty, but Luther Brown, now a fully-grown man and engaged to be married to George Corey's daughter Olivia, stated later that he had been searching for a lost heifer near the boundary between Corey's farm and Sawyer's, and saw the four figures silhouetted against the night constellations as they stood atop the hill.

As Luther Brown watched, all four disrobed; he was fairly certain of the identification of the three men, and completely sure of that of Zenia because of her obvious pregnancy. Completely naked they set fire to an altar of wood apparently set up in advance on the peak of the Hop Yard. What rites they performed before Luther fled in terror and disgust he refused to divulge, but later that night loud cracking sounds were heard coming from the vicinity of the Sawyer farm, and an earthquake was reported to have shaken the entire Miskatonic Valley, registering on the seismographic instruments of Harvard College and causing swells in the harbor at Innsmouth.

The next day Squire Sawyer Whateley registered a wedding on the official rolls of Dunwich village. He claimed to be qualified to perform the civil ceremony by virtue of his standing as Chairman of the local Selective Service Board. This claim must surely be regarded as most dubious, but while the Whateleys were not highly regarded in Dunwich, their detractors considered it the better part of valor to hold their criticism to private circumstances, and the marriage of Earl Sawyer and Zenia Whateley was thus officially recognized.

Mamie Bishop, in the meanwhile, had settled into her new home in Aylesbury and began spreading malign reports about her former lover Earl Sawyer and his new wife. Earl, she claimed, had been in league with the Whateleys all along. Her own displacement by Zenia had been only one step in the plot of Earl Sawyer and the Whateley clan to revive the evil activities that had culminated in the events of 1928. Earl and Zenia, with the collaboration of Squire Sawyer Whateley and old Zebulon Whateley, would bring about the ruination of the entire Miskatonic Valley, if left to their own devices, and perhaps might bring about a blight that would cover a far greater region.

No one paid any attention to Mamie, however. Even the other Bishops, a clan almost as numerous and widespread as the Whateleys, tended to discount Mamie's warnings as the spiteful outpourings of a woman scorned. And in any case, Mamie's dire words were pushed from the public consciousness in the month of August, 1938, when Earl Sawyer rang up Dr. Houghton on the party line telephone and summoned him to the Sawyer farm.

Zenia was in labor, and Earl, in a rare moment of concern, had decided that medical assistance was in order.

Zenia's labor was a long and difficult one. Dr. Houghton later commented that first childbirths tended to be more protracted than later deliveries, but Zenia remained in labor for seventy-two consecutive hours, and barely survived the delivery of the child. Throughout the period of her labor there were small earth temblors centering on the Devil's Hop Yard, and Zenia, by means of a series of frantic hand motions and incoherent mewling sounds, indicated that she wished the curtains drawn back from her window so that she could see the crown of the hill from her bed.

On the third night of her labor, while Zenia lay panting and spent near to death between futile contractions, a storm rose. Clouds swept up the valley from the Atlantic, great winds roared over the houses and through the trees of Dunwich, bolts of lightning flashed from thunderhead to hilltop.

Dr. Houghton, despairing of saving the life of either Zenia or her unborn child, began preparations for a Caesarian section. With Earl Sawyer hovering in the background, mumbling semi-incoherent incantations of the sort that had caused the Congregational minister to refuse a church wedding to the couple, the doctor set to work.

With sharpened instruments sterilized over the woodstove that served for both cooking and heat for the Sawyer farmhouse, he made the incision in Zenia's abdomen. As he removed the fetus from her womb there was a terrific crash of thunder. A blinding bolt of lightning struck at the peak of the Devil's Hop Yard. From a small grove of twisted and deformed maple trees behind the Sawyer house, a flock of nesting whippoorwills took wing, setting up a cacophony of sound audible over even the loud rushings and pounding of the rainstorm.

All of Dr. Houghton's efforts failed to preserve the poor, limited life of Zenia Whateley Sawyer, but her child survived the ordeal of birth. The next day old Zebulon Whateley and Squire Sawyer Whateley made their way to the Sawyer house and joined Earl Sawyer in his efforts. He descended the wooden steps to the dank cellar of the house and returned carrying a plain wooden coffin that he himself had surreptitiously built some time before. The three of them placed Zenia's shriveled, wasted body in the coffin and Earl nailed its lid in place.

They carried the wooden box to the peak of the Devil's Hop Yard and there, amid fearsome incantations and the making of signs with their hands unlike any seen for a decade in the Miskatonic Valley, they buried Zenia's remains.

Then they returned to the farmhouse where the child lay in a crude wooden cradle. Squire Whateley tended the infant while its father rang up Central on the party line and placed a call to Mamie Bishop at the rooming house in Aylesbury.

After a brief conversation with his former common-law wife, Earl Sawyer nodded to his father-in-law and to the Squire, and left them with the child. He climbed into his Model T and set out along the Aylesbury Pike to fetch Mamie back to Dunwich.

The child of Earl Sawyer and Zenia Whateley Sawyer was a girl. Her father, after consultation with his father-in-law and distant cousin Squire Whateley, named his daughter Hester Sawyer. She was a tiny child at birth, and fear was expressed as to her own survival.

Earl contacted the Congregational minister at Arkham, asking him to baptize the infant according to rites specified by Earl. Once more the dispute as to the use of Earl's strange scriptures — if they could be so defined — erupted, and once more the minister refused to lend his ecclesiastical legitimacy to the ceremony. Instead, Earl, Zebulon and Sawyer Whateley carried the tiny form, wrapped in swaddling cloths, to the peak of the Devil's Hop Yard, and on the very ground of her mother's still-fresh grave conducted a ceremony of consecration best left undescribed.

They then returned her to the Sawyer house and the care of Mamie Bishop.

There were comments in Dunwich and even in Aylesbury about Mamie's surprising willingness to return to Sawyer's ménage in the role of nursemaid and guardian to the infant Hester, but Mamie merely said that she had her reasons and refused to discuss the matter further. Under Mamie's ministrations the infant Hester survived the crises of her first days of life, and developed into a child of surprising strength and precocity.

Even as an infant Hester was a child of unusual beauty and – if such a phrase may be used – premature maturity. Her coloring was fair – almost, but not quite, to the point of albinism. Where Hester's distant relative, the long-disappeared Lavinia Whateley, had had crinkly white hair and reddish-pink eyes, little Hester possessed from the day of her birth a glossy poll of the silvery blonde shade known as platinum. Mamie Bishop tried repeatedly to put up the child's hair in miniature curls or scallops as she thought appropriate for a little girl, but Hester's hair hung straight and gracefully to her shoulders, refusing to lie in any other fashion.

The child's eyes showed a flecked pattern of palest blue and the faint pink of the true albino, giving the appearance of being a pale lavender in tint except at a very close range, when the alternation of blue and pink became visible. Her skin was the shade of new cream and was absolutely flawless.

She took her first steps at the age of five months; by this time she had her full complement of baby teeth as well. By the age of eight months, early in the spring of 1939, she began to speak. There was none of the babyish prattle of a normally developing child; Hester spoke with precision, correctness, and a chilling solemnity from the utterance of her first word.

Earl Sawyer did not keep Mamie Bishop imprisoned in his house as he had the dead Zenia Whateley Sawyer. Indeed, Earl made it his business to teach Mamie the operation of his Model T, and he encouraged her – nay, he all but commanded her – to drive it into Dunwich village, Dean's Corners, or Aylesbury frequently.

On these occasions Mamie was alleged to be shopping for such necessities for herself, Earl, or little Hester as the farm did not provide. On one occasion Earl directed Mamie to drive the Model T all the way to Arkham, and there to spend three days obtaining certain items which he said were needed for Hester's upbringing. Mamie spent two nights at one of the rundown hotels that still persisted in Arkham, shabby ornate reminders of that city's more prosperous days.

Mamie's sharp tongue had its opportunities during these shopping expeditions, and she was heard frequently to utter harsh comments about Earl, Zebulon, and Squire Whateley. She never made direct reference to the dead Zenia, but uttered cryptic and unsettling remarks about little Hester Sawyer, her charge, whom she referred to most often as "Zenia's white brat."

As has been mentioned, Dunwich village supported no regular newspaper of its own, but the publications of other communities in the Miskatonic Valley gave space to events in this locale. The Aylesbury *Transcript* in particular devoted a column in its weekly pages to news from Dunwich. This news was provided by Joe Osborn, the proprietor of Osborn's General Store, in return for regular advertisement of his establishment's wares.

A review of the Dunwich column in the Aylesbury *Transcript* for the period between August of 1938 and the end of April of 1943 shows a series of reports of rumblings, crackings, and unpleasant odors emanating from the area of Sawyer's farm, and particularly from the Devil's Hop Yard. Two features of these reports are worthy of note.

First, the reports of the sounds and odors occur at irregular intervals, but a check of the sales records of the establishments in Dunwich, Aylesbury, Dean's Corners and Arkham where Mamie Bishop traded, will show that the occurrences at the Devil's Hop Yard coincide perfectly with the occasions of Mamie's absence from Sawyer's farm. Second, while the events took place at irregular intervals, ranging from as close together as twice in one week to as far apart as eight months, their severity increased steadily. The earliest of the series are barely noted in the Dunwich column of the *Transcript*. By the end of 1941 the events receive lead position in Osborn's writings. By the beginning of 1943 they are no longer relegated to the Dunwich column at all, but are treated as regular news, suggesting that they could be detected in Aylesbury itself—a distance of nearly fifteen miles from Dunwich.

It was also noted by the loafers at Osborn's store that on those occasions when Mamie Bishop absented herself from the Sawyer farm, Earl's two favorite in-laws and cronies, Zebulon Whateley and Squire Sawyer Whateley, visited him. There were no further reports of odd goings-on at the Sawyer place such as that made by Luther Brown in 1938.

Perhaps Luther's unfortunate demise in an accident on George Corey's silo roof, where he was placing new shingles, had no connection with his seeing the rites atop the Devil's Hop Yard, but after Luther's death and with the new series of rumblings and stenches, others began to shun the Sawyer place from 1939 onward.

In September of 1942 a sad incident transpired. Hester Sawyer, then aged four, had been educated up to that time primarily by her father, with the assistance of the two elder Whateleys and of Mamie Bishop. She had never been away from the Sawyer farm and had never seen another child.

Mamie Bishop's second cousin Elsie, the maiden sister of Silas Bishop (of the undecayed Bishops), caught Mamie's ear on one of Mamie's shopping expeditions away from the Sawyer place. Elsie was the mistress of a nursery school operated under the auspices of the Dunwich Congregational Church, and she somehow convinced Mamie that it was her duty to give little Hester exposure to other children of her own age. Mamie spoke disparagingly of "Zenia's white brat," but following Elsie's insistence Mamie agreed to discuss the matter with Earl Sawyer.

On the first day of the fall term, Mamie drove Earl's Model T into Dunwich village, little Hester perched on the seat beside her. This was the first look that Hester had at Dunwich — and the first that Dunwich had at Hester.

Although Mamie had bundled the child into loose garments that covered her from neck to ankles, it was obvious that something was abnormal about her. Hester was astonishingly small for a child of four. She was hardly taller than a normal infant. It was as if she had remained the same size in the four years since her birth, not increasing an inch in stature.

But that was only half the strangeness of Hester's appearance, for while her size was the same as a newborn infant's, her development was that of a fully mature and breathtakingly beautiful woman. The sun shone brilliantly on the long platinum hair that hung defiantly around the edges of the bonnet Mamie had forced onto Hester's head. Her strange lavender eyes seemed to hold the secrets of an experienced voluptuary. Her face was mature, her lips full and sensual. And when a sudden gust of wind pressed her baggy dress against her torso this revealed the configuration of a Grecian eidolon.

The loafers at Osborn's, who had clustered about and craned their necks for a look at the mysterious "white brat" were torn between an impulse to turn away from this unnatural sight and a fascination with the image of what seemed a living manikin, a woman of voluptuous bodily form and astonishing facial beauty, the size of a day-old infant, sitting primly beside Mamie Bishop.

Elsie Bishop welcomed her cousin Mamie and her charge, Hester Sawyer, to the nursery school at the Congregational Church. Elsie chose to make no comment on Hester's unusual appearance, but instead introduced her to the children already present. These included her own nephew Nahum Bishop, Silas's five-year-old son. Nahum was a perfectly normal boy, outgoing and playful, one of the few such to appear in the blighted Miskatonic Valley.

He took one look at Hester Sawyer and fell madly in love with her, with the total, enraptured fascination that only a child can feel when first he discovers the magic of the female sex. He lost all interest in the other children in the school and in their games. He wished only to be with Hester, to gaze at her, to hold her miniature woman's hand in his own pudgy boy's fingers. Any word that Hester spoke was as music to his ears, and any favor she might ask, any task that she might set for him, was his bounden duty and his greatest joy to perform.

In a short while the various children of the nursery school were playing happily, some of them scampering up and down the aisle leading between the two banks of pews in the main body of the church. The two cousins, Mamie and Elsie, retired to the chancel kitchen to prepare a pot of tea for themselves. Although they could not see the school children from this position, they could hear them happily playing in the semi-abandoned church.

Suddenly there was a terrible thump from the roof of the church, then a second similar sound from the burying-ground outside, then a series of panic-stricken and terrified screams from the children. Mamie and Elsie ran from the chancel and found nothing, apparently, amiss in the church itself, but the children were clustered at an open window staring into the churchyard, pointing and exclaiming in distress.

The two women shoved their way through the panic-stricken children until they could see. What they beheld was the body of Elsie's nephew Nahum Bishop, grotesquely broken over an old tombstone upon which he had fallen when he bounced from the roof of the church. There was no question that the child was dead, the sightless eyes apparently gazing upward at the steeple of the church.

Before they could even turn away from the window, the two women were able to hear a light tread, one so light that, except for the total hush that had descended upon the church as the children's screams subsided, it would not have been heard at all, calmly descending the wooden staircase from the steeple. In a moment Hester Sawyer emerged from the stairwell, her manner one of complete self-possession, the expression on her beautiful little face one of mockery and amusement.

When the state police arrived Hester explained, with total self-assurance, that she and Nahum had climbed the steeple together, up the narrow wooden staircase that ran from the church's floor to its belfry. Nahum had averred that he would do anything to prove his love for Hester, and she had asked him to fly from the steeple. In attempting to do so he had fallen to the roof, bounced once, then crashed onto the old grave marker in the yard.

The police report listed Nahum's death as accidental, and Hester was returned to the Sawyer farm in charge of Mamie Bishop. Needless to say, the child did not return to the nursery school at the Dunwich Congregational Church; in fact, she was not seen again in Dunwich, or anywhere else away from her father's holdings.

The final chapter in the tragedy of the Devil's Hop Yard, if indeed tragedy is the proper designation for such a drama, was played out in the spring of 1943. As in so many years past, the warmth of the equinox had given but little of itself to the upper Miskatonic Valley; winter instead still clung to the barren peaks and the infertile bottomlands of the region, and the icy dark waters of the Miskatonic River passed only few meadows on their way southeastward to Arkham and Innsmouth and the cold Atlantic beyond.

In Dunwich the bereaved Silas Bishop and his maiden sister Elsie had recovered as best they could from the death of young Nahum. Elsie's work with the nursery school continued and only the boarding-up of the stairwell that led to the steeple and belfry of the Congregational Church testified to the accident of the previous September.

Early on the evening of April 30 the telephone rang in the Bishop house in Dunwich village, and Elsie lifted the receiver to hear a furtive whisper on the line. The voice she barely recognized, so distorted it was with terror, belonged to her second cousin Mamie.

"They've locked me in the house naow," Mamie whispered into the telephone. "Earl always sent me away before, but this time they've locked me in and I'm afeared. Help me, Elsie! I daon't knaow what they're a-fixin' ta do up ta the Hop Yard, but I'm afeared!"

Elsie signaled her brother Silas to listen to the conversation. "Who's locked you in, Mamie?" Elsie asked her cousin.

"Earl and Zeb and Sawyer Whateley done it! They've took Zenia's brat and they've clumb the Hop Yard. I kin see 'em from here! They're all stark naked and they've built 'em a bonfire and an altar and they're throwin' powder into the fire and old Zeb he's areadin' things outen some terrible book that they always keep alocked up!

"And now I kin see little Hester, the little white brat o' Zenia's, and she's clumb onto the altar and she's sayin' things to Zeb an' Earl and Squire Whateley an' they've got down on their knees like they's aworshippin' Hester, and she's makin' signs with her hands. Oh, Elsie, I can't describe them signs, they's so awful, they's so awful what she's adoin', Elsie! Get some help out here, oh please get some help!"

Elsie told Mamie to try and be calm, and not to watch what was happening atop the Devil's Hop Yard. Then she hung up the telephone and turned to her brother Silas. "We'll get the state police from Aylesbury," she said. "They'll stop whatever is happening at Sawyer's. We'd best telephone them now, Silas!"

"D'ye think they'll believe ye, Elsie?"

Elsie shook her head in a negative manner.

"Then we'd best git to Aylesbury ourselves," Silas resumed. "If we go there ourselves they'd more like to believe us than if we jest telephoned."

They hitched up their horse and drove by wagon from Dunwich to Aylesbury. Fortunately the state police officer who had investigated the death of young Nahum Bishop was present, and knowing both Elsie and Silas to be citizens of a responsible nature the officer did not laugh at their report of Mamie's frightened telephone call. The officer started an automobile belonging to the state police, and with the two Bishops as passengers set out back along the Aylesbury Pike to Dunwich, and thence to the Sawyer farm beyond the village center.

As the official vehicle neared Sawyer's place, its three occupants were assailed by a most terrible and utterly indescribable stench that turned their stomachs and caused their eyes to run copiously, and that also, inexplicably, filled each of them with a hugely frightening rush of emotions dominated by an amalgam of fear and revulsion. Sounds of thunder filled the air, and the earth trembled repeatedly, threatening to throw the car off the road.

The state police officer swung the automobile from the dirt road fronting the Sawyer farm onto a narrow and rutted track that ran by the decrepit house and led to the foot of the Devil's Hop Yard. The officer pulled the car to a halt and leaped from its seat, charging up the hill with his service revolver drawn, followed by Silas and Elsie Bishop, who made the best speed they could despite their years.

Before them they could see the altar and the four figures that

Mamie Bishop had described to her cousin Elsie. The night sky was cloudless and a new moon offered no competition to the millions of brilliantly twinkling stars. Little Hester Sawyer, her body that of a fully formed woman yet not two feet in height, danced and postured on the wooden altar, the starlight and that of the nearby bonfire dancing lasciviously on her gleaming platinum hair and smooth, cream-colored skin. Her lavender eyes caught the firelight and reflected it like the eyes of a wild beast in the woods at night.

Earl and Zebulon and Sawyer Whateley stood in an equilateral triangle about the altar, and around them there had apparently sprung from the earth itself a perfect circle of slimy, tentacled growths, more animal than vegetable, the only things that had ever been known to grow from the soil of the Devil's Hop Yard. Even as the newcomers watched, too awe-stricken and too revolted to act, the horrid tentacled growths began to lengthen, and to sway in time to the awful chanting of the three naked men and the lascivious posturings of the tiny, four-year-old Hester.

There was the sound of a shrill, reedy piping from somewhere in the air, and strange winds rushed back and forth over the scene.

The voice of Hester Sawyer could be heard chanting, "*Ygnaith . . . ygnaith . . . thflthkh'ngha . . . Yog-Sothoth . . . Y'bthnk . . . h'ehye-n'grkdl'lh!*"

There was a single, blinding bolt of lightning—an astonishing occurrence as the night sky was entirely clear of any clouds—and the form of Hester Sawyer was bathed in a greenish-yellow glow of almost supernatural electrical display, sparks dancing over her perfect skin, and balls of St. Elmo's fire tumbling from her lips and hands and rolling across the altar, tumbling to the ground and bounding down the slopes of the Devil's Hop Yard.

The eyes of the watchers were so dazzled by the display that they were never certain, afterwards, of what they had seen. But it appeared, at least, that the bolt of lightning had not descended from the sky to strike Hester, but had *originated from her* and struck upward, zigzagging into the wind-swept blackness over Dunwich, streaking upward and upward as if it were eventually going to reach the stars themselves.

And even more quickly than the bolt of lightning had disappeared from before the dazzled eyes of the watchers, the body of Hester Sawyer appeared to rise along its course, posturing and making those terrible shocking signs even as it rose, growing ever smaller as it disappeared above the Hop Yard until the lightning bolt winked out and all sight of Hester Sawyer was lost forever.

With the end of the electrical display the shocked paralysis that had overcome the watchers subsided, and the police officer advanced to stand near the ring of tentacled growths and the three naked men. He ordered them to follow him back to the police vehicle, but instead they launched themselves in snarling, animalistic attacks upon him. The officer stepped back but the three men flew at him growling, clawing, biting at his legs and torso. The police officer's revolver crashed once, again, then a third time, and the three naked men lay thrashing and gesturing on the ground.

They were taken to the general hospital at Arkham, where a medical team headed by Drs. Houghton and Hartwell labored unsuccessfully through the night to save them. By the morning of May 1, all three had expired without uttering a single word.

Meanwhile, back at the Devil's Hop Yard, Silas and Elsie Bishop guided other investigators to the altar that Hester Sawyer had last stood upon. The book that had lain open beside her had been destroyed beyond identification by the lightning bolt of the night of April 30. Agricultural experts summoned from Miskatonic University at Arkham attempted to identify the tentacled growths that had sprung from the ground around the altar. The growths had died within a few hours of their appearance, and only desiccated husks remained. The experts were unable to identify them fully, indicating their complete puzzlement at their apparent resemblance to the tentacles of the giant marine squid of the Pacific Trench near the island of Ponape.

Back at the Sawyer farmhouse, Mamie Bishop was found cowering in a corner, hiding her eyes and refusing to look up or even acknowledge the presence of others when addressed. Her hair had turned completely white, not the platinum white of little Hester Sawyer's hair but the crinkly albino white that had been Lavinia Whateley's so many years before.

Mamie mumbled to herself and shook her head but uttered not a single intelligible word, either then or later, when she too was taken to the general hospital at Arkham. In time she was certified physically sound and transferred to a mental ward where she resides to this day, a harmless, quivering husk, her inward-turned eyes locked forever on whatever shocking sight it was that she beheld that night when she gazed from the window of the Sawyer farmhouse upon the horrid ceremony taking place atop the Devil's Hop Yard.

*This was one of my earliest stories, written and published in 1969, and it's still one of my favorites. When I wrote it I offered it to Ed Ferman for* The Magazine of Fantasy and Science Fiction, *and to Chester Anderson, who had recently announced a new science fiction magazine with the intriguing name of* Pigs and Fishes. *To my delight, but also my discomfiture, both editors wanted it.*

*The idea of having a story in the first issue of a brand new magazine appealed to me, so I accepted Anderson's offer and tendered Ferman my regrets.*

*Mistake.*

*Big, big mistake.*

Pigs and Fishes *never quite happened so Chester Anderson transferred "Stream of Consciousness" to* Crawdaddy, *a music magazine which he also edited. Then a typographer at* Crawdaddy *revised the story to suit his own taste as he set the type, apparently without discussing this with Anderson and certainly without mentioning it to me.*

*Then whoever laid out the issue of the magazine jumbled the pages of "Stream of Consciousness," making it impossible to understand.*

*And finally,* Crawdaddy *went out of business without paying me.*

*Listen, don't cry for me, Argentina. Every author who's been around for more than a couple of weeks can describe experiences like this one. After all these years I can actually laugh about it (although it does still hurt just a little).*

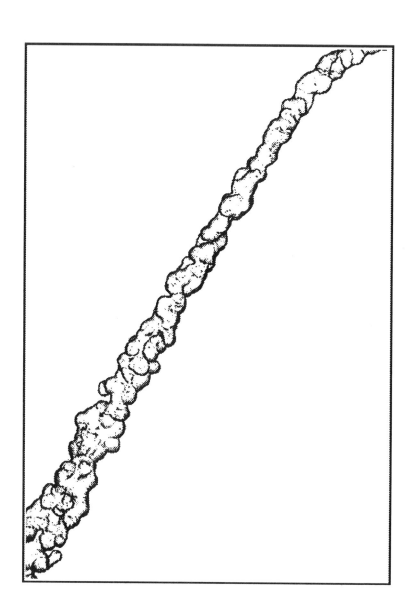

# Stream of Consciousness

S ALZMAN DINED WELL THAT NIGHT. RELAXED FROM
a day's labors he sipped two martinis in his favorite chair, his
feet elevated, the evening paper lying unread across his
knees, a mild drowsiness enhanced by the alcohol suffusing his
head.

His wife timed the serving of the meal nicely to coincide with
Salzman's completion of the second martini. As if in celebration,
except that there was no particular occasion to celebrate, she
served him his favorite dinner, a conglomeration of dishes seldom
eaten at one meal, but based on years of married intimacy between the two. A lobster bisque, red-pink and creamy with large
lumps of the crimson-flecked white meat sunk in the liquid. A
watercress salad, crisp and sparklingly reflecting the kitchen lights
in a dressing of oil and vinegar livened with bits of fresh garlic.

For the main course sea bass, slit, boned, then baked with a
stuffing of crabmeat and ground cheese, the platter steaming
and filling the yellow-painted room with its deliciously saliva-
provoking odor. Baked with it and served alongside the bass, sliced
water chestnuts, Mrs. Salzman's personal touch that added her
personal signature to the delicately flavored but otherwise anon-
ymous specialty.

Served with the meal a bottle of chilled Petit Chablis, a fine vintage fully mature at age five, an excellent traveler and a fitting companion to the refined flavors of the repast. Then coffee, brandy, a comforting Havana and a quiet evening with a Ballard novel. Then to bed.

Salzman woke so gradually that it was impossible to tell the precise moment at which sleep yielded to consciousness. In the darkened room, the soft and regular sound of his wife's breathing giving companionship even as she slept on, Salzman could not even be certain when he had opened his eyes. The involuntary act performed upon wakening showed only the plain darkened ceiling above his pillow so that only after some seconds' wakefulness could he be sure that he was truly seeing the room about him.

He had been wakened by a sensation, a pressure that represented a mild discomfort, surely something less than a pain, hardly something distressing, yet a feeling that persisted as he lay unmoving in the darkness, gradually regaining the full rationality of wakefulness.

It was distinctly a pressure, yes. In his lower abdomen, spreading across the pelvic area and demanding a relief downward; downward, that was, in relation to the axis running from his head to his feet; actually, while he lay supine, the true direction of the pressure was horizontal, toward the far end of the bed.

Salzman pushed himself upright, swung his feet over the edge of the bed and stood for a moment, then walked to the bathroom. He closed the door between the bathroom and bedroom behind him, so as not to waken Mrs. Salzman. He turned on the bathroom light, opened the toilet seat, carefully checked his pajama pants to assure himself that the fly was open, directed his organ toward the clear pool at the bottom of the toilet and urinated.

As the stream of waste fluid passed from his bladder he felt a sharply pleasurable sensation, a heated relief of the annoying pressure not wholly unlike the sensation of sexual discharge, although of much lesser intensity and wholly lacking in the emotional overtones of the latter.

Still somewhat bleary-eyed from the past period of sleep he looked downward and watched the stream of urine passing from his organ, through the vacant area above the toilet bowl, then into the water at the bottom of the bowl where it made a bubbling and intricately interactive series of ripples, the ripples in turn moving outward from the point of entry of the urine, rebounding off the porcelain walls of the toilet, then moving back into the center to

*had* he been standing here? — and then he would be finished and return to bed. Hmm, now that he was fully awake, Salzman wondered if it might not be worthwhile to waken Mrs. Salzman upon returning to bed, and attempt to interest her in a session of the marital pleasures before resuming his, and her, interrupted slumber. Yes, that would be comforting, friendly.

A thought stuck Salzman without warning. Here he stood, presumably completing a bodily requirement, looking forward with warm anticipation to sharing a strangely similar one with his wife, mentally calculating the time that would be required to complete his period in the bathroom, return to bed and waken his wife, perform the customary acts of foreplay and proceed finally to the marital union and its pleasurable completion, when the sun might go nova at any time. He shuddered with a momentary coldness at the thought of the world's ending before he had time for a complete act of intercourse with his wife, at the thought of the sun turning from its beneficent and effulgent role as giver of necessary light and warmth, into a searing huge globe of inconceivable heat and brilliance, burning the Earth to a glowing cinder in the few moments that would elapse between the initial achievement of the nova state and the final, total engulfment of the Earth into the sizzling, bulging body of the huge exploding star.

The end of the world had always been predicted as coming in fire or flood, a fiery nuclear blast if Man decided to end his world or a fiery nova if God decided to do it first, or a flood. . . . Good heavens, thought Salzman, am I, personally, going to flood the world? Am I God's chosen instrument for the destruction of the wicked? Will Man end, not in melted ice caps nor in unceasing rain, but in a small but steady stream of Salzman's urine?

He reached forward and depressed the chromium-plated handle that stood out from the tank at the rear of the toilet, watching the steady stream of his urine entering the bowl even as the contents of the toilet disappeared to the accompaniment of the usual flushing sound. As the bowl refilled with fresh water Salzman's stream continued to flow into the toilet.

That, at least, was no immediate peril. He could continue to pass his stream into the toilet, reaching forward and turning the handle to flush it periodically, for an indefinite time. Until fatigue, at present a mere nuisance factor, should prove a more formidable foe. That would be a long time.

Meanwhile he thought of a flooded world. What *was* that book of Ballard's, something about a universal flood, trained alligators paddling silently around in the streams and lagoons of a tropically aqueous London? Absurd. *The Watery World*, was it, or *The Drowning City*? Ah, he had it, *The Drowned World*, with those strange people living in the tops of flooded apartment houses and hiding out when big helicopters came to rescue them and carry them away to some place that was still, at least temporarily, safely above water level.

And that other book, what, *In the Wet*, by Nevil Shute, and that thing by Greenfield that he'd never bothered to read, *Waters of Death* or something like that. That old thing by Serviss, *The Second Deluge*, with its submarines sailing up the Valley of Kings and the unravelment at last of the Secret of the Sphinx.

Now that he thought about it a bit, Salzman realized that an aqueous apocalypse was really at least as popular as a fiery one. Both went back to the Bible, and both were popular to this very day in speculation and fantasy.

Of course it would take a very long time for *him* to flood the world single-handed. (Or, he thought in an aside to himself, whatever the right expression would be. Probably not single-handed. But that would do, he surmised. Mr. Salzman was not a vulgar man.)

But had he not already been a long time at this? Again he wished for his wristwatch, vainly regretting not having picked it up as he had risen from his bed to come to this room. It seemed to have been a very long time, but time was unquestionably a relative and subjective thing, especially when one did not have one's watch available. Had he been here for some minutes now, or only for subjectively elongated seconds? Or for several hours? What if he had begun this at midnight and it was now as late as four o'clock in the morning? Was that physiologically possible?

He must be dehydrating! The body was four-fifths water, he had once read or heard. Suppose he continued to pass water, on and on, until all the water in his body was exhausted. There he would be found in the morning, a mere thirty-pound husk lying dead on the tile floor beside an unflushed toilet, no urine in his bladder, no blood in his circulatory system, no saliva in his mouth, no mucous in his nose, no lubricant in his eyeballs. A pretty puzzle for some coroner to unravel!

Mr. Salzman reached with one hand, took a drinking cup from its little holder above the sink, turned the chromium tap and filled it with cold water, then drank the full cup. After three cups he put the light plastic implement back in place, flushed the toilet once again, took the cup once more and drank it empty twice, then again replaced it, slightly uncomfortable, thinking perhaps that he should have drunk water a bit less chilled, but relieved nonetheless to know that he was reprieved from the menace of dehydration for the time being.

In fact, now that the menace had retreated to a less personal and immediate distance he smiled to himself at the thought of a coroner trying to solve the riddle of his dehydrated corpse. It might even make a detective novel for Gardner to write: *The Case of the Dehydrated Husband*, featuring Perry Mason who would, as usual, save his client, solve the crime and unmask the real culprit in one dazzling chapter somewhere around page 200.

But really now, Salzman thought after he had savored the joke for a while, this is getting to be a real problem for *me*. How long can I stand here urinating? What happens when morning comes, anyway?

He held his penis between thumb and forefinger, squeezing it to stem the flow. For a moment it worked but the immediate pain was so intense that he was forced to release it. The stream immediately resumed its passage. He reached forward, found a rubber band on the shelf over the toilet and tried that. The results were equally unsatisfactory, in addition to which a small amount of urine sprayed onto the floor and onto his hands. He ran some water in the sink and rinsed his hands, dried them on his pajama bottoms. He would dry the floor before returning to bed.

Perhaps he could use a condom to contain the urine. None was at hand. But Mrs. Salzman's shower cap. . . . No, she would be furious, and with good reason. Besides, that was no real solution anyway. He abandoned that line of thought, wracked his brain in hopes of discovering a more productive approach to solving his problem.

If he couldn't just walk away from the toilet — and that he most assuredly could not — perhaps he could get help. "Darling! Wake up! Come into the bathroom, quickly! There's something the matter and you must help me! Call the doctor!"

No, he could not do it. Mrs. Salzman was a light enough sleeper that there would be no difficulty in awakening her, but her husband could not bear the humiliation of calling for help under the present circumstances. Were he bleeding to death he could call for help, would call for help without hesitation. But this? He blushed even at the thought.

Suppose the sun went nova?

Now a new menace, or more properly a newly-considered aspect of that same menace, overcame Salzman's worried consciousness. If the sun went nova at a given moment, the heat and light of the solar disaster must still travel the full distance to the Earth. That was a matter of some 93 million miles. At the speed of light, what was that, Salzman stirred his memory, ah, yes, 186,000 miles per second, it would take the flare some, ah, let me see, why, *exactly* 500 seconds, which was eight minutes and twenty seconds over.

So the problem was not merely, What if the sun goes nova, but, What if the sun has *already* gone nova? What if it went nova a minute ago and the first flaring holocaust is already ten million miles on its way, and going to get here in seven minutes and twenty seconds? What if the sun went nova two minutes ago and the Earth is going to be destroyed in six minutes and twenty seconds? What if the sun went nova seven minutes and twenty seconds ago and the Earth is going to end in one minute?

Billions of people all over the world, workers and soldiers, artists and policemen, children, old crones and gaffers, scientists and actors and politicians, astronomers who would never know that they had become part of a great astronomical event, spacemen who would never leave the Earth, criminals and beatniks and alcoholics and dope fiends and salesmen and mechanics and plumbers and sailors and deep sea divers and longshoremen and distillery workers, Chinese and Brazilians and Poles and Egyptians, white and yellow and black, the mighty and the humble, the wealthy and the penniless, all gone, gone, a glowing cinder for a moment and then even that gone into the raging, seething sun.

Salzman began to count. From one to ten, twenty, thirty . . . When he reached sixty he ticked off a number on a second imaginary counter in his brain, then went back to one.

Sixty again, reset the other counter to two, then start still again. When the second counter reached eight he went back to one once more, but this time counted only to twenty. Now the opposite face of the Earth was feeling the heat and seeing the light of the radiation that had left the sun when he started to count. He felt that if the sun had not by now gone nova the Earth was safe for an indefinite time.

Mr. Salzman, by counting off the 500 seconds it took radiation to travel from the sun to the Earth, felt that he had found a way to keep the sun from going nova. Any time now, that he felt the Earth to be in danger of destruction by the sun, he need only to begin that eight minute and twenty second countdown and the Earth would be safe.

He reached over and flushed the toilet. He had stopped urinating. He closed the fly of his pajama bottoms, rinsed his hands and dried them on a chenille towel hanging beside the sink, turned off the bathroom light and returned to the bedroom.

As he entered the bedroom he heard the continued steady breathing of the sleeping Mrs. Salzman. He decided that it would be unfair to awaken her now, and aside from this he felt somewhat shaken and quite tired.

Mr. Salzman climbed into his bed and stretched once, relaxing and preparing himself to sleep once again. Before he dropped off into slumber he felt a slight stirring in his bowels, but felt that he would wait until morning before eliminating the waste product of the previous evening's dinner.

It seems that every mystery writer in the world has had a crack at pastiching Sherlock Holmes. I've done it myself more than once. But anthologist and Holmesian scholar Marvin Kaye had a new twist to offer when he invited submissions for The Resurrected Holmes (1996).

Each author would write a Holmes story not in his own voice nor in imitation of Holmes' associate and amanuensis, Dr. Watson — but in the persona and voice of another author, attempting to write in Watson's voice about Holmes. I wound up writing "The Adventure of the Boulevard Assassin (or, On the Road)," by "Jack Kerouac."

Marvin was dubious about the story but his editor, Keith Kahla, was highly enthusiastic, as were a great many critics. Kerouac's biographer, Barry Miles, loved the story and wrote a glowing letter about it. Then there was the reviewer who stated that she found the pastiche of Kerouac brilliant, and absolutely dead-on accurate, and she hated Kerouac.

And where did that leave me?

# The Adventures of the Boulevard Assassin

IT WAS JUST ANOTHER FOGGY EVENING IN BAKER Street and Holmes and I were sitting in front of the fire and I was wondering if Mrs. Hudson had gone to bed yet because I was hungry and I would have loved to have a bite to eat, maybe an Austrian cream torte mit schlagg or possibly some of Mrs. Hudson's famous kippers and cream, I love her kippers and cream even though Holmes thinks they're suitable only for breakfast which is, I suppose, the proper way to eat kippers and cream or cream and kippers or creamed kippers or kippered cream but that was just something to think about, the fire was snapping and crackling away on the hearth beneath the slipper filled with shag tobacco and the bullet-holes spelling out Victoria Regina Queen of the United Kingdom of England Scotland and Wales Empress of India and the Dominions beyond the Seas Defender of the Faith and all the rest of our Glorious Monarch's titles when there was a knock at the door.

Who could be calling at Baker Street at this hour of the night and who was knocking to announce a visitor, I wondered, at a time when respectable husbands were happily home in the bosoms of their families? Billy the buttons, perhaps, or maybe it was Mrs. Hudson herself having read my mind and climbed the stairs to

161

221B to offer Holmes and myself a spot of tea, a crumpet, a kipper, a cake, a trifle, a bit of cheese, a fish, a wish.

It was Mrs. Hudson indeed, stout, gray, motherly. I wondered about her, wondered who Mr. Hudson had been, thought of her as a young girl, a bride, a schoolgirl, a child, imagining her the pride of some mother's eye long ago in Surrey or in Hampshire, in Scotland perhaps because Mrs. Hudson did speak with a distinct burr in her voice, seeing this tiny girl playing with a hoop or a ball or a doll, basking in the sunlight of a summer's afternoon, looking after a little brother or sister or looked after by a sibling who was older, larger, I hoped she wasn't bullied by a larger and older or older and larger or even younger and larger or older and not larger, sister or brother or uncle or aunt, maybe Mrs. Hudson's mother had a sister of her own—Watson! Watson, would you be so kind as to answer the door, can't you see that I am occupied.

Holmes was occupied the way he was too often occupied, I'd watched him, at first with the shame of a voyeur and he with the shame of a man caught in a shameful and solitary act, a solitary vice, but then after a while I found myself enjoying it, enjoying watching him, and I think he enjoyed being watched, the voyeur and the subject of his voyeurism sharing a mutual guilty pleasure, a mutual guilty secret, a secret pleasure and a pleasant secret, Holmes would roll up one sleeve and tie off a vein with a cloth tourniquet wound round a *toki* or Maori war-adz that I thought he must have taken from an assassin, a swarthy thug, a bad man, a killer, a killer, a killerkillerkillerkillerkiller somehow in the course of one of his famous investigations or maybe this would be an inspector here from Scotland Yard, someone come to ask the great Holmes to assist the official police in cracking one of the cases he so often cracked for them when they were unable to crack them themselves, thought they were uncrackable, unsolvable, impossible, riddles tied within riddles within puzzles, conundrums, teasers, gordian knots for the human brain, that's what the inspectors brought to Holmes and he never turned them away, he said he would, Holmes did, said he'd never take a case that didn't challenge him, interest him, pique his curiosity, anything to keep him from sticking needles in his arm, from tying off a vein with a tourniquet and piercing his own flesh with the sterile hypodermic lest he pick up some dread bacterium and shooting into his vein, into his arm so it would enter his bloodstream, would reach his heart, the mighty heart of Holmes that beat so in Baker Street you could hear it from Dover to Land's End I thought, to St. John O'Groats, to the Queen's farthest-flung garrisons in the four corners of the world and I laid down my paper, my *Evening Review and Advertiser* on top of a pile with the *Daily Express,* the *Morning Standard,* the *Illustrated London and World Dispatch* in which I had been comparing and collating the reports of a series of horrendous murders in the section of Whitechapel known as the Boulevard of Lost Hope in which a fiend apparently chopped fallen young women to bits with a heavy, sharpened stone. The murders had indeed horrified me and I was only able to perform my duty of clipping and collating reports relating each gory detail, each drop of blood, each horrendous wound, each staring eye, each ghastly face, each indescribable atrocity by reading adjacent titbits, stories about oddities and quiddities such as the search throughout the borough for a missing student reputed to be the sister of a foreign personage of note attending classes incognito in London preparing herself for a place upon the stage in her native land or possibly planning to run away from home and join a traveling circus the news-writer having dubbed the missing female the Mad Mime of Mayfair I found myself chuckling.

I crossed to the door, stepping carefully around Holmes, avoiding the hem of his mouse-gray brown purple dressing gown and opened the door wondering whether I should behold the little sallow rat-faced Lestrade or the brilliant Tobias Gregson, what's Gregson doing taking the Queen's shilling when he could make a fortune on his own but then it isn't my business to ask, he'll do what he wants, and instead of either of them entering the sitting room who should appear but a woman.

A woman!

Mrs. Hudson wanted to show me up but I showed myself up. Why, what is it you want? I want to hire a detective. I asked if there was any particular detective she wanted to hire, Mr. Holmes was doubtless the most successful and sought after private inquiry agent in all of London, perhaps in all of Her Majesty's Realm, but I was no mean gatherer of clues and devisor of theories myself, I'd solved several cases, I was the envy of Harley Street with my big house that I didn't even live in most of the time because I was more amused to spend my time in the company of my longtime friend Mr. Sherlock Holmes. Are you a detective, sir?

She stepped across the sill into our room. Holmes had filled his hypodermic syringe to the limit and stood gazing intently at it, holding it up to the gaslight and studying its appearance he pressed upward on the plunger and the finest of sprays of liquid arched upward between myself and the gaslight making a tiny, glittering, temporary rainbow in the air and landed against the pane and ran down it like a tiny rivulet of rainwater only this liquid was on the inside of the glass pane not the outside, it mattered not no not at all no not not not at no not at all that the light refracting through the clear liquid came from the gas lamp outside our window in Baker Street.

The woman reached a hand forward clutching for support and I caught her in my arms and lowered her ever so carefully but ever so slowly but ever so ever so carefully onto the sofa, taking note inadvertently, unavoidably, of her charming perfume, her softly coifed hair, her delicate figure, the tiny hand softened by heredity but hardened and roughened by unwonted labor, how could this woman have been treated so, what monster of a father or husband into whose care her welfare had been placed, fail to give her the treatment, the tender, sweet treatment that such a lovely creature must surely warrant. Oh thank you sir I fear I grew faint for a moment. Oh madam it was my privilege to be of assistance. Oh sir if you would be so kind as to assist me to the horsehair sofa which I perceive. Oh madam of course do lean on my shoulder do take my arm oh do place your lovely little thin graceful delightful hand in mine. Oh sir. Oh madam.

Holmes stood louring over us as I helped our new guest to the sofa and assisted her in arranging herself upon it. I was relieved to see that he had returned the hypodermic syringe to its velvet-lined wooden case with the polished brass hinges and fittings, polished, burnished, cleaned and rendered sparkling by Mrs. Hudson and by the upstairs maids she sent to keep order in the messy apartment that I had the privilege of sharing with Sherlock Holmes when I found it convenient to stay in Baker Street. Sometimes Holmes invited me, sometimes I invited myself, there was nothing to it, no way to tell when I was going to stay in Baker Street so I kept a set of clothes in the spare bedroom, actually several sets of clothes, actually the apartment was mine to start with and Holmes moved in because I needed a roommate to help me pay the rent because I was just out of the army, just home from Afghanistan, I had no London practice to provide me with funds, I ached from a Jezail bullet in my shoulder or was it my leg, sometimes it all seems so long ago and so far away, yesterday Afghanistan, today London, sometimes a man tries to find his way in the world, tries to earn a living and perform a useful service and find his place, and he comes up short of Sterling and has to take on a roommate and through such happenstance is formed a friendship which has been the bright spot of my life, ah, Holmes, the best and wisest of men but what a maniac, and if the fiend

Moriarty or his second Sebastian Moran doesn't get Holmes then
the cocaine surely will.

Holmes's older brother Mycroft has even tried to talk him out
of his addiction. I've seen them together, heard them converse, it
was like hearing gods converse, the wisdom and intellect of the
one played against the intellect and wisdom of the other until a
mere mortal witnessing the exchange was lost in awe and admiration not to say puzzlement over what in the world these two
towering minds could have to say to each other, things like, did
I hear it correctly, Father always liked you better because you
were older, you used to go fishing with him and he taught you to
play baccarat and took you to the casinos and I always had to stay
home and it wasn't fair it wasn't fair it wasn't fair and Mother
always loved you more because you were her youngest and you
were her baby and she would give you hugs and kisses and
sweetmeats and send me off with Father to go stupid fishing I
hate fishing No you don't you always said you loved fishing Well
I didn't so there I hated it I only pretended to like it because I
knew it made you mad you scrawny little rat Why you big fat
sausage You dopey crybaby You big mean bully I hate you I hate
you Well I hate you more Well I've hated you longer . . .

Our client sat reclining against the back of the horsehair sofa.
I offered her a glass of sherry and she accepted it, took the small
glass in her little, graceful hand, I saw she had a reticule with her
and she opened it and took a handkerchief from it and touched
it to her brow and to the corner of her mouth, her tiny, sweet-
looking mouth, I wondered what it would be like to press my lips
to those tiny, sweet lips of our guest, what that mouth would taste
like, if it would taste of sherry but she took a tiny sip of the sherry
and placed the glass on the table beside the couch and said, Mr.
Sherlock Holmes will you help me, and Holmes said, Madam, you
may speak freely in front of my associate Dr. Watson I trust him
in all things he is my strong right arm and amanuensis when the
Jezail bullet in his wrist doesn't hurt him so much he cannot hold
a pen isn't that so, Watson old man?

I said, Holmes, that is so. Ever since Maiwand, where the Fifth
Northumberland Fusiliers faced the fierce Afghan fighters and I,
as a medical officer and therefore a recognized noncombatant was
supposedly immune to enemy fire, nonetheless a savage pointed
his long single-shot Snyder-Enfield rifle at me even as I stood over
a wounded man, surgical instruments in hand, and fired point-
blank time stood still for me I felt that I could see the puff of
smoke emerge from the muzzle of the rifle and see the bullet

emerge, see its .577-calibre ogival cylinder moving through the thin Afghan air toward me and feel it crash into my shoulder or was it my leg and I fell slowly, toppling, dropping, twisting, sinking toward the floor, the ground, the hard-packed, sun-baked Asiatic earth and Watson, Holmes said, are you well, and I awakened in hospital in Peshawar staring up into the eyes of a lovely young nurse who placed her cool, tiny hand on my hot, fevered brow and, Watson, Holmes said, if you do not mind fetching your notebook and writing instrument, old man, so as to record the information to be provided by our client I think you will find the case one well worth your attention.

Was he turning this case over to me or was Holmes merely requesting my assistance in the capacity of amanuensis so that he or I might later consult my notes? Well, no matter, for to serve the west and bisest of men was itself sufficient privilege for the humble likes of John H. Watson, Doctor of Medicine, London University, class of 1878 anno Domini, former surgeon in the service of the Crown and Empire the woman was weeping she had retained the handkerchief which she had removed from her reticule and dabbed now daintily, daintily dabbing, dabbing, dabbing daintily dabbing at her eyes from which flowed copious freshets of tiny tears that caught the light, the gentle gaslight that illuminated our chambers in Baker Street and reflected it like prisms, ah, how could anyone, Watson, I say old man, if you don't mind, really, said Holmes and I fetched my notepad, bound as it was in Moroccan leather and furnished with the finest of vellum sheets, and my ormolu filigree gold-crusted pen and placed the book upon my knee which had been shattered by the Jezail bullet and held the pen above the vellum and looked attentively at the bise and westest of men and our client with her tiny lovely hands and the teardrops shimmering on the edges of her gracefully curved eyelashes and I listened to her tale and wrote my notes she had been abandoned she had married for love not money and her husband a man of good character but untidy ways and unpredictable actions had left her bed and board and she said that she wanted him back, she had no desire to seek vengeance for she truly loved him and believed that he truly loved her but was concerned that some slimmer waist or some more gracefully curved ankle had won his affection away from her and she was to go through the rest of her days neither spinster nor wife nor widow but in some unhappy unholy uncertain undefined condition Oh, Mr. Holmes, I know you can find my husband for me, I know you by your reputation and by your works and by the wonderful reports of them which Dr. Watson has written and which have been published in *The Strand* magazine and I know you could simply reach out your hand and find my husband for me but would he know me, would he care to return to me, is he lost to me and I to all hope of happiness in this mortal sphere, Mr. Holmes? And how can I possibly obtain your services if only I could have enough cents to hire you in my behalf.

The wooze and bizzest of men patted her on the hand and said not to worry, he would take her case, he would find her husband, he would return the bounder to her side for all that one who would abandon such as she was surely undeserving of her favor and companionship and to have no fear for lack of a fee with which to pay for his services for surely there were other cases more lucrative than this and with greater impact on world affairs but no less deserving of his interest and attention and she was to go to her home, to return to the scene of her erstwhile domestic bliss such as it had been for as long as it had lasted and Holmes would tend to all and she believed him and rose and he saw her to the door, to the street. I watched from the window as he placed her in the second or third cab that pulled to the kerb, maybe the fourth or fifth, tipped his hat, sent off the driver bearing his precious cargo and turning, I swear Holmes winked at me through the chilled fog and its glowing gaslights and returned to our abode.

Well, Watson, what do you think, he asked. You have observed my methods long enough, have you learned to apply them, did you observe, did you learn anything about our client? I said I had, and in fact I was able to reach out to the horsehair sofa where she had placed her tiny graceful charming sweet adorable lovely beautiful derriere but moments before and pluck from between the cushions a wisp of white linen trimmed in lace and hold it between myself and Holmes observing it carefully in the gaslight, turning it carefully in my hand whilst I sensed Holmes the yeast and booster of men observing me with similar care.

Well, Watson, what do you think, he asked. What have you learned from the lady and that handkerchief which seems to hold such interest for you?

I raised the scrap of cloth to my nasal organ and inhaled, savoring the suggestive aroma left behind by the erstwhile and presumably future owner of the handkerchief. Holmes old chap I said you think me a dull fellow I know and I am well prepared to accept your judgment of me as much as it hurts, yea, though it be more painful even than this Jezail bullet in my leg or is it my shoulder as long as you grant me the pleasure of your company but for once you are wrong, dead wrong, completely totally altogether yes wrong yes yes wrong wrong yes yes yes wrong wrong wrong Holmes.

Really Watson Holmes said please do go on.

The owner of the handkerchief is obviously an American I said you don't need to ask me why I say that I'll tell you and a woman of literary taste and discernment as well for look you here, Holmes, I said to him, holding the woman's handkerchief for him to see, Do you not perceive the letters W.W. stitched prominently near the edge of the handkerchief obviously our visitor is a great admirer of the American author Mr. Edgar Allan Poe, I would have said more but Sherlock Holmes interrupted me by inquiring, My dear Watson, what ever gave you that idea, and I responded that the letters W.W. must refer to Mr. Poe's famous story and its eponymous protagonist William Wilson.

To this the wiz and booziest of men nodded his head comprehendingly. So our guest carries a kerchief embroidered with the initials of her fictional ideal, is that what you're telling me Watson? Yes that is precisely what I am telling you Holmes. And is she seeking this Wilson Watson Holmes asked. No she is not she must know the difference between a fictitious and an actual personage she is searching for the creator of William Wilson Poe. Ah says Holmes I see and where do you think she will find this Poe. If she traveled from America to England in search of her ideal and has now hired you to locate him for her then surely she must believe him to be in England says I.

Really? Holmes asks. And what about her husband, did the lady not enlist my services in the search for her inconstant spouse. An obvious subterfuge says I. But my dear Watson says Holmes Poe is dead has been dead for many years has been dead for longer than our visitor has been alive, Oh really, says I to Holmes, Oh really, says Holmes to me, Then why does she carry a William Wilson handkerchief and whom is she looking for Holmes? All in good time says he all in good time and retiring to his dressing room announces that he is going to prepare himself for a party in Belgravia in honor of a certain visiting potentate from a nation in the East whose location makes its ruler's good will critical to the welfare of the Empire and it would be wise of me to do the same. So I do.

Holmes and I engage the seventh or possibly eighth or ninth or tenth cab awaiting at the kerb in Baker Street and Holmes placing his hat in inverted position upon his lap and his gloves in his hat and his stick across his gloves so that its tip strikes me repeatedly and uncomfortably in the ribs just below my old wound instructs the cabby to proceed to the home of the noble personage staging the gala in behalf of the visiting potentate by way of Whitechapel and the Boulevard of Lost Hope. That's way out of our way Mister the cabby argues but Holmes the boo and wheeziest of men whacks the cabby across the back with his stick and says do as you're told man who do you think you are which makes me feel better because whilst Holmes is whacking the cabby with his stick he isn't poking me with it in my old Jezail wound which is damned painful let me tell you when he does it.

Here is Whitechapel and here are its music halls and here are its fallen women and here are its depraved noblemen out for an evening in their evening clothes plumbing the lower depths of society and here are the drabs and here are the poor gin-besotted hags and here is Jack the Ripper and here are Dr. Jeckyll and Mr. Hyde and Holmes raps on the roof of the cab with his stick and the cabby opens the hatch pokes his head in and Holmes tells him to pull up and he does and Holmes tells him that we are going to step out of the cab for a time and he is to wait for us and he bows and scrapes, tips his hat, pulls his forelock, makes a leg, makes two or three legs, mumbles something, blows his nose, wipes his eyes on his sleeve, and agrees to do anything that the governor wants.

Holmes and I next found ourselves inside a music hall. Who should be performing there but the famous Gertrude Kaye, Queen of Musical Comedy, dressed in harlequin garb, delivering sweet songs, "White Wings," "Always Take Mother's Advice," "The Sea Hath Its Pearls." Next Fred Westcott does his acrobatic act, twisting himself into impossible positions, swinging over the audience on a trapeze, lifting a bottle of champagne from the table of a party of swells and depositing it upon that of a Whitechapel drab and her *patron du nuit*. Holmes drinks a few glasses of gin and vermouth, a vile mixture whose appeal utterly escapes me and says Come Watson we must be going which we do.

Outside the music hall we pass a form lying in the gutter, its head crushed as if by blows of a sharpened stone. Near our cab I espy a familiar female figure and exclaim Mrs. Hudson what are you doing here and she turns as if distracted, hiding something behind her skirts and Holmes rushes forward, knocking me gently onto the swill-covered cobblestones, says Mrs. Hudson what are you doing here never mind you ought not to be out in a section such as this on a night such as this I will send you home in my cab and he raps the cabby upside the head with his stick and says Take Mrs. Hudson to her home at once and return here for me and the cabby falling over himself fawning in gratitude ushers Mrs. Hudson into the cab and whips up his team and clop-clop-clop-clop-cloppity-clops away to Baker Street.

Whilst we wait for the cab to return Holmes asks me if I noticed anything peculiar about Mrs. Hudson or about the form we saw lying in the street and I say, Well no actually Holmes I did not but if you should care to enlighten me but he says Never you mind Watson all will be well.

Which I believe.

Whilst waiting for the cab to return Holmes and I smoke our pipes and discuss the affairs of the day. He asks if I have enjoyed any further thoughts concerning our former female visitor and I tell him that I remain convinced that she is an admirer of Mr. Poe's and Holmes shakes his head smiling ruefully and says Ah Watson Watson what would we do without you well enjoy the party in Belgravia and we shall converse afterwards.

The party took place in a magnificent Georgian house in Belgravia 'twixt box hedges and a stand of copper beeches. As Holmes and I entered the hall our hats and sticks were taken by liveried servants and we were escorted into the grand ballroom of the mansion. Men in white tie and tails conversed with ladies in daring décolletage whilst properly attired maids and butlers circulated graven trays of refreshments from which one was invited to sample. An orchestra, imported for the occasion from Vienna, performed Herr Millnöcker's new operetta, *Der Bettelstudent*.

It was obvious to the trained observer's keen eye, upon which I pride myself, that a number of qualified undercover men from Scotland Yard were posted throughout the establishment, passing themselves off to the best of their ability as partygoers whilst maintaining a close watch on the guest of honor who, I learned through a series of discreet inquiries beginning with a serving maid as I gently caressed her charmingly accoutered derrière whilst gratefully accepting a glass of champagne from the silver tray upon which she proffered it, was none other than a Kashmiri rajah who, at the behest of Her Majesty's Foreign Office and with secure promises of backing from the Crown and the Imperial Fusiliers, was prepared to lay claim in behalf of himself and his Empress upon Afghanistan.

My wound throbbed with pride!

I had hardly had time to absorb this astonishing announcement when there came a horrid crash from the far end of the ballroom and I whirled to see the stained glass windows there shatter and fall to the floor in a million pieces, causing a distressing

tear in the scarlet uniform jacket of a brigadier of my slight acquaintance, causing his lady to drop her champagne glass and
incidentally killing several of the Viennese musicians, two foot-
men, a butler and a group of maids.

A gaudily clad figure swung through the air above the heads
of the assembled ladies and gentlemen. As he passed above the
guest of honor the interloper reached down and pulled the rajah's
massive, jewel-encrusted turban from his head, revealing his
naked forehead and a streak of pale skin and blond hair. The rajah
was no rajah at all! I recognized him at once and exclaimed, "Von
Trepow! The famous Prussian intelligence agent and impersona-
tion artist!"

A crew of Scotland Yard men had him by the elbows now, and
the spy and impostor was cursing them in his barbaric native
tongue as he was dragged off to face interrogation and possible
trial by Her Majesty's courts. At the same time a lovely young
woman who had stood near the terrifying encounter raised a
gloved hand to her brow, turned in a slow spiraling swoon, and
wound up in my arms.

Even as this amazing series of events transpired there was
another crash as the jewel thief swung himself—or herself, for the
shapely lovely graceful attractive provocative adorable little form
of the miscreant made manifest her membership in the gentler
gender—through the decorative windows at the opposite end of
the great ballroom and disappeared from the sight of all bearing
the false rajah's turban with its real jewels with her.

I say I said what is this all about and then I looked closely into
the face of the woman whom I had caught not the jewel thief who
might after all be none other than the very Mad Mime of Mayfair
of whose exploits I had been reading but hours before and realized
that I was looking at our visitor of the same day, the woman who
had engaged Sherlock Holmes to find her inconstant spouse. Her
limpid eyelids fluttered, she raised a tiny lovely adorable little
hand provocatively to her forehead and whispered to me, "John,
is all well?"

Under the circumstances such undue familiarity might possibly be overlooked so I said Madam the spy is unmasked and she
said No that is not what I meant, Is all well between us? I said,
Between us, madam? She said, Do you not know me? I said, I
know only of your admiration for William Wilson. She said, What
are you talking about you boob? I said, Madam, your handkerchief
bore his insignia. She said It did not, it was an old one that I didn't
care about any more from before we were married the monogram

says *M.M.* for Mary Morston my maiden name you ox you were reading my initials upside down. But surely you are an American, I said, you said something about having enough cents to hire an investigator and cents are what they use in America if you were English you would have said shillings and she said, Dear darling dunderhead I did not say cents I said *sense,* which is clearly something that you lack but still John Hamish Watson my heart belongs to you.

Sherlock Holmes, standing nearby, sniggered up his sleeve and said See Watson now I will not have to explain things to you your wife has done it for me.

I looked at her more closely. I said Mary my darling girl I do indeed recognize you you are indeed my girl darling Mary can you ever forgive me and she said, Take me home, John, Mr. Holmes can find his own way without you and I said, Mary my darling girl you are right Sherlock it has indeed been fun but I am off now to spend the night in my own home in my own bed and Mary said coyly And with his own wife and lifted a glass of champagne which had somehow found its way into her hand to her lips and sipped at it the darling girl.

The night passed and in the morning I thought to pay a visit to my old friend Sherlock Holmes and thank him for his role in reuniting myself with my beloved bride. The hansom rattled away from 221 behind a team of smart dumb beasts and I admitted myself using my key to 221 Baker Street and climbed the stairs to 221B and softly entered the familiar flat where I had spent so many a contented hour only to discover no sign of my friend Sherlock Holmes, but in his place a tall, thin officer of the Kaiser's cavalry. He was an evil-looking fellow, his field-gray uniform pressed to perfection and glittering with polished buttons and gleaming decorations, a monocle screwed into one eye, an upturned moustache prominent on his saturnine face and a dueling scar prominent on one cheek.

Strangely enough, he was armed, not with a military sidearm of Prussian design, but with a Maori *toki.* He paced furiously before two female forms seated side by side upon the horsehair sofa.

I say I said Who the deuce are you and what are you doing here in my friend's apartment which is also in a sense my own apartment that is the apartment we have from time to time shared and where is my friend Mr. Sherlock Holmes and what in blazes is going on here why are there two Mrs. Hudsons sitting upon my sofa which is to say Holmes's sofa or our shared sofa?

The Prussian officer, a major I think or perhaps a *kapitan* why can't they wear pips on their shoulders like good English officers well never mind that's beside the point, said to me, never taking his eye from the females but out of the corner of his mouth he said Ah Watson so good of you to pay a visit I recognized your tread upon the stair of course your distinctive hesitant stride the product no doubt of that troublesome Jezail bullet in your hip or is it your toe we have a pretty puzzle here what say you Watson to the sight before your eyes?

I was flabbergasted. How in the world did this Prussian *kapitan* or major know so so much about me, how did he know about the Jezail bullet in my ankle or was it my shin for that matter how did he know I was John Watson MD I stared at him incredulously and he winked at me not an easy trick when you've got a monocle screwed into your eye and I realized that this was not a Prussian officer at all but my good friend Sherlock Holmes brilliantly disguised.

I shifted my gaze from the mock officer to the horsehair sofa. There side by side seated on the sofa sat to all the world's view two identical women two middle-aged gray-haired generously-proportioned sweet-faced women wearing identical dresses of gray homespun and button-topped shoes their hair drawn into buns at the napes of their necks their eyes twinkling merrily or perhaps I should say angrily or maybe even cleverly up at the gray-uniformed officer then darting to me then back to the officer to the weapon he held in his hands the *toki* the stone-headed war-adz of the Maori tribesmen of New Zealand What say you Watson he said again.

I was rendered speechless.

You see before you two Mrs. Hudsons, he said.

I nodded dumbly.

One of them is a menace is a murderer is a madwoman take your choice he said the other is our dear beloved Martha our housekeeper our cook our mother confessor if I may say as much and saying as much he bowed toward the two women seated side by side upon the sofa and they looked back at him now impassively which is which Watson Holmes asked.

How can this be? I stammered.

You see before you Fraulein Von Trepow Holmes said the sister of the notorious Prussian agent who was captured but yester-eve she is none other than the Mad Mime of Mayfair the jewel thief whose acrobatic appropriation of her own brother's turban led to his unmasking and as well I regret to say the notorious Boulevard Assassin Watson.

No Holmes I gasped. I thought I committed a dreadful *faux pas* by mentioning his name but he smiled at me a thin smile but a smile nonetheless as if to say Worry not old friend no harm is done — But then which of these women is our beloved Martha Hudson and which the Mad Mime and Boulevard Assassin? I exclaimed.

Aha said Holmes let us determine whether your reunion with your beloved bride — William Wilson indeed Watson you surprise me you really do you are a fortunate man indeed to have won the love of such a woman as the former Miss Mary Morston — has sharpened or dulled your mental faculties tell me Watson how would you determine the true Martha?

Mrs. Hudson I said thinking I had solved the conundrum Mrs. Hudson what is my favorite meal thinking that only the true Martha Hudson would know the answer to the question and even if the false Martha Hudson knew the answer her accented speech would give her away.

Both Mrs. Hudsons spoke I was barely able to distinguish the one from the other one of them said Why Dr. Watson of course it's my very own kippers and cream and the other said Why Dr. Watson of course it's my very own cream and kippers and both of them spoke in perfect English albeit slightly marked with a faint Scottish burr so much for the silence of the mimes Holmes I said I am baffled.

I shall perform a small test Watson Holmes said and you will tell me which is the true Martha Hudson and which the alas both mad and murderous Fraulein Von Trepow Watson and without so much as batting an eye without so much as a by your leave Holmes raised the Maori *toki* above his head as if to bring its sharpened stone down upon one or the other of the two women all the while shouting in brutal guttural German *Der Koenig und Kaiser ist ein Esel.*

One Mrs. Hudson sat stony-faced as if she had no idea that Holmes, a master linguist, had called the King of Prussia and Emperor of Germany a jackass while the other Mrs. Hudson grew red in the face, ground her teeth and glared up at Holmes. Well Watson said Holmes to me the answer is before you tell me Watson which is the true Mrs. Hudson. Why this one I said indicating the woman who had reacted to Holmes's insult to the continental monarch. No Watson said Holmes if you will be so good as to fetch a bit of rope Mrs. Hudson said Holmes to the woman I had selected as the Boulevard Assassin we shall tie up this pitiful creature the Mad Mime of Mayfair and slayer of gin-soaked drabs and hold her for the arrival of one of our famous inspectors.

No sooner had Mrs. Hudson complied with the request of the lost and wistest of men than the imposter began railing angrily at Holmes in German. By Jove Holmes you were right I exclaimed how in the world did you ever know I would have thought that the woman who reacted angrily to an insult to the Kaiser would surely be his subject while the woman who failed to react being a good British subject would have been our own Martha Hudson.

Ah Watson Watson said Holmes clapping me on the back with his free hand now that Fraulein Von Trepow was safely tied so he was able to put down the *toki* the Kaiser's spy is despite all her foibles and failings still a talented actress and was able to restrain herself utterly from reacting to my deliberately inflammatory remarks.

But Holmes said I why did the real Mrs. Hudson grow angry I didn't even know that she understood German. Holmes said Ah yes Mrs. Hudson has acquired a smattering of German through contact with the many scientists who have climbed these old stairs Watson not very much but enough to know that I had called the Kaiser a jackass a word not suitable I fear for polite discourse and further an insult to a monarch who whatever his failings and foibles is still the cousin of our own beloved Monarch and peeling away the false moustache and allowing the monocle to fall from his eye and removing the false dueling scar from his no longer Prussian cheek Holmes drew from a pocket in his Prussian colonel's uniform a revolver and added another bullet hole to the message in the mantelpiece.

*When the multi-talented Mike Resnick asked for a story to include in his* Alternate Tyrants *anthology (1997) I'd been writing mysteries for several years and had to readjust my thinking for a return to science fiction. There really is a difference in the way one looks at the world, interprets clues, constructs plots.*

*This story required an exercise in world-building, to create not an alien planet but an alternate history. What if the Roman Empire had never collapsed? What if some reform movement had swept the Western Empire, in particular, preventing the calamitous events of the Fifth Century CE, and Rome had continued its slow, methodical, orderly evolution, expanding its borders, developing its technology?*

*That's one of the classic alternate histories, contemplated as early as 1939 by the late L. Sprague de Camp in his brilliant novel* Lest Darkness Fall. *Indeed, what if the darkness had not fallen? L. Sprague de Camp was my friend for forty years, and now that he has left this planet, "Jubilee" is my personal festschrift in his honor.*

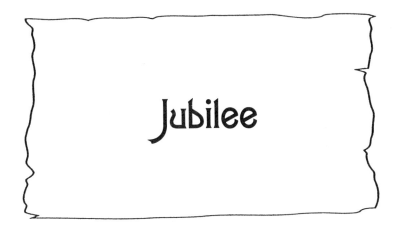

# Jubilee

EARLY AUTUMN SUNLIGHT BRIGHTENED THE KITCHEN in the modest domus on the Via Palmae. Aelius reached across the table to take Dulcis' hand. "Thank you for last night, Dulcis. I guess I was preoccupied at first. But you were very sweet. You . . ."

Before he could finish the sentence he was interrupted by the shock of Livia's cold nose against his thigh. He looked at the marsupial bitch. One of her pups had stuck its head out of her pouch and Aelius said, "Well, will you look at that. It's about time."

Dulcis rounded the table and knelt on the malachite floor. Its polished greenness retained the night's cool. This was going to be a scorcher. Sometimes the third month of the year was cool in Novum Ostia, when autumn set in early, but this year summer had been fierce and it refused to loosen its grip. The whole continent of Terra Australis seemed like a baked portion of the Jews' unleavened bread.

Livia whined and Dulcis reached up and scooped a dollop of wheat cereal and honey from Aelius' plate. She put the food into Livia's dish and the bitch trotted across the kitchen and snuffled curiously at the treat. She was still nursing two pups and her appetite, always good, was outstanding.

Aelius growled. "You're the one who's always saying not to feed her off our plates, Dulcis. We shouldn't do that, it only encourages her to beg. How many times have you told me that?" He lifted his glass and took a deep draught of freshly squeezed orange juice.

She stood behind his chair and leaned forward, her breasts pressed against his head, her face at an odd angle to his own. "You're right, my darling. As ever. But she has babies. Just look at that one. Pointed ears, and those big shiny eyes. The world is brand new to him. Let Livia have her treat."

Aelius grinned. He looked at his watch. "I'd better get a move on. Today of all days."

Dulcis kissed him on the ear, then moved away. Livia had cleaned up her treat and Dulcis scooped the remaining cereal from the pot into the bitch's dish. Livia sat on her haunches, watching Dulcis. The tiny dog disappeared back into his mother's pouch. Almost at once another miniature marsupial dog poked its head from Livia's pouch.

"There he is again," Aelius laughed.

Dulcis frowned. "No he's not. That's the girl."

"Oh, come on. You can't tell."

"Sure I can. The other one looks like a boy. This is the girl." Dulcis stroked Livia's sleek head, tugged gently at her pointed ears. She didn't try to touch the tiny head peering from Livia's pouch. Dulcis said, "What a good girl you are, Livia. What a good mommy. What beautiful babies you have."

Livia's tail thumped the malachite floor. She waited for Dulcis to step away before tucking into the second bowl of cereal and honey.

Dulcis said, "The babies don't even look alike. The boy has darker fur and he's much more aggressive. This one has to be a girl. Look—she has a beauty mark on her cheek. See, Aelius, the disk of golden fur against the black?"

Aelius shook his head. "Celadus will have my head if I'm late today of all days. Caesar Viventius himself is flying in from Terra Nipponsis to welcome the crew back from their expedition to Martes. This should be the biggest news day of the century."

"Then you're working with Celadus today?"

"I wouldn't exactly say working with him. You know, every once in a while Celadus gets on his high horse and decides to be an executive. You'd think he was a senator, not just a news broadcast editor."

Dulcis shook her head sympathetically. "Who'll you be with?"

"Celadus wants me at the caelumportis when Caesar's caelumvola touches down. I'll be reporting. And then just hours later *Isis* reaches ground. The first craft to visit another planet . . ."

"We've been going to Luna for 200 years."

"Indeed. If you consider a mere moon a planet . . ."

"By reason, Aelius, if you consider its size and . . ."

"Please, Dulcis, let's not quarrel."

"You're right, Aelius. I'm sorry. What were you saying?"

Again Aelius lifted his glass and poured the last of his orange juice down his gullet. "I'm just saying that this expedition has been titanic news. The journey itself, the landing on Martes of *Amaterasu*, the loss of the spatiumnavis, the rescue by *Isis* . . ."

"And the brave nautae who gave their lives . . ."

"All for the greater glory of Rome, my darling."

"Yes, all for the greater glory of Rome."

"Well, Caesar Callistus Viventius himself wants to be on hand to welcome the heroes back to Tellus. And who am I, a humble journalist, to speak other than words of praise, eh?"

"I just don't understand why it took 200 years after first visiting Luna, then setting up bases there, to build a spatiumnavis and travel to Martes. I mean, the navia are pretty much alike, aren't they, Aelius? You report on these things all the time. You ought to know."

Aelius smiled. "We Romans have always been timid about innovation."

"Some would say, thorough, or at most cautious, rather than timid."

"And who's to quarrel with success, eh?" Aelius took up his portfolio and headed for the door. The portfolio was marked with the double jubilee logotype in gilt and green enamel. You couldn't go anywhere without seeing the intertwined *D* and *M* that would surely provide collectible jewelry and plaques and junk dinnerware to make merchants rich for decades to come. He stopped and patted Livia on the head and was rewarded with a snuffle of her cold nose against his palm. He peered at the sunlight through the kitchen window and turned back for a light, broad-brimmed hat. His black, balding pate seemed a magnet for strong sunlight, and too much of it gave him fierce headaches.

As he stepped from the house he heard Dulcis ask once more who he was going to work with. He muttered, "Avita, you know." Indeed, Dulcis knew Avita, and Aelius knew that Dulcis did not care at all for Avita. Well, there was nothing that Aelius could do about it. Celadus was the boss, Celadus gave out the assignments, and Celadus said that Aelius and Avita were to work today's events together.

Aelius heard a dish break against the green malachite floor as he turned into the Via Palmae. He suspected that it was his favorite dish, but he did not turn back to investigate. He climbed into his little sun-powered car and headed for work.

As he guided the car along the Via Palmae he reviewed the day's plans in his mind. And he thought about Avita. She was a fine broadcaster. She had wonderful presence—the camera loved her, as the expression had it. Aelius did most of the research and writing for their reports, but Avita took an interest in the material. She didn't just mouth Aelius' words, as had some he had worked with.

His route carried him across the Via Fuligo and past a boarded-up shop front.

In a stuffy room behind the boarded-up shop, two men and a woman leaned over a table of native eucalyptus wood. All three were dressed in drab garb, without ornament. Each wore a dagger at the waist. There was little to distinguish their genders save the woman's long, stringy hair and the meager, pointed breasts that poked sharply through her coarse shirt.

Sheets of paper littered the tabletop. A pot of Aegptian-style ink had been allowed to stand open, and had dried into a black, powdery substance. A small amphora of local wine stood open near the table's edge. Despite the day's heat, a small fire burned on a clay-brick hearth and added its smoke to the room's stuffiness.

A muscular, scowling man spoke. "This is the day. This is the last time we'll go over this plan. And it's a one-time chance. If we fail today, it's all over. We're probably dead. By Mithras, they'll crucify us. Caesar Viventius will personally hammer in the nails."

"You're dramatizing, Trux. We all know this is important. Don't go acting as if you were on a stage." The speaker was the group's lone woman. She was not much taller than average, but her skeletal thinness was her dominant feature. Rather than making her appear tiny and fragile, it somehow gave her the appearance of a rickety giant, a stick figure who might reach down and clutch at her victim, throttling her prey like a vengeful phantasm.

Trux pounded a fist on the tabletop. "Dramatizing, am I, Tenua?" He pushed himself to his feet and leaned forward, looming over the others.

The second man, fleshy and dark-visaged, was sweating in the hot, airless room. Dark circles showed where perspiration had soaked his garment at armpits and chest. His belly was pressed against the eucalyptus-wood table. He reached for a heavy mug, lifted the amphora and poured himself a quantity of wine. He flashed bloodshot eyes from the looming Trux to the skeletal Tenua.

"We're in this for the money," the fat man said.

"We're in it for the people of Terra Australis and for the freedom of peoples in every land." Trux raised a hand as if he intended to strike the drinking mug from the fat man's grasp, but he held himself back. "Don't ascribe your own crass motives to others, Pinguis. There are still some idealists in this world."

Pinguis raised his drinking mug. He held it to his chin, then dipped his tongue into the dark wine like a great, fleshy cat sampling a puddle. "When the money arrives from our masters in Uwajima—"

Now Trux did strike the mug from Pinguis' hand. The mug smashed on the rough brick floor. The largest piece bounced into the fireplace. A trail of wine, like thin blood, led to the flames. "Our colleagues," Trux barked. "Our only masters are the tyrants of Italia, lording it over all the globe, pretending that all men are citizens of Rome, or can earn citizenship by serving the eagles. And we believe them. Fools believe them."

Pinguis gazed mournfully at the fragments of his smashed drinking mug. He reached across the table and wrapped fat fingers around Trux's empty mug. He filled it from the amphora and again dipped his oddly pointed tongue, catlike, into the wine. "Colleagues, masters, whatever. So long as their aurii are made of real gold. And so long as they pay up."

"They have so far, haven't they?"

"But once the deed is done, and they need us no longer, Trux? What then?"

Trux shook his head. "They will pay."

Throughout the exchange Tenua had watched in silence, a cynic's smile playing across her lips. Now she shook her head as if bemused by a pair of squabbling children. "Shall we go over the plan once more? Or shall we just sit here stifling while Caesar's caelumvola arrives from Terra Nipponsis and the spatiumnavis returns from Martes?"

The two men grumbled. Fat Pinguis, apparently satisfied that the wine was not poisoned, tilted his head back and drank deeply from his mug. A generous trickle of dark wine spilled over his chin and dripped onto his belly, adding a darker stain to the sweat-marked garment.

Trux said, "You're right, Tenua. Here, let's review this once more."

Pinguis sighed. "All right. I could do this in my sleep. But if we must, we must."

The largest sheet was a map of Nova Ostia and the surrounding countryside. The caelumportis where both Caesar Viventius' caelumvola and the spatiumnavis *Isis* would touch Roman soil this day was circled in red. The journey from Nova Ostia itself was not long. A ground vehicle could cover the distance in half an hour, easily.

"The explosives are loaded," Trux said. "If either of you have any doubts—Pinguis, Tenua—state them now. Once we cross the Pons Meretrix and head out the Via Brassica to the Pratum Grandis road and thence to the caelumportis . . ."

"The die is cast," Pinguis completed Trux's sentence.

"We have crossed the Rubicon," Tenua added.

"How apt, darling." Trux grunted an unformed word. "The first Caesar crossed the Rubicon and entered Rome. And we shall cross the Pons Meretrix, cross the River Diamantina, and it shall be our own Rubicon."

"The plan, Trux, the plan." Tenua's tone was impatient. She watched Pinguis fill his drinking mug still again and tilt it and his head simultaneously.

"The plan." Trux lifted a pen and moved it across the map. Its point scratched dryly. He cursed, dipped the pen in the inkpot and cursed more violently when he saw that the ink had dried. He looked around but saw no water to add to the dried ink. Instead he tipped the amphora and dribbled a fine stream of wine into the dried ink. He stirred the concoction with his pen, then tested it on the edge of the map and grunted with satisfaction.

Pinguis muttered, "A waste."

Trux traced the route that they would take from the shop on Via Fuligo, across the Pons Meretrix to the Pratus Grandis road and to the caelumportis. "Our friends from Uwajima will be represented at the ceremonies. Caesar wants this to be a celebration for all the world, but he wants all the world to remember that it's a Roman world and a Roman triumph."

"All right," Tenua put in. "We know that Caesar's caelumvola reaches the caelumportis an hour before noon."

"And the tyrant will have a fancy feast, as usual, before anything else." Pinguis managed a smirk.

"Of course you would think first of that," Tenua hissed.

"Squab," Pinguis said, as if he could taste the succulent bird. "Honeyed redfish. Quails' eggs. Breads and cakes. And I'll bet he's got a miniature wine cellar right there on his caelumvola."

Tenua shook her head. "Don't be a fool. He'll be served from the local stores, or from the private stock of a Nova Ostian senator."

Trux growled, "Shut up and listen to me. The spatiumnavis *Isis* is expected at the middle of the afternoon, and Caesar wants to witness its landing personally."

"Who wouldn't? It will be a great sight. There will be crowds there. I still worry about our being stalled in a jam on the road, or caught in a multitude at the caelumnavis." Tenua's voice had the odd tang of those born and raised in westernmost Terra Australis. Here in Novum Ostia she sometimes had trouble making herself understood, and had been taken more than once for some sort of outlandish barbarian.

Trux shook his head. "Not to worry." He spoke with the harsh simplicity of a native of the metropolis. He even pronounced the city's name *Novoscha*, as if it were some village in northernmost Dacia.

A knot in the burning eucalyptus wood on the hearth exploded with a violent report. Trux leaped as if prodded with a hot poker, reaching for the dagger at his waist. Scrawny Tenua lunged sideways, scrambling into a crouched position, her hands curled into claws like those of the rare marsupial tiger of Terra Australis' eastern forests. Fat Pinguis shoved against the table. His chair tilted on its legs and toppled backwards. Pinguis' weight landed atop the flimsy chair and smashed it to smithereens.

Each of the three looked at the others, then Tenua permitted herself a nervous laugh.

Trux completed his review of their plan. When Caesar's guests from Terra Nipponsis created a distraction, Pinguis and Tenua would rush toward Caesar and the nautae, freshly emerged from *Isis*. Caesar's guards were no fools. They would have remained undistracted by the Nipponsii, but would rush to halt Pinguis and Tenua. It was then that Trux himself would strike, hurling a concentrated bundle of Cathayan exploding powder at Caesar.

If Trux failed, if the others remained captive, they were armed as well with explosive bundles. They could detonate them, taking their captives with them to Hades. But Trux would not fail. He could not fail. He must not.

The assassination of the supreme tyrant would be the signal

for uprisings throughout the world. The age of Rome would be at an end. No longer would arrogant Italia dominate the globe and all its lands and seas. Peoples of every continent and country would determine their own destinies.

By Mithras, a long overdue age of gold would dawn at last.

The three plotters left their den by a rear exit, and made their way to a battered, grime-coated car. They climbed into it. Trux seated himself comfortably while Tenua took the steering yoke.

Once Rome was dismembered, Trux thought, they might very well go back to the old system of slaves, a system abandoned by Rome hundreds of years ago. It would be very pleasant, Trux thought, to own men and women. To be able to command their every action, their very lives or deaths. With the machinery that existed today, slaves were not needed. For those tasks that could not be taken over by machinery, free workers were more efficient and productive. If anything, the problem was one of finding enough jobs for the available workers, not the other way around.

All of that would change.

Tenua pulled the vehicle around the building containing the boarded-up shop and guided it through a littered alley. The morning sun blazed on the Via Fuligo. The vehicle accelerated from the mouth of the alley and turned toward the Pons Meretrix, toward the Pratus Grandis road, toward Caesar's caelumvola and the spatiumnavis *Isis* and toward the events that would change the destiny of the world.

The Via Fuligo intersected with the Via Brassica. Standing in an upstairs room, gazing into the bright morning on the Via Fuligo, Aelius watched the filthy, battered vehicle lurch by. It was headed toward the Pons Meretrix.

Aelius nodded to himself. He jammed his light straw hat onto his head and spun on his heel. "All right," he said, "let's go, Avita. Celadus is already at the 'portis, and if we don't hustle out there we'll miss the big show and he'll roast our hides for his dinner."

"You're so eloquent, Aelius." Avita was short and busty, and favored costumes that permitted taller men to see the shadowed valley between her breasts. She wore a locket there, suspended by a chain of fine electrum. The contents of the locket she refused to divulge. No man was known to have seen those contents, though many had tried.

They loaded their gear into an agency van. Heavier equipment, they knew, was already at the landing site, but they wanted to have their hand-held sight-and-sound recorders with them.

"*Isis* is returning directly from Martes, isn't she?" Avita asked.

Aelius watched her out of the corner of his eye. This was information that Avita already had. Perhaps she was going over it just to refresh her mind. "That's right."

Avita shook her head. She wore her hair longer than Dulcis. The perfect blue-black waves caught the morning sunlight like a flame. "I don't see why. I'd thought they would dock at Luna and then shuttle down. Wouldn't that be easier? And safer?"

"Politics, everything's politics. Caesar Viventius wants to be the first to welcome them. And he didn't want to go to Luna to do it. He wanted it here in Terra Australis. The double jubilee, all of that."

"Right, just remind me, why don't you?"

Aelius shook his head. He steered the van around an immense industrial freighter powered by solar panels the size of a small playing field. Beneath its belly, Aelius knew, were the heavy batteries that were charged during the day and permitted the freighter to run all night if need be. The freighter carried the double jubilee logotype on its side. The intertwined *D* and *M* worked with laurel leaves and gilt were covered with dust and grime. Even before the jubilee celebration had reached its climax, the tawdry decorations were chipping and fading away. Aelius muttered a curse.

"What was that?"

Aelius grinned. "I was just wishing that they'd ban those things from city streets. Make 'em unload in the suburbs, or at least get in and out of town at night. No matter."

"Did you ever wonder what the world would be like if the plot had succeeded?"

Startled, Aelius gaped at Avita, then looked back just in time to avoid crashing into the back of a grimy, battered conveyance containing a woman and two men. They had reached the Pons Meretrix and the battered vehicle had stalled in the middle of the arching span.

Aelius jumped out of the van and ran to the stalled passenger conveyance. The driver was a tall woman, almost skeletally gaunt. Beside her sat a powerfully built, square-jawed individual. A fat blob sprawled behind them.

"What's the matter?" Aelius demanded. "There ought to be a legionary here to keep traffic moving. Doesn't anybody do anything right in this town any more?"

The gaunt woman said, "The car's been sluggish all morning. Now it's stopped altogether." Aelius could hear the vehicle's motor humming feebly. Actually it sounded more like a moan.

"Look at this, look at your panel! For Jupiter's sake, when did you last clean the thing off?"

The man seated beside the driver muttered something Aelius couldn't make out. The man clambered from the car and peered at the panel. "Hades' name, you're right. Just a moment." He opened a compartment and produced an old shirt. He rubbed it across the solar panel. Again, again.

Aelius could hear the car's motor hum more steadily.

"Thank you, stranger." The square-jawed man climbed back into the car and the gaunt woman pulled it away.

Aelius muttered and climbed back into the van. Avita laughed. The van surged forward. Behind them, a row of vehicles had halted and their drivers had set up a clamor of complaint. The line now moved across the Pons Meretrix. Ahead, Aelius could see the ramp that carried vehicles from the Via Brassica onto the caelumportis road.

Avita said, "You never answered my question."

"What question was that?"

"If the plot had succeeded. If Marcus Brutus and Gaius Cassius and the rest had not been such incompetents. Or if Caesar Julius hadn't been smart enough to plant a spy among them and have the plot smashed before it could get into play."

Aelius shook his head. "Historians and fantasizers have wondered about that for a thousand years, haven't they?"

"But what do you think, Aelius? What do *you* think?" she repeated. She laid her hand on his thigh, emphasizing her question. Maybe it was just the bright sun warming them both through the van's glass, but Avita's hand felt red hot on Aelius' leg. Red hot, and yet not unpleasant.

He said, "I don't think history would have been much different and I don't think the world would be much different today. History is moved by great forces. Individual men and women are merely the instruments of destiny. If one tool is broken or lost, the Fates merely pick up another to do their work."

Avita shook her head. Her tresses swung with the motion. "I'm not so sure, Aelius. I think if the first Caesar had died, Rome would have followed a different course."

Aelius frowned. "How so?"

"I don't know for sure. I think the Republic would have failed. I think some strongman would have seized the reins of state, made himself the master of Rome."

"Maybe so." The van was on the caelumportis road now. Legionaries lined the road, their metal accouterments polished so they reflected the sunlight like beacons, the variously colored crests on their glittering ceremonial helmets marking their units and rank.

"Maybe so," Aelius continued. "But even so, what if that had come about? Rome was already the greatest power in the world. Really the only power that towered above all others. Carthage was long gone. Egypt, Syria, Judaea were all vassals of Rome. The Cathayans might have proved rivals of Rome, but when our nations had their encounter the Cathayans proved accommodating. And of course the people of the western continents were more than willing to make peace with our ancestors."

Avita snorted. "What do you mean, our ancestors? Does this look like the skin of an Italian?" She held her hand before Aelius' face. He saw the dark, sleek skin of one descended from the original inhabitants of Terra Australis.

"You don't have to be Italian to be Roman," Aelius said. "That's much of Rome's greatness."

Avita said, "Right. And when was the last time we had a Caesar who wasn't Italian?"

"It will come. It will come."

"Terra Australis has been a Roman province for 500 years. Most of us have been citizens for centuries. For what that may be worth."

"History will have its own way," Aelius asserted. The traffic ahead was growing denser. In the distance he could see the buildings of Pratum Grandis where the caelumportis had been built more than a century earlier. Even they were decorated with the grant double jubilee logotype.

Maybe Avita was tired of the subject, for she changed it. "What do you think the natae found on Martes? The government's been tight-lipped about it. Even the likes of us who always know everything first . . ." She left her sentence hanging between them.

Aelius shook his head. "I'll tell you one thing they didn't find, and that was Etruscans." He laughed scornfully at the notion that some of the wilder journalists of Novum Ostia had kicked around.

"Don't laugh, Aelius."

"You don't take that guff seriously, do you?"

"Well, I just don't know. The Etruscans went *somewhere*. Unless you think they went to Atlantis."

"Oh, please." Aelius snorted. "One silly legend on top of another."

"Well, what do you think, then?"

"I'm sure we'll find out."

But Avita wasn't quite ready to let go of the subject. "Something got *Amaterasu*. Whatever you think of Rome and Italia, Roman engineering is reliable."

"Sure. That's why that car stalled in front of us on the Pons Meretrix."

"You saw how they got started again, Aelius."

"And you think Etruscans destroyed *Amaterasu* but let *Isis* land and rescue the survivors and return safely to Tellus. That makes a lot of sense."

There was a glint high against the dazzling blue of morning. Aelius and Avita both saw it. Avita asked, "Do you think that's Caesar Viventius' caelumvola, coming in from Terra Nipponsis?"

Aelius shook his head. "Might be. Might even be *Isis* herself. She has to circle Tellus several times, slowing all the while, before she can land."

From the cabin of *Isis*, Terra Australis looked like a great sandy map, with reddish-gray outcroppings of mountain ranges, green forests in the east and glittering blue lakes and rivers. Beyond the greatest of Roman provinces the great western ocean spread in silvery splendor.

Lucius, Navicularis, stood with one hand against the metallic bulkhead, the other to his chin in characteristic pose. He had started the voyage four years before, launching with his crew from Luna. *Isis* had been constructed there, as had her sister spatium-navis, *Amaterasu*. Lucius had been clean-shaven then. Now he sported a reddish beard like those his ancestors had worn in Terra Occidens.

And now *Amaterasu* lay on the sandy, rock-strewn surface of another world, while *Isis* struggled to return, not to her place of birth on Luna but to the home planet Tellus. The engineers had calculated that a landing on Tellus was possible, but only at the hands of the greatest of naviculari.

Lucius turned to address his three chief officers. Sabbina, Gubernatrix; Septimus, Machinator; Drusilla, Nunciatrix. "Dear friends, you have come through Hades with me." He reached to clasp the hands of each in turn. "Now we face our final test." He turned his back to them and gazed through *Isis*' glass once again.

A junior gubernator sat at the controls. Junior at the beginning of our great adventure, Lucius thought. After four years and the greatest voyage in the history of humankind, Antoninus was far from junior, save in comparison to Sabbina.

"Sabbina," Lucius asked, "have you full confidence in the course you have plotted for us?"

The gubernatrix smiled wryly. "The mechanical computator has spoken, O Navicularis. The holy oracle says that the odds are in our favor."

"And the state of the navis itself, Septimus?"

"She'll not fly to pieces before we touch solum. After that, I imagine that Isis will wind up in a museum. I wouldn't want to try to fly her again, but she'll get us to Pratum Grandis all right." He paused. "If we're lucky."

Lucius made a low, inarticulate sound. Septimus' assurance was actually greater than he'd hoped for. "And you, Drusilla. You've been speaking with Novum Ostia?"

Drusilla said, "Caesar Viventius himself will welcome us back to Tellus."

Lucius smiled. "Of course."

"Of course, Navicularis. I suppose they're planning a hero's welcome for us all. A triumph in the grand old fashion."

Drusilla, her skin the burnished copper hue and her neatly braided hair the black of her own ancestors, nodded.

"All right." Lucius inhaled deeply, pressed the heels of his hands to his eyes and motioned Antoninus from the spatiumnavis' controls. Isis had crossed Tellus' terminator into darkness. Beneath her electrum and diorite coated hull province after province flashed by in blackness. The great cities of Tellus had illuminated their buildings and roadways and open air stadia, knowing that Isis was to pass overhead.

This was the welcome home of a planet whose dreams and prayers had ridden into the ocean of space with the navia Isis and Amaterasu, whose tears had been shed at the loss of Amaterasu, whose masses had thrilled at word of the rescue of Amaterasu's survivors, who waited now with bated breath to receive the men and women who had blazed their trail through the universe and returned to tell the tale.

Lucius' sure hands needed no testing to get the feel of Isis' controls. He was no remote commander. He had handled the spatiumnavis through her most difficult maneuvers, including the landing on Martes' mossy plain after the crash of Amaterasu and her takeoff and escape after the attack of the barbarians who had already slaughtered most of Amaterasu's brave nautae.

Maybe it was Rome's success that had led to those nautae's deaths. None on Tellus challenged a Roman citizen. Oh, there was the occasional robbery late at night when some unwary celebrant left a tavern reeling and defenseless. And of course there were the gladiatorial contests where outlandishly costumed and vaingloriously titled performers mocked the once serious combat of swordsmen and netmen.

But the majesty of Rome was respected everywhere. The notion that a Roman navis—spatiumnavis, he reminded himself —could be attacked by a gang of howling thugs . . . It was as much shocking as offensive.

"Machinator Septimus, the engines seem a trifle sluggish. Are you sure we have full power and function?"

Septimus studied his own console. "We are running on very lean fuel, Navicularis. There's none to spare. If I enrich the mixture we may not have enough to land safely."

Lucius nodded. Through *Isis'* glass he could see the spatiumnavis' engine nacelles, left and right, mounted on pylons beyond the ship's main edificium. Glittering with polish and enameled proudly with the eagles of Rome four years ago, the nacelles were now pitted with meteorites, scarred by *Isis'* passage through even the thin atmosphere of Martes, and, most shameful of all, gouged by the rocks and spears of the savages of an alien planet.

"We'll do what we must, then." Lucius shot a glance at Drusilla. "Nunciatrix, what is the state of our passengers?"

"As well as can be expected. Aside from the two we lost in passage, all still survive."

"Still in shock?"

"Resting, Navicularis."

Lucius smiled. The Greeks had contributed much to Roman culture, even to the language of the world state. One of Lucius' favorite words came from the Greek. *Euphemism.* He nodded, gazed downward. *Isis* screamed low over the western ocean. Terra Australis appeared on the horizon. It was afternoon in Novum Ostia. He made a conscious effort to relax, closing his eyes for a brief moment and rolling his shoulders to loosen muscles. He inhaled the ship's stale atmosphere, anticipating with pleasure the fresh, clean air of Tellus.

He caught a glint of the glassed towers of the Pratum Grandis and smiled in anticipation.

Avita finished her description of Caesar Viventius' arrival at Pratum Grandis and wiped her brow with a light cloth. Aelius never ceased to be amazed at her ability to look cool and elegant in the hot sunlight, blustery wind, or moments of plain or fancy stress.

Maybe that was the difference between talent and the rest of us, he though. We can write, we can direct, we can make the pictures and capture the sounds and deliver them to millions of Roman citizens and subjects all over the world. But we're not talent. That was a term reserved for people like Avita.

Caesar Viventius had made his expected speech to the assembled purveyors of information to the people of Tellus. Celadus had supervised his minions, Aelius and Avita among them, jostling for position and angles with the gatherers and disseminators of rival organizations, and he seemed pleased with Aelius' and Avita's performances.

Now Caesar Viventius and his party mounted the ceremonial stand from which they would observe the landing of *Isis* and to which the nautae would be escorted to be greeted by Caesar Viventius himself. Senators, magistrates and quaestors in their distinctively marked togas, lictors carrying their ceremonial bundles of rods, the procurator of Terra Australis and the praefectus of Novum Ostia jostled for position near Viventius.

Caesar's caelumvola stood nearby, guarded by legionaries in sparkling ceremonial armor. No sooner had Caesar and his party descended to the pratum than the aircraft was rolled to a covered shelter and rubbed and polished to a dazzling brightness. Then it was rolled back to stand near Caesar's pavilion, as much a symbol of his authority and the majesty of the state as had been the ancient Caesars' chariots with their curried and pampered teams of geldings.

Avita stood beside Aelius and laid her hand lightly on his arm. He looked down at the gesture but did not move his arm away. Avita followed his gaze toward the east. She knew that tracking instruments and recording devices had homed on *Isis* before this, but now she was able to make out the spatiumnavis' approach to the Pratum Grandis.

*Isis'* shape bespoke the strengths and traditions of Roman engineering. Avita could almost feel the solid strength of the craft as it dropped toward the field. She had looked at pictures of its departure for Martes and admired its lines and the fine sheen of its skin. The newly launched *Isis* had looked and moved like an Aegyptian goddess. Now the spatiumnavis looked and moved like an old woman, tired by a lifetime of labor and burdened with a lifetime of suffering.

The spatiumnavis circled the Pratum Grandis, dropping steadily toward the ground. The movement of the ship was deceptive. It seemed at any moment that *Isis* would touch the ground, but her skids, blackened and pitted, remained separated from the surface.

A glow like waves of heat rising from the sun-baked desert into the tired air emanated from *Isis'* engines. The navicularis must have touched the ship's controls, for the glow assumed a darkish color, then faded.

*Isis* touched the solum of Terra Australis, trembled like a creature in despair, then settled onto her skids. Squads of legionaries marched toward the ship. They surrounded *Isis* on all sides. A double column formed between the ship and Caesar Viventius' reviewing stand.

An ostium slowly swung open in *Isis'* hull, and legionaries hastened to station themselves in position to help nautae to the ground. The first to debark from *Isis* was the navicularis Lucius. He stood blinking in the bright sunlight of Terra Australis. For a moment his knees buckled and it seemed that he might fall, but he took the arm of a legionary and steadied himself. He turned and looked over his shoulder, into the darkness of *Isis'* interior, then swung back, smiled determinedly, and advanced between the rows of legionaries. Ahead of him stood Caesar's pavilion, and in it, Caesar himself.

Viventius watched the opening of the ostium in silence. The functionaries who surrounded him watched him like hawks, eager to pick up the first clue to Caesar's reaction and to show on their faces the emotions that Caesar felt.

Caesar turned his attention from his endlessly squabbling entourage to the men and women emerging from the spatiumnavis. No longer was he so certain that today's ceremony had been wisely planned. Indeed, it was the Ides, the five hundredth anniversary of the proclamation of the Roman province of Terra Australis and the millennial anniversary of the failed attempt upon the life of Caesar Julius.

It would be a close shave, but Viventius could greet these brave sailors of the sea of space and still return to Italia, to Rome herself, and preside over the grand jubilee celebration in the Eternal City. But it might have been better to send a delegation to welcome the brave nautae, to invite them to Rome for a triumph of their own.

Viventius rubbed his clean-shaven chin. Too late to change

plans now. He strained his eyes against the bright southern sun and peered into the face of the leader of the Martes expedition, Lucius Navicularis. The man looked haggard, exhausted, on the verge of collapse. The reports that *Isis* had sent back, and *Amaterasu* before her destruction, did not bode well for Roman colonization of Martes.

The planet of the god of war had lived up to its sanguinary tint and its bloodthirsty name. *Amaterasu* had landed safely while *Isis* remained in orbit around the planet. *Amaterasu's* officers and her nautae had behaved according to instructions, according to plan. They had maintained precautions, surveyed the area surrounding their landing site, determined whether Martes in general, and this region in particular, was inhabited.

And Martes *was* inhabited. *Amaterasu* had messaged to *Isis* and hence to both Luna and Tellus that Martes was inhabited. But by whom? By what? Had men of Tellus visited the red planet in the distant past, established colonies there, then been cut off from the mother planet as history's wheel slowly turned?

Such an event would not be unprecedented. There were records of lost and rediscovered colonies on Tellus. Why not on other worlds? Caesar's head reeled with the thought. What ancient states had arisen upon Tellus, what marvels had their machinators devised, and all lost to the modern world state?

The people of Terra Nipponsis, of Uwajima—suppose they were not truly native to those lands, but were the descendants of ancient visitors from Rome? What if Atlantis was a reality, and not merely a figment of the Greek imagination? What if the Hebrews' myth of a Garden of Eden was not wholly a myth, but an attenuated and distorted memory of—of what? What if the denizens of Martes were not descended from ancient visitors from Tellus, but in fact the very opposite was the case?

A senator—what was his name?—took Caesar's elbow. "Are you all right, sir?"

Viventius shook his head.

"Are you all right?"

"Yes. Yes. It was the glare, that was all. Thank you."

The senator, looking concerned, retreated.

Lucius Navicularis stood before Caesar's reviewing stand. He looked into the face of the chief of the world state, the leader of the Universal Republic. Caesar's cheeks were smooth and his hair, an alloy of silver and iron, was carefully curled and oiled. Lucius felt his own staleness and filth. Once he would have quivered at the thought of being received by Caesar Viventius himself. Now he would give his laurels and his triumph all for a long, hot soak.

To one side of Caesar's stand he could see a group of men and women in eccentric garb. He recognized them by their facial features and their clothing as Uwajimae. A violent, restless people who had never fully settled into the comfortable discipline of Roman citizenry.

A band was playing, horns blaring and drums pounding. Lucius felt heavy. He knew that returning to Tellus' gravity would have this effect, but still it was an effort to remain upright. He looked behind him and saw Sabbina, Septimus, Drusilla, his three chief officers, struggling to maintain a proper bearing in the presence of Caesar himself.

The band ceased its blaring and its pounding. Caesar was speaking. The words were meaningless to Lucius. He knew they would be the platitudes of Roman patriotism, steadfastness, courage, but while he could see Caesar's lips forming the words, all he could hear was a grating bleating sound like a goat making a speech.

The sun glinted off the musicians' instruments and off the armor and the weapons of the legionaries. Caesar's caelumvola shone like a sculpture of obsidian and electrum.

A trio of persons had broken from the crowd beyond Caesar's reviewing stand and were running toward the twin lines of legionaries that marked the path from *Isis* to the stand and that surrounded the stand itself.

The tallest of the Uwajimae pointed a object at the three who were running. A blocky, muscular man. A tall woman, little more than dark skin stretched over long, thin bones. A fat man, staggering and sprawling behind them.

A bright light flashed from the object that the Uwajiman had pointed. Lucius had never seen anything like it. The blocky man exploded like a knot in a fireplace. Bits of flesh and spatters of blood flew. The light fashed twice more and the tall woman and the fat man exploded as well.

Legionaries were already running to stop the three, but they arrived in time only to be splattered with blood and gore. A centurion had taken the Uwajiman in custody, had seized the object that had sent the bright flash toward the three who were now dead.

Pandemonium reigned on the Pratum Grandis.

Aelius and Avita had trained their gear on Caesar Viventius and

Lucius Navicularis, but now they too were running to the site of the sudden carnage, recording the event for the audience who depended on them for their daily news. Celadus was screaming at them but Aelius and Avita had anticipated his instructions.

For just a moment, Aelius swung back toward Caesar. He was surrounded by aides. A thousand years had passed, and this time it was not Caesar's own trusted friends but those who hated the Universal Republic who had attempted to assassinate the master of Rome.

A different plan, a different tactic, but the same outcome. Caesar lived.

*I sent this story to Ejler Jakobsson at* Galaxy *in 1970. I'd been a fan of that magazine and of its great editor (and my personal hero) Horace Gold in earlier years. Although Gold was long gone by 1970, and* Galaxy *was long past its glory years, I still hoped to appear in its pages.*

*Jake called me up about the story. He hated to write letters. He loved the story, he said, and he wanted to buy it, but he was concerned over its ambiguous quality. Would I tweak it a little bit, make it more definite, and send him another draft, and then we'd be in business.*

*Sounds okay, but the whole point of "The Heyworth Fragment" is its ambiguity.*

*What to do?*

*I revised the story in hopes of satisfying Jake. He was an old pulp hand, he liked things concrete and clear-cut and he was having a lot of trouble with this one. He phoned me again and we had essentially the same conversation we'd had the first time.*

*Huh. Back to the big red Selectric.*

*On the third attempt I visited Jake at his office. He was a cordial and hospitable gentleman. He read the newest draft and repeated his comments still again.*

*I don't know how many versions of the story I tried for Jake, but I guess I just couldn't (or wouldn't) give him what he wanted, and he just wouldn't (or couldn't) go for what I was willing to give him.*

*Finally I gave up and offered the story to Ted White, who ran it in* Amazing Stories *in 1972. I was grateful to Ted and I didn't hold a grudge against Jake—he was who he was, for better or for worse, as I suppose we all are. But I regret that I never did crack* Galaxy.

# The Heyworth Fragment

## Discovery of the Item

THE PORTION OF MATERIAL KNOWN AS THE "HEY-worth Fragment" first came to the attention of the auditorium projectionist during one of the regular Sunday evening film showings in the fall semester. The announced program for the evening was Luis Buñuel's classic featurette "The Andalusian Dog," and a full-length film, the little known but critically well-regarded *Rudolf Hess at Spandau.*

The projectionist was a graduate student, Tuck Heyworth, not at all given to practical jokes. In fact, Heyworth's serious outlook and total lack of humor were well known on the campus. At the time he disclaimed all knowledge of the origin of the fragment which has come to bear his name, and to this day swears total ignorance of the matter.

He submitted voluntarily to polygraph examination once the affair began to suggest serious implications, and all indications were that his ignorance was quite as abysmal as he alleged it to be.

According to Heyworth's statement, "The Andalusian Dog" was nearly over and he was about to thread up the first reel of *Rudolf Hess at Spandau,* when he discovered an additional reel of film on top of the feature film. It bore no label, but was wound on a standard 16-millimeter Goldsmith reel.

Assuming the film to be a short cartoon or other suitable addition to the program, Heyworth attempted to thread it on the second projector so it would be ready for screening at the end of "The Andalusian Dog." He was surprised that the film started without leader or titles, but later explained that this did not arouse his curiosity greatly as he assumed that the film was one produced by students, and that the technique of starting *in medias res* was used deliberately by the student film-maker.

Heyworth was unable to thread the film, however, and after making several futile attempts to do so set it aside as a defective print and proceeded to thread and show *Rudolf Hess at Spandau* as had been the original intent of the program committee.

When the showing of *Rudolph Hess at Spandau* was completed, Heyworth rewound the films and returned them to the distributor. However, as there was neither receipt nor shipping case for the unexpected reel, it was left behind in the projection booth. It was only some days later that Heyworth recalled the odd print, and attempted once more to thread it, purely for his own satisfaction.

He was again unable to do so, and upon examination of the print discovered that it was of nonstandard format. At this point Heyworth contacted the university's film department, and turned the print over to the department for their disposition. He showed no interest in the content of the film at this or any later time, contending when questioned later that only his inability to thread the film roused his curiosity and that only the technical aspects of the film's unusual format intrigued him.

Heyworth has since received his master's degree and resides in the area, working as a night supervisor in his father-in-law's ladies' purse factory. He has proven cooperative with regard to questioning concerning the fragment, but has been unable to provide any information further than that already reported.

## Irregular Format of the Fragment

Once delivered to the film department, the fragment was inspected for format. Almost immediately it became apparent why it had proved impossible to thread it in a standard projector, although the differences in format were sufficiently slight as to have baffled Tuck, who was not a film technician but only a cursorily-trained projectionist who was limited to naked-eye examination of the film in a dimly-lighted projection booth.

Although the film was wound on a standard 16-millimeter reel, and to the naked eye appeared to be of standard width, it was actually just over 17 millimeters wide. The precise width does not work out into exact units, fractions, or decimals in either the metric or English system, or in any other against which it was compared. This may be a significant datum, but there is no assurance but that the width was not set on some more obscure scale, or that it is not merely arbitrary.

The frame format is square rather than being in the three-by-four horizontal format to which standard the industry adheres, but again there have been many variant formats developed, ranging from the successful wide-screen productions of recent years to round, upright, and other shapes, including square frames.

Presumably because of the square frames, the sprocket holes, which are themselves square and slightly larger than normal, and which appear in an alternating pattern on either side of the print, are not spaced at the normal interval of three-tenths of an inch, (or six-tenths, as would be the case with the alternating arrangement of the Heyworth Fragment), but are approximately 20 millimeters apart.

The frames themselves occur at a frequency of just under 32 per foot. Once again, it will be noted that none of the dimensions of the print are commensurate with either English or metric measurements. All attempts to bring the measurements of the Heyworth Fragment into coincidence with inches or millimeters have failed.

It should be noted further that the "film" itself, or what is usually referred to as a film, was not one at all, strictly speaking. While the fragment appeared to the naked eye to be a standard celluloid-based motion picture print, later analysis proved it to be of an unusual organic-metallic compound. This compound, reproduced after some rather difficult laboratory procedures had been mastered, has been found to be a superior replacement for standard photographic emulsions, serving, in slightly different forms, as both original and print stock, with outstanding color fidelity and an unusual range of light sensitivities.

In the case of the Heyworth Fragment, however, once the format of the print was adequately ascertained, the question arose as to whether it would be more practical to convert a standard projector for the showing of the film, or to attempt to convert the film for showing on a standard projector. A third course of action, to dismiss the entire affair as a joke by students, with or without the collusion of Tuck Heyworth, was given consideration only until naked-eye examination of the film proved so intriguing that a proper screening of the film was definitely decided upon.

After some discussion, the chairman of the film department, Dr. Cashman, placed himself firmly on the side of converting the fragment. His argument, which came to be accepted throughout the department, was that once converted, the fragment could be duplicated and shown on any standard projector, but that if the projector rather than the film were modified, access to the single modified projector would be required for any study of the film. Further, the making of duplicate prints would be extremely difficult and tedious work because of problems entailed in working with the non-standard footage.

The fragment was painstakingly matted onto 35-millimeter stock and duplicated through the use of an optical printer. Once a duplicate master in 35-millimeter format had been made it was of course no problem to strike as many 35-millimeter prints as desired. When projected with standard equipment these prints showed a full, square "Heyworth" frame, matted on black. The color of the original print was reproduced with excellent fidelity.

Two additional problems were encountered in converting the print.

One of these was the sound track. Because of the organic-metallic stock used in the fragment, no visible optical or magnetic track was noted at first, and it was assumed that the fragment was silent. However, upon screening of the converted version, it became obvious that sound was required to make sense of the content of the film. The original was re-examined, this time more closely than ever, and there was found, embedded in the edge of the film, very much as a sound track is placed in normal prints, an alloy wire of extreme fineness.

Every attempt was made to read this wire as a sound track, and after extremely lengthy efforts, Dr. Bloch-Erich of the Department of Computer Sciences claimed to have decoded the wire's content. It was, he asserted, digitally recorded information, but not basically digital data. Rather, Bloch-Erich claimed, a continuous flow of analog data—possibly sound, possibly odor or other messages—had been recorded *in digital form* on the wire.

By converting the digital data from the imbedded wire to standard nine-track 2420 format and reading the tape into the university's Model 195 data processing system, Bloch-Erich stated that he could have the computer decode the information, transmit it to a modified 7774 audio I/O device, and convert it back to standard audio tape form. This in turn led to a further pair of problems.

One of these, Bloch-Erich complained, was that after his computer program had decoded, edited, and transmitted the audio content of the Heyworth wire, there remained a kind of data-detritus which Bloch-Erich was unable to explain. He guessed that the Heyworth film was intended originally for some sort of projector or other reader which could detect not merely pictorial and audio recordings, but others as well, and that the surplus code that remained after the audio data was filtered out contained messages intended to be perceived other than visually and aurally.

The second problem encountered by Dr. Bloch-Erich was that the audio track produced by his equipment, while sounding relatively coherent and, after suitable bench-work, synching accurately with the image in the fragment, made no apparent sense. This intriguing aspect of the fragment will be alluded to again. For the moment it should be noted that Dr. Bloch-Erich and his machines are attempting, thus far without notable success, to find some meaning in the (presumed) words.

The final technical problem to be dealt with was the frame-rate at which the film should be projected. As the fragment itself was found in a format approximating, although clearly not identical with, 16 millimeter, it was first assumed that the film was meant to be projected at 24 frames per second. The first converted 35-millimeter print was projected at this speed, but immediate discrepancies were noted in the movement of the actors, mechanical objects, and other objects in the film.

The more this problem was considered, the more baffling it became. Movements of hands, feet, or mouths could be observed, but to establish the proper speed was not simple. A man walking at a normal brisk rate will usually approximate the military march of 90 paces per minute, or two-thirds of a second per stride. But how could it be determined that a person in the film was in fact moving at that rate—perhaps he was meandering at half that speed, or pacing rapidly at a far greater rate.

The sound track, once Dr. Bloch-Erich had decoded it, seemed at first to offer assistance, but again, unless the voice characteristics of the actors were known, the proper speed for the tape could not be determined either. Did a particular figure speak in a *basso profundo*—or a piercing falsetto? If this were known, the projection speed could be determined, or vice versa. But without one item of information to start from, the other must remain equally a puzzle.

At length a tentative solution was reached when a scene was found in which water was poured. Giving this the normal 32 feet per second squared rate of acceleration established a frame-rate for the rest of the film that appeared fairly normal, and gave the voices a level not unacceptable to the ear.

There remained in several scenes apparent anomalies in the behavior of light, but these had to be accepted as "given" rather than adjusted for, as any further adjustments to the frame rate to allow for these items would have thrown all the rest of the contents of the fragment into a state of utter confusion.

## Content of the Film—Scenes

The fragment contains only five scenes, each running for approximately the same footage or duration. The intended projection time of the scenes is not known with assurance, as this depends obviously upon the intended projection rate, itself not fully ascertained. However, by the gravity test previously mentioned, the established frame rate indicates an overall running time of somewhat longer than two minutes, or approximately 25 seconds per scene.

It should be emphasized, however, that this is not firmly established. It has been suggested, for instance, that the fluid being poured is not water at all, but a clear substance of highly viscous consistency, which would pour far more slowly than water due to its own gooey nature. This suggestion is not taken very seriously, but in the face of so little data it cannot be wholly disregarded.

An even farther-fetched suggestion is that the filming was done on location in a setting where acceleration due to gravity is not equal to the familiar 32 feet per second squared. The individual responsible for this suggestion will remain unnamed as he himself regards the idea as ludicrous; nonetheless, it is a possibility not to be excluded from consideration.

The contents of the scenes themselves are as follows:

*First,* a room. Camera work in this scene, as in all, is technically proficient but static and unimaginative. The cameraman seems to have set up his equipment, obtained correct lighting and focus, and made his shot in a single take, entirely without camera or lens movement of any sort. Characters move in and out of the frame, block one another from view, appear off-center or even partially out of the frame, entirely without regard from the cameraman or director.

The room itself is bare, sparsely furnished, with apparent plaster walls in a nondescript pastel shade slowly crumbling away. Visible furniture consists only of a chair, or presumed chair, and another article of uncertain nature. The presumed chair is so identified because one character is seated upon it throughout the scene; the item of furniture is itself almost entirely blocked from view. The second article of furniture is made of a glossy material colored a dark orange; it stands upright beside the seated character, who at no time touches it although in several frames the character seems to be looking at the object out of the corner of the eye.

Neither ceiling nor floor is visible in the scene. The edge of something presumed to be either a window or a picture frame is seen, but only this much.

*Second,* an exterior landscape. The ground can be seen for some distance from the camera. It is covered with low vegetation, apparently low shrubs, some grasses and other small plants. Representatives of the Botany Department have been unable to identify the growth, but have given assurances that there is nothing extraordinary about them.

In the distance can be seen a roadway and beyond it woods. Again, the composition of the woods is unascertained. The roadway is apparently of a hard surface, light in color. Movement can be seen upon the roadway, but frustratingly it is at such a distance that it is impossible to determine the nature of the vehicles in use. Extreme magnification of the film does not provide sufficient resolution to identify the vehicles other than to establish them as being drawn rather than self-powered. The animals pulling them cannot be clearly seen, and debate has developed as to whether they are four-legged beasts drawing in tandem or even troika fashion, or (absurdly perhaps) previously unidentified creatures possessing more than four legs.

At one point it was even suggested that the creatures were not animals at all, but human beings tethered and forced to draw wagons of passengers and freight.

*Third,* a corridor. The relationship between this scene and the first, that of the room, is unknown. It is hypothesized that the corridor is located in the same building as the room, perhaps even that the room opens off the corridor. There is no evidence to support this idea.

The walls, floor and ceiling of the corridor are apparently of identical construction. No seams are visible, suggesting either that they have been concealed architecturally or that the corridor is made of a single fabric, as by casting in a mold or hollowing from rock. Light is provided by a series of convoluted strips, which seem to be embedded in the walls and floor. It has been suggested that the convolutions of the strips represent script of some sort, but all attempts to identify this have been unsuccessful and it has been tentatively concluded that the strips are arranged in abstract decorative patterns.

The corridor is lined at irregular intervals with what seem to be mechanical devices of roughly human conformation. These have been identified by various faculty representatives as suits of XIVth Century Germanic armor, positronic robots, astronauts' space garb, and (in one case) cryogenic mummy cases. Each faculty representative has prepared a justification for his identification, and in all cases the argument has seemed so powerful and thoroughgoing that, in the absence of contending suggestions, any one might be readily accepted. However, in the presence of the varied hypotheses, no one has achieved general paramountcy.

*Fourth*, another exterior shot. Unlike the previous exterior scene, this was apparently made at night. Also, it seems to have been made from a very high angle, indicating a very high boom mounting of the camera, or its mounting atop a very tall structure of some sort, or even an aerial mounting. This last possibility is not in concert with other aspects of the film, but even if it is considered, it must be noted that the characteristic absence of camera movement, while evidence of lack of ingenuity in normal circumstances, indicates in the case of aerial cinematography the development of extremely sophisticated techniques of aviation and cinematic equipment.

The camera is directed toward the horizon. There appears—again, most frustratingly, in the extreme distance—what seems to be a city. Tall structures rear skyward; they are dotted with lights of great brilliance and variety of color, which wink on and off in apparently non-random fashion. Attempts to decode the pattern thus displayed have led to the tentative conclusion that esthetic considerations alone cannot account for the blinking, although it is noted that the esthetic effect is also highly pleasing, and a number of undergraduates who had access to the converted film compared it favorably to the so-called "light shows" that are sometimes utilized in conjunction with their electronic concerts.

A small portion of night sky is visible beyond the city. Unfortunately the intensity of the city's lights obliterates the stars which might otherwise be visible. Brilliant objects can nonetheless be seen in the sky, moving toward the city. None reach it in the footage included in the fragment. Because these objects are visible only as points of variously colored light, it is not possible to determine their size, distance from camera, or velocity of movement. Any of these data would be most useful in determining the others, but lacking all it defies analysis to determine any.

*Fifth*, a close-up. The subject is the person seen seated in the first scene of the fragment. Because of the subject's unfamiliarly styled clothing it is impossible to determine his (?) sex. The subject faces directly into the camera. His face is covered with bruises and there are traces of wiped-away blood. One eye is puffed badly and the hair is disheveled.

The subject speaks to the camera imploringly; his voice is heard on the sound track. No words are understood, of course, but the tone leads one to believe that the subject has been beaten, perhaps tortured, and is pleading with the viewer for assistance or rescue.

After some time a hand or hand-like object enters the frame line and moves rapidly toward the camera. Before the hand or other object reaches the lens (or goes out of focus—the technical quality of these scenes is remarkable!) the fragment ends.

It appears fairly obvious that the five scenes comprising the Heyworth Fragment are not a complete film. What other material should have preceded and followed the five extant scenes is wholly conjectural.

## Remaining Questions

Because the fragment is so short and obviously incomplete it has raised many more questions than can presently be resolved. In particular the locale in which the footage was recorded is puzzling. The race of the characters—the person being interrogated, the interrogator, a woman seen weeping while devouring a raw joint of meat (?) in the first interrogation scene—is unknown.

Variations in skin tone and facial configuration between the interrogator and the interrogatee may be merely individual characteristics, or may be indicative of different racial stock. If so, which races are represented? In no case is skin color or configuration so unusual as to suggest that the persons are not Earth-humans, and yet they do not fit comfortably into any known line of human stock.

Similarly, the language spoken has never been identified. It sometimes sounds maddeningly familiar, yet no linguist—and the film has been screened repeatedly for the full Language Department—has made positive identification. Further, the speech of the interrogator is not identical to that of the interrogatee. Individual variation? Regional dialects? A "foreign" accent on the part of one of them? If so, which one?

To return to the second scene, what or who pull the wagons?

In the third scene, what are the figures lining the corridor?

In the fourth scene, what is the message of the lights, and what are the aerial objects moving toward the city?

In the final scene, what is the appeal of the interrogatee? Who was the cameraman and why does the interrogatee think it worthwhile to address his appeal to the camera? Was it an act of desperation, or did he really believe that the film would be seen by someone able to come to his aid?

In any case, why and how did the cameraman get away with his film? And, emphatically not to be forgotten among the many enigmas of the fragment, how did the film find its way into Tuck Heyworth's projection booth?

For the comfort of any persons who may find these questions and this entire affair disquieting, it should be noted that both the original Heyworth Fragment and all additional copies made, plus Dr. Bloch-Erich's tapes of the sound wire, have been delivered to the appropriate Federal agency. All may rest assured that the final disposition of the Heyworth Fragment will be handled with the full wisdom and responsibility of our democratically chosen leaders.

*I wrote this story as a kind of crime caper and showed it to my then-agent circa 1974. I hoped to hit one of the detective magazines—maybe* Ellery Queen's *or* Alfred Hitchcock's—*with it. But my agent despised the story. It would never sell, not to anyone, he said.*

*That put the kibosh on my hopes of cracking the mystery field, but I liked the story and tarted it up with some phony science fiction trappings and sold it on the first try to* Fantasy and Science Fiction.

*But I always regretted that. I should have had the courage of my convictions. So I've gone back to the original version of the story. A copy of the manuscript has resided in my files for all these years. What you see now is what readers should have seen a quarter century ago.*

*You'll notice a mention of auction prices for pulp magazines in this story. I will make no comment save to remind you that these are 1972 prices. Why is there never a time machine around when you need one?*

# Whatever Happened to Nick Neptune?

**F**IRST OF ALL, LET ME CLEAR UP A LITTLE MYSTERY. All this time people have been wondering who in the world Nick Neptune *was:* a pseudonym (there were some amazing guesses), a sort of collective front for a group of shadowy figures, even a real person. Well, Nick Neptune would be a slightly odd name, but there have been odder ones. The old novelist Edison Tesla Marshall, when he started writing, people wondered what enigma lurked behind that odd byline. Turned out that Edison Tesla Marshall was Edison Tesla Marshall, that's all. Old man and old lady Marshall had this kid and they were both admirers of the great scientists of the period, so they stuck those names on their baby.

So maybe Nick Neptune was a real name. Why not?

All of this is somewhat digressive. A habit you pick up when you're the editor of a small-time rural weekly. There isn't much hard news out in the sticks and somehow the local residents aren't interested in their country weekly's editor's views of world problems, so you learn to spin little philosophical essays around the changing of the seasons, the arrival of Christmas or Independence Day or Halloween, commencement week at the consolidated school, the death of a senior resident, whatever.

There, I'm doing it again. Sorry.

Who was Nick Neptune? Before I go any farther let me tell you who Nick Neptune was. *Me.*

Yes, I was Nick Neptune. I'll tell you my real name too. Chances are highly remote that my real name will mean anything to you unless you're a resident of Potawatomy County, Pennsylvania, and a reader of the weekly paper there. Yes, Potawatomy County is an odd name, too. It's been the name of that county since the Commonwealth was formed. Attained a brief notoriety back in 1884, when a local high school professor built some sort of strange machine in his basement and then disappeared along with his houseboy, a youngster from one of his classes, and the machine. But that's another story too.

Nick Neptune never drew a breath of air except as I used the name. I was Nick and Nick was me and I was, yes, the editor of *Nick Neptune's Adventure Magazine* for its entire run of one edition.

My real name is Sanford Hall, I live in the town of Pachyderm, Pennsylvania, and yes, that's a strange name too for a Lehigh Valley town, but that's the town's name and the folks who live there don't think it's really any stranger than Intercourse, Pennsylvania, Tarzan, Texas, or Yreka, California. It just takes a little getting used to.

I've lived most of my life in Pachyderm and I've worked all of my life, except for four years out-of-state attending college, for the county weekly newspaper, the Pachyderm *Tracks*. During those four years I made the acquaintance of Herman Minkowsky—you'd better remember that name, he was one of the key figures in the whole Nick Neptune affair—and after I earned my degree in journalism and came back to Pachyderm, old Fred Callister, the editor and publisher of the *Tracks*, handed me the front door key, told me, "She's all yours, Sandy," went home, lay down and died. Old Mrs. Callister said that Fred had been waiting for me to come home so he could be sure the paper was in safe hands before he passed on. Maybe so. Old Fred was a strong-willed man.

So I took over the paper. That was back in '46. I was just a fresh kid, barely out of college, but I'd worked for Callister as printer's devil, sweeper, ad salesman, delivery boy, switchboard operator (we never had but one phone, but old Fred called it our switchboard), high school sports reporter, copy editor and coffee gopher, so I figured I knew a little about how to run a weekly. The rest of the staff was Mort Van Vlack who served as both linotypist and our single pressman, and my own mother, Gladys Hall, who was business manager of the *Tracks.*

We never made a lot of money but we met our payroll every week and we never missed an edition come drought, flood, heat or snow.

Now Herman Minkowsky was a very different kind of fellow from the boys I'd gone to school with back in Potawatomy County. When we got to the university and were assigned as roommates, we must have reacted to each other like the country mouse and the city mouse. We had different ways and different styles and sometimes we could hardly understand each other's attitudes, but underneath it we were cousins, if you know what I mean. We were both going to major in journalism. We both had printer's ink in our veins. He was going to become a famous reporter for a big city daily, he said. I knew all along I was headed back to Potawatomy County and the Pachyderm *Tracks,* but we were both dedicated to our careers, and as we got to understand each other we developed a strong feeling of respect and even mutual affection.

After college we went our separate ways. Mine was exactly what I'd planned—back to Pennsylvania, back to my country weekly. Herman followed a different course. For a while he couldn't settle down, kept changing jobs and even kinds of jobs.

We didn't see each other again for years and years, but every Christmas we'd exchange a letter and bring one another up to date on our lives. My letters to Herman must have been pretty dull. Year after year I ran the Pachyderm *Tracks,* chronicling the seasons and the crops, the births and marriages and deaths in my little county.

Herman's letters told a different story. At first he was out to become a famous journalist and he landed as a copy boy for a daily tabloid. After that he switched to a magazine job, then went to work for a big company putting out their house organ. He wrote me that that paid a fortune compared to legitimate journalism but he hated it so much he quit cold after a while.

Then he went to work editing some pulp magazines, and that he really loved. He wrote to me that the pay was terrible, the work was overwhelming, his office was a little corner of a drafty loft, but he loved every minute of it. He even put me on for a free subscription, and I started reading the wild stories that he edited. Absolutely amazing, but they were such a contrast to my own small-town life that I kind of enjoyed them, and saved all the magazines up in the attic over the *Tracks* office.

When Herman's publisher quit after a few years (he decided to switch over to manufacturing sexy playing cards and bought a sixty-room mansion in Florida after three years), Herman decided to become a literary agent. He figured by then that he knew all the other editors and he knew all the authors, and he should be able to pick up enough clients to make a fair living, and he was right, and he did, although he never made it into the sixty-room mansion class.

Well that's the way things went along, like I said, for all those years, me getting more and more settled into my regular ways making a living with the *Tracks* and even expanding to take in some job printing for the local schools and the small businesses and social stationery requirements of Pachyderm, and Herman doing better and better in the literary agent business as some of his clients started breaking through into the big money brackets with a couple of best-sellers and then some movie sales. All of this communicated solely by means of our annual Christmas letters.

When all of a sudden Herman phoned me up.

My wife answered the switchboard — yes, I'd got married in '51, and it was for love, too, not just to stay out of Truman's war — my wife answered the switchboard and came to where I was typing out an essay on the meaning of summer, tapped me on the shoulder and said, "It's a long distance call for you, person to person. Better come talk."

I picked up the telephone and told the operator that, yes, I was Sanford Hall all right, and said to go ahead and this voice which I must confess I didn't remember at all said, "Sandy, this is Herman Minkowsky, how are you?"

Now I hadn't spoken with Herman Minkowsky in nearly thirty years, and I was so amazed to hear him asking me a question that all I could do was answer it, direct. "Pretty good," I said, "got a little arthritis in my left shoulder but I'm still pretty good.

"And how are you?" I said.

"Fine, fine. Listen, Sandy, are you still running that little paper?"

I said I was.

"And you have a job shop too?"

I said I did.

He said, "I think I've got a nice piece of job printing for you, if you can handle it."

"What is it?" I asked him.

"A magazine," he said. "I need a complete job—typesetting, some plates for illustrations, one color separation for the cover. I need printing, folding, and magazine binding. Can be either side-stapled or perfect bound."

"How big?"

"Not very big. Standard pulp size, ninety-six pages, and a very short run."

I thought about that for a minute, scratched some figures on a sheet of yellow copy-paper that lay on the desk next to my ancient L. C. Smith (the same one old man Callister had used when I was his copy boy), and told Minkowsky I could handle the job. I quoted him some prices, scaled to the length of the run.

Herman didn't make a sound for a few seconds. I thought he was running up a big phone bill, and I wondered if he'd been struck speechless by the price I'd quoted him. Still holding the phone to my ear I started working over the figures some more to see if I could squeeze a few dollars out of the price and not blow the job.

Suddenly Herman's voice came back through the earpiece. "Sandy, did I hear you right? Let me have that price again."

I repeated the figures.

"You have any profit in there, anything for you?" he said.

"A little," I allowed.

"Well, you've got the job, chum. There's just one thing, though. There are certain, ah, delicate aspects of this venture. You've got to keep it under your hat, all right?"

I looked across the Pachyderm *Tracks* office at my wife.

She was brewing a pot of tea on the office hot plate. It was a quiet afternoon in the *Tracks*'s weekly cycle. The latest edition had come off the press and Mort Van Vlack was out in our old Ford panel truck distributing the run to the paperboys and the few retail stores that carried the *Tracks*.

"Linetta," I called over to my wife, "Gladys is working on the books over home today. Would you go over there and get me a summary of our payables and receivables from her, and see what our bank balance is, too."

She gave me a look like she knew I just wanted to be alone in the office for a few minutes, which I did, but after all these years she and I respect each other enough to go along with that kind of thing.

As soon as she'd shut the door behind her I said into the phone, "Now look here, Herman, you're not getting into the pornography business, are you? Because if you are, that's your own

concern all right, but I don't want any part of it, do you understand?"

Minkowsky laughed loudly right into the phone, nearly tore
my ear off. He said, "Nope, no smut."

"Or maybe a little piracy?"

"No, no, no, nothing shady, Sandy. This is perfectly legal. It's
just that we're going to have a unique distribution system, and we
don't want any publicity leaks other than what we control ourselves, and we absolutely don't want any unauthorized copies of
the magazine getting into the wrong people's hands."

Those words sounded all right, but there was a kind of odd
feeling about it, if you know what I mean. I told Herman so. I said,
"Herman, I don't know what you're into here, but before I get into
it with you, I'll have to know a lot more about it. Not that I distrust
you, mind, but I have to know what I'm doing, is all."

Herman didn't say anything again, and I just pictured him in
my mind's eye, holding the telephone while the toll charges ran
up. Of course I pictured him as he'd looked in 1946, not the better
part of three decades later. But finally he said something more, in
a kind of solemn, reasonable, don't-push-me-past-my-limit tone of
voice.

"All right, Sanford," he said. "I can understand your feeling
that way. I'll make you a proposition." (How often had I heard him
say that in our old student days!) "I guess you're entitled to know
what this project is about. You come on to the city and I'll set up
a meeting of you, me, and, ah, one more person who is a principal
in the matter."

Now I held my silence and let him go on.

"This other, ah, individual will explain to you as much as we
possibly can reveal. If you're satisfied with his explanation and you
still want the job, it's yours. If you don't like anything about it, you
can drop out right then—but if that happens you'll have to forget
everything that happened. Have you ever signed a confidential
disclosure agreement?"

I hadn't, but it was clear enough what it was about, and I
certainly didn't mind signing. Even though I was acting in the
capacity of a printing contractor, I'd been through the business of
protecting news sources often enough to be familiar with those
sensitivities. Even in Potawatomy County, Pennsylvania, yes.

"But there's one more problem," I said to Herman.

He asked what it was.

"Trip to the city's an expensive proposition," I started.

"Don't worry about that," he said, before I could get any farther. "You'll be on full expenses plus, oh, we'll call it a consulting fee while we work this out. Will you come?"

Well, that changed things aplenty! We set up an appointment for the next week and I went back to my essay on the meaning of summer for the Pachyderm, Pennsylvania *Tracks*.

The next week we laid out the paper with a bunch of reserve news, press releases and book reviews by the local self-styled intelligentsia, put the issue to bed a day early, and Linetta and I headed for the city, leaving Gladys in charge of the office and Mort in charge of the plant. Such as they were.

We checked into a hotel pretty late, and in the morning Linetta headed for the department stores while I headed for Herman Minkowsky's office and the meeting with our mystery man. Herman's office was actually a suite in a converted apartment building; I looked at his receptionist and at the fancy equipment he gave her to work with, and decided that Herman was doing all right in the agent business.

Inside his private office I laid eyes on the great man, my college roommate, for the first time since June of 1946. He'd put on a roll around the middle and grown a beard which he kept neatly trimmed, and he dressed in the tweedy good taste that must mark him as a bona fide literary figure. For a moment I felt like a naive country boy with straw sticking right out of my Sears Roebuck collar, but Herman was around his desk and pumping my hand in a second, telling me how fine I looked and then leading me over by the arm to meet—the mysterious principal.

He'd been sitting unobtrusively in a wing chair facing Herman and I hadn't even seen him till now.

"Sandy, I want you to meet the man behind this project. One of my top clients, I'm sure you've read his stuff."

The man he was introducing me to rose from his chair. He was very tall, at least half a foot taller than my own six even, and thin, thin as a rail, with sparse blond hair and pale blue eyes and rimless octagonal glasses. I had the feeling that a stiff breeze could pick him up and carry him right out the window—if Herman ever turned off the air conditioning and opened a window, that is.

"Stinky," Herman said, "this is Sanford Hall, The Joseph Pulitzer of Pachyderm Pee Ay. Editor, publisher and job printer par excellence. I think he's the man to be Nick Neptune."

Stinky didn't put out his hand. He just looked me up and down, nodded, and sat down in his wing chair again. In a quiet, steady voice, he said, "Very well, Herman, if he has your confidence."

"Is that your real name, Stinky?" I asked the pale man.

Herman Minkowsky said, "You'd know Stinky's name if you heard it, Sandy. He doesn't put his photo on any of his books because he doesn't want people bothering him in the street. And he doesn't shake hands because he's afraid of infection."

"Well, then," I said, but Herman didn't let me get any farther.

"Stinky, Sanford has agreed to the confidentiality of this matter, whether he takes the job or not. Is it all right to proceed?" Herman gestured at me to sit quietly.

Stinky nodded yes.

"Sanford," Herman resumed, "as I told you on the phone, we plan to issue a new magazine. It will be published in the old pulp format and called *Nick Neptune's Adventure Magazine.* We'll probably only publish one issue, although we won't say that in public."

"And you want me to handle the production, right?"

"Yup."

"Well, I don't see what all the mystery is about, Herman. I can do the job for you. Might run a little short on fonts but the Pachyderm *Tracks* is about due to order a couple anyhow, we'll just get 'em in for this job and then turn 'em over to the paper afterward.

"Now why," and I leaned over and jabbed my forefinger at him, "all the cloak and dagger stuff?"

By now Herman was sitting back in a great big chair behind a behemoth of a desk. He stood up and walked around the desk so he was standing over Stinky and myself. "Okay, then, this is in strict confidence. We're going to create a collector's item!"

I dug my heels into his thick carpet and pushed myself back into my chair laughing. "Is that all?" I bellowed. "All of this fuss and money to make a rare magazine? Herman, you're out of your head!"

At that he exchanged glances with Stinky. Herman looked a little upset but Stinky didn't feel a thing, or if he did he didn't let it show in his face. He made a funny little gesture with one hand and Herman walked back behind his desk and sat down.

"Never mind what you think of the state of my head, Sandy," said Herman. "We just plan to publish a limited edition pulp magazine, and control the circulation very, very carefully. Stinky will run the business side, by which I mean mainly that he'll pay the bills."

I looked at the mysterious pale individual in a new light, but he still kept that perfect poker face. A piece of ice, I thought, wondering who he actually was.

Herman went on, "I'll provide the material to go in the book, and you'll handle the physical end of production. We'll also need a front corporation, and neither Stinky nor I can have our names associated with the magazine. The editor will be Nick Neptune officially. Of course there isn't any Nick Neptune, but if anybody has to stand up and act as Nick, it'll have to be you, Sandy, not Stinky or myself.

"What you get out of it is maybe a little fun plus—I went over your bid with Stinky last night and you'll get what you asked plus a nice bonus if you do a good job and keep the thing quiet. Now, we've had enough discussion. The project is *Nick Neptune's Adventure Magazine*. Do you want the job, yes or no?"

I said—well, you know by now what I said. I'd liked the idea of producing a magazine to start with, and my concern over ethics was, well—I'm no Pharisee, mind you, but I'm no crook either, nor a panderer. I was serious about not wanting to get involved in pornography, I didn't want to infringe any copyrights or work for a spy ring, and I might as well say that I've never printed hate literature and I expect I never will.

But *Nick Neptune's Adventure Magazine* sounded legal, moral, and not too fattening, and it was a nice piece of job work for the shop. So we spent the rest of the day working out details, and the next day Linetta and I were back in Pachyderm at the *Tracks* office conducting our business and waiting for word from the city as to when we could start work on the magazine.

It came pretty soon. Even though I was supposed to be Neptune, Minkowsky actually gathered all the material for the magazine, and with the connections he'd built up over the last twenty years he did an amazing job.

I don't know what kind of rates he paid, using Stinky's money of course, but he told me that he was able to get limited rights to a lot of stories authors were writing for other publishers. By the time the copy arrived in Pachyderm he'd put together a complete magazine without there being any outside publicity, by appealing to people who were his clients or from whom he'd bought back in his editing days.

He got a story from Robert Silverberg that Silverberg said he'd originally written for the old Palmer *Other Worlds* when Silverberg was just a beginner, and that had never appeared in that magazine for some reason. He got a really funny story from Isaac Asimov, a sequel to a famous old yarn called "Christmas on Ganymede."

He actually got a new Curtis Newton short story from Edmond Hamilton, and a John Star short from Jack Williamson.

And then, he scored his real coup—although to me it seemed a little bit morbid. He contacted the estates of four people, and managed to get unpublished pieces from Doc Smith, John W. Campbell, Robert E. Howard, and Edgar Rice Burroughs.

My own experience with pulp magazines was limited to reading the ones that Herman had sent me when he was editing a pulp, but even with my limited knowledge it seemed to me that he had put together an incredible package.

He even pulled some strings and got a bunch of unpublished art by great old pulp illustrators. His cover for *Nick Neptune's* was a marvelously atmospheric scene by the late Hannes Bok—a musty, mysterious Egyptian tomb, with ankhs and mummy cases and various sorts of funerary sculpture standing around. Just to look at it makes you feel as if something uncanny is about to happen.

There were a couple of drawings by Frank R. Paul, and some by Virgil Finlay.

Of course the artwork and the stories didn't exactly go together in all cases, but I went up to the city a couple of times for conferences—Minkowsky wouldn't come anywhere near Pachyderm, said he didn't want to be connected with the project in any way that could be traced—and we managed to sort out the stories and the illustrations so that they matched at least in general theme if not in detail of character and action.

Minkowsky asked me to write an editorial for the first issue. He was afraid that his own or Stinky's style might be a giveaway. I wrote it. It wasn't too hard, rather like a Pachyderm *Tracks* essay on the contributions of the American farmer.

Mort Van Vlack began setting the stories in odd moments and after hours. He was happy to get the overtime.

And *Nick Neptune's Adventure Magazine* was under way! The only snag we hit was with the cover. The *Tracks* plant isn't set up for color work, so we had to send out the separations on that Bok cover, with lurid chartreuse lettering overlaying it, and then farm out the printing, too. But Herman's notion of getting confidential disclosure agreements sealed up any leaks at that end. The color people thought *Neptune's* was a test project from a big publisher and they were eager to get the full-scale run when it came along, so they were happy to cooperate with this job.

So there we were, the covers all ready to use, the body material coming off the press, even a space cleared in the old wooden storage shed behind the *Tracks* office to store the run of magazines until they were trucked to the distributor. The only thing that struck me as odd was the fact that Minkowsky hadn't given me any information on who the distributor would be. Mort Van Vlack and I could have handled that ourselves, if Herman had wanted to distribute only in Potawatomy County, but that was absurd.

I had Gladys put through a call to Herman's office the day before the magazine would actually be ready. That was what he'd asked. When I told him tomorrow was the day, he said he had some arrangements to make but that he'd be out to Pachyderm the next afternoon to see the book and to give me some more instructions and my check.

Next day I was over at Evelyn's Oasis, across the square from the *Tracks* office having some lunch to work off a due-bill for Evelyn's regular ad in the paper. The phone rang and in a minute Evelyn said I'd better take the call. It was Linetta—she was spelling Gladys at the switchboard—and Linetta said there was a man to see me, very important, wouldn't talk on the phone.

I told her to give him a cup of tea and I'd be back as soon as I finished my hot pot roast sandwich.

Little while later when I strolled over to the *Tracks*, I saw a rental car parked inconspicuously in the alley beside the building, and when I got inside a stranger stood up and said, "You took your time getting back, Sanford. Didn't I tell you I was coming today?"

I gaped at the stranger. He had a bunch of red hair standing up all over his head, big, tortoise-shell eyeglasses without any lenses at all, and a funny fake moustache attached to the phony nose.

"Herman?" I said.

He frowned—I think he frowned, as much as I could see his face through the artificial shrubbery and the stick-on nose. "Shhh!" he hissed, grabbing me by the elbow and putting his mouth close to my ear. "Nobody is supposed to know. That's why I put on the disguise."

There I was, laughing at poor Herman again. He always had a flair for the theatrical, but it never rose above melodrama. Maybe that's why he did so well as an editor and agent. I said, "Okay, I won't give you away. You want to see the magazines?"

He said, "Where are they?"

I led him out the back door of the *Tracks* building and over to the shed. I opened the door and said, "There it is, Herman, the first issue of *Nick Neptune's Adventure Magazine*."

He said, "What do you think of it? Considering that you are Nicholas Neptune. . . ."

"Well," I told him, "for somebody who doesn't really know too much about pulp magazines, I think it's pretty good. The only thing is, it has a kind of old-fashioned look to it with that artwork, and the stories are pretty creaky in places."

"That's just fine," Herman said, "that's exactly what, ah, Stinky and I want."

I wanted to ask him who Stinky really was then. I had a number of guesses—B. Traven, James Tiptree, Jr., J.D. Salinger, even Howard Hughes. But Herman kept going before I could ask.

"Look here," he said, "I want you to do something. Where were you a few minutes ago, when your wife called you?"

"Over to Evelyn's," I told him. "Eating my lunch."

"Well look," Herman repeated himself, "I want you to go on back to Evelyn's. Get yourself some dessert. Better yet, have a drink, have a drink on me. Does Evelyn have a liquor license?"

Herman seemed to be getting more and more excited. I didn't know why he wanted to be left alone in the shed, but I nodded, yes, Evelyn sold liquor too.

"Okay," Herman said, "you go on back and have a drink for yourself and I'll be right after you."

Well, I don't consider myself a heavy drinking man, but if it was important to Herman I wouldn't mind sipping a shot of Jack Daniel's Black Label as long as he was paying for it. Maybe even a double. I walked back through the *Tracks* office, told Linetta where I was headed and went ahead.

I sat in the Oasis and looked over across the square, nursing some JD. Next to the *Tracks* office I saw Herman opening the trunk of his rented car. He took some stuff out, disappeared back toward the shed, reappeared in a couple of minutes, put some stuff back into the trunk and walked over to the Oasis.

He sat down at my table and told Evelyn to bring the bottle back and leave it and to bring a glass for him. That was about the oddest I'd ever seen Herman act. He kept looking across the street toward my office, like he was waiting for something to happen, and all the time he was drinking fine bourbon and talking away nervously.

"Tomorrow's a vital day," he told me, "you have to be Nick Neptune."

"What do you mean?" I asked him.

"I mean there's a man coming to see you tomorrow."

I must have looked a little dubious about that. "Don't worry," Herman said, "you don't have to do anything wrong, and you'll be well paid, Stinky has a fat bank account."

"Well," I said, "then what's going on?"

Herman finally took his eyes off the window of Evelyn's Oasis and looked me in the face, through those funny lenseless glasses of his, his red wig sticking up all over and his plastic nose and moustache bobbing with every word.

He said, "Did you ever hear of Louie Lupowitz?"

I thought for a moment. "Sounds vaguely familiar," I finally said, "he a pulp writer of yours?"

"Not quite," Herman said. "But close. He happens to be a collector. He's also been involved with adventure fiction for thirty years, since he was a kid. He's one of those characters with no particular talent but a lot of ambition. So for thirty years he's made a living driving a sewer-excavating machine up in Kingston, New York, where he lives.

"At the same time he's built what he claims is the best pulp and adventure fiction collection in the world. What the Vatican library is to pornography, Lupowitz's collection is to adventure stories. I've seen his collection, and he's got all the scarcest items. He is a fine collector."

"Sounds admirable," I said.

"He's also one of the nastiest bastards walking around," Herman said. "He's vicious, vindictive, he'll do anything to crush any other collector who has any chance to get something that he's lacking. There are stories about him that—when H.H. Ungano was on his deathbed, on his deathbed mind you, Lupowitz came to Ungano's house and told his wife that—"

Herman Minkowsky didn't get to finish the story of Lupowitz and Ungano's wife because I saw a huge cloud of smoke billowing up over the *Tracks* office across the square from Evelyn's. I jumped up and knocked over the table and the Jack Daniel's and I was out the front door of the Oasis like a shot, Minkowsky about one-half a step behind me.

I burst through the front door of the newspaper office expecting to find a raging inferno inside, and all I found was my wife sitting at the switchboard with a cup of tea in one hand and a pencil in the other, taking a classified ad over the telephone. Herman Minkowsky banged into me from the rear and I started moving again, through the little half-high swinging door in the counter, past my own desk and into the back of the building, the plant, looking for flames *there*, and all I found was Mort Van Vlack working over the *Nick Neptune's Adventure Magazine* plates with a sledge hammer. Herman and the mysterious Stinky wanted a controlled edition, they were going to get one.

I screeched to a halt, Mort said, "Howdy-do," and this time without Herman having to collide with me I took off still again, out the back door and down the steps to the old lot where the wooden shed stood. There it was, roaring in flames.

"Oh my God," I heard my own voice wail, "all the *Neptune's* books!" I spun on my heel to get back to the switchboard and phone over to Buffalo Falls for the volunteer fire brigade, but before I could get my call through they roared up in their old American-LaFrance engine. Turned out that Evelyn had phoned 'em from the Oasis as soon as she saw why Herman and I had run out so precipitously.

The volunteers kept the fire from spreading to the *Tracks* building or any other structure, and the shed itself, well, it was a total loss but it was so rickety and old that it was small loss at that. But the magazines! The magazines!

I turned to Herman Minkowsky and I said, "By God but I'm sorry, Herman. I should never have stored the magazines out here, I can't figure out how that fire started but whatever caused it, they're totally ruined. Any copies that weren't burned up, why look —" and I poked at a pile of charred and waterlogged and foam-soaked garbage " — any that aren't burned up are wrecked by water and chemicals.

"Herman," I said, "what are we going to do? What's Stinky going to say?"

Now the strange thing was, Herman didn't act upset at all. Excited, yes, but not upset. He got the strangest light in his eyes and he started poking around those charred remains and he pulled something out of the mess and held it aside. Then he said, "Sanford, don't worry about anything. This is just perfect."

I said I didn't understand how he could think that. Would Stinky pay to do the whole production job over? What was going to happen?

Herman said that everything was delightful, that I'd get my full payment for the *Tracks* doing the production work, plus the bonus he'd talked about, plus Stinky would pay for the loss of the shed, and not to make an insurance report or anything. He stuck the hunk of garbage he'd salvaged under his arm and said, "Just one thing, Sanford. I want you to promise on your honor to personally dispose of this mess," and he gestured to the burned-up magazines.

I said I would, and he shook my hand and started to leave. I walked him to his rented car — the volunteers had gone on back to Buffalo Falls by now — and just as he started to climb behind the wheel I said, "Wait a second, Herman. What should I say to Lupowitz?"

"What?" he said.

"I said, what should I tell Lupowitz. Is he still coming here tomorrow? You said before that I had to play Nick Neptune for that weird magazine collector."

Herman got the biggest, oddest grin on his face then, and he said, "I forgot all about that, Sandy," only it sounded to me more like he'd thought I would never ask.

"Here," he said, and handed me the battered remains of a magazine that he'd pulled out of the burnt-up shed. "When Louie arrives you tell him that you were Nick Neptune. You tell him the whole story of the magazine, only keep me out of it and keep Stinky out of it whatever you do.

"If I know Louie Lupowitz's collector's heart he'll ask you if any copies of *Neptune's* survived the fire, or if there are any proofs or unbound signatures or covers or anything—*anything*—he can get as a memento of the magazine. He'll try and charm something out of you, he'll try and wheedle something out of you, and if you resist long enough he'll try and buy something from you. How you handle Louie is up to you, Sanford, but when you get tired of playing with him, I want you to give him this. Give it to him, or sell it to him, whatever, but I want you to make sure he has it when he goes back to Kingston."

And he tapped that burned, battered, soaked carcass of a magazine with his finger tip, and he clamped on his safety belt and turned on his car engine and away he drove.

The next morning was business as usual, taking care of *Tracks* business that was. Mort was very upset about the fire and the whole *Neptune's* episode, but I told him what Herman had said, that Stinky would still pay, and that he—Mort—and Gladys and Linetta were all to keep quiet about it, especially if and when Louie Lupowitz showed up.

And he did. I was eating lunch at Evelyn's Oasis again, telling Evelyn how lucky I felt that the fire was only an old wooden shed with nothing valuable in it, when the phone in the Oasis rang and this time it was Gladys saying that a Mr. Lupowitz was here to see me and would I come right back. I could tell by her voice that she didn't like Mr. Lupowitz, but I told her to offer him a cup of tea and say I'd be back as soon as I finished eating my meal.

I had an extra cup of Evelyn's fresh coffee and strolled over to the *Tracks*. There, sitting at my desk and examining my notes (none of which could have interested him much, being the rough draft of my planned Christmas editorial), sat just about the un-pleasantest man I had ever laid eyes on.

Now I knew why Herman and Stinky disliked this fellow.

He seemed to combine a kind of surly, defensive manner with flashes of hearty hale-fellowship that didn't ring true at all, with a terrific desire to impress folks with his own importance and influence. I think he counted a little too much on me as a country bumpkin, too, which didn't set very nicely.

To top it all off he showed me something that he said was proof of his devotion to adventure literature and particularly to the late Edgar Rice Burroughs.

I said what was that and he reached inside his suit coat and pulled out a long, thin-bladed knife.

I must have jumped back five feet when he brandished that thing at me, and he just laughed a lot and said it was a genuine authentic Barsoomian stiletto, custom made according to the specifications in Burroughs's *Under the Moons of Mars*, and that he carried it with him wherever he went.

That didn't really impress me too much, but I had my instructions so I asked Lupowitz who he wanted to see and what it was that he wanted.

"I need to talk with Nicholas Neptune," he said.

I said I was Neptune.

He said, "Is that your real name?"

I said no, I was actually Sanford Hall, but that Nick Neptune seemed a more atmospheric name for the editor and publisher of my new magazine, and what could I do for him.

"I am universally recognized," Lupowitz told me, "as the leading authority on the history of adventure literature. I have written six standard books on the subject, and I am working on a new, authoritative revision of *The Latter-Day Pulp Period — 1953 to Date*, published by Latham & Latham. I need the full informa-tion on the background of your magazine, and how you got the material for it."

So I told him about the fire, and told him that we were unin-sured and that the backers of the magazine—who insisted on anonymity—had refused any more capital. "So you see, Mr. Lupowitz, I'm afraid you traveled all the way out here for nothing. There is no *Nick Neptune's Adventure Magazine* and there never will be, and I've just gone back to being a small-town editor."

Right then Lupowitz acted exactly the way Herman Minkow-sky had predicted. He asked if any copies of the magazine had sur-vived the fire and I told him no, and he said was I sure, and I said yes, and he said were there any galleys left and I said no, and he said were all the covers destroyed too and I said yes.

He asked if he could see the site of the fire and I showed him the charred place where the shed had stood. I'd cleared away even the remnants of the fire and there was nothing to see but some blackened earth and some burnt weeds.

He shook his head sadly and we'd started back into the newspaper building when something caught the corner of his eye. At the same instant he called, "What's that?" and dived for the top step at the back of the plant, where I'd carefully tossed the wrecked copy of the magazine Herman had salvaged yesterday.

Lupowitz came up clutching the horrible mess to his bosom like it was a piece of the True Cross, and said defiantly, "No copies left, hey? What do you think this is?" And he clutched the magazine tightly in his hand and shook it at me, giving a kind of clenched-teeth smirk of triumph that set my own teeth on edge.

"Oh, that," I said with studied casualness, "do you want that disgusting thing? Look at it!"

He held it in his hands, reverently but as if he'd never let it go, and carried it inside the building and to my desk. He put it down but he never relinquished contact with it, as if he'd established a claim and was never going to give up possession.

"Look at it," I said again. "The cover's completely gone, it was a Bok original."

Lupowitz groaned.

"The front pages are gone."

Lupowitz groaned.

"It's soaked with water and chemicals."

Lupowitz tore his hair.

"Almost half the type on every page is charred."

Lupowitz looked at me with tragic eyes. "Nonetheless," he said, wagging a long and grimy-nailed finger under my nose, "it is still a copy of *Nick Neptune's Adventure Magazine*. It is a first edition Burroughs," he said, which information he must have got from Minkowsky because he hadn't got it from me, "and a first edition Campbell and a first edition Doc Smith. We can assume with a full degree of assurance that all of the stories will in due course find their way to the dignity and permanence of hardcover publication."

"S'pose so," I said.

"But this—" and he held that ugly, smelly, charred, damp remnant of a magazine up in the air like it was Holy Grail—"is *unique!* *Unique!*" He cackled like the mad scientist in a bad old horror movie. "Oh," he said, his voice low and full of ugly triumph, "wait until Amundsen hears about this! Wait until Wollheim and Teitler and Coriell and Caz hear about it! Wait until they all hear about it!"

He looked at me and I swear I'd never in my life looked into the eyes of a genuine madman until that moment. "I need this item," he said. "I won't give it up! What will you take for it?"

"Take for it?" I said. "I don't want anything for it. Take it, take."

He shook my hand and it was like shaking hands with a character out of Dickens, Scrooge or Beadle, or better yet Uriah Heep. And then he dropped my hand and ran out of the building, literally ran, and jumped in a car and drove away and that was the last time I ever saw Louie Lupowitz, or even heard of him, until the day of his death.

But those adventure story people have some kind of grapevine all their own. I don't know how word spread—maybe it was Herman Minkowsky or his friend Stinky who leaked the news deliberately—but by night I'd had two phone calls from fellows who said they published special newsletters and wanted to talk to Mr. Neptune. I told them both that I was Neptune, we'd been burned out and there wasn't going to be any magazine.

Next morning at eight o'clock I had a person-to-person call from a fellow on the West Coast. Meant that *he* had got up at five o'clock to phone me! He introduced himself as the curator of the National Magazine Repository and said he wanted a copy of *Nick Neptune's Adventure Magazine,* said the repository had to have it for their archives. I told him there was no such magazine. He said that Louie Lupowitz had a copy—imagine that, less than twenty-four hours and he knew all about Lupowitz.

Well, I took his number and said I'd get in touch with him.

Within a week I had close to thirty telephone calls and a hundred letters from collectors trying to get copies of *Neptune's.* I phoned Minkowsky about it and he sounded happy as a bear in a bee tree with nobody at home, and said I should forward everything to him. He really sounded pleased when I told him about the magazine repository call.

"That's Amundsen," Minkowsky said, "I knew he'd be in touch. This is absolutely delicious, absolutely delicious! Good work, Sandy."

Well, I had his check by then, so I was pretty happy too. I have to admit that I still didn't understand, really understand, what the whole sequence of events meant. I mean, each thing that we'd done, I grasped—gathering the material for *Neptune's,* producing that one issue, the fact that it had been destroyed, Stinky's refusal to put up money for doing it over, Minkowsky's having me give that battered copy to Lupowitz and forward all the later inquiries to his, Minkowsky's, office.

But when I put it together it didn't really make any sense.

One more thing that made the back of my brain itch when I thought about it: I couldn't prove anything, so I never confronted him with it, but I was certain that Herman set the storage shed fire himself. All of the mysterious going back and forth between his rented car and the back of the newspaper plant, the way he acted so expectant in Evelyn's Oasis, and the very peculiar way he responded to the damage, paying for the shed, not even seeking insurance. . . .

Well, it was all a mystery but I was more involved in keeping my weekly going and in running the job shop on the side. We were heavily into the consolidated school's yearbook by then, and except for the *Neptune's* project that yearbook is the biggest and most lucrative piece of job printing in Potawatomy County, and we couldn't afford to do a bad job—or to get the books delivered too late for senior week at the school. Those kids take their yearbook very seriously and I don't blame them.

I still got an occasional letter or telephone call about *Neptune's*; they were all forwarded to Herman Minkowsky and what he did with them was none of my concern. June came and we made the yearbook deadline and collected our money for that, and Gladys and Linetta and Mort Van Vlack and I settled back for a relatively easy season of doing just the *Tracks* and the usual run of wedding invitations and at-home cards.

Then Herman Minkowsky telephoned again. His voice sounded full of glee, and somehow I felt a little quiver when I heard it, wondering what new bit of business was coming up. He told me right off. "Sandy," he said, "I hope you're not too busy right now with your giant journal."

Nope, I told him, it was actually a pretty quiet period.

He said, "Wonderful, great. Now listen, this is very important. You're going to be Nicholas Neptune again."

"You mean Stinky wants the magazine revived?"

"No, nothing of the sort." Over the long distance wire I could hear him draw away from the telephone and puff on a pipe. "This is just for one day," he resumed. "There's a national conference coming up, of people who collect pulp magazines, and we need Nick Neptune there. We'll fly you in, put you up at the conference hotel, and all you have to do is take about fifteen minutes to sit up at a dais. Then we'll fly you home again and you get all expenses plus another bonus from Stinky."

I thought about it for a minute. We had a folder of the high school senior essays in the reserve drawer. Gladys could run the *Tracks* if she had to, so I said, "Can I bring Linetta with me?"

Herman said, "Absolutely. I'll send you your tickets."

That's the way Herman operated. Direct and even a little bit arbitrary, but he was effective.

A week later the tickets arrived, I told Gladys and Mort what had to be done, and Linetta and I were off to the conference. They had it in the Muehlbach Hotel in Kansas City, and the minute we walked in the big revolving doors we were surrounded by the strangest bunch of maniacs I have ever laid eyes on, and that includes the frat boys and other assorted hell-raisers I knew in college.

There was a message waiting and I got Linetta settled and went on up to the penthouse suite where I found Herman Minkowsky lounging with a bottle of Jack Daniel's in front of him. I was happy to see that he'd left his disguise at home. He said, "Have a seat, Nick."

I did a double take, laughed a little unsteadily and sat down. I looked around the luxurious suite and was about to ask Herman what was happening now when, by golly, I saw a tall, pale man sitting on a chair so faint that he almost disappeared into the pastel appointments of the room.

"Hello again, uh, Stinky," I said.

He barely nodded.

"Now this conference," Herman launched into his talk, "is held annually in a different city each year. These magazine collectors travel thousands of miles to meet old friends and rivals, to brag about their acquisitions, to look at exhibits and to get a chance at some rare old copy of *Miracle Stories* or *Golden Fleece* or *New Story* magazine or *Zeppelin Stories*."

"*Zeppelin Stories?*" I repeated.

"Oh yes, or *Civil War Stories*, or *South Sea Stories*. There were a lot of very specialized pulps. Some were even devoted to the adventures of a single hero, issue after issue. *The Shadow, Terence X. O'Leary, Captain Hazzard*."

"Okeh," I said. "I don't believe it but I believe it, if you take my meaning."

Herman laughed at that, and I even saw the ghost of a tiny smile flitter around the edges of Stinky's mouth.

"But I still don't see what you need me for," I added.

"All right," said Herman, suddenly all earnest business. He leaned over toward me, all of the mass of him looking like he was going to launch himself physically into what he was saying. "There's going to be an auction tomorrow afternoon after the big luncheon. There are going to be some pretty choice items offered to the highest bidder. Now we need you to appear for a few minutes as a special guest, and personally auction this item." He turned slowly in his chair, picked up a fancy alligator-skin attaché case and unzipped it. He pulled out a pulp magazine sealed in a transparent polythane bag and held it up for me to see. The cover showed a brooding, mysterious scene in the depths of a musty, ancient Egyptian tomb. Splattered across the top of the picture in lurid chartreuse lettering was the title of the magazine.

"*Nick Neptune's Adventure Magazine!*" I gasped.

"Right." It wasn't the hearty businessman's voice of Herman Minkowsky that carried that one word, but the chilling whisper of Stinky from his chair.

I said, "But there were no copies left after the fire, except for—"

"The battered copy that you gave to Louie Lupowitz, that he's been flaunting and gloating over ever since."

"Well," I said.

"Well there's this one also," Herman said. "Unlike Lupowitz's battered fragment of a book, this one is complete, perfect, mint. And you're going to auction it off tomorrow."

I nodded pleasantly. All right, so that was Minkowsky's secret. All the while I was sitting in Evelyn's Oasis that day Herman had come to Pachyderm, while he was making his way between the shed and his car, I suspected that he was starting the fire that destroyed the shed and the *Neptune's* magazines. But now I realized that he'd done one other thing: removed a mint copy of the book before he set the fire. Well, fine, he didn't tell me everything and I didn't tell him everything either, so we were even on that score.

The icy voice of Stinky came slithering out of his corner. "Several hundred of the most fanatical collectors are gathered in the Muehlbach," he hissed. "Most of them are private hobbyists, a few represent libraries and similar institutions. *Neptune's* is going to be the sensation of the sale. It is a prize of prizes. It will draw Howard specialists, Burroughs specialists, Smith specialists. . . .

"But mark my words, Hall. Once you introduce this magazine the bidding will come down to two men before the first ten min-

utes are past. Those men will be Louie Lupowitz—" he said the
name as if it were filth in his mouth "—and Foster Fred Amundsen."

Minkowsky broke in. "Amundsen is the National Magazine
Repository. Or rather, the repository is Amundsen's attic. He's
been collecting for forty years. His collection and Lupowitz's are
the two best in the world."

I said, "All right."

Herman went on about Amundsen. "In manner he's the complete opposite of Lupowitz: cheerful, witty, sympathetic. But
there's a streak submerged in Foster Fred Amundsen." I was
amazed to see Herman Minkowsky shudder. I turned toward
Stinky. He was paler than ever, clutching the arms of his chair
until his knuckles were dead white.

"Under the skin," Herman Minkowsky resumed, "Amundsen
and Lupowitz are brothers. Rivals. And they hate each other's guts!"

There was a moment of stillness, then I shook myself in my
chair, reached across to take Herman's bottle of Jack Daniel's and
a glass. "I don't see that this is any concern of mine," I said. "I'll
auction off the magazine if that's my instructions, take my pay
and go back to Potawatomy County, and be well shed of the
whole affair, if the truth be known!"

"Fine," said Herman. "Just so you understand. And don't let
Amundsen pull anything on you about the repository. Remember
that it's just his private collection. He's made some sort of crazy
will that when he dies his insurance will perpetuate his collection
as a public archive of some sort, but Amundsen himself is just a
glory-seeking, greedy, self-aggrandizing, competitive pack-rat."

Stinky gave a loud hiss. I looked into his face and saw real
emotion there for the first and only time.

Hatred.

I stood up and left the penthouse. Downstairs I found Linetta
and we spent the afternoon and evening circulating among the
magazine collectors. I was a little bit leery of revealing to those
weird folks that I was Nicholas Neptune, so I just gave my real
name and we had a pretty good time. I found that most of the collectors were eager to talk about their hobby, and since I was more
inclined to listen than to talk we got along fine.

We got through the next morning and the luncheon the same
way. Then came the auction.

I sat in the audience with Linetta and watched fascinated as
single copies and runs of half-century-old magazines were sold for
unbelievable amounts. The money that people will pay for a copy

of *Triple-X,* of *Science Wonder Stories,* of *Ranch Romances,* absolutely flabbergasted me.

Finally the auctioneer, a huge fat man with a greasily-ingratiating manner, made the announcement I was waiting for. "Ladies and gentlemen," he said, "as all of us who follow the current magazine scene are aware—" and at this there was a faint ripple of boos through the audience "—the past year has seen a very bizarre and unfortunate incident.

"We all know the regrettable story of a new magazine that was to have appeared with previously unpublished stories by some of our finest authors." There was an undertone from the crowd, as groups of people called out names: Burroughs . . . Howard . . . Asimov.

"Until now," the auctioneer continued, "it was believed that only one copy of the magazine had escaped the conflagration that destroyed the warehouse where the first edition was stored. That copy, coverless, partial, charred and stained, is the proud possession of Mr. Louie Lupowitz, who is scheduled to make a speech about it later today.

"But this afternoon we have the good fortune to have with us the editor and publisher of *Nick Neptune's Adventure Magazine,* Mr. Nicholas Neptune himself."

I rose to a solid round of applause and strode to the platform. The auctioneer handed me an alligator attaché case that I recognized as Herman Minkowsky's. I took it from him and said to the audience, "I'm sorry that we never quite got off the ground, folks, but here's something that you may wish to bid for."

I looked around the room. Sitting near the end of one row of folding hotel chairs I recognized Louie Lupowitz. I smiled at him and he looked back at me as if he'd just bitten into a fresh lemon. Far at the opposite end of the room, surrounded by a crowd of admirers, average age about twelve, was a cheery looking man wearing a badge. The badge was so huge that I could read it from my place on the platform. It was a brightly colored, ornate monogram: *NMR.* Ahah! I said to myself, the National Magazine Repository. That must be Foster Fred Amundsen.

People were beginning to rustle around, so I unzipped the alligator case, reached inside, and pulled out the polythane-wrapped mint copy of *Nick Neptune's Adventure Magazine.* I held it before my chest and turned slowly so that everyone in the room could see it.

They were all on their feet, jostling for a better look. I just held the magazine until they settled back into their chairs.

Before the fat auctioneer could even call for bids jolly Foster
Fred Amundsen was on his feet. "The National Magazine Repository bids one hundred dollars," he said, and sat down.

Lupowitz was on his feet, furious. "One hundred twenty-five
dollars!" he shouted.

Right there the die was cast, and I could see what Herman and
Stinky had set this whole thing up for. While the fat auctioneer
ran the bidding, I let my eyes rove over the audience. There were
Herman and Stinky sitting quietly in the last row. They were
taking in every word. Herman even held a little cassette recorder
in his lap, pointing a portable microphone toward the front of the
room.

A fellow with a big Tarzan lapel button topped Lupowitz's
one-twenty-five, then a little old lady with a kind of hairy, barbaric
figure stitched onto her coat topped that.

There must have been close to a score of bidders, but just as
predicted they dropped out, one by one, until only Amundsen and
Lupowitz remained.

When the bidding passed five hundred dollars, Lupowitz asked
the auctioneer if personal checks were acceptable. The fat man
said, "For you, Mr. Lupowitz, of course." Louie went up another
fifty dollars.

Foster Fred Amundsen was perspiring freely, the jovial expression on his face replaced by a deadly determined one. I saw him
and Lupowitz exchange glances of purest hatred after every raise.
Amundsen said to the auctioneer, "Do you take credit cards?"

There was a brief exchange between the fat man and the
cashier-clerk who cleaned up each transaction as it ended. They
conferred, looked up, nodded, exchanged a few more words, then
the fat man said, "Sure, Foster, if you'll give us a minute to phone
for confirmation."

Amundsen raised the price over Lupowitz.

I watched Lupowitz and Amundsen, Minkowsky and the
enigmatic pale Stinky, trying to understand what I was seeing.
This was a lot more than a hobbyists' auction. A whole lot more.

Just what it was the two rival collectors had ever done to the
mysterious Stinky I expected I would never know—not unless I
could find out his true identity, which seemed very unlikely. But
what Stinky and Herman Minkowsky were doing to the two collectors I could see clearly, and it was something with a surface ele-
ment of humor to it, but something very serious underneath.

I could see it in Lupowitz's and Amundsen's faces, hear it in
their voices as they bitterly raised each other's bids. They had

quietly edged to the front of the room now, and they were standing hardly an arm's length from each other, directly in front of the
auction table, looking up at the fat auctioneer and at the copy of
*Neptune's* magazine I held.

Lupowitz had his checkbook in his hand. He looked at it carefully, slipped it inside his suit jacket, patted the pocket and said,
"Eight seventy-five."

He already owned a *Neptune's*. Until today, he had thought, a
unique item, the modern diadem of his entire collection. And that
supremacy was being challenged, and challenged by his archrival.

Amundsen was trembling visibly, making some sort of magical
passes with his fingers. He was staring as if hypnotized at the
magazine. He whispered, "Nine hundred."

This was his chance, not merely to break Lupowitz's monopoly
on *Neptune's* but actually to obtain a better copy than the one his
enemy owned.

Lupowitz went up another notch.

Amundsen followed.

Lupowitz leaned over toward Amundsen and whispered something I couldn't make out, then raised the bid again. It stood at
nine seventy-five.

Amundsen was drenched in sweat now. He turned from facing
the magazine, ninety degrees, to look squarely at Lupowitz. In a
voice I could barely make out he said, "One thousand."

The room was as silent as death for five seconds, then cheers
and applause broke out. When silence was restored the fat auctioneer announced, "Mr. Amundsen has bid one thousand dollars.
Are there any more bids?"

Silence.

"Going once."

Lupowitz began to shake visibly where he stood. He took out
that checkbook again and looked in it. He leaned over the auction
table so that I took a step back from it. "One thousand one
hundred dollars," he said.

No one spoke. Amundsen stood where he was, his armpits and
crotch dark with perspiration, his face running with it. Lupowitz's
face was drained of blood. He chewed at his lower lip. A wave
seemed to pass over him and his ears and neck turned beet red.
He began to reach for the magazine.

The auctioneer said, "Mr. Lupowitz bids one thousand one
hundred dollars.

"Going once to Mr. Lupowitz."

Every eye in the room was riveted on Amundsen's sweaty face.

"Going twice to Mr. Lupowitz for one thousand one hundred dollars."

Suddenly Amundsen raised his hand like a schoolboy answering a geography question. The auctioneer said, "Foster?" Amundsen said, "One-five."

The auctioneer said, "Mr. Amundsen bids one thousand five hundred dollars.

"Going once."

Lupowitz opened his checkbook and gazed at it with a griefstricken expression.

"Going twice."

Lupowitz stared glassy-eyed into his checkbook, then at Amundsen, then up at the magazine in my hands, then down at the checkbook again. His face seemed to be undergoing alternate waves of fiery redness and icy white. A low, keening sound began to rise from his throat, gaining ever so slowly in volume.

I looked at the back of the room. Everyone was standing. I spotted Minkowsky and Stinky standing close together, staring at the scene before the table.

The fat auctioneer said, "Going three times and gone to Foster Fred Amundsen for one thousand five hundred dollars!"

The collectors in the room began cheering in earnest. The sound coming from Lupowitz's throat rose to a scream. His face was bright red now, his eyes popping. He dropped his checkbook and reached inside his coat, his hand emerging clutching that weird Barsoomian stiletto he'd shown me the day he visited Pachyderm.

With a cry of, "Die, ulsio, die!" he plunged the stiletto into the breast of Foster Fred Amundsen.

The auctioneer went over the top of the table with amazing speed. At the same time people from the front row of the audience were swarming over the figures of Amundsen and Lupowitz. Amundsen had fallen to the floor and lay supine while Lupowitz crouched over him, jamming that wicked slim dagger into his chest again and again.

Finally they got him off Amundsen, leaving the knife stuck in that poor man's chest, blood all over both of them. Lupowitz stood there, four or five men holding him. "I am the—" something, he shouted, the last word was inaudible. "I! I! Louie Lupo—" and he collapsed forward, turning suddenly to dead weight and falling across Amundsen's body, dragging two men down with him.

They released his arms, then turned him over. He was dead,

an expression of sheer, bitter hatred still on his face. The auctioneer was there. He reached down and with two fingers of his one hand closed Foster Fred Amundsen's eyes; with the other he closed Louie Lupowitz's.

Of course that broke up the collector's conference. The hotel detective was on the scene in five minutes, he had the Kansas City regulars there in ten. There was a coroner's inquest but there was never any doubt, with all of the witnesses in that hotel ballroom, that the verdict would be murder followed by natural death. Lupowitz had worked himself up to apoplexy. Once he'd killed Amundsen he died himself, before he even hit the floor.

The only really complicated part of the case, ironically, was what would become of that mint copy of *Nick Neptune's Adventure Magazine*. The coroner seized it initially, as evidence in the investigation of the two deaths. Now he says he's willing to release it, but he doesn't know who is supposed to get it.

Minkowsky and his friend Stinky left the conference and the hotel as quickly as they could. They paid me off for my services, such as they were. I had a note from Herman saying that what happened at the auction wasn't my fault and I was entitled to my pay and expenses. I still don't know who Stinky is.

My guess—by this time I decided that I'd cover the auction and the violence in my capacity as editor of the Pachyderm, Pennsylvania *Tracks*—is that that National Magazine Repository, set up in Amundsen's will, will stand by his bid of fifteen hundred dollars and get custody of the mint *Neptune's* in due course.

But I also guess that it may take them years.

All of which brings me to the reason why I've told you this whole story, and again I apologize for my habit of going long-way round Robin Hood's barn to tell a story, but that's the way you get after a while when you have to fill a small-town newspaper every week and there just isn't that much hard news in the town where you live.

When all of those magazines were getting assembled back in the Pachyderm *Tracks* office, and I got together with Mort Van Vlack and we put 'em in cartons and carried them out to the storage shed behind the newspaper plant, the very first thing I did was the same thing I do any time any publication comes off of my press. I set two perfect copies aside to send to the Library of Congress to register the copyright.

Now once that fire struck the shed and the magazines were destroyed, and Herman told me that we never were going to print and distribute any more copies, then of course the magazine was

# Old Folks at Home

## Marvia Plum

THE SQUEAL CAME IN SIDEWAYS. THE REPORTING PERson called nine-one-one, Dispatch sent the paramedics, the 'medics reported the subject DOA under dubious circumstances, and the case got bucked to Homicide.

Enter Sergeant Plum.

Marvia was working swing shift, cruising Berkeley in a black-and-white, when the squeal came in. She monitored the traffic, phoned in to McKinley Avenue and told the watch officer that she was responding to the scene.

She arrived a microsecond behind the patrol unit. She spotted the maroon and white Paramedic ambulance in the courtyard of Autumn House, the converted Victorian mansion on North Jordan Boulevard that now served as a retirement home for three dozen still-ambulatory seniors.

She tipped her hand to Jeff Felton, pleased to see one of the department's sharpest experienced patrol officers, and wondered for the hundredth time why Felton had never put in for sergeant. He could have had the promotion in a walk, she was certain.

The Victorian had been retrofitted with automatic doors; they hissed open for Marvia and Felton. The lobby was filled with heavy, dark, old-fashioned furniture. The walls were covered with red flocked wallpaper that could as well have served in a turn-of-the-century bordello as in the home of a onetime president of the University of California.

Old people shuffled through the lobby—once the vestibule of the Victorian—like ghosts. They stopped and stared at Marvia and Felton, residents of different worlds viewing each other faintly through the gray fog of time, then tottered away to their separate destinations.

A buxom red-haired woman in a tight-fitting white uniform crossed the lobby to meet them. At first she appeared very young, then Marvia realized that she was closer to fifty than forty; the deception was the product of contrast with the old folks.

"I'm Anise MacDougald." She held out a pale hand. Marvia took it, introduced herself, asked Ms. MacDougald if she was in charge of the home. "I'm the manager."

The doors opened behind Marvia and she turned her head, saw the crime scene technicians coming through. The coroner's bureau would be the last to arrive, she knew. Their work required the least urgency. The chief crime scene tech nodded to Marvia, then stood a few feet away, awaiting instructions.

More gray-haired ghosts, their skin transparent and their thin bones visible—or was that Marvia's imagination at play?—gathered around them, drawn by the uniforms, the youth, the warm life of the newcomers.

"You better show us what happened," Marvia told MacDougald. "The paramedics are still there, right?"

MacDougald nodded. "Upstairs." She led Marvia and Felton to a linoleum-floored elevator. Marvia jerked her thumb at the evidence techs, summoning them to follow. In the elevator she asked MacDougald for a quick rundown on the incident.

"Mr. Collins pulled the panic cord. All our rooms have little panic cords, really bead chains. If somebody feels ill or falls down and can't get up, all he has to do is get to the nearest cord and pull it and we send somebody up to see what's wrong."

Marvia nodded.

The elevator stopped and the doors slid open. As they stepped into the hall, MacDougald added, "Mr. Collins pulled the cord. I ran upstairs myself. The old stairs are actually quicker than the elevator. He just pointed to Mr. Smithton. His roommate. We encourage our residents to double up. It keeps their charges down, you see. And the companionship is good for morale. Loneliness is such a problem for old people."

The door was open and Marvia stepped inside ahead of Mac-Dougald. One of the paramedics had stayed beside the man lying on the floor. MacDougald nodded to the still form as if they were exchanging a friendly greeting. "That's Mr. Smithton."

Marvia turned back toward the doorway. She gestured Felton forward. "You're in charge of the scene, Jeff."

Felton moved forward and stretched a yellow crime-scene tape across the doorway. He knelt beside the body, looked up at the paramedic and started asking questions.

Marvia stood with MacDougald, observing. The body was that of a man in his eighties. It was clad in gray trousers, slip-on shoes and a long-sleeved plaid shirt. The hands looked like claws. The sparse hair was gray except where blood stained it and ran — had run — onto the nondescript carpet.

At the sight of the blood Marvia knelt beside Jeff Felton and peered at the wound without touching Smithton. The surface wound was small but the shape of Smithton's skull indicated that it had been crushed by impact. A heavy cut-glass ashtray lay a foot or so from Smithton's head, one corner splashed with blood. A pair of figures in silhouette had been etched into the glass, along with a few words in languages that Marvia couldn't read.

Almost involuntarily she laid her fingers against Smithton's throat, searching for a pulse she knew would not be there. She stood up and came face-to-face with the paramedic.

The paramedic said, "Only thing I touched was the body, Sarge. Soon as I saw he was dead and saw the blood I figured it was for Homicide, not for us."

Marvia nodded. "You did right." She addressed MacDougald. "You said his roommate pulled the cord."

"Mr. Collins."

"Where is he?"

"The nurse took him to the medical room. We have a RN on duty at all times. She took Mr. Collins to the med room. He was very upset, I was very worried about him and I asked her to take him to the med room. If he calms down we'll have to put him somewhere, I don't know where we'll put him, I'll have to figure something out."

"Did he say what happened?"

"He just said that Mr. Smithton needed help."

"I want to talk to him right now."

MacDougald looked worried. "I don't know. We'll ask the nurse. I think we may have to send him to the hospital."

## Hobart Lindsey

American Financial Resources and International Surety Incorporated had been business partners longer than Hobart Lindsey had been alive; their billions spoke with authority. It was a long-standing policy at International Surety, not put in writing in so many words, but clearly understood: when AFR whistled a tune, IS danced a jig.

So the claim hit Lindsey's desk in a bright red folder that meant *immediate attention, top priority*. Lindsey opened it and read a few lines, then reached for the phone. Somebody had been running up bills on a stolen AFR emerald card. That was a common enough problem, but the stolen card belonged to AFR's regional VP. The card had no limit and the bills had piled up high and fast before the theft was noticed, and the VP was steaming.

AFR had a fraud policy with IS and AFR wanted its money. Lindsey's job was to soothe ruffled feathers at AFR, first, and to recover as much as he could of the loot—the merchandise purchased with the stolen card.

The card itself had been canceled, of course, as soon as the VP realized that it had been stolen, but that had taken almost forty-eight hours and the purchases were almost frightening by then.

Lindsey punched in the number for the regional AFR office and fought his way through the vice president's receptionist, her executive assistant, and her personal secretary. Finally he heard an angry growl and said, "Ms. Whelan."

"Speak!"

"This is Hobart Lindsey at International Surety. About your emerald card."

"Of course about my emerald card. What about the fraud claim?"

"Ms. Whelan, that's an awful lot of money. It's an awful lot of money in any case, but retail purchases in forty-eight hours, it's almost as if the thief was trying to run up bills."

"SOP, Lindsey, you ought to know that. Amateurs use stolen card to buy things for their own use. Professionals buy fencible items. We're dealing with a real pro here."

"Even so, Ms. Whelan. Two Mercedes, from two different dealers no less, and an Acura, jewelry, a Benny Buffano sculpture from a prestigious gallery, well, where else would you get one, half a dozen computers, top-of-the-line home electronics including a couple of HDTVs, it's an amazing list."

"There's more than that."

"I see there is." Lindsey fingered the list in the folder. "What did he buy from Patriot War Goods and Weapons?"

Whelan said, "I have no idea, except it cost a bundle."

"Ms. Whelan," Lindsey continued, "do you have any idea how the thief got your card? Have you made a police report? I don't see a copy of one in the case folder."

"I made a report," Whelan said. Her voice was raspy, as if she were an unreformed chain smoker or as if she'd been cheering at a football game for hours on end. "If you want to know about it I suggest you hustle your little tail over to my office and I'll tell you about it. I don't want copies floating around and I don't feel like describing this on the telephone."

Lindsey agreed and reached for his jacket.

AFR's regional HQ was at 101 California Street. Ever since a disgruntled investor had showed up there with a personal arsenal and gunned down a room full of people before blowing himself to kingdom come, the guards in the building had been both more numerous and more diligent than ever before.

Lindsey felt like an astronaut when he climbed off the express elevator. The executive assistant he'd spoken to—his voice was unmistakable—shook his hand. "Garrison," he announced. "Come with me."

Garrison—Lindsey didn't know whether that was his first name or his last—had the dimpled chin and glittering eye of the MBA on the make. His suit couldn't have been more than three days old, straight from Wilkes-Bashford, and Lindsey knew that it would be discarded in favor of a newer model long before it showed the first sign of wear.

Executive assistant Garrison escorted Lindsey into Ms. Whelan's sublime presence and faded into the scenery.

Whelan's official digs resembled a plush hotel suite more than they did a business office. "Jeannette Whelan," the VP grunted. Lindsey responded with his name. She pointed to a chair and he sank into it obediently. Before he could say a word she said, "I talked to your man Richelieu. He vouched for you. Good. What was your question again, Lindsey?"

Flustered, he opened his attaché case and pulled out the red manila folder. "Uh, the total amount of this claim—"

He looked up and she locked eyes with him. It was like looking into the face of a great white shark.

"It's, ah, a great deal of money." He dropped the folder; fortunately it landed back in the attaché case.

She nodded but didn't say anything.

"Ah, you were going to tell me why it took you two days to report the loss of your card. And the circumstances of the loss."

"Yes."

"Well." He blinked. The sky over San Francisco was crystalline blue and the sun was brilliant. "Ah, how did—?"

"Brilliant racket. I wish who ever did it had come to me for a job instead. We can use that kind of brains in this business. Too many dullards and too many slackers today. Dullards. Slackers."

Lindsey nodded. "And, ah—"

Whelan worked at a table, not a desk. The only break in the smooth surface was a thin-screen computer monitor. She folded the monitor down into the desk, pushed her chair back and stood up. She removed her jacket and hung it on the back of her chair. She was wearing a white sleeveless blouse.

She raised her fists and flexed her arms, showing long, graceful muscles. "What do you think, Lindsey?"

Lindsey blinked. "Ah, ah, very impressive," he stammered.

"Think I got these for Christmas?"

"No."

"Hard work. Two hours at the gym every night. The rest of this organization heads for the corner saloon for their liquid tranquilizers but I head for Starwest Fitness Center and my favorite torture chamber. They think they have the good life but thirty years from now I'll dance on their graves, Lindsey, and then go out and run the Bay to Breakers."

She pulled her jacket back on and slid into her chair.

"Very impressive," Lindsey repeated. "Very admirable. But about the credit card."

"Right." Whelan grinned in a manner that Lindsey was unable to fathom. "Last Thursday I left work at the usual time and headed for Starwest. I went through my usual routine."

"Please walk me through that."

Whelan heaved a long-suffering sigh. "Checked in, picked up a couple of towels, went down to the locker room and changed to my gym outfit."

"Did you carry a gym bag with you?" Lindsey asked.

Whelan shook her head. "I keep a couple of outfits at Starwest. They run everything through the laundry for me, it's part of their service."

Lindsey jotted a note.

"Back up to cardiovascular for my warm-up on the stationary bike. Did a few miles on the bike, then to the weight room. Pumped iron for forty minutes, then back to the bike for a cool-off. Then some stretches and mat exercises. Then a steam bath, sauna, shower, and back to the locker room."

"This takes two hours?" Lindsey asked.

"Just about."

An amber light flashed beneath the tinted glass cover of Whelan's desk. She tapped her fingertip on the glass and the light went into a polychrome dance, then winked out.

Whelan said, "That's when it got funny." She did not laugh when she said, *funny,* and Lindsey didn't think she meant amused at all.

"Couldn't open my padlock," Whelan said.

"Combination or key?"

"Combination."

"You sure you had the right numbers?"

Whelan's eyes widened. "You must be joking. Of course I had the right numbers. It's a perfectly standard rotary padlock and it had always been perfectly reliable. I tried the combination over and over, finally picked up the phone and summoned the manager. When I told her what had happened she asked the combination and I told her. Of course that meant I'd have to replace the lock, but that wasn't my concern at the moment."

Behind her, Lindsey could see into the windows of the office building across California Street. Someone was gazing down at the plaza below as if contemplating a jump. But in the sealed environment of these buildings that was no longer an option.

"Once she'd tried the combination herself a few times she conceded that I was right. She had to summon a handyman with boltcutters to sever the U-ring. She couldn't figure out what had happened. Neither could I. I suspected that something odd was going on, so I checked all my valuables."

"Including your AFR card?"

She looked offended that he even needed to ask that, but she replied, "Of course."

"And it was there?"

"In my card case. Everything looked normal."

"But it wasn't."

"Far from it."

"All right. When did you first realize that something was wrong, and how did you know?"

"Saturday night. Friday I went to the gym after work, picked up a new lock at the desk and had my workout. Saturday I slept in, as usual, spent the day with my succulents, and met a friend at the Iron Horse for dinner."

Behind her, sunlight glinted off a huge jet coming in from the Pacific for a landing at SFO. Lindsey nodded and waited for her to resume.

"Melanie Price. She's my oldest friend. We grew up together in Belmont, went to school together, roomed together at Stanford. She's in line for city editor at the *Examiner* in another year. If the *Examiner* is still around. We get together for drinks and dinner once a week and we go to the Iron Horse at least once a month."

This time the blinking light in her desktop was green. She tapped once and a message appeared in the glass. Lindsey couldn't read it upside down. Whelan scanned it, muttered, and tapped a reply on the glass. The desk went dark.

"Where was I?"

"The Iron Horse."

"We never split a bill. We just take turns picking it up. I gave the waiter my emerald card and he came back and said it was a canceled number. I couldn't figure that out. It wasn't as if I'd maxed out the card. Couldn't do that anyhow. My emerald is no-limit-no-question. One of the little perks of my job. The waiter said they'd gladly put it on a tab, heaven knows they know Mel and me at the Horse. But I said, never mind, I'll pay cash, and I did. Then I studied the card. It was my signature all right, or a damned good forgery. But it wasn't my number."

Lindsey shook his head. "I don't understand."

"Neither did I. Until I put two and two together. Mel helped me. I used to be a systems analyst and Mel was on the crime beat at the *Ex* so we both know how to solve problems. We traced it back to Starwest. The way we figured it out, somebody got into my locker while I was upstairs. Maybe she had bolt-cutters of her own or maybe she was trained as a safecracker and just opened the lock. My God, a little pipsqueak combination lock wouldn't even slow down a professional."

She raised one hand and looked at her wristwatch. It looked like a good one. Lindsey didn't doubt that.

"She must have timed it exquisitely," Whelan went on. "Either that, or just took one hell of a chance and got lucky. She took my lock off, took my emerald card out of my locker, substituted the phony. I don't know how she got my signature, unless she's some kind of instant copyist, or maybe had some kind of miniature scanner and electronic pantograph."

"How would that work?"

"I don't even know if such a gadget exists. But if it does, she could scan my signature off my emerald card and lay it back onto the phony card. Then she put it back in the locker and relocked the locker with an extra lock she brought with her. That would have bought her an extra hour by the time I got things sorted out with Starwest."

"Why do you keep saying 'she?' How do you know it was a woman?"

"It was the women's locker room. Starwest is a coed gym but the locker rooms aren't coed. Even San Francisco isn't that liberated."

Lindsey pondered. "But why was the extra hour important? You didn't discover the theft until Saturday night."

"The crook couldn't know that. For all she knew, the fake card scam—I think that was brilliant, by the way—might fail. And I'd cancel the card and send out an alert within minutes once I discovered what had happened. Even as it is, I know that most of the money was spent within three hours. If the theft took place at six o'clock Thursday, those big-ticket purchases were made within two or three hours. She must have had her program worked out to the minute. Not only did she get expensive goods, they're all fencible. I'll bet those cars are in Mexico already. Or in the hold of ships headed for Japan. Or Kuwait."

Lindsey frowned, concentrating. "One other question."

"Yes?" Whelan waited for him.

"The emerald card—your emerald card—has a no-question-no-limit, ah, feature. Is that right?"

"Yes, it is."

"Then why didn't the thief just grab a fortune in cash? She could use the card for cash advances, couldn't she? Why bother with these complicated transactions, buying cars and HDTVs and computers and converting them to cash? Why not just take the cash to start with?"

"I thought of that myself, Lindsey. And here's the answer. While the emerald card has no limit, the AFR card cash fund itself has a limit. Even American Financial Resources doesn't have an inexhaustible cornucopia of plenty. So AFR Central monitors the cash account balance in real time, through our computer network. If she'd tried to get too much cash, she would have alerted the system that something abnormal was going on, and somebody would have been called to look into it. Maybe even me!" That brought a smirk to her lips.

"So whoever did this knows the inner workings of the AFR system," Lindsey suggested.

"That's right. It might be an inside job. But whether it is or not—this is a smart broad we're dealing with." She ground out the words like small, sharp rocks. "But I'm a smarter broad. And I'm gonna burn her ass!"

## Marvia Plum

Marvia Plum left Jeff Felton in charge of the crime scene and had Anise MacDougald take her to the Autumn House infirmary. MacDougald introduced her to the nurse, Amy Brown. She had dark mocha skin and was overweight and friendly and was sitting beside Jack Collins, holding both his hands.

Marvia introduced herself, staring all the while at Jack Collins. For an instant she thought she knew him, then realized that he looked familiar because he looked so much like the dead Henry Smithton. Both men were short, probably shorter than they had been in earlier decades. Both had pale, transparent skin. Collins's hair was pure white while Smithton's had been iron gray.

Even their eyes were a similar color, but Collins's eyes had the sheen of life while Smithton's had the glaze of death.

Collins was staring straight ahead, moving his lips silently and nodding on occasion. Marvia had no idea what he was saying. She stood in front of him and took his hands from Amy Brown. She introduced herself and asked Collins if he would speak with her.

He raised his eyes to hers, paused, then nodded.

"Mr. Collins, do you want to tell me what happened?"

"The Nazi is dead," he whispered.

"The Nazi?"

"The Nazi is dead."

"Mr. Collins, your roommate is dead. Henry Smithton is dead. It looks as if somebody hit him in the head with a heavy glass ashtray."

Nurse Brown interrupted. "We don't allow smoking here at Autumn House. Health and safety code, Miz, uh, Officer."

"Did somebody do it to Mr. Smithton, Mr. Collins? Did someone hit him? Do you know who hit him? Or could it have been an accident?" Among younger men, it would surely not have been an accident. But among these frail, aged people, a loose shoelace, a ripple in the carpet, a momentary loss of balance, and you could have injury or death.

"I should have done it years ago," Collins said. "Years ago. The Nazi. But I was never certain. He could lie and lie. So could I." He smiled a secretive, inward-turning smile.

Should she mirandize him? Should she take him into custody? *Could* she take him into custody? It certainly looked as if he had wielded the heavy glass weapon, but there was no way she could book him into city jail. She'd have to take him to the county hospital and have him admitted to a locked facility—if she decided to take him into custody at all.

"Mr. Collins, can you tell me what happened today? What happened to Mr. Smithton?"

"He had a visitor. His daughter came to see him. She brought it."

Marvia turned to Amy Brown, then to Anise MacDougald. She tensed, sending her question telepathically first to the nurse then to the facility manager.

MacDougald answered. "I'll get the log." She disappeared from the infirmary, returned almost at once with a notebook. She laid it in front of Marvia, ran her finger down the page. "Here it is. Marjorie Dowling. Mr. Smithton's daughter. She brought him here, she visits regularly."

Marvia blinked. "Don't you control access to this building? All these old people must be—vulnerable."

"We do our best. We ask everyone to sign in and out. We keep a file of authorized visitors with each guest's records, with photos. But this isn't a prison, you know, Sergeant. We operate more or less on the honor system. But you see—*Marjorie Dowling—in—out*. She was only upstairs for fifteen minutes."

"What about the ashtray?"

Mr. Collins was tugging at Marvia's hands. "The ashtray, the ashtray," he whispered. "It was the monsters. Both of the monsters. Both of them!"

"I don't understand, Mr. Collins. What monsters are those?" If the old man was delusional, seeing monsters in ashtrays, he might have thought that Smithton was one of them. He would have picked up the ashtray. . . .

Could Collins have picked up the ashtray at all? Marvia wondered. The aged man with his pipe-stem arms, his thin, fragile bones and withered muscles? It was heavy glass, must have weighed the better part of ten pounds.

But if he was panicked by his imagined monsters, he might have found the strength to lift the heavy glass implement and bring it down just once, its sharp corner colliding with Smithton's thin temple. Once would have been enough.

"Did you do it, Mr. Collins?"

She was getting close to Miranda territory, she knew that. But if Collins was willing to speak freely, to offer a spontaneous statement, she should be able to use it. But that would mean she was putting together a homicide case, which would mean that he couldn't have been delusional.

"I should have done it a long time ago." He smiled up at her.

"Why is that, Mr. Collins?"

"You weren't there. You didn't see. He looked at the monsters and he—" He stopped speaking and a series of expressions raced across his features, anger, terror, grief.

Through all their conversation, Marvia had been standing in front of Collins, holding his hands in her own. Now he dropped his face and wept, his tears falling on the backs of Marvia's hands.

He pulled himself erect and dropped her hands. Nurse Amy Brown handed him a wad of tissue paper and he blotted his eyes. He reached for Marvia's hands and blotted them as well. "My apologies." A gentleman.

"Mr. Collins." She decided to try once again. "Who were these monsters you saw? Where were they?"

"In the ashtray."

"You mean—like in the ashes? Like seeing the devil in a flame?"

"No, no," he shook his head. "The devil, I'd take my dinner with the devil, drink wine with the devil before these two."

"Then I don't understand."

"I won't even say their names. My mouth I won't soil by speaking the syllables. I could never spit enough to clean my mouth if I said those names."

Marvia turned. "Ms. MacDougald, can you call upstairs to Mr. Collins's room and get Officer Felton on the line for me? Thank you."

A moment later MacDougald handed her the phone. She asked Felton to sign for the ashtray and bring it down to the infirmary in an evidence bag. The techs could safeguard the crime scene until the coroner's squad arrived to remove the body.

To Collins she said, "Sir, I have to ask you, do you understand what happened upstairs? Do you understand what's going on now, who I am?"

The old man smiled wistfully. "You know the best thing about Alzheimer's, Miss Police Sergeant? Those are sergeant's stripes, yes? At my age, your eyes aren't always so reliable. You know the best thing about Alzheimer's? You meet interesting new people every day."

Marvia said nothing.

Collins said, "Ah, at my age I can't even get a laugh no more.

Well, a Henny Youngman I never was anyhow. So, Miss Police Sergeant, ask me again the question."

"Do you understand what happened, sir? Do you understand where you are and who I am?"

"Oh, yes." He nodded. "Oh, yes, believe me I understand."

"It looks as if Mr. Smithton was the victim of a homicide. If you're willing to chat with me about it, informally, we can chat. If you want your Miranda rights, I'll read them to you and—"

The old man laughed. "I know my rights. I watch TV. What else do I have to pass the time? I see cop shows galore, Miss Sergeant. Don't worry about my rights."

The door swung back and Jeff Felton entered. At Marvia's direction he carefully placed the ashtray, still in its bag, on a counter.

Marvia said, "Mr. Collins, would you pick that up for me?"

Collins swung around and peered at the ashtray.

"You want me to pick that up?"

"Please."

The old man got unsteadily to his feet. Moving slowly, he crossed the short distance to the counter. He slid one hand under either end of the heavy ashtray. His powdery white face reddened with effort. The ashtray did not budge.

## Hobart Lindsey

International Surety had opened a prestigious regional head-quarters in the upper reaches of the Transamerica Pyramid. He walked there from 101 California, rose skyward in an express elevator and used his Special Projects Unit ID to borrow a private office.

He was concerned over the timeline in Jeannette Whelan's story. If, as she claimed, she had reached the Starwest gym at six o'clock on Thursday night, and if the thief had completed her illicit purchases within three hours, that meant that she had bought three automobiles, something close to a truckload of computers and other office equipment, and two of the most advanced television sets in existence.

Didn't the stores ever close around this town?

A few telephone calls settled that problem. The purchases had been arranged in advance. The customer had arranged to come back, pay for everything, and take delivery between six and nine o'clock Thursday night.

"Well, actually," a nervous Mercedes salesman told Lindsey,

"she was going to come in Tuesday night. She never showed up, but she postponed to Wednesday. She's a VVIP, you know, and we try to accommodate. She's a vice president up at AFR and she got stuck in a meeting and she actually had her executive assistant call us. A very impressive person, very authoritative. What was his name, now? Garrison, yes. Bernard, no, Barnard Garrison. He was all apologetic but I could tell that he didn't like apologizing. Still, he explained Ms. Whelan's situation and of course we said, well, certainly."

"Wednesday."

"That's right."

"She bought the car Wednesday?"

"No, her assistant called again Wednesday night and apologized again in behalf of Ms. Whelan. He said she was positively humiliated, she'd like to buy our whole staff dinner at the Carnelian Room to make up for the inconvenience, and could she pick up the car on Thursday. And we acceded, of course. My manager was hovering like a vulture and of course we agreed to do what the customer requested, and Thursday night Ms. Whelan arrived with her assistant. She paid on the spot and they took delivery and drove off."

"Paid how?"

"AFR emerald card."

"You didn't phone in to see if the card was legitimate?"

"But I did. I punched it into the system and it came up clean but just to be certain I called the AFR 800 number and spoke with a human being who told me this was one of their NLNQ's. I asked what that was and she said, and I quote on this, Mr. Lindsey, 'no limit, no question.'"

Lindsey thanked the salesman.

The salesman said, "Were we scammed, sir?"

Lindsey thought for a while before he answered. Finally the salesman said, "Sir? Are you there, sir?" And Lindsey said, "No, you weren't scammed. You sold the car. Congratulations. But I don't think you'd better count on that dinner at the Carnelian Room."

The story was the same with the second Mercedes dealer, with the Acura dealer, with three computer stores, two home-electronics stores, and the city's top-rated, cutting-edge, we-always-have-everything-first-and-you'll-pay-through-the-nose-if-you-want-it, television dealer.

Lindsey decided to visit Patriot War Goods and Weapons, Incorporated, in person. He picked up a cab in front of the Pyramid and gave the cabbie the address.

The cabbie was a grizzled veteran. His African features were covered with a week's worth of white bristles and a snowy fringe peeked out from beneath his old-fashioned cab driver's military-style cap. He craned his neck to get a good look at Lindsey. "You sure of this, mister?"

Lindsey said he was sure.

"Sir, I gotta take you anywheres you want, in the city limits. But I really don't think you wanna go to this address."

Lindsey looked at his watch. It had been a long day and it looked as if it was nowhere near being over. "Why don't you want to go there?"

"You're not from the city, are you?"

"Walnut Creek."

"You do better in Hunter's Point, you like me. You know what I mean?"

"Could I hire you to stand by, then, while I make this call? I wouldn't ask you to do anything improper. Just provide a little—"

"Local color?" The driver chuckled.

They cut their deal and the driver headed toward the Embarcadero, picked up the freeway and headed for his destination.

He pulled up in front of a ramshackle frame house. A couple of ragged kids offered to watch the cab for a small fee and Lindsey nodded to the driver.

They had to pass a metal detector to get past the front door. Lindsey had to hand his electronic pocket organizer around the sensor. There was no sign on the building, nothing to identify it as Patriot War Goods and Weapons. He wondered if this was a crack house, but inside he found himself surrounded by an astonishing array of military collectibles as well as modern weaponry. The proprietor was an African-American in a blue pinstriped suit, spotless white button-down shirt and maroon silk tie. He was standing behind a display case filled with glistening Samurai swords and World War II Japanese helmets. He set aside the slick journal he'd been studying and gave Lindsey a curious look.

"How did you get this address?"

Lindsey showed his International Surety credentials. "I'm following up a case of credit card fraud."

The black man shook his head. "I run a straight business here. I don't even like to take credit cards, I tell 'em to take a cash

advance and pay me in greenbacks. But once in a while I'll make
an exception."

"You made a large sale last Thursday evening, to a customer
who paid with an American Financial Resources emerald card."

The other shook his head. "No."

"Sir, we have records of the transaction. There's no point in
denying it."

"No point in buck you, fuster. Get out of my store, and take
your slave there with you." He started to come around the
counter.

Lindsey held up his hands placatingly. "You needn't get rough
with me. You order me out of here, I'll go. But the police will be
in here before you can blink your eyes, and you can expect a visit
from the ATF and very likely the IRS. Or you can just talk to me.
That's all I'm asking you to do, just talk to me."

Blue Suit backed a step and reached toward the display case,
his fingers inches from a Samurai sword.

"No need, brother. You want us out, we gone." It was Lindsey's
cab driver. Suddenly he was standing between Lindsey and Blue
Suit, and suddenly he was half a foot taller and thirty years
younger than he'd been when they arrived.

Blue Suit dropped his hand and leaned on the counter.

The cabbie was a small old man again.

Blue Suit said, "What do you want?"

"Someone came in here last Thursday night and made a large
purchase, and paid for it with an AFR emerald card. I've seen the
charge slip. The card was stolen."

"I checked with the company. The card was okay. They said
it was a no-limit-no-question card. I never heard of such a thing
before. If they try and stick me for it—"

"You won't be stuck," Lindsey reassured Blue Suit. "But I need
you to describe the customer. And an itemized list of what the
customer bought."

"It was some white woman. Never saw her before."

"Describe her."

Blue Suit pondered. Then he said, "The Whelan chick, sure.
Light brown hair, real light, with streaks. She colors it, definitely.
About fifty. Slim, maybe five-three, five-four. Wearing sweats and
running shoes, but no gym hanger-on, if you know what I mean.
She didn't look real happy, but she slapped down that card and
signed the slip, that's all I wanted from her."

The description didn't ring a bell with Lindsey. Blue Suit

called the woman the Whelan chick but she was surely not Jeannette Whelan.

"Was she alone?"

"Oh, no." Blue Suit shook his head. "She had her man with her."

Something gave Lindsey a hunch. "You didn't know her. Did you happen to recognize him?"

Blue Suit broke into a big grin. "Recognize him? Listen, I know him. His name's Billy Tarplin. My customers' names are sacred secrets to me, but not Billy Tarplin. That chump is too weird. Dresses like a fashion plate. Puts me in the shade, and I try to look good at all times, but he is just too far off the beaten track for my taste."

He paused, then added, "I told you I can always move Nazi merchandise? Billy Tarplin, he's my number one customer for that stuff."

"Do you have his address?"

"This is strictly a cash and carry business, but Billy's such a good customer, I have to send his orders out by truck. Late at night, too—you wouldn't believe the things he buys. He must be planning a revolution with some of his weapons. Heavy machine guns, bazookas, BARs. That chump even bought a 57-millimeter reckless rifle. But, hey, he didn't get anything from me, you understand what I'm saying?"

Lindsey agreed that he understood what Blue Suit was saying. "I just need to track down this one purchase, the purchase made on the Whelan AFR emerald card."

"Here, here's what they bought," Blue Suit told Lindsey. He showed Lindsey a customer order sheet. A ceremonial SS dagger, uniform cap with death's-head insignia, an array of World War II era German medals.

"I don't like Nazis," Blue Suit said. "I don't like Nazi paraphernalia. Brings out some nasty types. But it comes in from time to time and there's always a market for it. If I lose Billy Tarplin I'll never miss him. These Nazi nuts get off on that sick stuff, and Billy's the sickest of the bunch."

Lindsey was busy jotting information into his organizer. When he finished he handed the order sheet back to Blue Suit. "You won't get any trouble from AFR," he assured him. "I just need the address where you ship Tarplin's orders."

"You didn't get it from me," Blue Suit said. He pulled open a file drawer, riffled through folders and pulled out a sheet of paper.

Lindsey reached for it but Blue Suit pulled it back. "No way!"

But he held it while Lindsey tapped the address into his organizer. It was in San Anselmo in Marin County. This case was neatly triangulating the bay. "If you hear anything from Tarplin or, uh, Whelan, give me a call at once, please." Lindsey laid an International Surety card on the counter. "Or else call the police," he added.

"Yeah, sure." Blue Suit looked at the card without touching it.

"There will be a very large reward," Lindsey added.

Blue Suit picked up the card and slipped it into his pocket. Lindsey started for the door.

"Hey, hold it there." Blue Suit brushed past him. "I have to let you out."

The cabbie stepped through the doorway ahead of Lindsey. As Lindsey moved forward, Blue Suit said, "Oh, yeah, there was one more thing those two got. The man was mainly interested in the hard-core military goods but the woman asked me about this one other thing that came in with a batch of Nazi merchandise. I had it in the case and she was interested so I said she could just have it. I don't know what the hell it was doing with those other things anyhow."

Lindsey said, "What was that?"

Blue Suit said, "Some ugly old ashtray."

## Marvia Plum

"What do you think, Jeff?"

"I really don't think he could have done it. He didn't have the strength."

"Even for a moment? You know, the father who lifts a car off a child, that kind of thing?"

Felton shrugged. "Anything is possible, Sarge. But I don't think so. No."

Marvia studied Jack Collins. He was sitting quietly now, holding one of Amy Brown's competent hands. "I don't think so either," Marvia said. "But I think I'm going to request a hospital evaluation. What do you think, Ms. MacDougald?"

"Actually, I think it would be a good idea."

"Does Mr. Collins have any family we can consult?"

The old man reddened and rose halfway from his seat, then sank down again. "Stop talking about me as if I wasn't here! You got a question, ask me, Policer."

Marvia leaned back. "I'm sorry. You're right, sir. Would you object to a hospital evaluation?"

Collins tilted his head thoughtfully. "In America, I guess a hospital is a hospital, eh? Not a murder house. No, I don't mind. I got nothing to hide."

"And do you have any family, sir?"

"Not in this world. We got caught in the middle. In Poland. The ones Hitler didn't kill, Stalin killed. Our great friend and protector, Comrade Stalin."

Now Marvia was confused. "I'm sorry. Jack Collins? Is that a Polish name?"

"Jack Collins. So." He shrugged. "Jacob Chmelkovitz in Poland, Jack Collins in America."

"No children, grandchildren, no wife?"

"The monsters got them all. Why didn't they get me? I don't know, Policer, I don't know, I wish they had."

Marvia said, "Jeff, call this in, will you? Let's make sure Mr. Collins gets good treatment." She turned back to Collins. "They'll have an ambulance out here for you in a little while."

Collins shrugged again, turning his hands palm up as if to show that they were empty. "I could ride in your car, too, but I don't mind the ambulance neither."

Once Jack Collins was taken care of, Marvia went to the Autumn House office with Anise MacDougald. She asked to see their records on both Collins and the victim, Henry Smithton.

MacDougald hesitated briefly, muttering something about confidentiality, but finally acceded.

Collins's record was as he'd indicated. Born in Lodz, Poland, in 1914 as Jacob Chmelkovitz. One brother, three sisters. Married, 1932. Twin girls born 1935, no other children. Twins taken by Nazis for genetic experimentation in 1942, died. Parents died. Brother and sisters all killed in Warsaw ghetto uprising. Chmelkovitz liberated from Belsen, 1945. Displaced person, admitted to US on humanitarian grounds in 1947. Changed name to Collins, worked for Post Office Department, 1948 to 1979. Retired.

There were no photos of authorized visitors in the file.

Smithton's was far less dramatic. Born Bayonne, New Jersey, 1916. Worked in war plant assembling trucks during World War II. Married, 1948; daughter Marjorie born same year. Wife deceased. Daughter married and widowed, name Marjorie Dowling. There was a photo of Marjorie in the file, and one of another authorized visitor, a man named Barnard Garrison. Marvia asked MacDougald for copies of the photos; MacDougald ran them through a copier and gave her one of each. Since Dowling was Smithton's next of kin and his designated emergency contact, her telephone number and address were included. She lived in San Anselmo, up in Marin County.

Apparently Marjorie Dowling cared for her father, enough to visit him at Autumn House. Marvia would contact her with the sad news. She would also have some very serious questions for Ms. Dowling about the heavy ashtray that had crushed Henry Smithton's skull.

### Hobart Lindsey

"You a pretty standup guy for a overweight, middle-aged white man."

Lindsey decided to take that as a compliment and thanked the cabbie for backing him up in his confrontation with Blue Suit.

"Thanks are nice, they don't buy no groceries."

"You'll get a good piece of change for this day's work," Lindsey told him. It was IS money, not his own. He could afford to be generous. And the cabbie had certainly earned it. The cab was untouched when they reached it outside Patriot War Goods and Weapons, and the cabbie rather than Lindsey had paid off the kids who had guarded it so well.

The cabbie dropped Lindsey at the Civic Center station of the commuter line. He paid him off, reimbursed him for his time and the out-of-pocket expense that had gone to the kids, and added a generous tip.

"Any time you need some help, cap," the cabbie offered. He pulled a stub of a pencil out of his pocket, found a soiled envelope and wrote his name and telephone number. He handed them over. Lindsey thanked him and climbed from the cab.

The train would carry him to Walnut Creek along with hundreds of other commuters, shoppers, and students returning from a long day at San Francisco State or USF.

The train barreled through the tube beneath San Francisco Bay, roared above ground in West Oakland, ducked into a dark tunnel again, then emerged for its run to the suburbs of the East Bay. Lindsey sat with his pocket organizer in his hands, reviewing the case.

Somebody inside AFR understood the card system well enough to know that no-limit-no-questions wasn't as simple as it sounded. A scam artist with a stolen no-no emerald card looking for the main chance would have to buy and fence big-ticket merchandise rather than go for a killing in cash. How many people in AFR understood the system? There must be dozens, maybe hundreds, starting with Jeannette Whelan herself.

And somebody at Starwest, a woman, had to know Whelan's routine and be able to get in and out of the locker room fast, without being detected. Whoever was doing this had set up her caper for Tuesday, then had to postpone it to Wednesday and finally to Thursday before it worked. She was smart, quick, and sensible enough to put off her action twice, waiting for the right moment.

He didn't know who the woman, the false Jeannette Whelan, was, or where she was. But he had an address for Billy Tarplin.

He climbed into his car and started for San Anselmo.

It was a long drive from Lindsey's home to the Richmond Bridge, through downtown San Rafael and through one bedroom community after another in Marin County before reaching San Anselmo.

Billy Tarplin lived in a modest single-story home on a curving road. The neighborhood had the look and feel of a 1950s development. The original homeowners would all have sold their houses and moved away by now, or died off and left them to their adult children.

Ten-year-old cars lined the street. There was an almost tangible air of seediness and slow deterioration in the air. Most of the houses had small swimming pools. Children shrieked under the watchful eyes of overweight mothers smoking cigarettes.

Lindsey double-checked the house number, then rang the doorbell. He heard muffled sounds, as if someone was stumbling around inside the house, sobs and fragments of speech.

He tried the door and it swung open.

A woman handed him something and he took it instinctively. It was sticky. It was covered with blood. It was a ceremonial dagger decorated with a swastika and Nazi eagle.

The woman was sobbing and babbling. She was spattered with blood, blood in her blonde-streaked light brown hair, blood on her white T-shirt and khaki shorts, blood on her face, her bare arms and legs and running shoes.

Lindsey heard a car screech to a stop and a voice behind him call out, "Freeze!"

He turned toward the voice. The blood-covered woman was behind him now. He was holding the bloody dagger. A black and white police cruiser stood in the driveway and a uniformed police officer was pointing her service automatic at him.

"Bart?" There was shock in her voice.

"Marvia."

"Put the weapon on the ground."

He obeyed.

"What's going on here?"

"I don't know. I just got here. I opened the door and she handed me the knife."

Marvia Plum moved past Lindsey. She addressed the blood-soaked woman. "Are you all right? What happened?"

"It's all over now," the woman said. "All over. The Nazis are dead. Both dead."

Marvia asked, "Are you wounded?"

"No." The woman shook her head. She seemed calm now, and fairly coherent although dazed. "I—he's in the pool. Come on, I'll show you."

Marvia said, "Come on, Lindsey. Stay where I can see you."

The three of them walked through the house, out the back door into a modest, fenced yard. The pool was filled and the water was stained with a pink cloud. A fully clothed man was floating in the pool, face down.

Marvia holstered her weapon and picked up a long-handled leaf net. She used it to draw the man to the edge of the pool. "Come on, help me."

With Lindsey's assistance she dragged the man from the pool and turned him onto his back on the pool apron. She felt for a pulse but she knew in advance that she would find none. There were major wounds in the chest and abdomen, and one in the throat that would have been fatal if the others had not been.

"He was right," the blood-covered woman said. "I wouldn't believe him but he was right. So now—so now—so now it's all over, it's all right, it's all over."

Marvia led the woman to a chair. She directed Lindsey to another. She asked the woman her name even though she already knew it.

"Mrs. Dowling. Marjorie Dowling. Marjorie Smithton Dowling. Marjorie von Schmitt."

Marvia shook her head. "What's that? I don't understand." She understood every name except the last.

"I killed Billy," the bloodstained woman said. "I killed my daddy and I killed my boyfriend." She grinned crazily.

"That's Billy Tarplin?" Marvia asked. She knew the answer but still she asked.

"That's Billy."

Lindsey shook his head. "That's Garrison. That has to be Barnard Garrison." Marvia Plum shot him a sharply questioning glance. "I met him at Jeannette Whelan's office. He was her executive assistant."

"Who the hell is Jeannette Whelan?" Marvia asked.

"She's a VP at American Financial Resources. She was the victim of a credit card scam. Billy, what's his name, Tarplin, worked for AFR under the name of Barnard Garrison. He was the inside man on the scam. Mrs. Dowling here, I take it, was the outsider. Garrison got the information inside AFR. Mrs. Dowling stole a no-limit emerald credit card from Ms. Whelan's locker at the Starwest Fitness Center in San Francisco. They cleaned up on it. Cars, HDTVs—and Nazi paraphernalia."

For the first time he looked around the house, as much of it as he could see through the back door. The living room was festooned with Nazi flags, war posters, military regalia. He wondered where the uniforms were kept. It seemed doubtful that Garrison/Tarplin and Mrs. Dowling entertained their neighbors very often.

"—And the ashtray," Mrs. Dowling volunteered.

Marvia was suddenly attentive.

"He saw the ashtray. Billy was the only one who knew what it was. He said all along that he recognized my daddy from old photos, that he wasn't really from New Jersey, that he wasn't really Henry Smithton, he was really Heinrich von Schmitt. I always hated the Nazis, I knew what they did, and he said my daddy was a Nazi who came to America and hid out all these years with a false name. So my name is false too."

"Did Mr. Tarplin kill your father, Mrs. Dowling?"

"No. Billy didn't kill daddy. I killed daddy. Billy said, 'We're going to buy this ashtray. Nobody knows what it is but I know what it is.' Billy studied the history, he studied all the time. He said Stalin sent that ashtray to Hitler when they signed their treaty. Their pictures are etched in the glass, with the pledge of eternal friendship in German and Cyrillic. Daddy knew what the ashtray was. He was so shocked when I gave it to him, he knew what it was. He admitted who he was. He didn't deny it any more. I couldn't stand it. I couldn't live with that. So I killed the Nazi and I came home and Billy asked me what was the matter and I picked up his favorite dagger and I pricked him. And he bled. I pricked him and he bled."

Marvia led her back into the house, followed by Lindsey. She picked up the telephone and called the San Anselmo PD.

*My wife and I were walking our dogs in an unfamiliar neighborhood when we spotted an odd tower rising above some dense shrubbery. An iron fence surrounded the shrubbery; there was a heavy, padlocked gate at one point. The tower was an intriguing building, and we walked around the fence hoping for a more complete view of it, but we had no luck. From some angles the tower simply disappeared. From others it was visible but inaccessible. And there seemed no way to reach it or even to get a complete view.*

*The whole thing was reminiscent of H. P. Lovecraft's story "The Strange High House in the Mist." I knew there was a story there for me, as well, but I didn't know what it was until Scott David Aniolowski asked me to contribute a story to a book he was preparing. This was* Made in Goatswood, *"A Celebration of Ramsey Campbell." Campbell is one of our outstanding Lovecraftians, so I suppose "The Turret" is second-generation homage to the great HPL.*

*When* Made in Goatswood *was published in 1995, mystery writer Jane Langton commented that "The Turret" was "splendid, wild, wonderful, zany, absolutely crazy." What lovely words!*

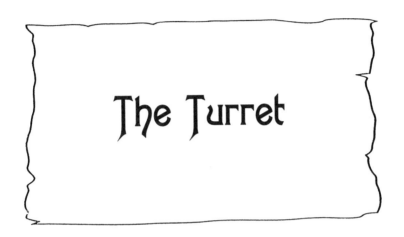

# The Turret

I WAS NOT REALLY SURPRISED WHEN MY EMPLOYER, Alexander Myshkin, called me into his office and offered me the assignment to troubleshoot our Zeta/Zed System at the Klaus Fuchs Memorial Institute in Old Severnford. The Zeta/Zed System was Myshkin Associates' prize product, the most advanced hardware-software lashup in the world, Myshkin liked to boast, and the Fuchs Institute was to have been our showpiece installation.

Unfortunately, while the Zeta/Zed performed perfectly in the Myshkin lab in Silicon Valley, California, once it was transported to the Severn Valley in England, glitches appeared in its functioning and bugs in its programs. The customer was first distressed, then frustrated, and finally angry. Myshkin had the Fuchs Institute modem its data to California, where it ran perfectly on the in-house Zeta/Zed and was then modemed back to England. This was the only way Myshkin could placate the customer, even temporarily, but we knew that if the system in Old Severnford could not be brought on-line and into production, the Institute could order our equipment removed. They could replace it with a system from one of our competitors, and further could even sue

Myshkin Associates for the lost time and expense they had put into our failed product.

"Park," Alexander Myshkin said to me as soon as I entered his office in response to his summons, "Park, the future of this company is in your hands. If we lose the Fuchs Institute, we could be out of business in six months. We're hanging onto that account by our fingernails. You've got to get that system running for the customer."

I asked Myshkin why our marketing and technical support teams in the UK had not solved the problem. "We have good people over there," I told my employer. "I know some of them, and I've seen their work."

Myshkin said, "You're right, Park." (My name is Parker Lorentzen; Lorentzen for obvious reasons, Parker in honor of a maternal ancestor who actually hailed from the Severn Valley. I had never seen the region, and was inclined to accept the assignment for that reason alone.)

"You're right," my employer repeated, "but they haven't been able to solve it. Somehow I don't think they *like* visiting this account. They don't like staying anywhere in the Severn Valley and they absolutely refuse to put up in Old Severnford itself. I've never been there myself, but I've seen the pictures, as I'm sure you have."

I admitted that I had.

"The countryside is beautiful. Rolling hills, ancient ruins, the Severn River itself and those smaller streams, the Ton and the Cam. I'll admit, a certain, well, call it *sense of gloom* seems to hang over the area, but we're modern people, enlightened technologists, not a pack of credulous rustics."

"True enough, chief. All right, no need to twist my arm." I gazed past him. Beyond the window the northern California hills rolled away lush with greenery. I found myself unconsciously touching the little blue birthmark near my jaw-line. It was smaller than a dime, and oddly shaped. Some claimed that it resembled an infinity sign; others, an hourglass; still others, an ankh, the Egyptian symbol of immortality. My physician had assured me that it was not pre-cancerous or in any other way dangerous. Nor was it particularly unsightly; women sometimes found it fascinating.

My mother had had a similar formation on her jaw. She called it a beauty-mark and said that it was common among the Parkers.

"Thanks, Park," Alexander Myshkin resumed. "You're my top

troubleshooter, you know. If you can't fix a problem, it can't be fixed."

Within twenty-four hours I had jetted across the country, transferred from my first-class seat in a Boeing jumbo to the cramped quarters of the Anglo-French Concorde, and left the Western Hemisphere behind for my first visit to England, the homeland of half my ancestors.

I stayed only one night in London, not sampling that city's fabled theatres or museums, but simply resting up, trying to rid myself of the jet-lag inherent in a body still running on California time even though it had been relocated some eight or nine time zones. I boarded a wheezing, groaning train that carried me from fabled Victoria Station through Exham and the very peculiar-looking town of Goatswood and thence to its terminus at Brichester.

My luggage consisted of a single valise. In this I had placed my warmest clothing, a tweed suit and Irish hat that I had purchased years before in an English shop in San Francisco and reserved for trips from California to areas of less salubrious climate. I carried an umbrella and, slung from my shoulder, a canvas case containing a notebook computer.

In Brichester I spent my second night in England. The inn where I lodged was old and run-down. It contained a pub on its ground floor, and I looked forward to an evening of good-fellowship, a tankard of beer (perhaps more than one!) and a platter of good English beef before bed.

Alas, I was disappointed on every count. The beef was tough, stringy and overdone. The beer was watery and flat. But most disheartening of all, the local residents, for all that they appeared just the colorful and eccentric folk that I had hoped to encounter, proved a taciturn and unforthcoming lot. They responded to my opening conversational ploys with monosyllabic grunts, and rejected my further attempts at camaraderie by pointedly turning their backs and engaging in low, muttered dialogs, casting unfriendly glances from time to time at the obviously unwelcome interloper in their midst — myself.

After chewing futilely at the beef until my jaws ached, and giving up on the poor beer that the innkeeper served, I finally retired early, not so much from fatigue, for my body was beginning to recover from its jet-lag, but simply because I could find no comfort in the surroundings of this disappointing pub and its hostile clientele.

hurled a large rock after my car. The rock struck the rear of the car, and for a moment I thought the driver was going to stop and berate the children, but instead he pressed down on the accelerator and sped us away from there, muttering something beneath his breath that I was unable to make out.

The driver brought the car to a halt in a decrepit dockside district of Severnford. Full night had fallen by now, and the quays and piers before us seemed utterly deserted. I asked the driver if he would wait for a ferry to carry us to Old Severnford, and if he would then drive me to the Klaus Fuchs Memorial Institute.

He turned around then, gazing at me over the rear of his seat. I had switched on the car's tiny domelight, and it reflected off his mirrored glasses. "Last ferry's run, mister," he husked. "And me'uns don't fancy spending no night by these docks. You get out. Get out now, and you're on your own."

I started to protest, but the driver leaped from the car with surprising agility for so bulky and aged an individual. He yanked open the door beside which I sat, caught my lapels in two thickly-gloved hands, and lifted me bodily from the car, depositing me in no dignified condition on the cracked and weedy sidewalk. He hurled my valise after me, jumped back into his vehicle and sped away, leaving me angered, puzzled, and utterly uncertain as to how to resolve my predicament.

I recovered my valise and tested my notebook computer to reassure myself that it was undamaged. I then pondered my next move. If the Severn ferry had indeed ceased its runs for the night, I could not possibly reach Old Severnford before morning. I did not know my way around the town of Severnford itself, and with a shudder of apprehension I set out to explore.

At first I walked beside the river. A moon had risen, apparently full, yet so cloaked by heavy clouds as to appear only a vague, pale disk in the sky, while furnishing the most minimal of watery illumination to the earth. But as my eyes grew accustomed to the darkness, I realized that there was another source of illumination, faint and inauspicious.

A glow seemed to come from beneath the surface of the Severn River. Seemed? No, it was there, it was all too real. I tried to make out its source, but vague shapes seemed to move, deep in the river for the most part, but darting toward the surface now and again, and then slithering away once more into the depths. And a mist arose from the sluggishly flowing water, and gave off a glow of its own, or perhaps it was that it reflected the glow of the river and the vague, luminous shapes therein. Or yet again,

were there shapes *within the mist* as well, floating and darting like
fairies in a garden in a child's book?

The sight should have been charming, almost pretty, but for
some reason it sent a shudder down my back. With an effort I
turned away and made my way up an ancient street, leading at a
slight uphill slant from the river and the docks and into the heart
of town.

Perhaps I had merely strayed into the wrong part of Severnford, or perhaps there was something about the town itself that
set off silent shrieks of alarm within me. I could find no establishment open, no person to ask for assistance. Instead I paced
darkened streets, chilled and dampened by the night. Once I
thought I heard voices, rough and furtive in tone, murmuring in
a language I could neither comprehend nor identify. Twice I
heard scuffling footsteps, but upon whirling clumsily with my
valise and computer weighing me down, I saw nothing. Thrice I
thought I heard odd twitterings, but could find no source or
explanations for them.

How many miles I trudged that night, finding my way from
alley to courtyard to square, I can only guess. I can only say that
the first pallid gray shafts of morning light were as welcome to me
as any sight I had ever beheld. I was able, by heading steadily
downward, to find my way back to the docks.

In the morning light the mist was lifting off the Severn, the
hills on its far shore looked almost welcoming, and the disquieting
shapes and lights beneath the river's surface were no longer to be
seen.

I located the quay where the Severn ferry made its stops and
waited for the morning's first run. I was rewarded soon by sight
of an ancient barge, something more suitable to a motion picture
about Nineteenth Century life than to a modern enterprise.
Nonetheless cheered, I climbed aboard, paid my fair, and waited
with a small party of taciturn passengers until the ferryman saw
fit to weigh anchor and transport us across the slowly flowing
water.

I tried my cellular telephone from on board the ferry, and by
some miracle of electronics managed to get through to the Fuchs
Institute. I spoke with Karolina Parker, who expressed concern as
to my welfare and my whereabouts. As briefly as possible, I
explained my situation and she said that she would personally
greet me at the pier in Old Severnford.

She proved as good as her word. I found her a delightful young
woman, perhaps a few years younger than I, but showing so

marked a family resemblance as to remove all doubt as to our being related. I explained to her about my Parker ancestors, and she astonished me by planting a most uncousinly kiss on my mouth, even as we sat in her modern and comfortable automobile.

I was still puzzling over this remarkable behavior when we arrived at the Klaus Fuchs Memorial Institute. Karolina Parker introduced me to the director of the institute, whose friendly greeting was tempered by his assertion that I was expected to resolve the troubles of the Zeta/Zed System posthaste, if Myshkin Associates was to retain the Fuchs Institute as an account.

Without stopping to arrange lodging in the town of Old Severnford itself, I set to work on the Institute's Zeta/Zed machines. The system was taken off line, which did not please the director, and I ran a series of diagnostic programs in turn on the mainframe processor, the satellite work stations, and the peripheral units that ran under system control.

As long as I used only sample data for testing, Zeta/Zed performed to perfection. It might be thought that I would be pleased with this result, but in fact the opposite was the case. If the system had malfunctioned, I possessed the tools (or believed that I did) to narrow down the area of malfunction until a specific site in the hardware or software remained. This could then be examined for its flaw and repaired or replaced.

When nothing went wrong, I could correct nothing.

"Very well," my hostess, Karolina Parker, suggested, "let's go back on-line while you observe, Mr. Lorentzen." I was as surprised by the coldness of her address as I had been by the warmth of her greeting in the car, but I could think of no response better than a simple, "All right."

Zeta/Zed was placed back on line. Almost at once error messages began flashing on the main monitor screen, but the system did not shut down. I permitted it to run until a batch of data had been processed, then attempted to print out the results.

The high-speed laser printer hummed, then began spitting out sheet after sheet of paper. I tried to read the top sheet, but it seemed to contain sheer gibberish. The printout comprised an almost random pattern of numbers, letters, and symbols which I knew were not part of any font supplied by Myshkin software. I asked Karolina Parker about this, but she insisted that no one had tampered with the software and no virus could have been introduced into the system as it was swept by anti-virus software regularly.

What could be the answer?

I asked Karolina Parker the source of the Institute's power supply, and was told that the Institute generated its own power, the Severn River turning a generator housed in a separate building. In this manner the Institute was independent of the vagaries of the local power system, antiquated and unreliable as it was known to be.

Furnished with a sparse cubicle from which to conduct my affairs, I soon sat alone with the enigmatic printouts. I had been furnished with a meal of sorts from the Institute's commissary, and I sat eating a stale sandwich, pausing to wash it down with occasional swigs of cold, stale coffee, trying to make head or tail of these pages.

After a while I found a passage that seemed less chaotic than what had gone before. The printing was in Roman letters, not mathematical formulas, and by concentrating on the "words" (which were in fact not any words I recognized), moving my lips like a child just learning to read, and letting the sounds that were suggested pass my lips, I realized that this was the same language I had heard the previous night as I wandered the streets of Severnford.

By quitting time I was tired, nervous, and eager to find a warm meal and a soft mattress, if such amenities even existed in this accursed Severn Valley.

To my astonishment, Karolina Parker offered me a ride home in her automobile, and even offered me room and lodging in her house. I insisted that such hospitality, while appreciated, was excessive, but she replied that everything should be done to make my visit pleasant. We were, after all, family!

Karolina Parker's home was a pleasant house set in the center of a modest but beautifully tended parklike estate. The house itself was of late Tudor style, with half-timbered beams and diamond-pane windows. There was a great fireplace in the living room, and through the front windows I could see the peculiar topiary shrubs that stood outside like unfamiliar beasts grazing an alien landscape.

My hostess explained to me that she lived alone, and showed me to a comfortable bedroom which she said would be mine during my stay in Old Severnford. She suggested that I refresh myself while she prepared dinner for us both.

An hour later I was summoned to dine in a charming informal room. Karolina apologized for her impromptu mode of entertaining, but I found both her manner and the meal which she served me the high points of my until-now dismal journey. She had decked herself out in a pair of tight-fitting blue jeans and a T-shirt with a portrait of Klaus Fuchs himself blazoned on it. Over this amazing outfit she wore a frilly apron.

She served me a delicious ratatouille accompanied by an excellent white wine (imported from northern California, I noted with some pride) and a crisp green salad. How this attractive young woman could work all day at the Institute and still entertain in such delightful fashion afterwards, was quite beyond my power of comprehension.

After the meal we repaired to the living room and shared coffee (hot, fresh and strong!) and brandy before a roaring fire. Oddly portentous selections of Carl Philipp Emanuel Bach and Georg Philipp Telemann came from the speakers of a superb sound system. Karolina and I spoke of computers, of her work at the Fuchs Institute and mine at Myshkin Associates. We tried to trace our common ancestry but ran into a blank wall somewhere around the year 1665. At no time did we speak of our personal lives. I did not know whether she had ever been married, for instance, or seriously involved with a man, nor did she query me with regard to such sensitive (and for me, painful) matters.

The sound system must have been preprogrammed, for after a while I found myself drawn into a complex composition by Charles Ives, and then into one of the stranger sound pieces of Edgar Varese. Our conversation had turned to the history of the Severn Valley, its peculiar isolation from the rest of England, and the odd whispered hints that were sometimes heard regarding the dark countryside and its inhabitants.

I fear that my stressful journey and my lack of sleep the previous night caught up with me, for I caught myself yawning at one point, and Karolina Parker, gracious hostess that she was, suggested that I retire.

"I'll stay downstairs to clean up a little," she volunteered. "You can find your room again, of course?"

I thought to offer a familial hug before retiring, but instead I found Karolina returning my gesture with a fierce embrace and another of her incredible kisses. I broke away in confusion and made my way to my room without speaking another word. I locked the door and placed a chair beneath the doorknob before disrobing, then climbed gratefully into bed and fell asleep almost at once.

I do not know how much later it was that I was awakened by— *by what?* I asked myself. Was it a careful rattling of the doorknob of my room? Was it a voice calling to me? And in words of what language—the familiar tongue which Americans and Britons have shared for centuries, or that other, stranger language that I had heard in the streets of Severnford and had myself spoken, almost involuntarily, as I struggled to decipher the peculiar printouts of the Zeta/Zed System at the Fuchs Institute?

Whatever it was—whoever it was—quickly departed from my ken, and I sought to return to sleep, but, alas, I was now too thoroughly wakened to do so easily. I did not wish to leave my room; I cannot tell you why, I simply felt that there were things, or might be things, in that pleasant, comfortable house that I would rather not encounter.

So instead I seated myself in a comfortable chair near the window of my room and gazed over the Severn landscape. I could see but little of the village of Old Severnford, for this was a community where the residents retired early and stayed in their homes, the doors securely locked and the lights turned low, perhaps for fear that they attract visitors not welcome.

Raising my eyes to the hills above, I saw their rounded forms as of ancient, sleeping beings, silhouetted in absolute blackness against the midnight blue sky. The clouds that had obscured the moon and stars earlier had dissipated and the heavens were punctuated by a magnificent scattering of stars and galaxies such as the city lights that blazed all night in the Silicon Valley could never reveal.

I permitted my gaze to drift lower, to the Severn Hills, when I was startled to perceive what appeared to be an artificial construct. This structure was in the form of a tower surmounted by a peculiarly made battlement or turret. I had thought the Severn Hills uninhabited save for a few examples of sparse and ill-nourished wildlife, hunted on occasion by locals seeking to add to their meager larders.

Even more surprising, the turret appeared to be illuminated from within. I strained my eyes to see clearly that which was before me. Yes, there were lights blazing from within the turret—if blazing is a word which may be applied to these dim, flickering, tantalizing lights. If I permitted my fancy to roam, the lights would almost form themselves into a face. Two great, hollow eyes staring blindly into the darkness, a central light like a nasal orifice, and beneath that a wide, narrow mouth grinning wickedly with teeth—surely they must be vertical dividers or braces—eager to invite . . . or to devour.

I stared at the turret for a long time. How long, I do not know, but eventually the night sky began to lighten, the moon and stars to fade. Were the lights in the turret extinguished, or was it the brightness of morning that made them fade?

A chill wracked my body, and I realized that I had sat for hours before the open window, clad only in thin pajamas. I climbed hastily back into bed and managed to catch a few winks before the voice of Karolina penetrated the door, summoning me to a lavish breakfast of bacon and eggs, freshly squeezed orange juice and a rich, hot mocha concoction that offered both the satisfying flavor of chocolate and the stimulation of freshly-brewed coffee.

In Karolina's car, on the way to the Klaus Fuchs Memorial Institute, I sought to gain information about my peculiar experience of the night before. I realized that my suspicion of my dear, multiply-distant cousin (for as such I had chosen to identify her, for my own satisfaction) had been the unjustified product of my own fatigue and depression, and the strangeness and newness of my surroundings.

Almost as if the turret had been the figment of a dream, I grappled mentally in hopes of regaining my impression of it. To a large degree it eluded me, but I was able at length to blurt some question about a turreted tower in the hills.

Karolina's answer was vague and evasive. She admitted that there were some very old structures in the region, dangerous and long-abandoned. In response to my mention of the flickering lights and the face-like arrangement in the turret, Karolina became peculiarly agitated, insisting that this was utterly impossible.

I averred that I would like to visit the tower and see for myself if it were inhabited, even if only by squatters.

To this, Karolina replied that there had been an earthquake in the Severn Valley some years before. A fissure had opened in the earth, and the row of hills in which the tower was located was now totally unreachable from Old Severnford. I would have to abandon my plan and give up on my hopes of learning about the turret and its lights.

I spent the day at the Fuchs Institute working diligently on the Zeta/Zed System. Since my attempts of the day before had led me only to frustration, on this day I determined to take the problem on a smaller, more intensive basis. I powered down the entire system, disconnected all of its components from one another, and began running the most exhaustive diagnostic programs on the circuitry of the central processor.

During a luncheon break I thought to ask another employee of the Institute—*not* Karolina Parker—about my experience of the previous night. But strangely, I was unable to recall just *what* I had experienced, that I wished to inquire about.

This was by far the most peculiar phenomenon I had ever encountered. I *knew* that something odd had happened to me, I *knew* that I wanted to seek an explanation for it, but I was absolutely and maddeningly unable to remember just *what* it was that I wanted to ask about.

Humiliated, I terminated the conversation and returned to my assigned cubicle to study manuals and circuit diagrams associated with Zeta/Zed.

That night Karolina furnished another delicious repast, and we shared another delightful evening of conversation, coffee-and-brandy, and music. Karolina had attired herself in a shimmering hostess gown tonight, and I could barely draw my eyes from her own flowing, raven hair, her deep blue orbs, her pale English skin and her red, generous lips.

When the time came for us to part to our rooms and retire for the night, I no longer recoiled from my cousin's ardent kiss, but luxuriated in it. As I held her, our faces close together, I saw that she, too, carried the familiar Parker mark on her chin. I placed my lips against the mark, and she sighed as if I had touched her deeply and erotically. Images and fantasies raced through my mind, but I banished them and bade her goodnight, and climbed the flagstone staircase to my quarters.

I wondered whether I really wanted to lock my door tonight, whether I really wanted to place a chair against it, but I finally did so, and climbed into bed, but this time I was not able to sleep, so I attired myself more warmly than I had the previous night, and placed myself in the comfortable chair before the window.

In the darkness of the Severn Valley my eyes soon adjusted themselves, and the utterly murky vista that greeted me at first once more resolved itself into rows of hills, clearly old hills smoothed and rounded by the passage of millennia, silhouetted against the star-dotted heavens. And as I simultaneously relaxed my body and my concentration, yet focused my eyes on the area where I had seen the turret rising the night before, once again I beheld its shape, and once again I beheld what appeared to be faint, flickering lights in its windows, making the suggestion of a face that seemed to speak to me in the peculiar tongue of the night-prowlers of Severnford and of the enigmatic computer print-out.

I did not fall asleep. I wish to make this very clear. What next transpired may have been a vision, a case of astral travel, a supernatural or at least supernormal experience of the most unusual and remarkable sort, but it was absolutely *not a dream.*

Some force drew me from my chair in my room in my distant cousin Karolina Parker's home. That which was drawn was my soul.

Now you may think this is a very peculiar statement for me to make. I, Parker Lorentzen, am a thoroughly modern man. I hold degrees in mathematics, linguistics, philosophy, psychology, and computer science. I could, if I chose to do so, insist upon being addressed as Dr. Lorentzen, but I prefer not to flaunt my education before others.

I opt philosophically for the kind of scientific materialism that seeks explanations for all phenomena in the world of physical reality. I know that there are great mysteries in the universe, but I think of them as the *unknown* rather than the *unknowable.* Research, careful observation and precise measurement, computation and rigorous logic will eventually deliver to inquisitive intelligence the final secrets of the universe.

Such is my philosophy. Or such it *was* until I visited the turret which my cousin Karolina claimed was unreachable.

At first I was frightened. I thought that I was being summoned to hurl myself from an upper-story window, from whence I would fall to the garden below and injure myself. I looked down and the weird topiary beasts seemed to be gesturing, urging me to fly from the house. I knew that this was impossible — in my physical being — but by relaxing ever more fully into my chair, while concentrating my vision, my mind, my whole psychic being on the distant turret in the Severn Hills, I felt my soul gradually separating from my body.

Why do I use the word, *soul,* you may ask. Did I not mean my mind, my consciousness? Was I not having an out-of-body experience, a controversial but nevertheless real and not necessarily supernatural phenomenon?

But no, it was more than my mind, more than my consciousness that was leaving my body. It was my whole *self,* which I choose to refer to as my soul. For all my scientific skepticism, I have been forced to the conclusion that there is some part of us that is neither material nor mortal. Just what it is, just how it came into being, I do not pretend to know. I have heard every argument, faced every scoffing comment — have made them myself, or did so when I was a younger man — but I cannot now deny the reality of this thing that I call the soul.

For a moment I was able to look back at my own body,

comfortably ensconced in the chair. Then I was off, drifting at first languorously through the open window, hovering briefly above the topiary figures in my cousin's garden, then rising as if on wings of my own, high above the town of Old Severnford, and then speeding into the black night, soaring toward the hills to the west of town.

I did see the fissure that Karolina had described, a horrid rent that seemed to penetrate deep into the earth. Its walls were strewn with boulders, and brushy vegetation had made its way down the sides of the fissure, attracted, perhaps, by the heat that seemed to radiate from its depths, or from the water that I surmised would gather in its depths.

As I approached the turret I had seen from my window, I could again perceive the flickering lights within, and the face-like formation of the illumination. From the distance of my cousin's house, and against the blackness of the Severn Hills, the tower had been of uncertain shape. Seen from a lesser distance, it assumed a clear shape and a surprisingly modern architectural aspect. It seemed to rise almost organically from its surroundings, a concept which I had come across more than once while browsing architectural journals.

Entering the largest and most brightly illuminated window, I found myself in a large room. It was unlike any I had ever seen before. As familiar as I am with every sort of modern device and scientific equipment, still I could not comprehend, or even describe, the titanic machinery that I beheld.

Figures utterly dwarfed by the machines tended them, tapping at control panels, reading indicators, adjusting conduits. Lights flashed on the machinery, and occasionally parts moved. Just as the building itself had exhibited an almost organic quality of architecture, so the machines within it seemed, in addition to their other characteristics, to be, in some subtle and incomprehensible way, *alive*.

Strangest of all was a gigantic, rectangular plane that filled an entire section of the monstrous room. Its surface was of a matte gray finish and had a peculiar look to it as if it were somehow *tacky*, as sticky as if a thin coating of honey had been spread on it, and let to stand in the sunlight until it was mostly but not entirely dry.

I approached the gray rectangle by that peculiar sort of disembodied flight that I had used since leaving my body in my cousin's house in Old Severnford, and hovered effortlessly above the gray plane. From my first vantage point at the window of the turret

me. But one does well to tread carefully before suggesting such an explanation to the customer. It can be offensive, and can alienate an important executive even if it is true.

I spoke with Alexander Myshkin by telephone. He was disheartened by my lack of progress on the Zeta/Zed System problem, but urged me to pursue my theory of external sources for the failure of the system. "You're a diplomat, Park, my boy. You can handle these Brits. Be honest with 'em, be tactful but be firm."

Following another frustrating day, Karolina Parker and I returned to her house. Once away from the Institute, I was able to recall something of my strange experience. Karolina suggested that we repair to a local restaurant for dinner rather than return directly home. Astonished to learn that an establishment existed in Old Severnford which Karolina considered worth visiting, I agreed with alacrity.

The restaurant was located in a converted country manor—in another context I would even have termed the venue a chateau. Waiters in formal garb attended our every whim. The preprandial cocktails which we shared were delicious. Our table was covered with snowy linen; the silver shone, the crystal sparkled, the china was translucently thin and delicate.

The meal itself was superb. A seafood bisque, a crisp salad dressed with a tangy sauce, tiny, tender chops done to perfection and served with delicious mint jelly, baby potatoes and tiny fresh peas. For dessert a tray of napoleons and petit-fours was passed, and we ended our repast with espresso and brandy.

Our surroundings had been as splendid as our meal. We dined in a hall with vaulting ceilings, ancient stone walls and a flagged floor. A fire blazed in a huge walk-in fireplace, and suits of armor, ancient weapons and battle flags set the establishment's motif.

A single disquieting note was sounded when, in the course of my table talk with Karolina, I happened to mention the turret. Karolina gestured to me to drop the subject, but I realized that I had already been overheard. The table nearest ours was occupied by a dignified gentleman in dinner clothes, with snowy hair and a white mustache. His companion, a lady of similar years, was decked out in an elaborate gown and rich-appearing pearls.

The gentleman summoned the waiter, who hustled away and returned with the maître d'hôtel in tow. After a hurried conference with the elderly gentleman, the maître d' approached our table and, bending so that his lips were close to my companion's ear, hastened to deliver a verbal message to her.

Karolina blanched, replied, then nodded reluctantly as the maître d' took his leave.

I had not fully understood a word of their brief conversation, but I could have sworn that the language in which it was conducted was that strange tongue I had heard in the streets of Severnford, and read from the faulty computer printout at the Fuchs Institute.

In any case, Karolina immediately settled our bill—she would not permit me to spend any money—and hustled us to her automobile. She spoke not a word en route to her house, but spun the car rapidly up the driveway, jumped from her position at the wheel and hastened inside the house, casting a frightened look over her shoulder at the topiary garden.

Once in the main room of her house, Karolina did an extraordinary thing. She stood close to me and reached one hand to my cheek. She moved her hand as if to caress me, but as she did so I felt a peculiar pricking at my birthmark. Karolina peered into my face while a frown passed over her own, then she stood on her toes to reach my cheek (for I am a tall man and she a woman of average stature) and pressed her lips briefly to the birthmark.

I placed my hands on her shoulders and watched as she drew back from me. She ran her tongue over her lips, and I noticed a tiny drop of brilliant scarlet which disappeared as her tongue ran over it.

*What could this mean?* I wondered. But I had no time to inquire, for Karolina made a brusque and perfunctory excuse and started up the stairs, headed for her room, with a succinct suggestion that I proceed to my own.

Once attired for repose, I found myself drawn to the comfortable chair which stood before the open window of my chamber. My eyes adjusted rapidly to the dim illumination of the night sky, and almost at once I found my consciousness focused on the illusion (if it was an illusion) of a face, gazing back at me from its place high in the Severn Hills.

Almost effortlessly I felt my soul take leave of my body. For the second time I flew across the topiary garden, across the village of Old Severnford, across the modernistic buildings of the Fuchs Institute. The brush-choked earthquake fissure in the Severn foothills passed beneath me and the tower loomed directly ahead.

Strangely enough, it seemed to have changed. Not greatly, of course, and in the pallid light that fell from the English sky it would have been difficult to make out architectural features in any great detail. But the tower looked both *older* and *newer* at the same time.

Hovering motionlessly in my weird ethereal flight, I studied the tower and in particular the turret which surmounted it, and I realized that the architectural *style* had been altered from that of modern, Twentieth Century England, to the form and designs of an earlier age. As I entered the turret through its great illuminated window, I briefly noted the cyclopean machines and their scurrying attendants, but sped quickly to the gray rectangular plain I had observed the previous night.

I sank toward its surface, bringing myself to a halt just high enough above the plain to make out the struggling souls there imprisoned. They had increased in number from the night before. Further, I was able to distinguish their appearance.

Again, you may wonder at my description. If a human soul is the immortal and disembodied portion of a sentient being, it would hardly be distinguished by such minutiae as clothing, whiskers, or jewelry. But in some way each soul manifested the *essence* of its owner, whether he or she be soldier or peasant, monarch or cleric, houri or drab.

And the souls which I had seen on my first visit were the souls of modern men and women, while those I beheld on this, my second visit to the turret, were clearly the souls of people of an earlier age. The men wore side-whiskers and weskits; the women, long dresses and high hairstyles and broad hats. No, they did not wear hair or clothing—it was their essences, as of the England of a century ago, that *suggested* as much.

How they had come to the turret and how they had become entrapped on the great gray plain I could not fathom, but their agony and their despair were manifest. They seemed to reach out psychic arms beseeching me to aid them, but I was unable to do so; I was totally ignorant of any way to alter their condition.

My heart was rent by pity. I flew to the attendants of the cyclopean machines, intending to plead with them to help these poor trapped creatures, but I was unable to communicate with them in any way. I studied them, hoping to discern some way of reaching them, but without success.

At last, in a state of despair, I began to move toward the great open window. I turned for one last look back, and had the peculiar sense that the attendants of the machines were themselves not human. Instead, they resembled the vague, yellowish creatures I had seen swimming beneath the surface of the Severn River.

A shudder passed through my very soul, and I sped frantically back to Old Severnford, back to Karolina Parker's house, back to my body. I reentered my body, dragged myself wearily to my bed, and collapsed into sleep.

Again in the morning my recollections of the strange experience were vague and uncertain. By the time I reached my cubicle at the Institute I was unable either to summon up an image of the night's activities, or to speak of them to anyone. I did, at one point, catch a glimpse of myself, reflected in the monitor screen of the computer workstation beside my desk. I must have nicked myself shaving, I thought, as a drop of blood had dried just on the blue birthmark on my jaw-line. I wiped it away with a moistened cloth, and was surprised at the fierceness of the sting that I felt.

Struggling to resolve the problems of the Zeta/Zed System, I had arranged an appointment with the chief engineer of the Fuchs Institute, a burly individual named Nelson MacIvar. When our meeting commenced, I surprised MacIvar by inquiring first as to why the Institute had been situated in so out-of-the-way a place as Old Severnford, and on the outskirts of the town at that.

MacIvar was blessed with a thick head of bushy red hair, a tangled beard of the same color, save that it was going to gray, and a complexion to match. He tilted his head and, as my employer Alexander Myshkin was sometimes wont to do, answered my question with one of his own.

"Why do you ask that, Mr. Lorentzen? What bearing has it on this damned Zeta/Zed machine and its funny behavior?"

I explained my theory that some exterior factor might be causing the system's problems, and reasserted my original question.

"You think this is an out-of-the-way place, do you?" MacIvar pressed. "Well, indeed it is. And that's why we chose it. I've been here for thirty-two years, Mr. Lorentzen, I was one of those who chose this spot for the Institute, and I'll tell you now, if I had it to do over, I'd have chosen a far more out-of-the-way location. The middle of the Australian desert, maybe, or better yet the farthest Antarctic glacier."

I was astounded. "Why?" I demanded again. "This location must make it hard enough to bring in supplies and equipment, not to mention the difficulties of recruiting qualified workers. The people of the Severn Valley—well, I don't mean to be offensive, Mr. MacIvar, but they don't seem to be of the highest quality."

MacIvar gave a loud, bitter laugh. "That's putting it mildly, now, Mr. Lorentzen. They're a degenerate stock, inbred and slowly sinking back toward savagery. As is all of mankind, if you ask me, and the sooner we get there, the better. This thing we call civilization has been an abomination in the eyes of God and a curse on the face of the Earth."

So, I was confronted with a religious fanatic. I'd better change my tack, and fast. "The water that drives your generators," I said, "Miss Parker—" MacIvar raised a bushy eyebrow "—Dr. Parker, then, tells me that you use the Severn River for that purpose."

"Yes, she is exactly right."

"Do you make any further use of its waters?"

"Oh, plenty. We drink it. We cook in it. We bathe in it. The Severn is the lifeline of this community. And we use it to cool our equipment, you know. Your wonderful Zeta/Zed machines can run very hot, Mr. Lorentzen, and they need a lot of cooling."

I shook my head. "Have you tested the river for purity? Do you have a filtering and treatment system in place?"

"Yes, and yes again. Just because we're out here in the country, Mr. American Troubleshooter, don't take us for a bunch of hicks and hayseeds. We know what we are doing, sir."

I gestured placatingly. "I didn't mean to cast aspersions. I'm merely trying to make sure that we touch every base."

"Touch every base, is it? I suppose that's one of your American sports terms, eh?"

By now I felt myself reddening. "I mean, ah, to make sure that no stone goes unturned, no, ah, possibility unexamined."

MacIvar glared at me in silence. I asked him, "What happens to the water after it's been passed through the heat-exchange tanks?"

"It goes back into the river."

"Has this had any effect on the local ecology? On the wildlife of the valley, or the aquatic forms found in the river itself?" I thought of those graceful yet oddly disquieting yellowish shapes in the river, of the glow that emanated from their curving bodies and reflected off the mist above.

"None," said MacIvar, "none whatsoever. And that is an avenue of inquiry, Mr. Troubleshooter, that I would advise you not to waste your precious time on."

With this, MacIvar pushed himself upright and strode ponderously from the office. Something had disturbed him and I felt that his suggestion—if not an actual warning—to steer clear of investigating the Severn River, would have the opposite effect on my work.

At the end of the working day I feigned a migraine and asked Karolina Parker to drive me home and excuse me for the remainder of the evening. I took a small sandwich and a glass of cold milk to my room and there set them aside untouched. I changed into my sleeping garments and stationed myself at the window. At this time of year the English evening set in early, for which I thanked heaven. I located the flickering face and flew to it without hesitation.

The tower had changed its appearance again. From its Victorian fustian it had reverted to the square-cut stone configuration of a medieval battlement. Once within the great turret room I sped by the cyclopean machinery and its scurrying, yellowish attendants and headed quickly to the gray plain.

Hovering over the plain, I dropped slowly until I could make out the souls struggling and suffering there. More of them were apparent this night than had previously been the case, and from their garments and equipage I could infer their identity. They were members of Caesar's legions. Yes, these pitiable beings were the survivors—or perhaps the casualties—of the Roman occupation force that had once ruled Britain.

After a time they seemed to become aware of me and attempted variously to command or to entice me into placing myself among them. This I would not do. One legionnaire, armed with Roman shield and spear, hurled the latter upward at me. I leaped aside, not stopping to wonder what effect the weapon would have had. It was, of course, not a physical object, but a psychic one. Yet as a soul, was I not also a psychic being, and might not the spear have inflicted injury or even death upon me?

The legionnaire's conduct furnished me with a clue, however. He had seen me, that I knew because he aimed his throw with such precision that, had I not dodged successfully, I would surely have been impaled on the spear-point. Even as the legionnaire stood shouting and shaking his fist at me, I willed myself to become invisible.

The look of anger on the ancient soldier's face was replaced by one of puzzlement and he began casting his gaze in all directions as if in hopes of locating me. I knew, thus, that I was able to conceal myself from these wretched souls merely by willing myself to be unseen.

Remaining invisible, I proceeded farther along the gray plain. There were many more souls here than I had even imagined. Beyond the Romans I observed a population of early, primitive Britons. Hairy Picts dressed in crude animal skins danced and chanted as if that might do them some good. And beyond the Picts I spied—but suddenly, a sheet of panic swept over me.

How long had I been in the turret this night? I looked around, hoping to see the window through which I had entered, but I was too near the gray plain, and all I could perceive in any horizontal direction was a series of encampments of captive souls, the ectoplasmic revenants of men, women, and children somehow drawn to the turret and captured by the gray plain over a period of hundreds or thousands of years.

I turned my gaze upward and realized that the turret room was indeed open to the sky of the Severn Valley, and that night was ending and the morning sky was beginning to turn from midnight blue to pale gray. Soon a rosy dawn would arrive, and in some incomprehensible way I *knew* that it would be disastrous for me to be in the tower when daylight broke.

Thus I rose as rapidly as I could and sped over the gray plain, past the machines and their attendants, out of the turret and home to my cousin's house.

At work that day I met once again with Nelson MacIvar. He had appeared vaguely familiar to me at our first meeting, and I now realized that this burly, oversized man bore an uncanny resemblance to the great child who had thrown a rock at my car as it carried me from Brichester to Severnford. I came very near to mentioning the incident to him, but decided that no purpose would be served by raising an unpleasant issue.

Rather should I save my verbal ammunition for another attempt to get MacIvar to order tests of the Severn River water used in the Institute. By this time I had come to believe that the water was impregnated with some peculiar *force* that was interfering with the operation of the Zeta/Zed System. This force, I surmised, might be a radioactive contamination, picked up at some point in the river's course, perhaps as a result of the fissure at the foot of the Severn Hills nearby.

When I thought of that fissure and of those hills, a feeling of disquietude filled me, and I had to excuse myself and sip at a glass of water—that same damnable Severn water, I realized too late to stop myself—while I regained my composure. *Why* I should find thoughts of that fissure and of those hills so distressing, I could not recall.

This time MacIvar grudgingly yielded to my request, insisting that nothing would be found, but willing in his burly, overbearing way to humor this troublesome American. I reported this potential break to Alexander Myshkin by transatlantic telephone, and spent the remainder of the day more or less productively employed.

Again that night I feigned migraine and excused myself from my cousin's company. She expressed concern for my well-being and offered to summon a doctor to examine me, but I ran from her company and locked myself in my room. I stared into the fiery orb of the sun as it fell beneath the Severn Hills, then willed myself across the miles to the turret.

As I approached it tonight I realized that it had changed its form again, assuming the features of a style of architecture unknown and unfamiliar to me, but clearly of the most advanced and elaborate nature imaginable.

I flashed through the window, sped past the machines and their attendants, and hovered above the gray plain. I had reached a decision. Tonight I would pursue my investigation of the plain to its end! I swooped low over the plain, passed rapidly over the Victorian village—for such is the way I now labeled this assemblage of souls—over the Roman encampment, over the rough Pictish gathering, and on. What would I find, I wondered— Neanderthals?

Instead, to my astonishment, I recognized the ectoplasmic manifestation of an Egyptian pyramid. I dropped toward it, entered an opening near its base, and found myself in a hall of carven obsidian, lined with living statues of the Egyptian hybrid gods—the hawk-headed Horus, the jackal-headed Anubis, the ibis-god Thoth, the crocodile god Sobk—and I knew, somehow, that these, too, were not physical representations created by some ancient sculptors, but the very *souls* of the creatures the Egyptians worshipped!

I did not stay long, although I could see that a ceremony was taking place in which worshippers prostrated themselves, making offerings and chanting in honor of their strange deities. I sped from the pyramid and continued along the plain, wondering what next I would encounter.

In Silicon Valley, Alexander Myshkin and I had spent many hours, after our day's work was completed, arguing and pondering over the many mysteries of the world, including the great mystery of Atlantis. Was it a mere legend, a Platonic metaphor for some moral paradigm, a fable concocted to amuse the childish and deceive the credulous? Myshkin was inclined to believe in the literal reality of Atlantis, while I was utterly skeptical.

Alexander Myshkin was right.

The Atlantean settlement was suffused with a blue light all its own. Yes, the Atlanteans *were* the precursors and the inspiration of the Egyptians. Their gods were similar but were mightier and more elegant than the Egyptians'; their temples were more beautiful, their pyramids more titanic, their costumes more fantastic.

And the Atlanteans themselves — I wondered if they were truly human. They were shaped like men and women, but they were formed with such perfection as to make the statues of Praxiteles look like the fumblings of a nursery child pounding soft clay into a rough approximation of the human form.

These Atlanteans had aircraft of amazing grace and beauty, and cities that would make the fancies of Wonderland or of Oz pale by comparison.

And yet they had been captured and imprisoned on this terrible gray plain!

I sped beyond the Atlantean settlement, wondering if yet more ancient civilizations might be represented. And they were, they were. People of shapes and colors I could only have imagined, cities that soared to the heavens (or seemed to, in that strange psychic world), wonders beyond the powers of my puny mind to comprehend.

How many ancient civilizations had there been on this puny planet we call Earth? Archaeologists have found records and ruins dating back perhaps ten thousand years, fifteen thousand at the uttermost. Yet anthropologists tell us that humankind, *homo sapiens* or something closely resembling him, has been on this planet for anywhere from two to five *million* years. Taking even the most conservative number, are we to believe that for 1,985,000 years our ancestors were simple fisherfolk, hunters and gatherers, living in crude villages, organized into petty tribes? And that suddenly, virtually in the wink of the cosmic eye, there sprang up the empires of Egypt and Mesopotamia, of ancient China and India, Japan and Southeast Asia and chill Tibet, the Maya and the Aztecs and the Toltecs and the great Incas, the empires of Gambia and of Ghana, the mysterious rock-painters of Australia and the carvers of the stone faces of Easter Island?

This makes little sense. No, there must have been other civilizations, hundreds of them, thousands, over the millions of years of humankind's tenancy of the planet Earth.

But even then, what is a mere two million years, even five million years, in the history of a planet six *billion* years of age? What mighty species might have evolved in the seas or on the continents of this world, might have learned to think and to speak, to build towering cities and construct great engines, to compose eloquent poems and paint magnificent images . . . and then have disappeared, leaving behind no evidence that ever they had walked this Earth . . . or at least, no evidence of which we are aware?

Such races did live on this planet. They had souls, yes, and so much, say I, for human arrogance. This I know because I saw their souls.

How many such races? Hundreds, I tell you. Thousands. Millions. I despaired of ever reaching the end of the gray plain, but I had vowed to fly to its end however long it took. This time, if daylight found me still in the tower, so must it be. My cousin might discover my body, seemingly deep in a normal and restorative slumber, propped up in my easy chair. But she would be unable to awaken me.

Yes. I determined that I would see this thing to its conclusion, and from this objective I would not be swayed. I saw the souls of the great segmented fire-worms who built their massive cities in the very molten mantle of the Earth; I saw submarine creatures who would make the reptilian plesiosaurs look like minnows by comparison, sporting and dancing and telling their own tales of their own watery gods; I saw the intelligent ferns and vines whose single organic network at one time covered nearly one third of the primordial continent of Gondwanaland; I saw the gossamer, feathery beings who made their nests in Earth's clouds and built their playgrounds in Luna's craters.

We humans in our conceit like to tell ourselves that we are evolution's darlings, that millennia of natural selection have led Nature to her crowning creation, *homo sapiens.* Let me tell you that the opposite is the case. The story of life on Earth is not the story of evolution, but of *devolution.* The noblest, the most elevated and most admirable of races were the first, not the last.

But still I pursued my flight, past wonder on wonder, terror on terror, until at last I saw the gray plain, the gray *plane* curve upward, rise into the brilliant haze that I recognized as the primordial chaos from which our Solar System emerged. And the souls that were captured by the turret—what was their fate? For what purpose were they caught up in every era of being, and drawn backward, backward toward that primordial haze?

A great mass of soul-force formed before my ectoplasmic eyes. A great seething ball of sheer soul-energy that accreted there in the dawn of time, now burst its bonds and rolled down that great gray plain, sweeping all before it, destroying cities as a boulder would crush an ants' nest, shaking continents to their foundations, causing the globe itself to tremble and to wobble in its orbit around the Sun.

But even this was only the beginning of the havoc wrought by this great ball of soul-energy. From the remote past to the present —our present, yours and mine—it roared, and then on into the future, sweeping planets and suns in its path.

And when the roiling concentration of soul-force reached that unimaginably distant future, when all was dim and silent in the cosmos and infinitesimal granules of existence itself floated aimlessly in the endless void, it reversed its course and swept backward, roiling and rolling from future to past, crushing and rending and growing, always growing, growing.

It reached its beginning point and reversed itself still again, larger and more terrible this time than it had been the first, and as it oscillated between creation and destruction, between future and past, between the beginning of the universe and its end, the very fabric of time-space began to grow weak.

What epochs of history, human and pre-human and, yes, posthuman, were twisted and reformed into new and astonishing shapes. Battles were fought and unfought and then fought again with different outcomes; lovers chose one another, then made new and different choices; empires that spanned continents were wiped out as if they had never existed, then recreated in the images of bizarre deities; religions disappeared and returned, transmogrified beyond recognition; species were cut off from the stream of evolution to be replaced by others more peculiar than you can imagine.

A baby might be born, then disappear back into its mother's womb only to be born again a monstrosity unspeakable. A maddened killer might commit a crime, only to see his deed undone and himself wiped out of existence, only to reappear a saintly and benevolent friend to his one-time victim.

And what then, you might wonder, what then? I'll not deny that my own curiosity was roused. Would humankind persist forever? What supreme arrogance to think this would be the case! Mightier species than we, and nobler, had come and gone before *homo sapiens* was so much as a gleam in Mother Nature's eye.

In iteration after iteration of the titanic story, humankind disappeared. Destroyed itself with monstrous weapons. Was wiped away by an invisible virus. Gave birth to its own successor race and lost its niche in the scheme of things. Was obliterated by a wandering asteroid, conquered and exterminated by marauding space aliens —

Oh, space aliens. Alexander Myshkin and I had debated that conundrum many a time. Myshkin believed that the universe positively *teemed* with intelligence. Creatures of every possible description, human, human-like, insectoid, battrachian, avian, vegetable, electronic, you name it. Myshkin's version of the cosmos looked like a science fiction illustrator's sample book.

My universe was a lonely place. Only Earth held life, and only human life on Earth was sentient. It was a pessimistic view, I'll admit, but as the mother of the ill-favored baby was wont to say, "It's ugly but it's mine."

Well, Myshkin was right. There were aliens galore. At various times and in various versions of the future — and of the past, as a matter of fact — they visited Earth or we visited their worlds or space travelers of different species met in unlikely cosmic traffic accidents or contact was made by radio or by handwritten notes tossed away in empty olive jars.

One version of posthuman Earth was dominated by a single greenish fungus that covered the entire planet, oceans and all, leaving only tiny specks of white ice at the North and South Poles. Another was sterilized, and thank you, weapons industry, for developing a bomb that could kill everything — *everything!* — on an entire planet. But spores arrived from somewhere later on, and a whole new family of living things found their home on Earth.

I saw all of this and more, and I saw the very fabric of space-time becoming feeble and unsure of itself. I saw it tremble and quake beneath the mighty assault of that accumulated and ever-growing soul-force, and I realized what was happening. The cosmos itself was threatened by whatever screaming demons of chaos cavorted beyond its limits.

At length a rent appeared, and I was able to peer into it, but the black, screeching chaos that lay beyond it I will not describe to you. No, I will not do that. But I peered into that swirling orifice of madness and menace and I mouthed a prayer to the God I had abandoned so long ago, and I swore to that God that if one man, if one soul could counter the malignities who populated the fifth dimension, or the fiftieth, or the five millionth, it would be I.

Did I say that the soul is the immaterial and immortal part of a living, sentient being? And did I say that I had realized, in despite of my lifelong skepticism, that God was a living reality? Perhaps I should have said that *gods* were living realities. I do not

Three thousand copies of this book have been printed by the Maple-Vail Book Manufacturing Group, Binghamton, NY, for Golden Gryphon Press, Urbana, IL. The typeset is Elante, printed on 55#Sebago. The binding cloth is **Arrestox** B. Typesetting by The Composing Room, Inc., Kimberly, WI.